NOTHING NEW UNDER THE SUN

JC RYAN

vinci
BOOKS

By JC Ryan

Carter Devereux Mystery Thriller Series

Nothing New Under The Sun

The Wolves Of Freydis

The Alboran Codex

The Nabatean Secret

The Labyrinth of Minos

Vinci Books

vinci-books.com

Published by Vinci Books Ltd in 2025

1

Copyright © JC Ryan 2016

The author has asserted their moral right to be identified as the author of this work in accordance with the Copyright, Designs and Patents Act 1988. This work is a work of fiction. Names, characters, places and incidents are the product of the author's imagination or are used fictitiously. Any resemblance to actual persons, living or dead, places and incidents is entirely coincidental.

All rights reserved. No part of this publication may be copied, reproduced, distributed, stored in any retrieval system, or transmitted in any form or by any means, including photocopying, recording, or other electronic or mechanical methods, nor used as a source for any form of machine learning including AI datasets, without the prior written permission of the publisher.

The publisher and the author have made every effort to obtain permissions for any third party material used in this book and to comply with copyright law. Any queries in this respect should be brought to the attention of the publisher and any omissions will be corrected in future editions.

A CIP catalogue record for this book is available from the British Library.

Paperback ISBN: 9781036703271

Printed and bound in Great Britain by Clays Ltd, Elcograf S.p.A.

Prologue

Ten miles off the Coast of Florida, USA

Carter Devereux leaned over the rail of the barge, dallying with one of the women who operated the crane while he looked down at the diver coming up to the surface.

A diver's masked face broke the surface a few yards away from him. It was Ahote – he couldn't get his mask off quick enough. "Carter!" he yelled. "What do you have for testing for gold?"

Carter's heart started racing. "I've got a few basic chemicals. What do you have?"

"Get them over here!" Ahote yelled again, unable to contain his excitement.

Carter spun around and ran down the stairs to get the testing kit from below deck. He arrived back just as Ahote climbed on board.

"Sabrina is bringing up something big!" Ahote shouted above the noise of the crane's engine.

Although Carter could speak several languages, and

1

understood several more, he couldn't make out any of the rest of Ahote's babbling – it could have been English or Hopi, or maybe even a few others. Carter could not comprehend anything else he was saying.

Just when Carter was about ready to grab Ahote by the shoulders and shake him to calm him down, Sabrina emerged from the water indicating to the crane operator to start the pull.

Sabrina climbed on board stripping off her mask and tanks, dropping them on the deck. Turning to look at Carter, she smiled.

Carter remembered the smile from the last time he'd been with Sabrina - on an unauthorized night dive – and grinned. Sabrina was part Greek with a fiery temper but had a sweet side that rarely surfaced unless they were alone.

Sabrina was an Olympic class swimmer, tanned, with long black hair and a bust line that could stop traffic. Somehow, Ahote always found the hottest women to work for him, much to the consternation of his wife, Bly.

"I've got it!" the winch operator cried out as the net broke the surface. It landed on the deck with a dull thud as seawater poured everywhere.

Ahote, a Hopi Indian, whose name translated as 'restless soul' ran to the object in the net and started scraping away the encrustation. He found something sparkling and gave it to Carter. "Here, test this!"

Carter was on summer break from a Boston University where he was working on his Master's degree in archeology. He'd found records of a sunken Spanish galleon off the coast of Florida and convinced his grandfather, Will Devereux, to fund the undersea expedition.

Will, intrigued at what they might find, employed Ahote's

salvaging company to undertake the actual diving operation to locate the galleon with the aid of underwater radar. They failed to find the galleon, but instead found the remains of an unnamed Viking dragon-prowed longship two days ago.

Carter opened the lid of his chemical kit box and started the test. A few minutes later he shouted, "I don't believe this! ... It doesn't happen! Ever."

"We got gold?" Ahote shouted, dropping to his knees next to Carter.

"It's not possible" Carter shivered with glee as the rest of the crew surrounded them. He turned to Ahote. "Is your wife still on the mainland?"

"Yes, she is. Why do you want to know?"

"Have her bring the champagne," he said. "It's solid gold! All of it! You never find gold on a site! Unless... unless..." He never finished that sentence.

Sabrina grabbed his head and planted a passionate kiss on his mouth – holding him for a long time.

While he was trying to tell everybody they all were going to be rich beyond measure, Sabrina dragged him down below deck, peeling off the rest of her diving suit as she went.

When Ahote's wife Bly arrived with the alcoholic beverages as requested, Sabrina was coming up from the lower deck wearing only the bottom part of her bikini.

Bly was busy tying up the rope to the side of the barge when she spotted the topless Sabrina. "What in God's name is going on?" she yelled at Ahote. "I hope you have a damn good explanation for this!"

"Gold, my love. Pure gold is what's going on." Ahote grinned.

Bly's aggressive demeanor vaporized like mist before the

sun as she started breaking out the champagne - the party raged through the night.

Ahote and Bly finally disappeared into the wheelhouse and stayed there. Bly reappeared the next morning wearing a big smile.

There was more gold than anyone would ever have thought possible at the bottom of the Viking ship. Even after the taxman had taken his share, there was well over $100 million that the crew divided before going their separate ways.

The last Carter heard from Sabrina was a post card from her resort in Fiji. She had a special Christmas card made up of her standing next to the rough young men she kept on hand to do a variety of jobs at her resort.

How a Viking longship came to be off the coast of Florida was anyone's guess. The discovery of the ship caused a rumpus across the historical and archeological communities. Archeologists were still debating over how the ship ended up thousands of miles from the Viking lands in Europe and as many miles from the only known Viking settlements in Nova Scotia.

Viking longships were built for fast attack and not long sea voyages, making them unsuitable for hauling anything heavy for long distances.

Part I

Part 1.

Chapter One

A DOZEN WHITE ROSES

Ten years later.

Carter Devereux held the sword and worked on focus which was crucial in the Chen style of *T'ai Chi Ch'uan* and even more so in the use of weapons. His master had finally allowed him, after years of studying the non-weapon styles, to take up the art known as the way of the sword.

For 30 minutes, he practiced the *Jian* - thrusting sword - position. There were at least 49 positions to learn with this weapon and he intended to come to terms with them all. He visited his master's training hall, the Center of Harmonious Gratitude, located over a Chinese restaurant in downtown Boston, twice a week. It was small, just under a thousand feet, but Master Hong took very few students. Carter would spend hours holding the postures Master Hong imparted to him despite the nauseating odor of a variety of unfamiliar foods cooking below and whiffing up through the floor. He dared not disrespect his Master by showing his aversion to the smell, as it was Master Hong's primary income.

He put the sword down and went back to the stances of the weaponless style. Master Hong stressed the fact that no one ever completely mastered a martial art; they only became less cumbersome at it. Carter had progressed better than most - his dedication was legendary among Master Hong's students.

Carter made his first appearance at the center eight years ago, shortly after his twenty-seventh birthday. He had wanted to pursue an oriental martial art ever since watching an old Bruce Lee movie on late-night television when he was a kid. Someone told him about the old Chinese man who taught a very traditional form of *T'ai Chi Ch'uan*, or 'Tai Chi' as most westerners called it, which roughly translates into 'The Supreme Ultimate Fist.' The style was thought to have originated with Buddhist monks who needed a method of protection while they traveled across the ancient Chinese Empire. It was considered a 'soft' martial arts style since the practice reacted to violence as opposed to initiating it.

Master Hong had an extraordinary philosophy regarding whom he would teach. He felt non-Chinese should not be allowed to learn the secrets of the tai chi style he taught. Therefore, first, when prospective students turned up he would ignore them, and they tended not to come back. Second, should they come back; he would show them some pain. They would leave humiliated and not show up again. Finally, if they returned for the third time, he would teach them since it meant they must have been Chinese in an earlier life and deserved to be taught.

Carter's first day at the center, not knowing the old man's philosophy, was his most difficult. He found himself ignored - forced to sit on the sidelines and observe, not knowing what was going on. The second appearance Master Hong unleashed every student on him until he had engaged each one in combat. He'd barely managed to climb the stairs to his condominium afterward, but he had no intention of giving up. The third time he'd arrived at the center, Master Hong smiled and started to teach him the basics.

Carter concluded his morning practice with a set of deep breathing exercises. For him, tai chi was a daily ritual he had not neglected since the day he started eight years ago. He showered, had a light breakfast, packed his briefcase, and made his way to his office on the University campus.

When he arrived at his desk, it was almost eight. He prided himself on arriving before the clerical staff and working well past office hours. His dedication had served him well over the years and awarded him a tenured professorship of archeology at the young age of 25. Having an opulent grandfather whose money funded several of the tall buildings on the campus grounds didn't hurt either. Nonetheless, Carter achieved his academic and financial successes through sheer brilliance, hard work, and enthusiasm for his subject.

His grandfather's prosperity meant he never had to worry about funds while studying. While other students were stuck in pointless internship positions over the summer breaks, Carter could spend his on archeological digs in the Middle East, South America, and undersea exploration.

To those who called him a lucky man, he always imparted a bit of wisdom learned from his grandfather; "Luckily good fortune is often found in partnership with conscientiousness."

He turned his attention to the box on his desk, which had intrigued him since its arrival an hour earlier, taking his time to examine it. When the shipping department brought it to him, they saved the packaging so he could see where it had originated. The return address was in Spanish and listed Peru as its point of origin. The rest of the return address was smeared and hard to read, causing Carter to surmise the sender didn't want the location known. He wasn't concerned - any package coming to the University was examined by campus security and passed through an X-Ray machine. The anthrax scares ten years ago had mandated this additional level of safety.

The box was wood with a thin strand of string tied around it in a constrictor knot. *Who went to such trouble just to secure a box?* Thinking better about it, Carter took several pictures of the box with his smartphone. Instead of cutting the string from the box, he used an awl from his desk to untie it. He would keep it with the box in case he wanted to know more about the source.

The lid hinged on one side of the box. Security might have been able to tell him the contents before he opened it, as they surely would have seen the insides as it passed through the scanner, but it would have ruined the surprise for him. Inside, he found cotton packing. Again, he was intrigued. No one packed objects in cotton these days - too expensive. Most of the time they used vermiculite, Styrofoam peanuts, or bubble packing, but the sender considered the contents of this box special enough to use cotton wadding.

He peeled back the cotton to expose a golden hummingbird. With a cotton glove on his hand, he picked it up. Although the figurine was about an inch long and three-quarters of an inch wide, it felt heavy enough to be gold. He would test the metal composition later, but Carter was willing to bet this was 24 karat gold.

Who sends a gold artifact through the mail? The postal systems of the world were rife with underpaid workers who just might be tempted to list an uninsured package, as a 'loss' if they thought something inside was valuable. He looked at the packaging from Peru - there was no postal insurance stamp on it. *Someone was willing to take the risk of this artifact's loss in the mail just to get it to me.*

He pulled a loupe out of a drawer and looked closer. *Wait a minute; this isn't pure gold.* The gold on most of it was shaded red, which meant it was some kind of alloy. The gold used in the construction of the figurine was altered to give it the red hue before the hummingbird was made. The eyes were black. From the way they glimmered under the light, Carter decided the eyes of the bird were obsidian, plentiful in South America, but difficult to fashion.

He pulled his special digital camera from the desk and mounted it on a small tripod to photograph the bird. For the next hour, he took a series of photographs at different levels of magnification and uploaded them to his desktop computer for closer scrutiny.

As he enlarged the shots, Carter could see the marks of hand tools on the bird. Someone had spent a long time fashioning this creation. He would need to confer with other researchers in his department, but if this artifact was as old as he suspected, it was a major find. He couldn't tell the exact age, but he was sure it was not created in the last 500 years.

The level of detail was hard to believe. This hummingbird was far more realistic than anything he'd seen before. The feathers were created so that each one had a level of precision only visible with magnification. He toyed with the idea that this might be some kind of fake artifact meant to fool him, but a phony one would not have this level of skill in its creation. Three-dimensional printing had just appeared on the market, but to build this artifact up from a computer design would have cost more than any hoaxer's budget would tolerate. It would take an SLS machine to do this job, and he was unaware of anybody who had developed one that could print with gold. And, why reproduce the marks and errors of a skilled artisan? No, this hummingbird figure had to be real, and pre-Columbian.

He gently returned the hummingbird to its box and looked at the container. Nothing on the package showed where it had originated, other than the Peruvian postal stamp. Could this be one of those 'ooparts' - out-of-place artifacts? Most of those turned out to be misidentified or fakes, such as the famous crystal skull of the Incas. He had to put the box in a safe place. The gold in it alone would make the artifact a tempting object for anyone who wished to score a quick buck.

He got up and prepared a mug of coffee from the machine behind him. *Wonderful thing technology, it gave the human race nuclear weapons and coffee machines.* As he added the cream from his small office refrigerator, Carter looked again at the photographs. He had another thought and uploaded a copy of the images to his online secure cloud repository where he stored most of his valuable documents.

He sat back with his hands folded behind his head, contemplating lost advanced civilizations antedating written history. His grandfather, who raised him and instilled in him a sense of wonder for ancient civilizations, regularly suggested there was more to the past than anyone cared to admit.

Carter had a collection of documents about lost civilizations, ancient astronauts and the wisdom of the Great Old Ones. He remembered a movie he watched as a young child where an archeologist found the lost battle-ax of a conquistador revived after being struck by a lightning bolt. In Europe there were so many tales of sleeping kings and Holy Grails, it was a wonder one couldn't just stick a shovel into the ground and find one or more of them.

But then again, there were plenty of artifacts that just didn't fit the era or strata where they were discovered, or didn't make any sense to modern day scientists. There was the ancient battery discovered in Baghdad by Wilhelm Konig in 1938. It was anyone's guess what it was used for. *Was this an invention by the ancients, or were they working from an older design they couldn't understand?* The Byzantines had invented napalm, but no one today knew what its exact composition was. He also knew about a team of investigators who built a model aircraft based on pre-Columbian figurines in an attempt to prove the ancient Tolima civilization had jet aircraft technology. The model really did fly. Also, there was the ancient Indian flying machine or 'vimanas' to contend with ... *those drawings were too technical; the information was much more than what would be relevant only to pilots for them to be fantasy.* Similar unexplained objects were also discovered in Costa Rica, Brazil, and Argentina.

Then there were the gold spirals found in the Ural Mountains of western Russia around 1991. Gold prospectors had brought them back from a trip to the Narada River. Some of them were as small as 1/10,000 of an inch. *The initial studies on the spirals inferred the micro-objects were shellfish, but this proved to be incorrect. It was indeed gold. No one was able to figure out where the objects had been made, or how.* Some researchers thought they might be over 20,000 years old.

The hummingbird figurine had come from Peru, where

the Lost Golden Garden of the Incas was supposed to be located. The Spanish conquistadors claimed to have discovered a city with an entire garden constructed out of gold, silver, and gemstones. They reported every aspect of the garden, which was sacred to the Inca royalty, was made from precious metal and precious stones. Even the roots of the plants were reproduced in gold or silver. The garden even displayed animals, hand tooled from gold which resembled the originals in every way, shape, and form.

"We did not know if they were living objects fashioned from gold or statues," the Spanish Knight Don Carlo Del Mache had written back to the King of Spain in the year 1565.

Most astonishing of all were reproductions of tigers and lions, animals not native to Peru or anywhere else in South America at any time in the past. The Spaniards were thunderstruck by what they saw as they entered the sacred city. *Present day archeologists wonder if the conquistadors were mistaken in their accounts. Others speculated that the Incas had traded with the Middle East using some sort of unknown technology.*

The Inca royalty had tried to hide what they could from the greedy invaders since the Spaniards tended to melt down the gold and send it back to Spain. The monks accompanying the conquistadors considered all the artwork produced by the Incas to be pagan idolatry. Some people felt the Spaniards account of the garden of gold was mistaken for the sacred Inca city of Coricancha. *I wonder if the hummingbird came from this golden garden of the Incas.*

Carter pulled out his smart phone and called his grandfather, Will Devereux. This little piece of archeological mystery was something that would definitely excite Grandfather Will. His grandfather traveled in less rigorous archeological circles and could often be found in the company of travelers and seekers of adventure. Just last year he'd financed a trip to the Greek Islands to locate the lost Minoan civilization of Atlantis. They hadn't found anything, but his grandfather vowed to return next year with a submersible.

"Carter!" the voice on the other end of the line greeted him. "How good of you to call! We're looking forward to your visit next week. Anything new and exciting in Beantown?"

He smiled at his grandfather's little slight at Boston. Will Devereux, although American born and bred regarded himself as a Quebecois these days and they looked down on the upstart nation to the South. They often said, "Vermont should never have joined that rebel alliance. Nothing good has come out of the state since they declared independence from Quebec in the 18th century."

"I've got something to send you, Grandfather. Look in your cloud account; I've uploaded some pictures of a hummingbird artifact that arrived in the mail earlier today. It appears to be pre-Columbian, and I'm sure you'll find it interesting."

"Why, thank you, Grandson. I'll look for it. See you up here next week."

At approximately 10:00 on that same morning, Carter was involved in a collision. Although it was not the kind normally reported in the local news, it would have a greater impact on the future of human civilization than any other collision reported in the news on that day.

Carter taught an undergraduate class, Introduction to Historical Methods, and needed to get to the lecture hall before his students arrived. Unlike most of his colleagues, he didn't mind teaching the introduction classes. He found them an excellent way to put the students on the path to scientific reasoning and it helped to identify the bright minds that would in due course make significant discoveries. One of his former students was a featured commentator on one of the educational channels and credited Professor Devereux as his inspiration to further his studies and obtain a doctorate degree.

Books and laptop computer in hand, Carter was doing his best to keep the golden hummingbird off his mind when he turned the corner and ran into another moving object. Books and flash drives flew through the air, but they both were able to grab their laptops before either of them hit the ground. Carter took three steps, righted himself, and turned to see whom he slammed into. It bothered him he'd been so careless. His pursuit of tai chi was supposed to keep this from happening. Master Hong would have laughed at his student's maladroitness had he been present.

Carter whirled around to help the person whom he struck, praying it wasn't a senior administrator. An incident like this would not be a good thing for a person of that position to have in mind during budget talks. The person he collided with was down on bended knee and slowly rising, having retrieved what had been lost. As Carter walked toward the figure, he could only see a green business suit. Then she turned around to face him.

He was speechless. Standing before him was one of the most beautiful women he had ever faced.

She was a vision in scarlet. She appeared to be in her late twenties and was nearly six feet in height. For a moment, Carter, who stood six-four, was enveloped by a vision of an ancient warrior princess emerging from a burning castle. The woman he faced had flaming red hair tied back with a dark green ribbon. She possessed a heart-shaped face, her eyes were emerald green, and the nails that gripped the books and laptop matched them. Her physical proportions conformed to the golden ratio.

Most of the college staff dressed down at this University, feeling the title of 'Assistant Professor' allowed them to look any way they wanted. Carter was one of the few who wore a suit and tie, as did this vision of beauty in front of him. Could she be an instructor of some type? Hardly, with her look of professionalism.

"Could you watch where you are going?" she snapped at him. "You damn near knocked me over. Do you have any idea how much that laptop cost me?"

"I'm really sorry," he apologized. "I was on my way to a class full of freshmen ..."

"I've got a class to teach too," she retorted, "and I'm late already." She turned and walked away.

Carter stood watching her divine form and then noticed she had a bit of a limp.

"Did I cause that?" He ran to catch up. "My apologies again. Are you hurt? Can I help you carry your stuff?"

"Don't worry I'll survive. Try and not collide with any more people today." She turned again and continued on her way, high heels clicking on the concrete.

"I think I've just met a goddess, a Valkyrie," He mumbled as he watched her vanish into the trees. A smile played on his face at this thought of the fierce Norse warrior maiden of antiquity, a daughter of royalty, with flaming crimson hair who would choose those who die in battle to spend the night with her in heaven.

He made sure to take a more conservative turn around the next corner and continued to his lecture room.

Dr. Mackenzie Anderson was angry. It was her first lecture, and not only was she late, but her foot was now stinging, and that annoyed her intensely. "Wretched fellow - tall dark and handsome - far too pretty - probably a bear of very little brain."

He returned from his class, dropped some forms off to the department's secretary, and checked to make sure the golden hummingbird remained locked in his desk – no reason to leave it lying about. Then, all thoughts of it vanished as he sat down at his computer and pulled up the staff profiles on the University Intranet. A few minutes later Carter located his goddess again.

There she was in all her glory: Dr. Mackenzie Anderson, the adjunct researcher in human molecular biology, Department of Genetics. He looked at her stunning picture and rubbed his eyes to make sure this was the same angry woman he'd encountered. She had been with the department since receiving her doctorate three years ago. Why wasn't this woman pulling down the big money working for a pharmaceutical company?

He picked up his phone and made a call. "Hello," he said when a voice answered on the other end. "I would like to have a dozen white roses delivered to someone at the University, and I would like the arrangement delivered today."

Chapter Two

FREYDIS

Carter piloted his Piper Seminole to match the flight plan he'd filed with the Canadian customs office after he landed in Quebec City. The customs officers knew him from the frequent stops he made on his way to his grandfather's property in the mountains to the north. The twin-engine plane only needed one pilot to fly it and had a range of 1,000 miles on a tank of gas.

His grandparents raised him as a collision with a gas truck killed his parents when he was just eight years old. His older brother and sister, who were in the car, died in the fiery explosion as well. No one knew how it happened - the accident investigators claimed the truck had lost control on a dry road and swerved into the oncoming lane, colliding with the smaller car driven by his father. As fate would have it, Carter was visiting with his grandparents at the time of the accident and never returned home.

They sold his parent's house and placed all the contents in storage. Carter melded into the lives of his loving grandparents, Will and Diana, attending school and developing a lifelong love of archeology imparted to him by his grandfather

His grandfather's ranch, Freydis, consisted of 50,000 acres with no access roads. Grandfather Will liked his privacy and didn't feel like having to run people off his land. He'd purchased it after Diana passed away suddenly and he wanted some peace and quiet. It became a summer retreat for Will and his still young grandson, Carter. A couple, Ahote and Bly, about 20 years younger than his grandfather, were the only other permanent inhabitants in close proximity.

Freydis had its own airstrip, which showed up on a satellite photo, but nowhere else. Will and his friends' mode of transport to and from the farm was a four-seater Piper Cub airplane.

The older Devereux had been part owner of a private satellite company. His company had placed several secretive satellites in geosynchronous orbit for a few discrete affluent customers looking to organize a private and secure communication network - a place to hide data and communications from their corporate competition. When Internet technology took off big time in the late 90's, several of the new companies came to him for help with their own communication networks. Grandfather Will's fortune continued to expand, and he sold his share in the company to a group of investors for an untold amount of money. Carter wasn't certain how much his grandfather was worth, but he knew the old man had no money worries at all.

Although Grandfather Will was a trained aerospace engineer, he had a love of archeology. When he cashed out of his company, he was able to move north permanently to his summer retreat on the land he bought after Diana's death. In his spare time, he was a regular backer of archeological expeditions to unexplored places on Earth. His face routinely appeared in any number of journals and websites devoted to the frontiers of archeology.

Ahote was raised on a Hopi reservation in Arizona. He'd met Will many years ago, and they became good friends. Ahote and his wife, Bly, sold the salvaging company as soon as they'd cashed out enough of their share of the gold to live comfortably. They visited Will on the ranch for a few days where they fell in love with the place, bought the adjoining property, and moved into the nice comfortable log cabin about a mile away from Will's place.

Ahote's seafaring and wild days were over. He settled down to the things he really loved: Bly, hunting, fishing, and horseback riding in the woods. Bly took to farm life like a duck to a pond. She soon had a few goats, milk cows, chickens, and a flourishing vegetable garden.

While Carter had banked most of his take from the salvage of the Viking longship, he did use some of it to complete an underwater survey of the site. But, even after the divers examined every bit of sand, bringing up and cataloging every artifact they found, they still couldn't figure out why the Viking ship was there. It led him to question much of what he learned about human history while at college. Additionally, why did the documents he uncovered at the Spanish Naval Academy list the wreckage as that of a galleon hauling gold? Even more than that, what was a Viking longship doing down as far south as Florida, and using gold for ballast?

Until the time when Ahote and Bly settled on their property, Will's ranch went nameless. One night shortly after their arrival over a bottle of good red wine, the three of them agreed that such a beautiful place couldn't go without a name any longer. After a few more glasses of wine and consideration of many possible names, Ahote came up with the winning suggestion.

"The Viking longship Carter and I discovered was also nameless, so Carter called it Freydis, after Freydis Eiriksdóttir, who took part in the Norse exploration of North America. Apparently she was a warrior with fiery red hair." Ahote laughed.

"Then Freydis it will be." Will settled the matter.

As Carter taxied the plane to the end of the runway, he could see his grandfather standing at the hangar to greet him. He contacted the air traffic controller at Quebec City to let them know he'd safely touched down and confirmed when he would return to the United States. He dreaded the return trip. US customs agents were much tougher than their Canadian equivalents.

"So where's the lady friend?" he heard his grandfather say as he opened the door to the cockpit and looked around inside

"Gramps!" he laughed. "Is there anything you don't know?" He pulled his bag and briefcase out with him. The satellite link from the ranch was top notch, and he planned to get some work done while visiting.

"I make it my business to know things," his grandfather grinned as he helped Carter transfer the bags to the electric cart he used to get around on the property. To keep the land as undisturbed as possible, Grandfather Will utilized the most modern alternative power sources available. All power was supplied on Freydis by two wind generators, a number of solar panels and a hydroelectric generator operating from a stream not too far from the enormous log cabin that hooked into universal power supply batteries. He did have a diesel generator as an emergency backup, but Carter couldn't remember ever seeing it in operation.

Later, with a mug of espresso in hand, they retired to the library where Will brought up the images of the hummingbird on the computer screen. "These photos are remarkable."

Since Will had devoted himself to studying the archeology of the unexplained, he'd assembled one of the best personal libraries in the world on the subject. Although the Internet made private libraries less important for research, he still had many books and manuscripts not found anywhere else, spending large sums of money to have them authenticated. He was fooled once and only once when someone sold him a fake papyrus that showed the journey of an Egyptian Pharaoh of the New Kingdom to North America. It never happened again. Since then he had several experts on retainer to authenticate any book or document of interest to him.

"You think this might come from the Lost Garden of Gold?" His grandfather asked while scrolling through the pictures.

"I'd have to know more about its origins. There was nothing on the packaging other than a postage stamp from Peru. It could have come from anywhere in that country. Tracing it back would be almost impossible. Someone didn't want me to know where it was shipped from."

"I tell you, if this is a fake, it's the best one I've ever seen. Look at that one; you can even see the cut marks on those feathers." Will scratched his gray beard and looked at the pictures some more. "Think this might be an Oopart? Even if it's only a few hundred years old, you still have an important find."

"Grandfather," Carter smiled, "I know you keep trying to find Atlantis and the Seven Cities of Gold, but really, most of those things have reasonable explanations. I'm just as interested in lost civilizations as you are, but in my position, I need hard physical evidence. I respect all the work you did at Skara Brae, but I need more verifiable evidence than you do to keep me out of trouble in the scientific community."

"If anyone ever uncovers it," Will continued while looking at the pictures, "It will be you." He turned off the slide show.

"So, pray tell, you did lock this hummingbird up before you left?" Will looked at him with raised eyebrows, "I'd hate it to turn into another Thunderbird photograph." He referred to the famous cryptozoology photograph of cowboys holding up a dead flying dinosaur from the 19th century. Many people claimed to have seen it or a reprint in the 1960's, but the photograph was never found.

"It's in a safe in the security department," Carter told him. "The security people don't even know what's in the box. I told them I had an artifact I suspected of being coated with gilded mercury. They were told it might be toxic if it was, so no one will go near it."

"It's not good to tell lies, son," his grandfather smirked, "but if it keeps the hummingbird safe, maybe, this time, the end justifies the means. So, do you want to go see Ahote and Bly? They've been asking about you."

The electric cart swiftly took them to Ahote and Bly's cabin at the edge of the estate. Ahote had a horse barn behind his cabin where he kept the animals; a few of them belonged to Will and Carter.

Ahote and Bly were out on the steps to greet them as

they pulled up to the front of their beautiful cabin built out of local wood. Ahote strode out and embraced him.

"Welcome back, Dr. Gates!" he shouted while patting Carter on the back. 'Dr. Gates' was the nickname Ahote gave him after they'd discovered the Viking gold off the coast of Florida. It referred to the main character Ben Gates from the popular movie series 'National Treasure'. Ahote swore Carter was born under a lucky star and that everything he did turned into gold. After kissing Bly, they walked into the cabin and sat down to the dinner prepared for them.

They talked for a long time. Naturally, the subject of Ooparts came up right after dinner. Ahote mentioned the Viking ship - it was foremost in his mind as something that wasn't supposed to be where they found it.

Bly had little interest in archeology or ancient civilizations. She was happy enough to get out of the Louisiana Cajun town where she'd come of age before going to work for Ahote. Bly, a stunning beauty in her young days, hired on as a cook for the crew, but soon ended up taking care of more than just Ahote's breakfast in the morning. After three months of her careful ministrations, Ahote found out he'd put a bun in the cook's oven and married Bly two months before baby number one arrived. Numbers two and three arrived three and four years later, but by then they had found the lost Viking ship, and money wasn't the problem it had been at one time. The kids stayed at boarding schools most of the year and journeyed north to stay at the cabin, where there was plenty of room when school wasn't in session. Pictures of the family, friends, and Hopi artwork, including an entire display of Kachina dolls, decorated the cabin.

"If anything ever made me wonder about the origins of

humanity," Ahote told them, "it was the Viking ship. Did you ever figure out how it got there?"

"No," Carter answered. "It never made any sense. Why would a Viking longship be at the bottom of a gulf reef in shallow water when the map I found listed it as a Spanish treasure galleon? No one has figured it out yet."

"And that's not all," Grandfather Will brought up, "there are these spiral metallic gold objects which were discovered in Russia over 20 years ago..." As his grandfather continued talking about his favorite subject, Carter drifted off thinking about the stunning woman he sent flowers to before he left. He prayed she didn't take it the wrong way. There were stiff rules against any sort of harassment at the University. Nevertheless, the vision of a red hair goddess kept appearing in his mind.

Sabrina, the diver, was not his first sexual encounter. Carter had been all over the world; he cut a fine profile to the women and had his share of dalliances. He knew he was considered a 'catch' at the University since his position was secure and his reputation firm. Most of his colleagues knew about the Viking gold discovery but didn't talk about it. He remained humble with the knowledge that he'd been privileged most of his life. The exception was the loss of his parents, which turned him into an orphan. How many men had been through similar incidents and had no rich relatives to fall back on?

"Will told us you may have a woman in your life?" Bly probed.

Carter, summoned back to Earth, turned to his hostess. "He told you? Gramps is there anyone who doesn't know by now?"

"Her parents ... and most of the people outside your department, with the exception of hers. Son, I've seen her photograph. She has a profile and pedigree Hollywood couldn't dream up. Why she isn't on the big screen is a loss to humanity."

Carter shook his head in amazement. He knew Grandfather Will had plenty of connections at the University. He endowed all kinds of funds connected with the college. When gramps made an appearance, he received the red carpet treatment. So it didn't surprise him he had every man and his dog looking out for his grandson.

Later, when they returned to the cabin, Carter had plenty of time to think. He went through some tai chi poses without the use of the sword, focusing instead on the open-handed techniques he had worked so hard to internalize. As he'd predicted, Master Hong frowned when Carter told him about smashing into the young adjunct instructor at the college.

"She must have been there to balance you out," he told him in his broken English, referencing the Chinese philosophy of Daoism where all things were kept in harmony.

After the long day, he went to bed and was soon asleep.

The next morning Carter took himself off for a trek with his horse. He rode through the forests and mountains of his youth where many times he'd spent days camping out in the wilds, smelling the pine of the trees and rejuvenating.

Will's orders were; "You've been in the city too long for your own good, take a day out and go live a little. I'll be here when you get back."

He left, wandering the tracks of the animals, seeking what was hard to find, reaching deeper and deeper into his own being as he trekked further and further afield.

Before long, winter would be upon them, and the ground would be white. Bears would hibernate and wolves with their coats winter white would roam in search of food. For now, autumn hesitated over the land, slowly turning the leaves to yellow, red and gold, reminding him of the days when he'd come here alone.

Once when he'd stayed too long, he had been trapped by a sudden snowstorm and had to wait a day before he could make his way through.

Of course, there was no panic. Will and Ahote taught him everything he knew, and he gleaned even more from his own experiences; it would be a rare moment that Carter might find himself lost or trapped.

From his vantage point where the climb eased out, it was possible to look down on hills that melted into a broad old glacial valley and river.

The water was sparkling in the sunlight as it rippled over rocks. Trees were changing color from dark green to gold, red, and yellow. They swept up and over the ranges like paint pots spilling their colors down the hills.

Far away, he could make out a couple of wolves traveling up and away from the water, maybe having caught the scent of prey.

In the city, time was controlled in regulated segments of breakfast, lunch, and dinner, time to work, and time to go home. Here it was one continuous rhythm measured in sunrises and sunsets, full moons, and distant dark nights scattered with stars.

His mind turned to green eyes and red hair. She was beautiful, and she was haunting him. He'd have to do something about that when he returned.

Chapter Three

THE NEXT PHASE

On the way back from Canada, Carter had a lot of time to think about the conversations he had with his grandfather. The old man had some thought-provoking ideas about human history, this was for certain, and he did have a point - we know a lot less about the history of civilization than anyone is prepared to admit.

There were many of the Oopart discoveries out there that Carter didn't buy, and were easily explained. Such as the old pictures floating around on the Internet that was supposed to 'prove' the possibility of time travel. It showed a woman talking into something, which appeared to be a cell phone, as she strolled down the street in the 1930's. People claimed it was a cell phone, which wouldn't be used for another 50 years. Carter wondered *where was the transmission tower located if the woman was using a cell phone in the 1930's. Without physical evidence, what did you have? Nothing but speculation.*

However, as a student of archeology, he was well aware of the way knowledge could change over time. *Throughout human history, there were periods when knowledge would grow and decline like the ebb and flow of the sea. The knowledge that once existed gets lost in time, sometimes for centuries, even millennia before being rediscovered, and some of it is often lost forever.*

Greek fire, an incendiary liquid substance that water could not douse, was used as a weapon during the peak of the Byzantine Empire. By the 10th century, the knowledge of its composition was lost. *To this day, no one knows the recipe for Greek fire. It took more than nine centuries, until the 1940's, before napalm, the closest counterpart of Greek fire, was developed.*

More than two millennia ago, the Maya, who closely studied the movement of the planets and the stars, created a calendar so precise it had not lost a single day in over 2,500 years. They calculated the length of the solar year to 365.2422 days; our civilization only recently calculated it as 365.2420 days - almost no difference.

It was with a tinge of sadness that Carter's thoughts turned to the catastrophic loss of knowledge when the legendary Library of Alexandria in Egypt burned to ashes in about 48 B.C. The library, a massive repository of knowledge reported to have held over a million scrolls, dated back to about 300 B.C. The cause of its destruction remains shrouded in the smoke of history. Some blame Julius Caesar while others assigned blame for its ruin to marauding Arab conquerors. *Regardless the culprit, it did not negate the fact that those flames forever destroyed a treasure-trove of knowledge, gathered from across the ages.*

Carter found some solace though, in the realization that some knowledge refused to be buried or destroyed, such as those gold spirals found in Russia, the Viking longship off the coast of Florida, and the golden hummingbird from Peru. Enough remained to make him realize that Charles Fort, the great prophet of 'The Unexplained' might have been onto something. *Every year new finds force the archeological community to rethink its standpoint. Perhaps the scientific world is on the verge of another discovery about the distant past.*

He landed the plane at the private airport outside Boston and finished checking in with the flight deck a few minutes later. Customs didn't give him as much trouble as he feared because the same officer was there to inspect his luggage and plane as the last time. He showed her his passport and continued to the parking lot to his car. A few minutes later Carter was on his way back to Boston and the latest round of college classes he taught.

He thought about his vision in red, Mackenzie Anderson. The roses were sent just before he left so she would have received them the previous Friday, which meant she'd had four days to think about him. Perfect. It was time to move this operation into the next phase.

The following morning, he was in a coffee shop waiting for his friend Pete O'Connor to arrive. He'd known Pete for years. Pete worked for the University in the IT department as the senior network engineer. He'd done a few special favors for Pete in the past, and Pete had done some for him. Sometimes Carter needed information available only to those on a restricted list. Pete had found ways to add his name to a few lists, and the information he gained from them was valuable. In return, Pete had enjoyed a few special favors from Carter. Now Carter needed another one of those special favors but wasn't sure who owed whom right now.

Pete lumbered into the coffee shop, ordered a latte, and sat down in front of Carter. He had the appearance of a used dust mop, the uniform of advanced IT workers. He struggled to get the steaming mixture past his bearded lips as he greeted Carter, who smiled and wondered if Pete had any other clothes besides the t-shirt and jeans he always saw him wearing.

"So what is it this time, Doc?" he asked. "You need to get into the catalog of a museum? Afraid someone is trying to sell your grandfather another piece of the True Cross?"

"A little different this time, Pete," Carter smiled. "You can access the electronic schedules and calendars of everyone in the university, can't you?"

"Well, yes," Pete said with a suspicious frown while slurping his coffee. "Hypothetically, but if the person you're interested in doesn't use the university system to do their scheduling, it's going to be a lot harder. What do you need done?"

"I want to set up a coffee date with a lady who works as an adjunct researcher in the Genetics Department. However, I want it to appear that she sent me the invite from her computer, and I am the one accepting it."

Pete closed his eyes and frowned. The background chatter emitting from the coffee shop was bothering his concentration. A few seconds later a police cruiser roared down the street, siren blazing. Carter could tell the noise was not making it easy for his friend to think.

"So let me get this straight," he said, "you want me to hack this lady's computer, a computer on the university network, and place an appointment to meet you for coffee? And then you'll accept the invitation once she's sent it out?"

"Yep, that's the size of it," Carter affirmed with a grin.

"This one is going to cost you, Doc," Pete told him. "I could lose my job if they ever caught me doing this. If I trip an alarm I don't know about, they'll be showing me the door the next day."

"Pete, I wouldn't have asked you if I couldn't pay."

"Six months' free beer," he told Carter, "and you have to set the tab up at Kilkenny's over on Dou Street. I'll be going over there tonight, so you'd better get the arrangements made today. I no get free beer tonight; you no get the date."

"Agreed. But only one beer at a time and no buying rounds for your buds."

"No problem, Doc," Pete agreed. "Bastards can pay for their own beer. Well, give me the particulars because I have to head over to the office. A bunch of smart-ass kids tried to breach the firewall around some professor's grading chart. The university will have a few less students this time tomorrow." Carter handed him a piece of paper with Mackenzie's information and watched his friend walk out of the coffee shop with the paper cup in his hand.

The next morning Mackenzie had just finished arranging the desk in her cubicle the way she liked it to appear. Not being a full-time instructor or member of the staff at the University meant she didn't warrant her own office. She did have one lab bench where she staked out her territory and a small cubicle in a large room full of them. She liked to arrive promptly, before the custodians, to make sure she had everything ready for the day. She did this right after her workout routine at a small gym near her apartment.

She scrolled down her electronic schedule to the class she was teaching that day to see who her teaching associate would be. They'd given her another 'intro' class; she gritted her teeth in preparation. At least it beats trying to explain the basics of genetic determination at the community college. She made certain her syllabus was up to date, and everything she needed to take to the lecture hall was on the flash drive.

Mackenzie chuckled over a story one of the senior professors in her department had told the other day. He found the latest advances in technology to be better than the older ones. One day in the 1970's, he taught a class in biochemistry and had to endure the latest fad in note taking - the multi-colored pen. Some genius had produced a cheap pen where you could trigger a different color with a new stem every time a plastic lever was depressed. All he had to say was "Now this is very important" to hear the 'clack-clack-clack' of hundreds of red points being depressed.

As she stood to leave, something caught her eye. She had an email from Professor Carter Devereux accepting a coffee date for this evening at 5:00. *What?* Mackenzie shook her head. She couldn't recall setting up an appointment with him. She turned to the vase of roses on her desk. *Isn't this the idiot who body-slammed me outside the other day?*

She'd accepted the roses but had to endure the joshing from her colleagues. She looked at her calendar in confusion. There it was, the date scheduled in with all the other appointments. She had made the invitation. Mackenzie scrolled back on the screen and found the formal email she'd sent out to Professor Carter thanking him for the flowers and asking to meet with him. *That's bizarre, I'm sure I would remember doing that.*

She continued to stare at the screen, worried she was suffering from temporary memory loss. For a few moments, she contemplated an excuse to cancel the meeting but then decided if she had made the appointment, she would need to keep it. The coffee shop where they were supposed to meet was located a few blocks north of campus. She shrugged; maybe I made it and forgot all about it. She was overdue for her annual physical; *perhaps I should bring this incident up when I see my doctor.*

At 5:00 that evening, she found herself at the counter of 'The Coffee Bean,' one of the many hip little coffee shops that dotted the better parts of Boston. She looked the place over with the eye of a biologist, making sure the food license on the wall was up to date.

She ordered her coffee and looked around for the professor. He was already at a corner table. Tall as he was, Prof. Carter Devereux was difficult to miss. He even had the same metal frame glasses on he'd worn at the time of the collision.

"Did you have any trouble finding the place?" he stood as she arrived and sat down with her cup.

"No, it was easy enough. I asked a few of my students. They come here often." She was still very much in doubt about this whole event and decided that the best defense was to attack. "So why did you want to meet with me?"

Carter did not blink an eye. "I believe you asked me out." She was studying his face for any signs of a lie. Carter smiled; *Pete has earned every dime of his beer tab.*

She tried her best not to act confused although she was still perplexed that she had no recollection of setting it up. "Yes," she tossed her hair back over her shoulder. "I wanted to thank you for the roses. Do you always send roses to the women you run over?"

"This was the first time," he laughed "For both running someone over and sending roses."

She nodded slowly. *I must definitely talk to my doctor about this bout of amnesia.*

"So how goes the research? I see you're working in Thor Veblen's lab. Is he still obsessed with chloroplast batteries?" The chair of her department had invested a lot of money in a company years ago that was supposed to make batteries based on the way plant cells created energy. It was a catastrophic failure, but Dr. Veblen continued to put time and his own money into the concept.

"I don't think so," she said. "He's getting close to retirement and continues to talk about the glory days of gene sequencing. We try to take care of him. He is a living legend and still brings a lot of money into the department."

"Good to hear he's still alright. I know he is getting on in years. What about your research, what are you doing? I couldn't tell from your online profile."

"Genomic analysis," she said while sipping her coffee. "We're trying to identify and characterize genes in hopes of improving blood cell function. It involves a lot of sequence work, so it's time-consuming."

"Sounds interesting; you want to improve the human race?"

"Remember your high school biology?" she said with a little sarcasm. "Red blood cells take oxygen to the body. You improve their function; you improve the body; asthma, sickle cell anemia, all kinds of respiratory diseases would be wiped out."

"So you're trying to find a way to make respirocytes," Carter concluded. Mackenzie looked up with interest. *So, he knows something about what I am doing. He obviously came to this meeting much better prepared than I am.*

"How does a professor of archeology know about respirocytes?"

"I found reference to it a while ago when I was doing some research on the supposed extreme age and gigantic size of humans and animals in ancient times. It seems as if constant high oxygen levels in the atmosphere and the blood could have had an impact on longevity and maybe even bigger and stronger bodies. Or have I got it wrong?"

"You are absolutely right; it would certainly have a positive effect on human health. I'm amazed that archeologists would be interested in the topic."

"Well, archeologists have to look at all the possibilities, and sometimes have to find an explanation for the unexplainable."

She was impressed. Mackenzie hadn't had the time to look at all the research Carter was doing, but her colleagues mentioned he was one of the top researchers in his area who was continually working in the field to find new sites of interest. In one year alone, he'd been to five different digs in four different countries. Shovel bums everywhere looked up to him as some kind of maestro.

Later on, the conversation moved to the topic of evolution. Mackenzie was a strict Darwinist - someone who thought Richard Dawkins had written the definitive study of the subject, and she embraced his beliefs.

"You know that most scientists believe that humans migrated from Africa to Europe ..."

"Yes, about 60,000 years ago it is thought," Carter interjected.

"... but I just think it's hard to really determine what happened all those years ago on the Serengeti plains." Mackenzie mused.

"Steven Pinker, the evolutionary psychologist, believes that even language is part of an evolutionary process, that it is an instinct shaped by natural selection and adapted to our communication needs."

"This seems to me to flow right in with Spencer's 'Survival of the Fittest.' Evolution is a progressive process; from our evolution into intelligent beings to the development and evolution of our language, our species has progressed, adapting and gaining new skills as needed to survive."

"Mm-hmm," Carter acknowledged while sipping his coffee.

Mackenzie continued, "I agree that evolutionary theory might need adjusting from time to time, to consider new information, but I still believe that evolution makes the most sense from a scientific point of view."

"I see what you are getting at," Carter acknowledged, "but I think there is more to the story than what is already known. For instance, consider the mechanism needed just to clot blood. Doesn't all that irreducible complexity argue for the existence of intelligent design?"

"I see we've been reading our Michael Behe," she smiled, bringing up the name of the controversial biochemist whose theory was that humans were too complex to have evolved by natural selection. "I don't know if I would go in that direction. It's a slippery slope and the next thing you know people are arguing about the earth being less than 10,000 years old. My grandparents were hard-shell Baptists and believed Darwin was the spawn of Satan. So every time I hear people try and find holes in evolutionary theory, I just smile."

"What about punctuated equilibrium?" Carter, enthralled by the woman with the flaming red hair, was enjoying every moment of their conversation. He just needed to keep the conversation active.

"Stephen Jay Gould was big on that one," she replied. "It makes for some nice reading, but Dawkins felt the gaps in the fossil record had more to do with migration than evolutionary activity. And please don't get me started on Lynn Margulis and her Gaia hypothesis."

"What if we are survivors of a previous civilization?"

Carter asked. "It's something I've always wondered about. My grandfather is a big believer in the idea of humanity descending from lost antediluvian civilizations."

"Care to elaborate?"

"Well, as you know, life on earth is a balancing act. Life is only possible because of a complex web of interconnectivity between a number of key components and factors. It's a very fragile environment in which life will end if enough key components collapse."

Mackenzie nodded. "Yes, that's true."

"And it's not just theory." Carter continued. "Such life ending events have in fact happened at least five times in our geological past, although scientists are still gathering evidence for two of them. Four hundred million years ago, a cataclysmic event wiped out almost all of the marine life on earth. Yet as we know, some life did survive. Another event, at the end of the Permian Period, wiped out close to 90 percent of the world's species on land and sea. That one came within a razor's edge of ending all life on earth. Yet again, some life survived and continued. The most recent catastrophic event wiped out the dinosaurs, creating the opportunity for mammals to thrive. Again, some life survived. So it's not too farfetched to think of us as survivors."

"You have me thinking," Mackenzie laughed. "If you look at it like that then maybe we are survivors."

Carter smiled. "The mystery is what did our planet look like before those devastating events? Who and what inhabited earth back then? We don't have much knowledge about those times. Most of it has been lost."

Mackenzie nodded. "Yes, that's true. We have a few bones and fossils, and that's about it."

Where has this woman being hiding all my life? Looking at her beautiful skin and flaming red hair was stirring passions of tenderness in his mind. He wanted to text Pete right now to give him a bonus. Phase 2 was a dazzling success, time for phase three.

Before he could move onto phase three, she asked, "So you're dead set against Darwinism then?"

"No, I'm trying to keep an open mind, but I'm definitely not convinced about it either. I have a few ideas but don't want to bore you with that."

"No please, I would like to hear about it." She insisted.

"Only if you promise not to hold it against me."

"I promise."

"My suppositions are based on probabilities. First 2,000 different and very complex enzymes are required for a living organism to exist. The mathematical probability of building just one of those enzymes by chance is about one in ten followed by 40,000 zeros. Now multiply that number by 2,000 to account for all the enzymes.

"Second, there are 20 amino acids in protein; to form a medium protein, 300 amino acids are arranged in a particular sequence. The possible arrangements of the 20 amino acids are 2,500, followed by another 15 zeros. In other words, if evolutionary theory is to be believed, every protein arrangement in a life form has to be worked out by chance until the right sequence is found - by chance.

"Third, DNA needs enzymes to function and enzymes only operate in the presence of protein chains. In other words, they have to be there together at the same time - a chicken and egg situation.

"Finally, if you were to calculate the odds of the first simple cell forming, you have to keep in mind that the simplest cell would require about 100,000 DNA base pairs and a minimum of about 10,000 amino acids, to form the essential protein chain. Not to mention the other things that had to be present in the primordial soup that would also be vital for the first cell to be formed - all by chance.

"The odds are stacked a bit too heavily against evolution for my liking."

Mackenzie had to put her hand under her chin to stop her mouth from hanging open. *Where did he get all that information and how on earth did he manage to remember it all?*

Carter looked at her and knew it was time for phase three. "Dinner?" he asked. "I know a nice place that cooks a healthy meal. It's run by this man from Berkley who specializes in macrobiotic cooking." He could see the look of intrigue in her face.

"I'll pay this time," he offered. He could tell by her eyes she'd been sold on the idea.

"Okay," she agreed. "This time, but next time you have to let me pay."

Nice, he thought to himself. *She's already agreed to another date.*

The restaurant, known as 'The Green Café,' overlooked the park. Although the weather was a little nippy, Carter had the hostess seat them at an outside table. He watched Mackenzie flip through the menu and order a daily special, consisting of smoked Black Forest ham with Swiss cheese and green bell peppers. He ordered something similar but tried to keep his carbohydrate intake down. She let him order the wine, and they ate their meal discussing the office politics at the University. The sun was slipping toward the horizon by the time their dessert arrived.

He received his share of approving looks from onlookers walking past them on the sidewalk. Mackenzie struck a fine pose with her height and figure. The dress she had on that day was exceptional. She knew how to look good, no argument there.

"So I guess I get to invite you out for the next coffee date?" He asked. Mackenzie finished her tiramisu and put the fork down.

"Only if I am allowed to choose the restaurant," she returned. "You like Thai food?"

"Love it." He smiled.

Carter watched a jogger running down the street on the other side. He wondered what the man might be able to do if respirocytes were ever created. Would the Olympic committee ban them the way steroids were banned from most competitions? Would athletes cross the border into Mexico to find illegal respirocytes therapy? It was too soon to be thinking about such matters. Or was it?

He walked her to her car that evening and, like science professionals everywhere, they exchanged business cards. He walked away a very happy man.

Chapter Four

THE TRUE SONS OF THE PROPHET

Carter saw his grandfather almost weeping over a news story, which showed an ancient temple complex obliterated by a series of explosions detonated by ISIS supporters. He stood in horror as they watched a video, made by ISIS fighters, showing how easy it was to plant the barrels of explosives and rig the charges. The ISIS militants chanted as they pulled the switch, exploding a structure thousands of years old, turning it into dust.

"They'll do the same if they ever come here," Carter growled.

"I pray to God that day will never come," his grandfather said.

The Islamic State controlled vast sections of the Middle East. It had survived numerous disastrous attacks to become the largest and most extreme Islamic group in the world. It was known by the acronym ISIS and ISIL in the western countries, but as 'Daesh,' from the Arabic words for its name, in most of the Middle East.

At its height of expansion, ISIS controlled an area

approximately the size of the state of Pennsylvania. It controlled the major desert roads through its territories and had about 35,000 square miles under occupation.

Much of the territory under ISIS control followed the fertile Tigris and Euphrates rivers through Iraq and into Syria, an area dominated by Sunni Muslims. One of the most disturbing things about the ISIS fighters was the large contingent of foreign volunteers fighting with them - volunteers representing 35 different countries.

ISIS originally painted itself as the defender of the Sunni Muslim community against American and Shia aggression, so young foreign men considered it a noble task to volunteer. They had an efficient propaganda machine and consistently requested help from young men to 'do their duty.' Even Canadian nationals fought alongside ISIS militants.

The western convert provided strong propaganda value for ISIS. An immigrant returning to fight for them might be useful, but a westerner not raised in a Muslim household was even better. Foreign fighters found themselves with better pay and living conditions than the local volunteers. They also had the pick of non-Muslim women captured in raids.

One of the most significant aspects of ISIS was its insistence on the draconic enforcement of Sharia law in all areas under its control. It had taken the enforcement of Sharia law to a point not seen anywhere outside the Taliban's rule over Afghanistan. Religious police patrolled the streets with weapons seeking out the slightest infraction, acting swiftly and mercilessly.

The destruction of ancient artifacts brought ISIS and its related groups into conflict with the archeological world. To them, the monuments of eras before the rise of Islam were nothing more than stones and precious metals forged to honor false gods - devil worship. Thus, it continued the policy of the Taliban, destroying priceless Buddhist statues in Afghanistan.

The archeological community could do little but sit back and seethe as the new barbarians destroyed irreplaceable objects and artifacts.

It was a bleak day near the town of Raqqa when Hassan Al-Suleiman stood watch over his small group of faithful mercenaries. He was a tall, swarthy man, nearing the middle of his fourth decade, with deep-set black eyes under bushy brows and an equally bushy well-trimmed beard. He was imposing, with an air of command that few would challenge. An educated man, he traveled to Europe to study before the fall of Saddam. He continually honed his fighting skills to a sharp edge. Hassan had the mind of a leader, the courage to lead, and was determined to go far and take his followers with him.

Leaving their little town near Baghdad to seek glory and booty had been his plan. Staying and having nothing was not his idea of the life that Allah had set out for him. He was convinced he would achieve great things. Providing he stood up and volunteered; Allah would be on his side and would aid and abet him.

Their Sunni elders handed the men flowers as they piled guns and ammo into whatever cars they could find, then mounted their old trucks and drove away from their hometown. Hassan left with a force of 150 proud and willing men.

Now his force had dwindled down to 20.

Death and defection had destroyed their numbers. Arriving in Mosul before the main fighting began against the Shia heretics and Iraqi Army, Hassan drove them to refine their fighting skills and be the best and most efficient volunteer group the ISIS command could send into the field.

He quickly learned that courage was no substitute for common sense, watching with despair as his friends were cut to pieces when they were sent directly against the American-supported positions.

At last, when he could stand it no longer, he walked up to the well-fed and well-connected ISIS officer and slapped him in the face. His force had been reduced by fifty percent in the last 24 hours and Hassan would no longer tolerate them being used as cannon fodder. He had watched the better-armed ISIS groups withdraw, sit back, and use the new weapons while his men died in their stead.

"You are worse than the accursed infidels the devil has sent against us!" Hassan shouted at the officer as the armed guards hauled him away. "At least they come out and fight! Go back and hide behind the skirts of your mother, you half-breed dog!" his heels dragging in the dirt, leaving skid marks leading back to the fat officer he was abusing.

Warned that another outburst would cost him his life, Hassan gathered his men and told them they were moving out immediately. He left the cover of the ISIS command post near Mosul and headed in the direction of Syria. He knew without a doubt that another group could use some battle-hardened fighters who did not fear death, but were smart enough not to court it. There would be no more wasted deaths among his men.

Two days later, passing refugees informed them that the ISIS post where they had fought, and many had died, was destroyed by a Russian bombing run less than 24 hours ago. The Russians, supporters of the 'official' Syrian government, were joining the coalition against the Islamic State and had no qualms about obliterating anything on the ground near their target.

When Hassan's men heard the news, they swore eternal loyalty to the man who had saved them from being vaporized in the field. On that day, his group began calling themselves The True Sons of the Prophet.

Hassan soon discovered they could sell their services to the highest bidder. What did he care if one group supported ISIS one day and the next they fought against the Islamic State? They were all dogs as far as he was concerned.

It was not in his plan to be fighting under the command of others forever. He needed some time to consolidate power and shape his followers into an even better fighting force. Later there would be time for women and wealth, but for now, all he cared about was conquest.

Hassan was no fool. He knew he would have to play his closest supporters against each other in order to obtain what he wanted: an empire of his own.

He stood next to his armored car, captured from a Syrian government troop, and surveyed the landscape around the small town on the bank of the river. Seeing the man standing so tall and severe in his dark blue dishdasha, his keffiyeh moving in the slight breeze around his head, drew the villagers out in curiosity to survey his armored column, which had arrived the evening before.

He had instructed his men, who had now grown to a force of 200, not to bother the local people. He wanted a chance to talk to them and gain their trust. From what he was told, this town was full of Shia Twelve offshoots that had lived there since their Imam had taken them down from the mountains 50 years ago. Good. They would have need of an armed force to protect them.

The village was close to the fighting between ISIS and

the Syrian government and ISIS was on the run, leaving him a power vacuum to exploit. Soon the American special operatives would try to make contact. Hassan let it be known he was open to talking with them. They had better weapons and the supplies he planned to acquire.

"When do you want me to take a squad and make contact with the locals, Amyr?" Ali asked him. Hassan allowed himself a rare smile. Ali had been with him since they left their town over a year ago. He'd seen the worst man had to offer and had survived countless campaigns against all matter of enemies. Now Ali was calling him by the ancient title used to address a prince. This was all as it should be.

"It's still early morning," Hassan told him. "I heard the first call to prayer so they must be up and about. Take five of your best men and go find the elders. Tell them we are here to protect them from those who would bring harm. Tell them we do not require much, just places for our fighters to stay and they will be handsomely rewarded."

"Yes, My Prince," Ali said and began to walk away.

"Ali!" Hassan called after him. Ali turned and looked back with a question on his face.

"Let them know we will protect them in the face of danger, that I am bringing them peace and prosperity. And let them know I will personally shoot any deserter."

"Yes, My Prince," Ali responded and returned to walking in the direction of his men.

Chapter Five

THE CEO

About a month after his first coffee date with Mackenzie, Carter was enjoying a morning coffee meeting with her, thinking that the Mackenzie project was moving along nicely. He was at the stage in his life where he was ready to settle down with the right woman, and his definition of the right woman was the red-haired, green-eyed deity sitting across from him who worked in the University's genetics department.

On the way to his office after the meeting, Carter saw a familiar face in the lobby -- someone from his past. A man much younger than himself was reading a copy of *Archeology Today*. As Carter approached him, it struck him who he was. Jacob Wilson, an energetic man from Ohio who had been determined to earn his Ph.D. in the history of the Inca civilization. Having a burning desire to document the rise and fall of the Incas, he spent several summers in the Andes researching sites at high altitudes. Jacob would return in the autumn fired up for more work and with tales of eating guinea pigs with the locals. He was on good terms with the

Peruvians and hinted he might spend the rest of his life down there if someone would pay him to do the research.

"Jacob!" Carter yelled at him from down the hall. "Jacob Wilson! Well, I'll be damned; you are a surprise! What brings you north?" The last he heard, Jacob was camping on top of some mountains doing fieldwork. By now, he felt the man would be running an entire department.

"Glad to see you as well, Prof," Jacob greeted him, while pumping Carter's hand. "It's good to be back at the University. I have a lot of fond memories of this place."

"Enough with the 'Prof' nonsense," Carter returned. "You're a doctor of philosophy as well. So, do tell, what brings you all the way from the Andes? Has a revolution broken out? I was under the impression the government was stable down there."

"No, nothing of the kind. Did you get the bird?" Jacob asked him. He was older than Carter remembered and had lost a lot of weight, not surprising considering the conditions under which he worked.

"You were the one who sent it?" Carter asked, his voice dropping in volume. "Son, you've had me hypnotized for many weeks with that artifact. Come on into my office, let's talk."

Carter unlocked the door, showed his former student in, and pointed him to a chair. He started the coffee maker and sat down behind his desk. At last, he was about to find out the tale of the golden hummingbird.

"So tell me the whole story. I want to know everything about it."

"I've been working on a dig outside Cusco," Jacob began, "and I started to hear rumors about the field supervisor selling artifacts to collectors. I'm not talking about letting people take small arrowheads and pieces of broken pottery home as samples; I'm talking major discoveries made out of worked metal. The kind of things we need to catalog. I didn't say anything to my coworkers."

"So how did you find out?" Carter asked while fingering his silk tie. "This is a serious allegation. I trust you have the evidence because the right people will demand it. Who's the field supervisor and what company is undertaking the dig?"

"The man's name is Mark Freeman, and we're all working on a long-term contract with Resource Alliance Unlimited - RAU," he explained. "They're a big outfit with an office in Manhattan. They've landed contracts with several universities to do the cultural resource studies out in the field. Look, I know we don't make a lot of money out there and what I bring home barely pays for my student loans, but what he's doing is completely unacceptable."

"Evidence, Jacob, evidence," Carter pointed out. "What did I teach you all those years ago? You can't prove a thing without physical evidence."

"I've got it on my smartphone," he said. "And I uploaded it to an Internet cloud account just in case. Can I get you to access something on your computer?"

"Let's see it," Carter said. This was serious stuff. The Peruvian government would have all the grounds they needed to kick the University out of the country if it was participating in artifact theft, even unknowingly. In most cases, anything of significance leaving the country required the approval of the local government prior to its departure.

They sat down in front of Carter's computer. Jacob typed in the passcode to his account and in a few minutes, they were looking at some shaky hand-held videos of a man meeting with several other men out in the field. Money passed between the men and bundles were handed over.

The man with the bundles was unshaven and Caucasian. The men with the money looked to be locals and were wearing the latest in hiking wear. The video wasn't long, but Carter could hear them talking in English. The man who was unshaven said something about having more cash the next time as the other two wandered off and out of the frame. The screen went black.

"Do you think he knew you were taking the video?"

"No, he doesn't suspect a thing. The local day-jobbers told me about what was going on. They knew I speak one of the local languages and came to me when they found out. He offered to cut them in on the deal if they took the bundles down the mountain, but he refused to pay them enough. They're more pissed about the lousy money he offered them than about the artifacts being sold outside the country."

"We'll deal with this right away," Carter thundered. "Now the bird, I want to know more about the bird. Where did you find it? I think it might be connected to the Lost Golden Garden the conquistadors wrote about."

"I've been thinking along similar lines," Jacob beamed. "I was working up on the cliffs digging some holes so we could screen the results. Those damn survey holes can be a pain to dig up in the mountains where there's nothing but rock, but it has to be done. Anyway, I noticed a cleft in a rock, so, inquisitive as I am, I went up a few hundred feet on my own and checked it out. And that is when I found the gold bird."

Carter nodded for him to continue.

"It was wedged between two rock facings. Somehow, the rain and wind had never reached it up there. I put it in my pocket, making a note in my field pad about the location coordinates and decided to see if anything else was there. I took out a flashlight and shined it inside. The opening was big enough for me, and I didn't see anything dangerous inside, so I went in on my own. I wasn't in very long, but I found several other figurines, also made out of gold and silver. They all appeared to be from the same artisan and time, so whatever is up on the mountain came from the same source. Anyway, I left the site intact and came down to my shovel and the hole I was digging. I brought the bird back with me but didn't say a word to anyone about it. I was afraid the bird, and its flock, would end up in someone's private collection or melted down for the gold."

Carter was listening attentively.

"I went to the nearest post office and mailed it to you the first chance I had. I told the postmaster it was some local rocks for a friend, and he believed me. I didn't put much in the way of a return address on it because I have no way of knowing how far up the chain this artifact theft scheme raises. I don't think Freeman is the only one involved. He has to have some help from local smugglers. I had a vacation coming up, so I took it the following week and told everybody I needed to visit my mother."

"You did right, Jacob," Carter encouraged him. "And don't worry about the bird. I've got it stashed in a safe place."

"So what do we do now?" Jacob asked.

"We go to see the project sponsors, and we present the evidence. I know some of their board members."

Two days later, Carter and Jacob found themselves on the top floor of a building overlooking Manhattan. In the distance, they could see the empire state building in all its glory.

It was a lovely morning, the sun was already high in the sky, sparkling on the ocean and revealing distant ships at sea. However, the whole atmosphere was sullen by the information they needed to deliver to the executives of the RAU.

Passing a wall with exotic art prints, a secretary looking to be all of 19 years old escorted them to a conference room. The door opened, and she ushered them in while asking both academics if they needed anything to drink. Both said no and heard the door shut behind them.

"Good morning Professor Devereux and Doctor Wilson," an older man greeted them. "I understand you have some important news about our operation in Peru?"

Another man rose from the table, whom Carter recognized as James Epstein, the CEO of a company he'd worked with in the past. He introduced himself to Jacob and then the other people who were at the table. Carter knew them all through his grandfather. With Epstein were Jonathan James, the man in charge of sales, and Esmeralda Levy, who handled the finances.

"I'll get right to the point," Carter told them with Jacob remaining silent in the background. "Doctor Wilson," he pointed to Jacob, "is a former student of mine and he's been working on your site for the past two years. He has uncovered strong evidence that the man you placed in charge of the site is selling artifacts to smugglers. I don't have to tell you what will happen if this knowledge ever becomes public."

A cone of silence descended over the room.

"I trust you have the proof to back up these allegations," Esmeralda Levy broke the silence.

Jacob opened up his briefcase and pulled out a tablet computer onto which the incriminating video had been loaded the night before. He pushed an icon on the screen, and the video began to play. He handed it to her while the others gathered around to watch.

"I know this man," was all James Epstein had to say to the other two. When the video finished playing, he returned the tablet to Carter. The looks on their faces were grim.

"I thank you for bringing this serious violation of our corporate policy to our attention," Jonathan said. "I really don't know what to say."

"We'll have to act right away," Levy declared. "If word of this gets out, it could destroy the company."

"We need to recall Freeman immediately," James told the others. "But he can't know why. We'll have to tell him it has to do with the budget forecast. Once he gets off the plane, we can have him arrested, but only then. If he suspects we know, he could alert his contacts and then more artifacts could be lost." The other two members of the board nodded in agreement.

"There's more," Carter continued. "Jacob found a significant artifact higher up in the mountains, and he was afraid to tell anyone about it lest Freeman sold it too." Turning to Jacob, he suggested, "Why don't you tell them what you found?"

The executive members sat mesmerized for the next fifteen minutes while Jacob went over the delicate discovery he'd made in the cave and what it all entailed. He talked about the legend of the Lost Golden Garden from the days of the Inca royalty, how it disappeared after discovery by Spanish explorers. To boost his claims, he brought up the pictures Carter had taken. After putting the display on scroll, he handed the tablet to them. They stood in amazement as the various digital pictures scrolled past.

"Where is this artifact?" Esmeralda asked. "I'd like to see it for myself."

"We're keeping it concealed in a safe place pending the investigation into the smuggling operation," Carter stated.

"I can attest to its authenticity. I've had the gold composition tested by the chemistry department."

The five of them talked about what to do next. It was Carter's idea to call a meeting with the University right away while the board summoned Freeman back to the United States. They all agreed that the severity of what had been uncovered warranted immediate action.

"Can you set up something with the Dean?" James asked him. "Let him know this is bigger than another fundraising event; this is deadly serious. The credibility of the University and our company is at stake. If this gets to the media before we get it under control, the results would be catastrophic."

"I'll set something up in the next few days," Carter told them. "In the meantime, get your man on the first plane out of there. Just don't let him know why."

Three days later, Carter and Jacob were in the boardroom of the University. The Dean of the school of Archeology and five members of the Board were meeting in private with Esmeralda Levy. Before the meeting began, she took an important phone call and informed everyone that Freeman was en route from Peru to JFK airport.

"The FBI has been informed, and we've sent them the video evidence," she explained. "When he goes through customs, they'll take him into custody. As soon as I get word that he's been arrested, I'll phone a contact in the Peruvian National Police. They won't be too happy to hear what I have to tell them, but at least, we'll have done our part."

Once again, Carter passed around the video evidence of Freeman selling artifacts to smugglers. After the Board had looked at it, he plugged the tablet into a video projector and showed them the pictures of the golden hummingbird. Jacob was able to show them some additional photographs he'd taken of the cave opening in the mountains. While everyone was allowing the significance of the find to sink in, Jacob told the legend of the Lost Golden Garden.

"From what you are saying this could be one of the biggest finds of the century," the Dean stated. "I can't recall anything of this size being uncovered in my lifetime."

"Yes, sir," Jacob agreed. "We are sitting on top of something huge down there. I didn't tell anyone at the Institute of Peruvian Studies about it. I'm afraid they'll want to be in charge of this dig every step of the way if we've found something of the size I think I may have discovered."

"We'll need to handle this very diplomatically," the dean continued. "We're already in trouble with the smuggling operation taking place on our watch."

"I would like to point out, there may be more Peruvians involved in these thefts of artifacts than North Americans," Esmeralda commented.

"It won't matter," the Dean responded. "The Peruvians will view it as an insult to their sovereignty. In their minds, the *gringos* would have tried to rip them off again."

Jacob looked to Carter, who nodded. Carefully, Jacob took out the original box from his briefcase, which he used to ship the golden bird north. He opened it after putting on cotton gloves.

"I have the artifact I discovered in the cave," he told them. "I will bring it around the room so everyone can see. Professor Devereux has already had the gold content analyzed." He slowly walked around the room showing the golden hummingbird to everyone at the conference table. When finished, Jacob returned it to the box and removed his cotton gloves.

He walked over to the table and set the box down. "I've

placed the artifact here for everyone to see. It's up to you to decide what needs to be done next."

There was silence and then the Dean turned to a Board member on his right and spoke quietly. Next, he turned back to Carter and Jacob. "Would you two gentlemen please excuse us for a minute?" he requested. "We need to have a conversation in private. I'll bring you back in a few minutes." Carter and Jacob walked out of the room and closed the door behind them.

They waited in the lobby without speaking to each other. A few times Jacob and Carter exchanged looks, but they knew nothing more needed saying.

The door to the conference room creaked open after 30 minutes. "Could you two gentlemen please come back in?" The Dean requested. "We have something to tell you."

They walked back in just as the Dean was taking his seat. The box with the golden hummingbird was still in the location where Jacob had left it.

"We've come to a decision," the Dean told them. "And it is a unanimous one; I want you to know there was no dissension on this matter.

"We've decided to ask Dr. Wilson to take charge of the site, reporting directly to Professor Devereux as the CEO of the expedition.

"Dr. Wilson knows more about the Inca civilization than anyone outside Peru. Ms. Levy phoned her contacts with the Peruvian National Police, and they were grateful for our help. They've suspected a smuggling operation was taking cultural artifacts out of the country for the past year and have undertaken some investigations on their own. They agree Dr. Wilson should be in charge of the site and will do everything possible to help him. We smoothed things over by offering to send the golden hummingbird to the Peruvian embassy in Washington, D.C. The ambassador himself is arriving tomorrow to pick it up.

They've promised not to publicize the smuggling operation because they don't want to compromise the investigation."

Jacob had a bewildered look on his face.

"You have our full trust behind you, Dr. Wilson. Professor Devereux, we owe you our gratitude for helping him bring this to our attention. If you accept our proposal, Dr. Wilson, we want you to leave right away and travel to the site. Because we don't know the full extent of the corruption at the dig site, we'll send a security team down there with you. They have an office in Lima where they will hire some local guards to accompany you. The local police will, in all probability, arrive first, but we feel you will need protection while you're down there."

The Dean stopped and looked at Jacob for an answer.

Jacob was pale but managed to signal his acceptance by nodding his head.

The Dean smiled and continued, "next week, we are going to issue a joint press release with the Peruvian Embassy. We'll state the nature of the smuggling operation and explain how you stopped it through your courageous efforts. The government of Peru will take credit for anyone they arrest as part of the smuggling ring."

Carter looked at Jacob's stunned face and wondered if his had the same expression.

"Professor Devereux, I take it you don't have any objections about the role of CEO as suggested? I'm sure you'll be able to do most of your work remotely via a satellite communications link."

"No objections sir. I will be honored to work with Dr. Wilson on this."

"Thank you, that's what I expected."

Outside Jacob turned to Carter, "What just happened in there?"

Carter chuckled, "Well I didn't see that coming either. Seems you and I are now in charge of that dig my friend."

"How come it happened so fast?" A still dumbfounded Jacob wanted to know.

"Think about it. Who knows the site better than you do? You have demonstrated your loyalty and trustworthiness. You are the best choice, Jacob." Carter laughed, "Welcome to the real world of archeology, Jacob. Let's go find that lost Gold Garden."

Chapter Six

ONE BRIEF MOMENT OF TIME

Later that evening Carter told Mackenzie about the emergency meeting of the University Board and the company responsible for the survey work outside the Peruvian city of Cusco. He avoided most of the details of the possible legal complications arising from Jacob taking the golden hummingbird out of the country and focused instead on how well the man handled himself in front of the board. Nor did he mention Wilson was a former student of his. Mackenzie sat spellbound as she listened to his account of the meeting.

"Wow, and poor Jacob thought they were going to charge him. He walked out of it not only a free man but the champion of the hour."

"We discussed what the outcome might be beforehand," Carter told her. "He's very serious about making certain the artifacts don't fall into the hands of smugglers. It's been an issue for years, and the stigma of people selling relics is something the profession wants to avoid."

"Still," she brought up, "he might have been suspended from his job or even gone to jail."

"I would have made sure he had the best legal representation possible," Carter said. "But, yes, he looked into the abyss when he walked into that meeting this morning. I could see his hands shaking when he brought the golden hummingbird out to show everyone."

They were in a small restaurant overlooking Boston Harbor and the lights of the city illuminating the metropolitan area. In the distance, they could see the changing color of the leaves on trees in the park and joggers running along the paths trying to avoid each other. Through the open windows of the restaurant, they felt the fresh air and heard the sounds of traffic in the distance. As Carter looked out at the busy scene before him, he remembered the waterway had once been much larger. Filling in a good portion of the harbor is what extended the Boston City area to what it was today.

"So," Mackenzie continued, "from what you say, it sounds as if you're the official head of the survey with Wilson being your representative in the field."

Carter nodded. "The first order of business is to find out how far up and down the chain the rot has traveled. He suspects Freeman's contacts were in the city and some people involved in the dig were passing information about the better artifacts. We need to find out about everyone involved before another shovel hits the ground. Right now, the entire site is under the jurisdiction of the Peruvian National Police. Every person who was working there has been moved off-site."

"How are you going to restart the survey? Something tells me you'll have to be patching up a lot with the Peruvian government."

"It helped when we offered to give the hummingbird to the ambassador. At least they are still happy to keep us involved. They know the University can lend the prestige they need to the survey, but at the same time, they are not happy about what happened. They have made it clear we'll be kicked out of the country if it ever happens again."

"That's understandable," she said as she took a sip of her wine.

"I want to fly up to Freydis and talk to my grandfather," he continued. "I want to think this one through with him. We might have to bring in a new company to continue the work. I really don't want to, but if the Peruvians don't allow me to use RAU, I will have no choice."

She nodded. "Freydis? What's that?" She put down her wine glass and looked at him with curiosity.

Carter smiled warmly. "It's the name of my grandfather's ranch up north in Canada. He's owned it for years."

"How did he come up with the name?"

"Freydis was Leif Ericksson's sister, born around 950. The Viking sagas refer to her as Freydís Eiríksdóttir. She was with Leif Ericksson when he traveled to North America if you follow the accounts in the sagas. She had red hair and was a wild and adventurous woman!" He teased.

"Somehow I missed reading those but it sounds like I should," she laughed.

Mackenzie tossed her flaming hair back as she remembered something and looked deep into Carter's eyes.

"Do you have any plans for next Saturday?"

"No. Why? Do you have something in mind?"

"My brother Ray is home on leave at the moment, and mom wants me to come over for dinner. You want to come along and meet the family?"

Carter did some quick calculations in his head and

figured he would have four days with Grandfather Will and two more to prepare for the survey with Wilson.

"Sure, but only if your mother is expecting me."

"Oh yes, she is. In fact, she wants you to come so she can meet you. We had one of those mother-daughter talks if you know what I mean."

Carter smiled. He knew exactly what she meant.

The leaves were beginning to line the streets as winter started to show its teeth and he took her hand in his as they walked toward the car. His heart beat faster when he felt her snuggle up close to him.

Stopping under a tree, his crimson-haired goddess turned her green eyes to him, and Carter felt the stir in him; he had to be with this woman. She was the one he'd waited for all his life; he just didn't know it until that momentous collision several weeks ago. She leaned into him and electricity sparked through his body as her lips touched his - voices chanted in a language unknown for centuries, echoing in his ears as he enjoyed the essence of the stunning woman in his arms. Time stopped for both of them.

If Carter could collect and preserve one brief moment in time, this would be it.

"I could do this for the rest of my life," he spoke softly as his lips disengaged from hers. She rubbed his back and continued to look into his eyes.

"I feel the same," she whispered.

"What are we going to do about it?"

"You're going to have to catch me to find out!" she laughed as she broke out of his arms and ran full speed toward the car.

Carter ran after her. When he caught up, she was leaning on the car still laughing, her red hair spread about her shoulders. He opened the door for her and saw her settled. Walking around to the driver's side, he whispered to himself with glee, "I've just chased the mother of my children."

Chapter Seven

THAT'S MANDATORY

The next day Carter left for Freydis. The flight in the twin-engine plane didn't seem to take as long as it usually did - he had a lot on his mind. He needed to talk to his Grandfather about his new responsibilities and Mackenzie. Gramps would want a complete account of each, so he rehearsed what to say as he passed over the Canadian landscape.

As usual, Grandfather Will was waiting for him by the hangar at the end of the runway. He helped him unload his luggage while peppering him with questions saved up about the golden hummingbird. As they drove off to the main house, Carter tried to answer them as best he could.

"The trees," Carter told him as they drove along the path. "I don't think I've ever seen them so beautiful before."

"It's because you're in love!" his grandfather laughed.

Nothing escapes him.

After pouring the coffee, they moved to his grandfather's study to discuss the events of the past few days.

"So your friend Jacob," Carter's grandfather began, "he's in Peru right now?"

"He's the only non-Peruvian national they'll let onsite," Carter explained. "The entire area is cordoned off by a detachment from the National Police. I talk to Jacob every day. He has an encampment outside the fence they erected. Even he has to check in every day with a guard who carries an Uzi. The government down there is deadly serious about taking care of this site."

"Given what happened, I can understand why. Are they going to keep the same company?"

"Yes. It took a lot of persuading, but the Peru Ministry of Culture, in charge of antiquities, finally agreed to allow them to continue on a probational basis. However, they will only be allowed to continue *after* the police have finished their work, which means everyone on the site will be thoroughly vetted before they are accepted. They will be checking the logs very carefully in the future. Everyone now realizes how big this discovery might become someday."

"Would you be willing to talk to your satellite company friends? We'll need a secure communications link to the camp. I'd also like to see if we could photograph the area from orbit. A lot can be determined from a geosynchronous satellite image."

"You still have to do the ground work. But yes, I'll talk to the people I know."

"Thanks! That will be very helpful."

"By the way, we're going over to Ahote and Bly's place tonight. They offered to cook dinner when I told them you were coming."

Later, as they made their way toward their friends' cabin, Will stopped the cart and cocked one ear to the distance. "Do you hear that?" His grandfather was absorbed.

"Hear what, Gramps?" Then he heard it too. The

sound resembled a train whistle, but it continued to wail in the distance. Carter was quiet, trying to identify it and then realized. "Wolves! There are wolves out there. They're howling."

Grandfather Will nodded with a smile. "They weren't around when I bought the place. They're slowly coming back and repopulating the environment. It's good, they'll help to restore balance among the deer population."

He stepped back into the cart and continued the trip. Ahote greeted him with a slap on the back, yelling to Bly that their guests had arrived.

"Will and Dr. Gates have arrived on schedule!" he announced.

Still sitting around the table after dinner, Ahote asked, "So what do you think the chances are that this golden hummingbird predates the Inca civilization?" He'd been around Carter and Will Devereux long enough to pick up their interest in ancient civilizations.

"It's something I'm still thinking about. In some ways, this artifact is an Oopart." Carter explained. He wished there was a better acronym. It sounded like a comic strip character. "The detail is too fine to match the Inca technology; they didn't seem to like making precise copies of animals – at least not according to any artifact I've ever seen produced by them. I am cautiously optimistic that this hummingbird could be from a civilization before them."

"Don't forget Puma Punku in Bolivia," Will brought up. "The Tiwanaku culture managed to build an entire infrastructure there. The construction techniques they used were beyond anything else we've seen in South America. Some of those stone blocks are polished better than what you'll see at a modern stone yard. You think there might be a connection between them and what your friend Jacob found?"

"It's possible, but I can't say how much. Each could be the remnant of something much older. Or, they could be two distinct civilizations. We just don't know. No one knows why the Tiwanaku culture abandoned the Puma Punku complex approximately 1,000 years ago. They left no written records, and no legends exist from the people in the area to explain the abrupt abandonment. The best guess is crop failure from bad weather, a plague, overpopulation, or war. No one really knows."

Ahote refilled their wine glasses and looked at Carter, encouraging him to continue.

"There is so much we're still learning about the history of this planet. Every so often, someone makes another discovery that undermines what we thought before. In most cases, it's a simple matter of going back to adjust what we already know and then going forward again. But, every now and then, something really big is unearthed, which forces archeologists to rethink it all. We may be on the verge of a paradigm shift because of this golden hummingbird and the other artifacts Jacob found in that cave. We can't ignore the possibility that some halfwits might want to destroy it just because the finds might threaten the way they think about the past."

"Putting it that way, I can see why it's important," Ahote remarked. "Are you afraid someone will try and melt the artifacts down for their gold content?"

"It's always a fear. Much of what the conquistadors found ended up melted into bars. We don't even know the origin of that gold we found in the Viking longship. Heck, we still don't even know what the ship was doing that far south."

The next day, his grandfather showed him some of the improvements he was making around the homestead. While they walked, he turned the conversation to something different. "So tell me about this woman that's spun the cobwebs in your brain," Grandfather Will grinned.

"Mackenzie?" Carter came out of his latest daze. He'd been thinking about their last date and the dinner that he was to attend with her family when he returned to Boston. "As you know, she holds a Ph.D. in molecular biology and is an adjunct professor in the Department of Genetics at the University. Quite a woman let me tell you. She's a tall drink of water; not much shorter than me."

"Well then I will have to meet her," his grandfather replied.

"So you don't mind me bringing her up here?"

"That's mandatory before you'll get my blessings." Will chuckled. "She can have the spare bedroom- can't have her getting the wrong ideas about a trip to Freydis."

"Glad you understand, Gramps. I believe she is 'The One' and I don't want to rush things. Up to now, I've put off so much to further my career, and I think it's time to settle down. You know, raise a family, and give you some heirs. None of us are going to live forever."

"We do need to be thinking about the future," the older man agreed. "So few people do these days."

"I do all the time," Carter said. "I haven't thought a lot about raising kids. It's something I need to sit down and talk to her about if ..."

"So you are really serious. I like that."

"Oh yes there is no doubt in my mind; this is the woman

I want to marry. She is going to be the mother of your great grandkids." Carter beamed.

"I'm sure you've made the right choice, but I would like to meet her just the same. You'd be surprised how people can act when taken out of their habituated environment. It's one of the reasons for basic training in the military. You take a bunch of guys from all over the country with diverse socio-economic backgrounds, toss them together in the same bunkhouse, let them suffer together, and out comes a fighting force which will crawl through the depths of hell for each other."

"She knocked me off my feet, and I'm sure she is going to have the same impact on you." Carter laughed. "You just wait and see when she sets foot on Freydis."

Chapter Eight

FAMILY DINNER

Carter put in extra work on his tai chi the day he was supposed to go over to Mackenzie's house and meet her parents. Carefully balancing the practice sword in his hand and visualizing a tiger on the attack, he saw it freeze before it leaped, just as Master Hong had taught him. The vision of the magnificent beast in the corner of his training room stared at him as he went into the final stage of his form. It watched Carter as he turned his back toward it. The tiger was real in his mind; a sleek creature created by nature to kill any weakness. As he returned to a natural standing position, relaxing his arms, to smooth and store energy, the tiger quietly turned, vanishing into the jungle. They would see one another again.

He finished showering, thinking about the divinity with red hair whom he would be accompanying to dinner that evening. Although the lovely vision of Mackenzie was foremost in his thoughts, Carter had many issues raging in his mind. Thoughts of the golden hummingbird figurine now floated to the surface. His conversations with Grandfather

Will manifested what he'd been trying to express for many years. What if human civilization was much older than anyone suspected? Had there been some primordial civilization or civilizations? All his findings were pointing in that direction. Then again, without physical evidence, there was only speculation, as he taught his students. There could be no substitution for the scientific method unless it was a matter of faith and that was best left to the theologians.

When he knocked on Mackenzie's apartment door, she met him dressed for the evening. Her fiery red hair tied back in braids, she wore a rust colored skirt, which matched her hair, and a light jacket over a sheer top. The effect was striking yet very practical.

"Good evening, Dr. Anderson. You are quite the vision in scarlet. Are we ready to introduce me to your parents?" he said with a smile.

"Why, Professor Devereux," she told him in a faux southern accent, "I do declare if you aren't the finest thing I have seen all day."

"Then let me escort you to the carriage, Miss Scarlet," he returned with a grin, leading her on his arm to the car. She honored him with a peck on the cheek as he opened the door for her.

An hour later, they drove to the top of a hill and pulled into the driveway of her parents' house. It was a modest one level home, apparently built at the same time as the other houses in the neighborhood. The archeologist eye in Carter noted the similar construction methods used, and then he wondered if ruins of an older civilization lay buried beneath the quiet neighborhood. Would future archeologists and anthropologists try to determine several layers of development such as Boston One, Two and Three?

The door opened, a tall man rushed forward and lifted

Mackenzie off her feet in a bear hug. "Sis!" He shouted, "It's so good to see you!" Turning to Carter, he put his hand out and said, "I'm Ray."

Ray, with fair skin and red hair, was the very image of his sister. Plenty of Irish immigrated from the emerald isles to Boston over the centuries and brought their genes with them. Many places in or near the Boston suburbs had names such as Roxbury, Dorchester, and Cambridge, that mirrored the original points of their ancestors.

"Come on in. Mom's in the kitchen fussing over dinner and Dad's wondering what you would like to drink."

"And you must be the professor!" a voice called out behind him. Carter turned to look at a slim, but older version of Mackenzie. Mary was a beautiful woman. He extended his hand. *This is what Mackenzie will look like in 40 years;* he thought to himself. *How odd to travel forward in time.*

"Steven," another voice came from right beside him, he turned to look at an older man holding two drinks. He was somewhat darker in complexion than his wife and daughter, but it was still easy to tell he was her father. "Steven Anderson. I hope you like whiskey." He said handing one of the drinks to Carter.

"Welcome, we've been looking forward to meeting you for some time, Professor."

"Please call me Carter."

"Good, I'll do that," Steven replied.

When they were all seated Steven looked at Carter, "You think the Patriots are going to make it into the playoffs this year?"

"Depends on whether or not they get the receiver everyone's been talking about. You know, Christopher Michael, that boy from Ohio." Carter responded, taking a sip of the whiskey.

"We'll see how they do as the season goes on."

There was a short lull in the conversation and then Steven continued. "So Mackenzie tells me you're a professor of archeology at the University?"

"Yes, I do profess to try and uncover the past Mr. Anderson," Carter smiled.

"Please," he begged, "Call me Steven. My dad was Mr. Anderson."

"In that case, seeing that everyone has now relinquished their titles, you can call me Mr. Anderson, one of us has to carry on the family name." Ray deadpanned.

"Carter," Mackenzie chuckled, "if you do, you'll find yourself in a heap of muddle in minutes. Be careful, he's a charlatan."

"Ah now Sis, don't give all my secrets away so fast."

When the laughter subsided, Carter looked at Steven, "Mackenzie says you're into astronomy?"

"Yes, I teach astronomy at the local high school along with some of the other physical sciences, but astronomy has always been my first love. I have a telescope out back on the porch if you want to see it later - built it from a kit. It's difficult to see much because of the city's afterglow, but Venus is supposed to be looking good tonight."

"I always liked going to the sky shows at the museum with my parents. I would very much like to have a look through your telescope later."

"I like to put them on every few months for my students," Steve continued. "We have a planetarium at the school." Steven sipped his drink. "So what does being an archeologist entail? I'm sure it's not always as glamorous as the movies make it."

"Hardly," Carter replied. "What most archeologists do these days involves going out to a site in front of construction projects to try to find artifacts worthy of examination and preservation before they are bulldozed. Very few people get the opportunity to work on an active archeological site."

Mary returned to the living room to announce that dinner was ready, and they all moved to the dining room. Sitting down to a table laden with fantastic foods and excellent wine, the conversation soon turned to weather, sports, and local politics.

Carter enjoyed the company of the Andersons, thinking them a wonderful family.

After dinner, back in the living room, Mackenzie got a cunning little smile on her face when she said, "Dad, Carter's been telling me some of his speculations about ancient Atlantis."

"She jests," he defended.

Steven inquired on a more serious note. "Mackenzie mentioned that you believe there have been advanced ancient civilizations before us? I'm eager to hear more about that."

"It's a little more complex than what you might have expected to see on '*In Search Of*,'" Carter laughed, referencing the old 70's TV series about unexplained phenomena. "I don't even get to play the funky 'chukka-wah-wah' music in the background."

They all laughed but continued to look at Carter in anticipation, encouraging him to continue.

"It's my favorite topic, but it can be boring to others, I usually overdo it."

"We're ready Professor Devereux; bring it on." Mackenzie laughed.

"Well, you asked for it." He started. "It's estimated that the earth is about 4.6 billion years old and that life in one form or another has been around for the last 3.6 billion years.

"According to 'official' science, the Homo species evolved from primates, about 1.7 to 2 million years ago. 'Wise man' or 'knowing man' in Latin, known as Homo sapiens appeared on the scene after two spontaneous evolutionary leaps, one about 450,000 years ago and another about 200,000 years ago.

"My problem with 'official' science is that it took 1 billion years for the first life to evolve and from that moment onward for 3.6 billion years all life forms in water, air, and on land developed. Modern humans, however, are only present in the last two hundred thousand years of that entire timeline. In other words, if the 3.6 billion years represent one hour, then each second represents ten million years; that means humans only arrived in the last one fiftieth of the last second. I doubt that very much."

"That is a fascinating analogy, and it certainly makes me wonder," Steven replied. "So is it your theory that we could have been around for a bit longer than that?"

"Biologists will tell you for such major changes to occur, evolution needs many millions, if not billions of years for them to take place and the 'official' version that humans basically evolved 'overnight' is not probable.

"I'm worried I'm boring you with this stuff."

"Carter, it's fascinating, please don't stop." Ray implored on behalf of all of them.

"How about hot chocolate for everyone?" Mary asked.

"Good idea." They all replied in chorus.

"Don't go any further until I'm back." Mary laughed. "I don't want to miss out on anything."

Mackenzie followed her mother to the kitchen under the

pretense of giving her a hand. "What do you think mom?" She asked the moment they were in the kitchen.

Mary had a big smile. "Don't let him get away Mackenzie; there are very few men of his caliber left in this world. The way he looks at you warms my heart. He is in love with you. Did you know that?"

"Oh yes mom, I know, and the feeling is mutual!" She had a sparkle in her eyes.

"What about dad? Do you think he approves?"

"Your Dad likes him; don't you worry about that for a moment. He already gave me the thumbs up during dinner when you two weren't looking."

Mary and Makenzie returned to the living room and passed around cups of the rich, steaming liquid. With the hot chocolate in hand, the discussion continued.

"Lately, I've been looking at out of place artifacts, 'ooparts' as some people like to call them, artifacts that do not seem to belong where they were found. There are things out there we can't explain no matter how deeply we dig into them.

"Things such as micro gold spirals found in Russia, 20,000 years old, which appear to be made by humans using a technology we have no record of and can't even fathom.

"Researchers regularly find human and dinosaur footprints in the same strata. They even find human tracks next to, and inside, those of dinosaurs, and dinosaur footprints on top of human footprints. We've found the remains of early human beings, which shouldn't exist among dinosaurs, but they do."

"I bet many of those discoveries don't go down well in some circles," Steven remarked.

"You can be sure of that," Carter said. "We need to

know more. We need more studies and more evidence about our real history. Evolutionary theory is fine, but it's still theoretical by its very nature."

"Oh, so we're back to that again?" Mackenzie mocked. They'd had plenty of talks about the subject. She'd lead him in the direction of all the major thinkers, but he still wasn't satisfied. There had to be so much more.

"Look," he said. "All I'm saying is there has to be a reason for the sudden shifts in the human species. Why does punctuated equilibrium exist? One day Neanderthals are all over Europe, and then suddenly we have Homo sapiens showing up. Did someone flip a switch? It doesn't make sense."

"So you're trying to say there is a lost Neanderthal civilization?" Mackenzie grinned.

"No, I'm not saying aliens from Mars came and turned cavemen into their servants," Carter said disgustedly, shaking his head.

"I saw that movie too," her father laughed.

"But we need to consider the evidence which indicates deterioration in human size, mental capacity and physique, and a decrease in the size of animals as well. In addition, the fossil data shows a much wider distribution of plants in ancient times. Many desert sites today have fossils that show forests and jungles once existed there."

"And why is that important?" Mary asked.

"It's difficult to deny there was a sudden increase in human achievement at one point. You have primitive dwellings in Egypt one year, and then suddenly, a few decades later, the basic pyramids are constructed.

"We know Zoser's Step Pyramid was a test run for what came later, but it's still a remarkable achievement. The Egyptian polymath Imhotep designed it. Some people believe he was the first architect and engineer in history. The Ancient Egyptians even deified him. Have you ever seen a statue of Imhotep? He's always presented as a man studying a set of plans. The question is - did he just find the scroll or was it something he made up? Where did he get the knowledge? We don't know. I like to think he found something that gave him the knowledge to show the kings of Egypt how to build those pyramids."

"So what you are saying," Steven mused, "is ancient man may have had physical and mental abilities that we can't even suspect?"

"Yes," Carter agreed. "They may have had abilities way beyond our understanding. We don't know because so little physical evidence remains and few people care to explore this line of research. I must admit; it's a minefield filled with people pushing ideas and concepts with little basis in reality. Nonetheless, if you haven't found much in a cave it shouldn't discourage you from continuing to look."

"I don't see what benefit can come from this way of thinking," Mackenzie played him again. "It's all speculation, and even you admit there is little in the way of physical evidence."

"Because someday we might find out modern man has been reinventing the wheel. Look, what use is space travel? How much money was spent taking man back and forth to the moon? Why do we still invest in space exploration?"

"Because it's there and we want to know more about it?" Steven volunteered.

"Precisely." Carter nodded with excitement. "We have an innate interest in what has come before and what is beyond our understanding. Why is this? Are we hoping the remnants of a lost civilization hold the kind of knowledge we seek? It's as Shakespeare said: *There are more things in heaven and earth, Horatio, than are dreamt of in your philosophy."*

"You see," Carter continued with enthusiasm. "I do believe in the intelligent design of the universe, although it may be controversial in some circles. Call it 'The Great Watchmaker,' God, or whatever name you will - even Newton was doing his research to understand how God made the universe work. Many scientists are still deeply religious people."

"Didn't Newton spend most of his time on alchemy?" Mackenzie wisecracked. She had him there.

"Granted, not everything he did worked out," Carter agreed. "But he did lay the foundation for modern physics and math, although his calculus notation mystified everyone but himself."

"It sounds as if you are saying evolutionists are trying their damnedest to make humans out of monkeys while historians are doing their damnedest to make monkeys out of humans!" Steven said, and everyone cracked up in laughter.

Taking a deep calming breath and smiling, Carter tried to bring things to a conclusion, "My apologies. You got me off on a favorite subject of mine, and now I can't shut up."

"That's quite alright," Mary smiled. "It's not every night we have an esteemed university professor over for dinner who willingly indulges our curiosity with an exposition of the origins of the human species."

On their way back from her parents' house, Carter asked Mackenzie if he'd talked too much.

"Oh, no," Mackenzie replied. "They enjoyed it. I like

seeing you come out of your shell every now and then. You're usually very quiet around strangers."

"Your family is nice. I enjoyed being around them."

"I'm so glad to hear that." Then she changed the subject. "So how long are you going to be in Peru?"

"Five days," he said, coasting his car to a stoplight. "I'll be working with Jacob and a speleologist whom he's convinced the government of Peru to allow on the site. We need to do a survey of the cave where he found the hummingbird."

"Oh," she said in her best sad little girl voice, "I'm going to miss you very much, Professor."

She'd started using that voice lately, and she knew the effect it had on him. "Now cut that out," he laughed. "Grandfather has made some satellite communications arrangements for me. I'll have a good connection down there, and we'll be able to talk over the Internet."

"That'll help, but I'll still miss you."

"And I you. I promise to talk to you every day."

The light changed, and he pushed the gas pedal, moving forward.

"I want to go back up to Freydis and talk with my grandfather when I get back. Gramps has offered to look at what the survey team might need down there. The Peruvian National Police will not allow us to move any item in or out of the site unless they've had the chance to photograph and record it. The local newspapers have already gotten wind of what happened with the smugglers, and they're screaming every day about national treasure being lifted by the Nordeamericanos. I'm not as worried about bad publicity as I am over who it will attract."

"What do you mean?"

"There are already two squatter camps close to the site.

The PNP are keeping them away, but word has spread about gold in the hills. Some of those people down there survive on less than a dollar a day, and we're going to tell them the hills are off-limits to prospectors? I'm worried about an army of poor farmers digging up the mountains looking for gold. There are generations of families down there who specialize in tomb raiding. Every so often, something will show up on the black market with an Inca origin, and you know another group of tomb robbers found something. They practically use those tombs as bank accounts."

"So this is why you need to get started right away," she concluded as they pulled up to her apartment.

"Mackenzie, as I said before, when I get back I'll be going back to Freydis. I plan to be gone three or four days, and I was wondering if you would like to come with me?"

"Oh yes, very much but only if your grandfather is expecting me!"

"He is expecting you - for some time already."

"Ah, I see. The grandfather-grandson-talk, if you know what I mean." She took the words out of his mouth and started laughing.

When they arrived at her apartment, he took her into his arms and kissed her long and tenderly before leaving for his place.

Chapter Nine

INSHALLAH

Hassan looked over his troops. They were fine men, ones he had recruited from the local towns and villages. He walked down the line, inspecting their battle armor and weapons, brushing a speck of dust from one man, adjusting the way another carried his assault rifle. Of all the men who'd come to him for training, these were the best. They were the men who would help him carve out his empire in this beleaguered land; they were men who followed his orders without hesitation.

He was proud of them.

In the past year since moving The True Sons of the Prophet into the small Syrian valley, he had become the absolute ruler of the valley. Tribal elders were bringing their daughters to him for marriage but instead of choosing from among them, he sought a woman he'd met when he was studying in Europe. She was well educated, wise in ways that he respected, and the sort of woman worthy of the position she would hold in his house - and she was willing to accept his offer.

Marrying her was more than just a convenience. As a young man, Hassan decided she was the woman he would wish to be his wife, but life had intervened. Only this past year had he finally found time in his busy schedule to locate her and propose marriage.

From her point of view, this very fine and imposing man was a woman's dream of a husband. He was making a place for himself in history, and she would rise with him.

Also tall, with stunning hazel eyes, Adeela matched his needs perfectly.

During the day, she kept her long black hair hidden beneath her hijab but at night, it flowed down to her waist and was his to adore.

Members of every mosque in the valley praised Hassan. He was pleased with his progress. Ruling this valley hadn't seemed a sure thing when he'd arrived a year ago with his ragged remnant of men from the Mosul conflict.

He'd left Mosul because he was sick and tired of the incompetency of the ISIS command structure. The self-proclaimed Commander of the Faithful had turned out to be a complete idiot on the battlefield, leading many of Hassan's men to their death.

Hassan no longer subscribed to the crazy ISIS ideology of worldwide Muslim domination. He had neither the intention nor desire to get into a war with the rest of the world - not America, not Russia, not Europe. It was a foolish notion of ISIS and others to think they could rule the world.

He had a vision to consolidate the Muslim world – one true faith – into one big consolidated Muslim Empire. When he finished his great work, no one would ever try to rape his land again. Never. There was enough oil, food, and wealth to keep the faithful rich and prosperous into the distant future. His study of history had taught him that the leader who reached too far was the one who ended up at the end of a noose.

Hassan had moved his men away from direct confrontation with the forces piled against the ISIS troops at Mosul one day prior to the Russian air strike that eradicated the command post.

ISIS had nothing to stop the continuous bombing runs carried out in the name of the official governments of Syria and Iraq. Stuck out in the open desert, they became an easy target for their opponents. The terrorist attacks carried out in the heartland of their enemy had inflamed their adversary to pursue a scorched earth policy against them. Many of the cities and towns where ISIS had drawn their support now lay in ruins.

His troop numbers grew daily, but Hassan was careful. He didn't want inexperienced frontline troops wasted against his opponents. He preferred to train the new recruits until they were ready to handle a weapon. The other militias and terrorist groups in Syria made the mistake of using village idiots. Not Hassan, he wanted the best of the best. His top commanders received the best weapons and booty he could send them, and he made sure they understood he was their supreme benefactor. The imams he recruited understood Hassan would tolerate no disunity in his ranks. Anyone who crossed him received only one opportunity to repent. A second infraction brought summary execution.

Today he was supposed to have received visitors from the House of Saud. However, his commanders told him it wasn't a good idea to become reliant on these oil-rich sheiks, as they would supply him with money and weapons only as long as they needed him. Then, when Hassan and his men were no longer of use to the Saudi's, they would abandon them. Hassan listened to their counsel and turned the sheiks away. He was going to choose his own friends when the time was right.

Hassan was sick and tired of the inter-tribal wars and sectarian violence that ripped his land and his people apart. He was tired of foreigners of all stripes who saw the rich fertile land as an apple waiting to be plucked. He was also tired of the fools who followed any idiot with a gun. Hassan knew there had to be a way out of the cycle.

For now, he had another problem to deal with. One of his men, a trusted commander, had started talking against him. It was Ali, the man who traveled across the war-torn lands with him, the man who stayed by his side to arrive in this little valley in Syria. Ali had forgotten to whom he owed his success. Hassan could not tolerate this.

It was late in the morning during a hot spring day when he had Ali brought to him in the field tent he used as a command post. Most of his men were staying in houses rented from the villagers. Over the past two years, fighting factions tossed the village from one to the other causing many people to flee and the population to dwindle. Hassan currently had his men fixing the bullet-riddled walls and looking for abandoned land mines. They'd already repaired irrigation canals and resealed the roads.

When Ali walked into Hassan's tent, his prince was sitting behind a small table holding an open laptop computer and a stack of papers. Hassan was a tall, lean man whose eyes burned deeply into all those who received his gaze. Ali was a head shorter than he was. Hassan remained seated in his chair. Two of his commanders sat next to him, smoking cigarettes and drinking tea. Hassan didn't smoke. It was a waste to him, but he was smart enough to allow his men their tobacco ration. Besides, there was always money to be made selling tobacco to those who wanted to buy.

"Peace be upon you," Hassan said to Ali as he entered the tent, using the traditional greeting.

"And peace be upon you, My Prince,' Ali responded as he stepped up to Hassan's table. "You have summoned me, My Prince. I assume you have a task suited to your servant's abilities?"

"I do, Ali," Hassan told him. "I do. But first let me recite a little story." The commanders sitting with Hassan had already been instructed not to show any sign that they understood what was about to take place. They sat with stone faces.

"I had a very close confidant," he began. "He was a trusted ally who came from my own town near Baghdad. We grew up together, and when the call came to take up arms to fight for the faithful, we both answered the call. We traveled to Mosul together and endured the ineptness of the ISIS leadership as they sent us into one pointless battle after another just to prove they had the best weapons money could buy. This man and I grew close and when I assumed leadership of our group he backed me in every way possible."

"I called him brother and there was nothing I would not have done for this man. When I realized Allah had anointed me to create a new group to fight for our lands, I gave him a leadership position in The True Sons of the Prophet. He was with me as we crossed into Syria and became my right hand."

Ali became pale as he realized what direction the story was headed.

"In due time I was able to win the trust of the people and villages in this valley," Hassan continued. "It was not easy, and my blood brother helped me when I needed to be firm and show my people we were not going to rape and pillage in the manner of every other group. He even helped me find the infiltrators who joined us just to do me harm. I allowed this man to hear my inner thoughts and left my own personal gun out where he could see it."

"But I am afraid my dear friend had aspirations of his own. He began talking at night with men from outside the valley, men with connections to the other militias. He approached other men under my authority and cast doubt on my ability to lead our forces against the enemies of the valley. He paid money in private to those who do not love me. I can only assume he has turned against me and become an enemy. I can no longer look the other way and pretend I do not know what happens when my back is turned."

"Ali, what is my policy for those within my ranks who would oppose me?"

"You allow them one chance to repent," Ali was shaking as he stood on the hot ground. The air in the tent was very still, and Ali noticed several of the other commanders had moved to the entrance of the tent.

"And what happens if the miscreant continues to oppose me?"

"There is no second opportunity," Ali said, the sweat was staining his white skullcap and running down his cheeks into his beard, "because you have them shot."

"So what would you counsel me to do with someone who has betrayed me ten times?" Hassan's powerful voice filled the tent as he rose to his full height. His eyes drilled into Ali's, chilling him to the marrow of his bones.

"Ten times," Hassan's voice resonated. "Ten times! I have had confirmed testimony you are working behind my back to bring me down. I trusted you Ali; I gave you privileges because you had followed me from the wretched town we both had the misfortune to call home. You, whom I have called brother, have betrayed me. You broke my heart you bastard son of a whore pig! Of all people, how could you be the one to betray me?" Hassan's face was purple with rage by this point, and spittle flew from his mouth as he spoke.

"Please," Ali begged while dropping to his knees in front of Hassan, "forgive me, my Prince. I was wrong. I beg you to understand I did it all for The True Sons. I only wanted to make sure we would always have a place in Allah's army."

"You lying, filth-eating dog!" Hassan roared down at him. "It is clear you think you are the one who should lead The True Sons. I should have you ripped apart in front of the troops to show them no one can work against me. No one! I should have your guts dumped for the vultures to pull apart!"

Hassan grew quiet. The sight of his former comrade quivering beneath him filled him with disgust, confirming that what he had to do was right. "You were my brother at one time," Hassan said, "therefore I will be merciful to show everyone I am compassionate. Stand up, filthy dog."

Ali struggled to regain his footing and found himself one inch away from Hassan, who gazed down at him. Hassan turned to one of the other commanders. "Bring the woman," he said to the man nearest the entrance.

The man returned seconds later, pushing before him a young Syrian girl who wore no veil. It was easy to see she was a beautiful woman. Her olive skin silk-like, and her eyes deep purple. Her black hair poured down her back. She could be no more than eighteen and was terrified.

"This is your favorite, is she not?" Hassan said to Ali. "I

hear you have visited her parent's house often and made all kinds of promises about what you will do for them when you are in control of The True Sons. Is this not correct?"

"My Prince, I..." Ali stammered in fear.

"Silence, Swine!" Hassan whispered. Ali cringed. Nothing was more fearful than Hassan's whisper - no one ever knew what would come next. He watched as Hassan reached down to his holster and withdrew his own pistol. In one swift move, Hassan shoved it into Ali's hand. "You know what to do, dog. Do it or you will not see tomorrow's dawn!"

With the pistol in his hand, Ali turned to the terrified girl. The commander standing behind her stepped aside moving out of the line of fire. With tears in his eyes, Ali raised the gun at her and pulled the trigger.

There was an impotent click. The gun was not loaded.

Everyone but Ali burst out in laughter. Even the girl who had appeared to be terrified began laughing. Hassan walked over to her and put something in her hand. She quickly stepped outside, leaving the tent to Hassan and his laughing men.

"Take this traitor out of my sight," Hassan said to his commanders.

Hassan sighed and reloaded his pistol before putting it back in his holster. He returned to his computer and didn't move a muscle when he heard the two gunshots.

Hassan spent the rest of the year planning and consolidating his forces in the valley and helping the people rebuild their houses and land. He welcomed his first son at the end of that year.

He needed time to decide where best to concentrate his efforts against the other groups in Syria. For six months, he refrained from venturing outside the valley. He let the

Western powers know that none of his people planned to travel outside the borders of Syria or Iraq. He used his time to plan and decide where to strike when the time was right.

His move came early one winter morning on the high peaks overlooking the next few valleys. The militia groups there were a motley combination of Shia, Sunni, and Druze. They coexisted in their valleys living in different villages, each one daring the other to make a move. They charged tolls and collected taxes becoming de facto governments while the official Syrian government was busy fighting against the troops affiliated with ISIS to the South and East. Hassan waited until they were complacent and low on ammunition; then sent out his ultimatum.

He offered them a place in his own organization, telling the local militia leaders they could integrate their units into his growing army. His long-term plan was to break up the tribal divisions, but that was not something they needed to know right now. He gave them three days to respond.

The responses came in less than 24 hours.

The militias told him he was a foreign devil who had no place in their land. They said he could continue his little state in the valley no one cared about, and they would overlook his insolence this time - but only this one time.

Hassan struck early the following day. His forces swarmed down the hillsides overwhelming the feeble fighters sleeping at their posts and disarmed them. There were only a few shots fired, and two militiamen died while trying to load their guns. Hassan recruited local people to tell him where the major roads and fortifications were located. In just one day, he was in control of two more valleys and many more troops.

The Western media did not notice. Nor did they notice when he took more territory a few months later. Hassan expanded his territory slowly but surely, making certain he brought peace and stability to the people in the areas under his control. His disciplined soldiers did not rule by fear – he and his soldiers had the respect and trust of the people. He dealt with any transgression by his troops swiftly and in public. The people saw real and fair justice in practice.

In Riyadh, Saudi Arabia, a very wealthy and highly influential man took notice of the emergence and growth of Hassan's group. "I want more information about The True Sons of the Prophet, their leader Hassan Al-Suleiman, and all his officers. I want to know everything about them. No detail must be left out: where were they born, their parents and grandparents, everything about all their friends and family, where they grew up, their education. Nothing should be regarded as insignificant. I also want to know what the people living under their rule think of them. Do you understand my instructions?"

"Yes, sir I do. It will be attended to right away and reported to you weekly."

"Excellent. I am looking forward to your progress reports." When his subordinate left, the rich man sat back and thought, *Hassan and his True Sons of the Prophet seem to be the ideal group to back and strengthen. They could become a vital instrument in my plan.*

One of the ISIS groups to the South had contacted Hassan - they needed his help on a particular job. They were willing to pay good money for him to send a demolition team to an area under their control. ISIS was obsessed with destroying the old monuments left behind by the Romans and Persians in places where they held power in ancient times.

It would be an easy job, and they would receive half of the pay in advance. Hassan's group would not need to supply the explosives; ISIS would provide them. Hassan could not understand their obsession with these old ruins. To him, it seemed a waste of good dynamite. But, if they were going to pay, he could spare a few men to do the job and, Inshallah, Allah permitting, return quickly.

Destroying the old buildings and monuments only angered the West for some reason he could not fathom. The infidels cared more for old sandstone blocks than they did for starving people of the world.

He sent a team of five, but only after the ISIS delegates paid half the money upfront. They were instructed to get the rest of the money and bring it back once the job was finished. Hassan let ISIS know that if they didn't pay the remainder of the money, the next bomb would be detonated beneath them.

Chapter Ten

APPROVED!

Carter waved to Jacob Wilson as he entered the terminal of Alejandro Velasco Astete International Airport. Once through customs, Jacob shook his hand and introduced him to the speleologist, Andres Ramos, who was joining them. Andres was from a University in Lima, came highly recommended and spoke fluent English.

The trio took a cab to a truck rental place and rented a Land Rover. The land was full of green fields and farmers working in their plots. On the hillsides, herds of sheep and llamas grazed under the watchful eyes of their herders who wore bright ponchos and broad-brimmed hats. Every now and then, the locals would wave at them as they drove past. Carter could feel the difference in altitude as they passed backpackers headed toward the ruins of the Inca civilization of Machu Picchu.

They made it to the site near dusk after having to pay a farmer to pull their Land Rover out of the mud when Jacob failed to slow down at a curve. The farmer made some comment to Andres about how he wished the gringos would always drive too fast around the curve. It was good business for him, and he needed the money.

As Jacob pulled up to the site, Carter could see the fence erected by the Policía Nacional del Perú. The detachment guarding the site was under the command of the Special Operations Division, which tended to cover thefts of cultural artifacts. They drove up to the gate, and after checking their documents, the guard admitted them into the site. In the distance, Carter could see the squatters in the camps watching their vehicle.

"There are more of them," Jacob said.

"Word spreads fast," Andres commented.

Carter could see the black-uniformed guard glare across the valley at the squatters. He didn't envy the man his job. If things got out of hand, the guard would be expected to defend the site; and asking someone to protect a hole in the ground full of broken statues with his life was a bit of a stretch.

The police had allowed Jacob to move his camp into the fenced area, and he was in the process of interviewing locals to work on the site. It helped that he was on friendly terms with the local people and spoke the dialect. The PNP commander was embarrassed to admit he couldn't understand the dialect of these mountain people, although everyone spoke Spanish. It would be a long process to build a new team to work on the site as the government had dismissed everyone previously working there. Jacob and Carter were the only non-Peruvians allowed to visit the site for now. On the way, Andres told them he'd been approached by a police detective and ordered to report anything suspicious to the PNP post.

"Welcome to home sweet home" Jacob grinned as he helped them carry their luggage to their tents. "Don't mind the bugs; they are friendly at night."

An electric lantern provided light in the tent, and a field pit took care of sanitary needs. The site was primitive, but Carter was used to living and working out in the field. Not too far away, he could see into the open tent barracks of the guards. They joked with each other and smoked cigarettes while watching a soccer game on a DVD player.

The next morning, the three men began the climb to the cave complex where this whole adventure started. It was a stiff climb, but they were all in top physical shape and didn't mind crawling over rocks. Soon, they were out of sight of both the guards and treasure hunters.

Carter looked over the scenery and turned to his companions. "This was a seabed millions of years ago. You can tell where one tectonic plate moved over another. Don't you agree, Andres?"

Andres, whose Indian origins were clear with his coal black hair and eyes, looked over the horizon and nodded. "You can see the remains of volcanic activity. The geology of this place has been active for millions of years."

"It's beautiful," Jacob commented. "I feel like I'm standing on a movie set up here. All we need is the opening score."

They spent the morning taking readings and measurements of the landscape. With a GPS, they could be precise with measurements of the rocks and mark their locations. Jacob had a digital camera, which he handed to Andres to do his recording. They worked for several hours documenting everything before breaking for lunch.

"Jacob," Carter said, "this place is begging for a much

larger survey. Note the rise of the land up toward the cave complex. It's not natural."

"Yes," Jacob acknowledged, "I agree with you on that one. Any ideas as to where it all comes from?"

"I have a few thoughts," Carter responded. "But it's too early to talk about them. Give me a bit more time."

"I'm looking forward to seeing the caves," Andres stated. "This is the first time I've been around here. I've heard a lot about this place and have wanted to see it for a long time."

"Tomorrow," Jacob said. "Bright and early. I have the location stored on the GPS. I warn you it's going to be a bit of a squeeze getting into the cave."

When they returned to the camp at the end of the day, Carter made a call to Mackenzie on the satellite link. "I'd love to see the place!" Mackenzie exclaimed. "It sounds historic!"

"You can't help but see the fundamental unity of all things once you've witnessed these mountains. I miss you, and I'm so much looking forward to taking you up to Freydis."

"I'll be ready to leave when you get back. Guess I'll need a passport."

"Yes, even to Canada these days. You can get one fairly quickly at the Boston Passport Agency."

The next morning Jacob took them to the cave complex as he had the day before. After a few hours of rock climbing, they came to the opening he remembered from his previous encounter. He checked the GPS and squeezed into the entrance, followed by his two companions.

Jacob shone his light on the cave walls once they were inside. All of them were wearing helmets to protect their heads from any sharp rocks or sudden falls. They looked around and stared at the rockslide, which had covered the original cave.

"Weren't there some other artifacts up here?" Carter asked.

"There were," Jacob acknowledged. "I retrieved them last week, took photographs, and turned them over to the commander. I know it's not a good idea to enter a cave alone, but Lima was starting to give him a hard time about results, so I had to do it. Don't worry, it's all documented."

"Notice the rock structure," Andres mentioned as they traveled deeper into the cave. "It's volcanic, but it folds over itself. The lava was viscous, not free flowing - probably trapped full of air. I think a lot of this may have been caused by trapped air as it traveled over previous rock falls we can't see."

"So you don't think it's as old as the ancient seabed outside?" Carter asked.

"No, I think this happened much later - say 30,000 to 40,000 years ago."

They spent the next three days taking photographs and measurements of the cave complex. Sometimes the guards offered to accompany them, but Andres had enough contacts in Lima to keep them out of their way. Each day as they climbed down from the hills back to the fenced site where the digs had ceased, the commander would be on hand to politely ask if they had made any important discoveries. Each day they told him the survey work was a long and slow process.

On the final day, as they made their way back to the tents, Commander Mario called Andres over, and they exchanged a few words in Spanish. He seemed disappointed when Andres returned to his companions.

"What was that all about?" Jacob asked him.

"He was begging me to give him some information he could use to shut down the post," Andres snickered. "Our dear commander reckons this is the most boring detail he's ever had to endure."

While driving Carter back to the airport, Jacob told him, "Even the manager of the truck place was asking me about what we're looking for in the hills. I noticed the artifacts I handed over to the commander the other day are now on the front page of the Cusco newspapers. I hope it doesn't bring more gold hunters up here."

Carter was back in Boston for two days before he and Mackenzie drove out to the hangar at the private airport where he kept his airplane. This would be her first flight in a small airplane, and she gave it an odd look when she saw it.

"We're flying to Canada in that?" she asked, watching as the tug towed the Piper from the hangar.

"It's not as bad as you might think. The weather is supposed to be good, and I'll let you know if we come up on any air pockets."

"Wow," she said, running her gloved hands over the wing. "I've never been in one of these before."

Carter helped her climb into the cabin, showed her how to buckle into her seat and then got in on the pilot's side. He made certain she heard him communicate with the control tower. Her green eyes were wide as he taxied the plane down the runway, and she almost gasped for air when he pulled back on the controls to lift the plane into the air. The ride was slightly bumpy as the plane climbed into the air, but smoothed out once it gained altitude and leveled off.

"That was so...awesome," was all she said. Mackenzie

watched the ground slowly disappear as he took the plane to cruising altitude. They flew across New Haven, over Baxter State Park and were soon crossing the Canadian border on their way to Freydis, north of Quebec City.

"So I get to meet your family. Anything I need to know?"

"They're human," he told her, "at least the last time I checked. Not sure how far up or down the chain of evolution, but you should be able to establish that fairly quickly I presume. One never knows what could happen to humans living in isolation as they do."

"Eight thousand feet in the air, nowhere for me to go," she said noting the altimeter, "and you're trying to be funny."

"Everyone tries to be a comedian - only a few of us succeed. And I have a captive audience!"

They stopped briefly in Quebec City to allow the Canadian Customs to inspect the plane, and then they were on their way again. Carter was lucky; the agent who checked his luggage and plane was the same as the time before. The officer, a young woman of Indian origin, was no-nonsense and stamped both of their passports while asking the usual declaration questions and checking his flight plans.

Captivated by the change of scenery and the serene beauty presented by the mountainous land and snow covered peaks, Mackenzie's mouth was hanging open when they touched down at Freydis. She stared in wonder at a man approaching the runway in a small vehicle. He brought the vehicle to a stop on the edge of the runway just as they touched down. She looked at her light jacket and jeans.

"I hope I look alright" she suddenly worried. "I wasn't sure how to dress for the trip and focused more on comfort in the airplane instead of how I would look to your family."

Carter gazed at her. *Look alright? How could gorgeous possibly not look 'alright'?*

"You look perfectly beautiful, and they're going to love you!" he reassured her as they taxied to a stop.

"Flatterer," she said with a smile.

As Carter helped Mackenzie out, he looked around. His grandfather was just a few yards away but still sitting in the cart, staring at them, not moving – that was odd.

Will had a strange grin on his face as he saw Mackenzie. "All Carter has to do now is to tell me her name is Freydis, Eric the Red's daughter," he mumbled.

For a few moments, Carter was worried but relaxed when he saw his grandfather finally start walking toward them.

Will had a big smile when Carter introduced Mackenzie, and he hugged her warmly. For the old man, it was love at first sight.

"Welcome to Freydis!" he boomed.

Will Devereux stood back from Mackenzie, looked her over, then faced his grandson and said one word:

"Approved!"

"You made my day, Gramps! I told you she would knock your socks off." Carter laughed.

Mackenzie was sporting an enormous blush.

They put the luggage in the cart and made their way back to the cabin. Carter could see the fascination on Mackenzie's face as her eyes rolled across the landscape around them. Will showed her to her room and then started the coffee machine. They visited a while and then Will excused himself saying he wanted to take a nap as he'd been up all night reading about the Incas.

Carter and Mackenzie took the opportunity to go for a walk around the homestead. He wondered if he should tell her about the security cameras all over the grounds that his grandfather used to watch the wildlife. He decided not to - he let her think they were alone, and no one could watch them. In fact, he thought he knew the location of most of the hidden cameras, but remembered the old man had a tendency to move them around when he found a new species of animal he wanted to watch.

"This is so beautiful," Mackenzie said as she held his hand. "Does he raise cattle?"

"No," Carter laughed, "There are a few horses, but Freydis is a ranch in name only. Gramps couldn't think of anything else to call his fortress of solitude, so he called it a ranch. He keeps the trees trimmed so he can see the mountains and has enough cutting and collection done to prevent forest fires, but he leaves most of it alone. I think it's listed on the register as a natural habitat for wildlife."

"So how does he get supplies in and out of here?"

"He shares an airplane, a Piper Cub, with Ahote and Blythe, whom you'll meet later. They use it to fly out for supplies every so often. He and Ahote both have pilot licenses. If there's a big project on the ranch, he'll hire some of the local trappers and hunters and fly them in. He has a few ATV's if he needs to get something in and out on the ground, but he doesn't use them too often. There's also a horse stable and the vet makes his calls by plane."

It was that time of year between late winter and early spring where most of the snow on the ground had melted, the buds were on the trees and in a few weeks, the new growth would begin. Without the heavy foliage blocking the view, it was easy to see far into the distance.

"This place is beyond beautiful," Mackenzie marveled.

Carter nodded, "You should see it in autumn. There's nothing like it anywhere in the world; I'm sure."

That evening Grandfather Will made dinner with the help of Blythe and Ahote. Both of them gave Carter an approving wink, pointing to Mackenzie when her back was turned. They were all listening with fascination while Mackenzie talked about her research work. In some ways, Mackenzie had the strangest feeling that this was home, almost as if she had been here before.

The following day, Carter took her out horseback riding. He was surprised to learn that Mackenzie knew how to ride. He never asked because he thought she was a city girl. He watched her with pleasure, moving as one with the horse, comfortable and confident. Her favorite uncle, she told him, had a horse farm in North Dakota where she spent her school holidays. She learned to ride, care for, and love horses there.

They traveled along the banks of a creek and watched the clean water from recent snowmelt flow downstream.

"Is it deep enough to swim in?" she asked.

He laughed. "Yes it is, but you wouldn't want to right now. It's too cold! Later in the year when the temperature warms up, you can swim in it. Would you like to do that?"

"Of course," she said, smiling at him.

When they turned to go back, Mackenzie noticed a scar on a hill in the distance where a landslide long ago removed a cliff. Now, the iron in the rock showed red in the rays of the sun, streaking orange and gold colors down to contrast the evergreen trees at the bottom.

Beautiful. Breathtakingly beautiful. She thought to herself.

"Would you like to live here?" he asked.

"Oh yes, once in a while I'd have to fly back to civilization to make sure it was still there, but to watch the seasons come and go here must be magical."

Carter smiled to himself as they rode side-by-side back to the cabin.

"So Mackie," Grandfather Will had a twinkle in his eye, "how did my grandson manage to entrance you?" He knew exactly how they met; his informers on campus told him all about it, but he wanted to hear it from her.

She liked her new nickname. "Do you want me to tell, or do you get the honors?" Mackenzie asked looking at Carter.

"You can tell him," Carter had a proud smile on his face. "I'm almost sure I'm going to get it wrong." *Not to mention the fact that there is classified information involved if I tell it*, he thought to himself.

"Your grandson slammed into me outside a building. I'm still not sure if it was deliberate or not. I was coming around the corner and pow! I nearly dropped the laptop I'd bought the day before."

"And you're the martial arts aficionado," Will laughed at Carter. "I thought karate maestros were supposed to know how to intercept a blow in advance."

Carter rolled his eyes. He'd given up years ago. It was something his grandfather associated with movies from Hong Kong and would never understand. Grandfather Will kept asking him about levitation whenever he brought up martial arts.

"Well, I can assure you, on that day he didn't display any of those skills," Mackenzie continued. "And then I received a message from him accepting a coffee date. Which was weird because I still don't recall sending an invitation."

Carter couldn't help but grin over that one. "I did apologize with flowers. Didn't I?"

"That's what saved his bacon. It's all good now," she laughed. "He's been the eternal gentleman ever since. I even had him over to my parents' house for dinner, and they're still talking about him."

Chapter Eleven

TU ERES MUY BONITA!

Two months later, Carter flew into the airport at Cusco with three new team members. The government of Peru had approved Jacob's request for additional help to work on the site. He'd spent the time since Carter's last visit making supplementary maps of the mountain ranges around the cave complex and creating an inventory of what the previous team had accomplished.

The company furnished him with three more field archeologists, all still needing the approval of the Peruvian Ministry of Culture. Although the government in Lima was pleased Jacob furnished them with the new finds, a level of mistrust still existed. The last communication Carter received from Jacob told him the gold hunters had given up, for the most part, and left after deciding there was no immediate treasure to be found. The squatter camp was still there, although greatly reduced in size. The PNP post was still there too but was now staffed by junior trainees who spent most of their time playing dominoes and watching DVDs.

Carter asked if Commander Mario was still in charge.

"He's still here, and his mood hasn't improved either. He claims he didn't deserve this horrible post. But on Saturday night when he was inebriated, I discovered that his mood actually has something to do with a superior officer's wife."

Carter inquired if anyone new had joined them from the Peruvian side of the operation. Jacob was pleased to inform him he had managed to score another cave specialist from one of the other colleges.

"Her name is Juana Maldonado. Andres drove up with her the other day and introduced her to us. Of course, the commander looked over her documents very carefully, but they checked out, Initially, I was a little concerned for her safety because of all those guards hanging around. But, she's got them wrapped around her pinky. They're even fixing her lunch today."

"I'm planning to stay for five days, but it can be extended if necessary," Carter informed him. "At least until I have a grip on everything. We'll have to see how it all goes. At least now we have enough people to move forward a bit faster."

The next morning the team of seven set out toward the cave complex. After three hours of tedious rock climbing, at least an hour of which they spent backtracking to prevent any of the gold hunters following their trail, they arrived at the cave entrance. Jacob examined the ground, but couldn't find any signs that anyone else had found the opening.

"Looking good," he said. "I just hope the PNP will be ready to send someone up here if we find anything because you can bet your last dollar if we do, the treasure hunters will be crawling all over this place."

One by one, they entered the cave and, taking out their

trowels, the archeologists went to work. Hours later, they were still sifting through the dirt and recording anything held back by the screen. A few more were busy brushing the dirt away from the square lines they set up. Carter didn't expect quick results - these things usually took time, a lot of time. However, the government and everyone else would want to know if they found any more artifacts over the next few weeks.

Carter was looking at an interesting shard in the screen, trying to determine if it was man made when he heard Juana cry out in Spanish. Everyone ran to see what she'd found. She talked in rapid-fire Spanish and Carter, who was fluent in seven languages including Spanish, translated for those who couldn't speak it.

"Gold!" he announced. "She's found something made out of gold!"

She explained that she was working to collect rocks from the entrance of the cave with Andres when she pried away a small stone and saw the flash of metal. Locating the spot Juana indicated, Carter put on latex gloves and dropped to his knees. Documenting everything as he worked, he brushed away the dirt and picked out the rest with a dentist pick. With four flashlights trained on the artifact, he gently picked up a small figurine of a cat.

A murmur went through the team as the cat came into full view. Digital cameras went into action taking scores of pictures.

"It's a Jaguar," Jacob announced, and everyone nodded in agreement. "Not surprising. There are plenty of them around these parts, although usually not found at this altitude."

"Nice," Carter said. "We've got another two hours before we need to get back to the base camp. Continue sifting and marking out the squares. We may find something else. Make sure someone marks the area around where the jaguar was found."

In the next two hours, five more gold figurines were discovered: a butterfly, two orchids, a turtle, and a wolf. The team was giddy with excitement. No one had expected to make a find of this magnitude so early in the survey.

"You hear about these sorts of discoveries," Mark Anthony, an archeologist from Boise said to Carter as they worked one of the figurines out, "but you never really get to see them."

"You found a wolf?" Mackenzie exclaimed when they spoke that evening. "I didn't know wolves ranged that far south."

"There are still maned wolves in the rain forests down here, but they're not true wolves – they more resemble foxes. Ten thousand years ago, there were dire wolves in South America, but what we found today is as close to a timber wolf as you can imagine."

"So you think these small crafted animals are relics of some prehistoric civilization we don't know about?" Mackenzie asked.

"I'm not saying a thing yet," he laughed. "We're still examining them."

Carter was not surprised the next day when Commander Mario instructed them to take two of the guards up with them. The guards helped as best they could while being vigilant for any unwelcome treasure hunters. After all the excitement of discovering the six golden figurines, they were disappointed when they made no further discoveries in the days that followed.

Although Carter had asked for and received permission

from, the government and the university to stay as long as he felt necessary, he decided the survey was in good hands with Jacob at the helm and went back to Boston after day four.

Six days after Carter left, Jacob, Andres, and Juana found what looked like the end of the cave - a wall 20 feet wide and 50 feet high. The trio stood before it in silence, their lanterns shining on it. The cave had extended down quite far, further than any of them expected it to go. Each day they had advanced a little bit further, mapping and photographing everything as they went. Andres declared it was a tectonic cave - created by a series of faults in the earth strata - not carved by water flowing through limestone. They needed to be especially careful because these types of caves were prone to sudden drops.

While the other two took a series of photographs of the rock wall, Jacob walked around restlessly and felt the disillusionment growing. *Is this the end of the road? Seven gold figurines, no petroglyphs, no treasure?*

He shook his head; *this can't be the end. There must be more.* He went right up to the wall and touched it, inspecting it in the light. The wall was one continuous slab. He walked to the side, looked at and felt of the rock wall on the left. Then he walked back to the wall in front and felt it. It didn't feel the same. This wall in front of him was smooth – much smoother than the wall on the left. He went to the wall on the right and did the same.

He called his team, "Can you all please bring your lights and inspect these walls? Feel this wall," he pointed to the one in front of them, "then compare it with the walls on the left and the right."

For a few minutes, Andres and Juana felt and inspected the walls as requested and then turned to Jacob.

"I'm not sure it makes sense," Juana shook her head, "but I think humans made this wall in front of us."

Andres nodded slowly, "I agree with Juana, this is not a natural wall."

Jacob smiled, "Thanks. For a moment, I thought I was going crazy. Let's see if we can find more evidence of its human nature."

They all turned their lights to the wall as Jacob started inspecting the full length of it, and soon found what they were looking for - signs of tool use where the cave walls on the left and right met the front wall. Scars from hammering showed at the points where the walls met.

"So what do you make of this?" Jacob asked.

"This was made to bar anyone from going further into the cave," Andres replied while Juana nodded in agreement.

"Why did they build a wall?" Jacob asked. "Wouldn't it have been easier just to collapse the cave and bury the entrance?"

"You assume they had explosives," Andres said thoughtfully. "I think they may have wanted to get back in eventually and needed to keep the cave open."

"I've never seen material like this," Andres stated while examining the wall. "I can't figure out what they would have used in its construction. We'll have to take a sample."

Jacob nodded in agreement.

It took Juana and Andres 20 minutes of intense work with a mallet and chisel to get a small inch-long sample from the wall.

"You're not going to believe what we found today," Jacob told Carter on the satellite link to Boston that evening.

"Try me," he told his friend on the other end of the line.

"The cave dead-ends on a solid wall," Jacob explained. "It's ginormous, and our two cave experts agree with me that it's not natural. The wall is made out of an inorganic material we're unable to identify."

"Can you see the picture I'm sending you?" Jacob asked. "Look at that wall. Ever seen anything like it?"

"Can't say I have. Did you say you got a sample?"

"A small piece, Andres and Juana worked for 20 minutes to get it loose. Whoever built that wall wanted it to be impenetrable."

"Can you ship a small piece of it up here for the University to examine? I'll run it over to the geological department and have a non-destructive analysis made of it."

"I don't see why not. Andres is going to his office in the city tomorrow, and if the commander can get approval, we'll have him run a parcel to the airport."

Five days later Carter held the sample in his hand. He placed it under his microscope and looked at it under various levels of magnification.

He knew that long before the Romans created cement, the ancients were using it. Only the ancients cement could be laid down in thin layers and was incredibly hard and durable. It didn't crumble over time as cement does nowadays.

Carter sat back and brought to mind what he'd read about ancient cement a while back. The stone blocks of the Great Pyramid of Giza were joined with a type of cement that was painted on. Although modern chemists were able to analyze this cement, they were unable to reproduce it. Thin as a sheet of paper, photographs failed to reveal it, yet it would hold a vertical joint as large as 5 x 7 feet. Some reports stated that the cement was so strong that the limestone blocks would break before the cement would give way.

The wall in the cave was hard, and it looked as if it was fused together. Whatever its composition, the wall had not been poured and allowed to set. He toyed with it being some kind of cementitious matter but, if it were, it wouldn't have such a dense, crystalline structure.

Deciding this wasn't his area of expertise, Carter sent it off to the Department of Geology to see if they could identify the sample. He attached a note to it advising them this was the only piece he had and requested they save as much as possible.

"Could you find a way around the wall?" Carter asked Jacob the following day. "Any small openings or holes?"

"I can't find a way through it, and I don't think it's wise to try and dig under it until we know the wall is not supporting part of the cave."

Carter looked at the photograph of the wall again and made a decision. "I'm coming back down to look at this thing. I have to see this wall in person to make a decision on what to do. You know if we don't find a way around, someone will find a means to haul dynamite in there, and then we might lose everything. I don't need another Oak Island Mystery to worry about." Carter said as he referenced a pit discovered on an island off the coast of the US, which had claimed the lives of several treasure hunters trying to reach the bottom.

"Your call, Carter," Jacob told him. "We're going back tomorrow to see if we can find a way around."

"Be careful, Jacob. I'll send you my flight arrival time."

Five days later Andres was driving Carter back up into the hills in the survey's Land Rover. "Can't seem to find a way around it," He said, speaking of the wall. "In the meantime, we've mapped the whole cave complex back there, and it ends at the wall. I've had Juana and some of the people you brought down go all over the thing again. Nothing strange about the cave. It was formed from lava flow over cracks in the strata, just like we thought."

Carter was looking at the rock wall with Andres, Jacob, and Juana. The air was damp and clammy, a little cooler than he expected from a cave, but this cave wasn't formed the way caves usually form. He shone the light on the smooth lava and jagged rocks around him. He'd brought an old and reliable tool along to find a passage.

As the others watched, Carter pulled a candle out of his backpack and lit it. The flame grew bright in the cave as he walked around the base of the wall, holding it up and watching it closely.

"Found it!" Carter announced a few minutes later, pointing to the flattened candle flame. They gathered around to look at it and felt the draft coming from an opening further up the rock face where the cave met the wall. It was difficult to see even with all the lights trained on it.

"Nothing like a bit of old-fashioned technology," Carter commented.

"So who wants to go with me?" he asked, and the entire team raised their hands.

It took them fifteen minutes to hitch ropes onto each other and shin up the wall to the opening. The way was difficult, and Carter soon found himself with no more than six inches on either side as he worked his way down through the passage. He felt the air moving from the other side, which was a good sign. The tunnel appeared to have been deliberately cut into the rock to allow someone to get to the other side of the wall. It seemed as if a rockslide had uncovered this opening in the past, although it was not easy to see.

"Can somebody give me a compass reading?" Carter called back. "We've been climbing through here the past half hour, and I want to make sure we're headed in the right direction. It does us no good if this tunnel leads back to the surface."

"We're headed southwest," Juana called back in Spanish.

"Okay, that means we're moving in the right direction."

"We're still the same distance under the ground," She said after looking at the altimeter.

"Good, I'm chalk marking our progress to be on the safe side," Jacob said.

Carter stopped when the tunnel opened up to a larger platform. He got up and stepped forward, shining the light on a large carving in the rock, and motioned everyone forward. The rest of the party stepped out and looked in astonishment at a series of animal carvings on the rock face."

"Griffins. At least, they look like griffins. What are they doing here?" Jacob mused.

The team shone their lights on the mythological animals and took a series of digital photographs. *"Tu eres muy bonita!"* Carter heard Juana exclaim at the detailed carving in the wall.

They stepped away from the griffin carvings and turned their lights ahead of them to the void where they had emerged. The combined light of the flashlights they held was unable to illuminate the entire cavern before them, but

Jacob started shaking and almost dropped his flashlight at what he was able to see.

"Madre de Dios!" Juana cried as she dropped to her knees and crossed herself.

Emerging from the edge of the intense darkness was a city.

They could see the nearest buildings and streets revealed in the beam of their flashlights. At the edge of the light, the buildings continued with what looked like courtyards and empty fountains with more buildings stretching out in the distance. The opening was large, too large to see the entire city with the light they had. The only thing Carter had ever witnessed remotely similar to this was the cliff buildings the Pueblo Indians constructed in the American Southwest. But, this was not made from baked clay. Each building was constructed of dressed stone, and some were several stories in height. A series of steps led from the platform down to the subterranean city. Nothing moved inside the city, and no light came from any of the structures.

"You dream, you believe, you want to think there are wonders waiting for you," Jacob muttered, "but you never really expect to find the Lost City of Kor or Atlantis. And today, it's happened. Dear God, it's happened!"

Lightheaded with excitement he brought up his digital camera and started taking pictures. The flash didn't extend very far, but it would be enough to give others an idea of what lay in front of them.

"King Solomon's Mines," was all Carter whispered.

"What?" Andres asked him. The cave specialist was trembling with excitement.

"I was just remembering an old movie I saw when I was a kid."

They remained on the platform in absolute silence for a

long while, taking in the overwhelming scene in front of them – the sound of Jacob coughing broke the spell.

Carter slowly moved forward and started to descend the stairs to the city. Then he realized the power on their equipment would soon run out and they would find themselves trapped inside.

"Okay, everybody," he announced, "This is the seventh wonder of the world, and we will go down in history as the first modern people to feast our eyes upon it. But if we don't get out we'll be trapped inside."

The crew reluctantly joined him, moving back into the tunnel. They had made the greatest archeological discovery of the new century. Carter worked hard to focus on the task ahead as he led them out of the tunnel and back to the other side of the wall. He noted Jacob's marks in chalk as he crawled carefully through the narrow tunnel.

Carter breathed his relief when they entered the main cavern.

"We have to tell everyone," Andres said as soon as they were on the other side of the wall. "This is big, huge! I still can't believe what I just saw in there!"

"Let's get ourselves calmed down," Carter said taking a deep breath. "I feel as if I just won the biggest lottery in history. I also know that most people who win the lottery end up broke and busted. So let's keep a little perspective on what we just found; shall we? There will be years of work surveying the city inside this cave. Our number one priority is to protect the artifacts. The squatter camp is still out there. We have only Commander Mario and his troopers to protect the find, and that's it. What do you think will happen when word gets out there is a city up in the mountains?"

"But it's not gold…" Andre tried to interrupt.

"You, I, and the rest of the team know that. But if this gets out, the story will get wings and feet and soon the entire city will be made out of gold. I doubt that our fearless commander has enough men to stop a riot at this stage."

"Sorry Carter I was a bit too quick there. Your suggestion is wise," Andres apologized.

They all agreed that it was crucial to remain quiet until Carter could contact the University and get their instructions.

They realized the entire area outside and inside the cave would soon be swarming with police, as it was necessary to protect the discovery.

There would also be news crews, archeologists, anthropologists and other 'ists' that they could not even think of now.

Carter had one burning desire before the place became crowded.

Chapter Twelve

THERE IS ONLY ONE HAPPINESS IN LIFE

Two days later Carter sat on the edge of the stone platform above the ancient city again. Grandfather Will sat on his left; Mackenzie on his right, and the rest of his crew stood behind them, shining lights down to the scene below. No one said a word.

When Carter told his grandfather and Mackenzie he'd made the most important discovery of his life and wanted them to come down to see it and share the moment, there was no stopping them. Both of them wanted to know more, but Carter was unable to say much for fear of it leaking to the media. He hinted that the discovery was on the level of the discovery of the Tomb of Tutankhamun, the Egyptian pharaoh of the 18th dynasty.

Will immediately chartered a private jet for Mackenzie and himself from Boston to Cusco and a helicopter from there to the dig site in the Andes Mountains. By the time the jet touched down at Cusco airport, the news of the amazing find in Peru had broken in the media. They were about six hours ahead of the first rush of visitors to the site.

"We don't have a lot of time," Grandfather Will said as they got into the helicopter. "All hell is breaking loose. I just took a call from a friend in Lima. They've mobilized the Fourth Mountain Brigade of the Peruvian Army to lock the area down tight. I'm praying we get to the site before the rest of the world tries to do the same thing."

When they landed at the encampment, still under the protection of the PNP post, Carter and his friends were standing in front of the tents watching another helicopter circle overhead. They could clearly see the emblem of the Peruvian Armed Forces on the side of the Russian Mi-26 helicopter as it hovered in the air.

Over the past 24 hours Carter, Jacob, and even the Dean of the University had called in all the favors they had with their contacts to get authorization for Will and Mackenzie to enter the site. The guards, formal and stern looking in their black uniforms, carefully checked their passports. Once cleared, they were allowed to enter the enclosure and were introduced to the rest of the team.

"Things are heating up in these mountains," Carter said after the introductions, one arm around Mackenzie's shoulders. "But we expected it would happen."

Over at the police barrack tents, a party was in progress. They could hear shouting and bottles opening. "What's going on over there?" his grandfather inquired. "Sounds like they're celebrating."

"Commander Mario brought in 12 cases of beer," Carter told him. "He's thrilled; they're sending his replacement soon. When he received the order to turn the site over to the army, I thought he was going to cry."

Carter and his team were already prepared to leave for the lost city in the mountains. They helped Will and Mackenzie move their luggage to their tents, outfitted them with backpacks, helmets, and rock-climbing equipment, and headed for the cave. Will was familiar with rock climbing. Mackenzie, a novice, needed to be shown how to secure the gear, but she was a quick study and soon had all the buckles and straps figured out.

Three hours later, they entered the cave and traveled past the tunnel behind the wall.

Silence reigned as they looked at the ancient city. The buildings were made of stone, but there was no degradation or damage on any of them. The air on the city-side of the wall appeared to be much drier. They could see roads and courtyards. The only thing missing were people.

"Oh … my … God Carter! This … this … I don't … is this real … how can it be …" Mackenzie stuttered, tears streaming down her beautiful face as she put her arms around him.

Will slowly turned and looked at his grandson in awe. He whispered with a trembling voice, "My son, I am so proud of you," tears ran down his wrinkled face.

Carter stood with them and wrapped his arms around the two most important people in his life.

"No one has seen this in more than a thousand years." Will's voice was still shaking.

In silence, Jacob pointed his light down the ramp to where it descended 30 feet to meet the ground level of the city. He motioned to Carter to lead the way and the team slowly moved down the steps, taking pictures nearly every step of the way.

They walked to the first structure, which appeared to be a house, and entered it with care. Inside, they found tables, chairs, benches, and even flatware for eating. An eerie stillness hung over the ancient city.

Will looked at a cup; it had a blue china appearance and reminded him of the ones he'd seen in China and Southeast Asia on his trips overseas. He walked around the room of the house looking closely at everything but being careful to touch nothing. Carter's words were still ringing in everyone's ears, "Remember the first rule of archeology – don't touch anything." Nothing would be disturbed – every item would be documented and photographed. He saw gold painted plates, rich in floral design, similar to the ones in the Kuching province of China.

Carter stood in place, trying to wrap his mind around it all. He was in a city in a cave - untouched for millennia. This had to be the most significant discovery in centuries. He couldn't bring his mind to think any further. He wondered if this was how his namesake, Howard Carter, had felt entering the tomb of the boy king of Egypt, Tutankhamun.

"Strange," Jacob broke the silence. "There seems to be a definite Asian influence on these patterns. Do you think it possible they were trading with the Chinese Empire?"

The next room they entered housed many objects they couldn't identify. They had to remind themselves not to touch anything, to be content with photo records made using their digital cameras. Some of the objects appeared to be of carved jade, others made from lapis lazuli or Tanzanite, and some possibly of onyx or obsidian.

The final structure they entered had gold items on display. It resembled a goldsmith's shop. The door stood wide open, seeming to invite them to walk through to the inside. As they explored the shop, their lights reflected off rings, armbands and other decorations they could not identify. In the corner stood an entire bench with the goldsmith's tools still in position. The artisan had left while in the process of pounding a ring into shape on a small anvil.

Carter's intuition led him past the door, careful not to interfere with anything in the shop. He had to know if what he suspected lay in the courtyard beyond him.

He returned to the group seconds later, putting his arm around Mackenzie. "I want my grandfather to be the first one in there."

He looked at Will. "Grandpa I saved this moment for you."

Will nodded his head and stepping through the door, moved carefully into the courtyard.

The old man froze as his flashlight illuminated what appeared to be petrified trees and flowers in the courtyard. He took a few steps; the courtyard filled with light from the flashlights as the others joined him.

He stopped at a low wall and looked over - a beach, but the water was gone. The boats were stranded, motionless on what must have been soft sand at one time but had condensed into sandstone with the passage of time.

Then, their lights found it, the Garden of Gold!

Carter heard a collective gasp from his crew. The old man walked forward slowly – alone. The garden was a reproduction of a real garden just as the conquistadors claimed; it matched a living one down to the last detail. Here a dragonfly covered with jewels rested on a golden leaf. There a silver hummingbird held its flight, attached to a golden tree limb. Small flowers of gold, pounded to the finest gauge, worked inside stalks of silver, decorated the garden.

Their cameras began flashing away. Andres conferred in Spanish with Juana as Mackenzie examined a small insect fashioned from gold, silver, and rubies. Grandfather Will moved his gaze in slow motion over what lay in front of him. He felt a part of a dream. Words were ineffective to describe what lay in front of his eyes. His thoughts were those of the Tsar of Russia's delegates to the cathedral in Constantinople: *"We thought we were in heaven."*

The last daylight showed through the cave entrance when they emerged, each of them changed forever by the experience, quiet as they made their way back down to the camp.

"The delegates from the company, press, government, university and every other person who wants to see this will be here tomorrow," Carter said. "Remember this day and how we were privileged to be the first ones to see it in over 1,000 years. I know I'll remember this day for the rest of my life, just as I'm sure you all will too." Everybody nodded for Carter had voiced their feelings as well.

They looked up at a circling helicopter. In the distance, they could see the treasure hunter camps, and below, the military vehicles beginning to pull up to the campsite.

Commander Mario met with Carter and Jacob at the base camp and introduced them to the Peruvian Army officer who was assuming control of the location now that the military was in charge.

Carter tried not to show his disappointment. The commander might have been an old rascal, but he was an easygoing man. The new man in charge, Lt. Cervantes, appeared to be an overzealous young officer who was trying to advance his career.

"You need to understand, Professor Devereux," he told Carter firmly. "This entire area will be under the control of the Cultural Ministry. We received your message yesterday, and the President activated the battalion to take full control of the area where the underground city is located. My superior is on his way here and will arrive tomorrow. Not one artifact will be allowed to leave these mountains unless we approve it."

"I understand your concern, Lieutenant," Carter told him, trying to stay out of the way of the soldiers who were setting up more field tents. "We need your help to protect the site from the gold hunters whose ranks will grow as the word spreads. But we also need to get in there and do our work. Surely the minister can understand what we have to do."

"What she knows is that the people who were here before tried to profit from my country's heritage," he snapped back. "I have no intention of hindering your work, but I will insist on strict control measures." He marched off yelling at some men who weren't moving fast enough, obviously as an example to Carter and Jacob about the sort of authority he wielded.

Later that evening after the stars were out and the sounds of military hardware grew silent, Mackenzie sat on a field chair outside her tent taking pictures of the mountains illuminated by the light of the full moon. Earlier, one of the soldiers had asked her politely not to take photographs of the helicopter as it landed and lifted off.

"Want to take a walk with me? Carter asked. "I'd like to spend a bit of quiet time with you."

Mackenzie smiled, there was nothing she would rather do than be with Carter.

"I'm guessing I won't be allowed back in the cave since the cavalry has taken control." She sighed with disappointment.

"The company people are showing up tomorrow, and I hope something can be worked out. Gramps has some friends in Lima; perhaps he can swing a deal that will make it possible."

They joined hands and walked along the fence line until they reached the gate where Carter showed his pass to the NCO on duty. Begrudgingly the man let them through to walk outside the perimeter. Mackenzie glared at him as they passed. "They're just trying to do their job and protect the find," Carter tried to soothe her.

Soon the fire from the camp was just a glow in the background. Looking up at the sky, Mackenzie asked, "Is it my imagination, "or are there more stars here in the southern hemisphere?"

"Could be. They are certainly brighter due to the lack of background light and the mountain air. Not much pollution around here either." He was silent for a moment as he stared up at the sky. "Can you make out the cross and two stars pointing away from it?" he asked, pointing toward the constellation.

"Is that the Southern Cross?"

"Yes, it is. In the Southern hemisphere, as long as you can find it you will always be able to find due south and never get lost. Just like the North Star in the Northern Hemisphere."

She stared in the direction of the cross and then turned back to him. "I don't know how to even begin to thank you for bringing me down here. I'll never forget that moment. Not ever."

He took her in his arms and kissed her. "Have you ever been kissed under the Southern Cross before?"

"Never," she beamed.

"Then may this not be the last time," he said before he kissed her again.

The smell of burning wood drifted to them from the fire in the camp.

"Did you know you can also tell the date and time by the Southern Cross?" Carter asked.

"Really? Can you show me how to do it?"

"Tomorrow," he said. "I need some light and a piece of paper. I'm visually oriented, so I like to look at things while I work them out."

"You never cease to amaze me, Carter," she laughed. "One day you're lecturing me about evolution, next you talk to my parents about the origin of the universe and human civilization, now you're showing me basic survival skills. Is there anything you don't know?"

Carter laughed. "So you agree then. I know how to make a good first impression."

"I never said that! Running me over and stepping on my foot did not impress me, Professor Devereux. Not at all." She giggled.

"Well, at least we know what happens when an unmovable object encounters an unstoppable force." They both laughed.

Continuing to walk in silence, it was a few minutes before she stopped and turned to him. "So how many languages do you speak?"

Carter was quiet for a few seconds. "Seven."

"Really?"

"I would say nine, but I read Mandarin much better than I speak it. Turkish throws me a bit, but I can carry on a conversation in most of the northern dialects."

"Okay, surprise me with something in a foreign language."

"*Mon amour pour toi est aussi grand que le monde.*" He responded.

She turned to him and looked into his eyes while she put her arms around his neck and whispered. "*Il n'y a qu'un bonheur dans la vie, c'est d'aimer et d'être aimé.*"

There is only one happiness in life - it is to love and be loved.

Chapter Thirteen

IN HARMONY WITH THE UNIVERSE

Twenty-four hours later the Peruvian Army helicopter brought in representatives from the University, the Ministry of Culture and Jonathan James of RAU. They were the first of many visitors that would follow. The helicopter descended slowly onto the landing zone outside the campsite, sending clouds of dirt into the air. The soldiers grew excited by its appearance as it gave them something to do besides sit around on trucks with their carbines loaded, trying to look alert.

"So where is this Garden of Gold?" the university representative asked Carter shortly after the greetings. Carter learned her name was Dr. Randi Sams, connected with the Department of Anthropology. He could see the look of excitement on the faces of Jonathan James and Maria Gallo, who accompanied the ministry members.

"You'll get to see it soon," he told them.

Later that afternoon, a squad of soldiers escorted them up the hills to the cave. After making sure they were all wearing safety gear, Carter and Jacob led the guests to the city. Once again, gasps echoed through the cave as the lights illuminated the ancient buildings. Cameras were snapping as their guests descended the steps and were escorted around the city and finally to the Golden Garden. The place had the same effect on the emotions of the newcomers as it had on Carter and his crew.

The army left a squad of soldiers guarding the entrance and made sure they had several radios to communicate with the remote campsite. Lt. Cervantes told them, in Spanish and English, that he intended rotating the guards every eight hours and was posting sentries at all points leading to the cave. For, as he said, the squatter camp with the gold hunters was growing by the day.

Jonathan sat next to his old friend Will at the dinner table that night. When Carter and Mackenzie sat down opposite him, he commented. "I was telling your grandfather earlier how proud he must be of you. I'm convinced this is going to be far more significant than the discovery of Tutankhamun's Tomb. If our speculations about the age of this place are even remotely accurate, this will require a rewrite of human history."

Will nodded his head in agreement and Mackenzie was glowing with delight.

"Have you heard people are saying the city is over 30,000 years old?" Jonathan inquired.

Carter shook his head. "I would really like to believe that, but you know as well as I do that we won't know a thing until the carbon dating begins."

Will smiled. "Who knows, it could be older. At least no one is calling it Atlantis."

"At least" Carter agreed with a smile, and then continued. "Our survey tasks just went up tenfold. I have convinced the representative from the ministry that we need a lot more help, and she assured me the Cultural Ministry is going to do their part. Dr. Sams is still shaking from the experience."

"That's good to know," Jonathan said.

Carter turned, looking in the direction of the mountains. "There's a lot of gold in that site. I just hope and pray Lt. Cervantes and his men are capable of keeping the looters away. It would be beyond disastrous if those artifacts were melted down."

The media descended on the site a week later, a few days after Mackenzie and Grandfather Will flew out. The morning of their departure, Carter took Will aside for a grandfather-grandson-talk. Mackenzie could see them talking and Will smiling from ear to ear. But, she could only wonder what they said as the two of them remained tight-lipped.

Carter stayed a week more until he felt confident the site was under control and Jacob had a suitable survey team assembled, and then returned to Boston.

The Cusco site made news headlines around the world, and within a few weeks, the place was swarming with legions of photographers, journalists, scientists, archeologists, real and pseudo-academics and many more. As Jonathan predicted, the discovery caused upheaval in archeological circles when geologists indicated that the age of the city was between 30,000 – 40,000 years.

Some of the many 'ists' of course immediately cried foul. Others were more sensible and investigated for themselves, then changed their views. Still others stayed away and prayed that another volcano eruption or an earthquake would bury the place so deep it would never be found again.

Mary Anderson loaded the dishwasher after dinner and listened to news coming from the TV in the family room where Steven sat. They hoped to catch more announcements about Carter and his team's discovery in Peru. It had dominated the evening news for several nights in a row until the usual doom and gloom of earthquakes and war stories returned.

The phone rang, and she answered. It was Carter, asking if he could come over a bit later – on his own. Mary smiled.

When she walked into the family room, Steven inquired about the call. "Carter is coming over a bit later." She paused and, getting no reaction from Steven, she added. "On his own."

Steven's attention was still on the TV, and it took a few moments before he realized what she just said. He looked at Mary questioningly. "On his own?"

"Steven, are you ready to give our little foxy's hand away in marriage?"

"What? Who will dare to …?" Steven said and stopped mid-sentence when the realization dawned on him.

Mary laughed when she saw the expression on his face. "Well?"

He switched the TV off; there was a long silence, and then he spoke. "Mary, no father is ever ready for that. But if it is a man like Carter who is asking, no father will ever say no."

When Carter arrived, Steven sat down across from him at the kitchen table; Mary went to the counter and started the coffee machine.

"So, Carter," he said. "What brings you out our way?"

Carter was nervous. Knowing that this moment had always been awkward for every young man through the ages didn't ease his tension at all. He almost stuttered but managed to get control of himself before he spoke. "Steven and Mary, I am deeply in love with Mackenzie and I'm here to ask you for your blessing to ask her for her hand in marriage."

In the hour since Mary told him what to expect from Carter's visit, Steven had enough time to come to terms with the fact that his little daughter had become a grown woman. He smiled for a few seconds after Carter's question, wondering if he should ask the man about his ability to take care of his daughter, and tell him what the consequences will be if he does not treat her well.

Carter saw the smile on Steven's face, looked at Mary and saw tears welling up in her eyes – realizing they were tears of happiness.

Steven looked at Mary and then at Carter and said, "I always knew my little girl would grow up some day and, even if I went looking, I couldn't have found a better man for her than you." He got up and shook Carter's hand.

Mary wiped the tears from her eyes as she hugged her husband then walked around the table and embraced Carter in a motherly hug.

Steven said with a big grin on his face, "Carter, there's just one point I need to clarify with you. We gave you our blessing to go ahead and ask her, but she is the one who will say yes or no."

"Point taken Steven," he laughed "but if she says no will you back me up if I tell her you two actually made the decision on her behalf, and she has no choice?"

Mary just laughed. "You can try, but I'm not taking any responsibility for what happens to you if you do."

Carter left his future in-laws a relieved man. They promised to keep his secret from everyone, especially Mackenzie.

He really hadn't expected there would be any trouble with them, but for him it was important – he still believed in the good old tradition of good manners and respect towards a girl's parents.

"A solitaire," Carter was telling the jeweler the next day. "I think a solitaire would be ideal - a size six ring." Mary had given him Mackenzie's ring size.

Carter was in the diamond district of Boston. One could find almost any gemstone or jewelry they wanted in one of the many family-owned jewelry businesses in this part of town. Some of them had been diamond cutters for five generations or more.

Because of the need for security, the various stores clustered together in a series of interlocking shops and buildings. In one building alone there were over 60 different companies catering to the jewelry trade. On every corner, there was a police officer and two security guards. Millions of dollars in gemstones and precious metals changed hands there every day.

His grandfather told him which jewelry store to visit and recommended an old master jeweler to talk to about a unique design. If everything went as planned, he would return in a few months to buy the wedding ring too. Carter walked into the busy store earlier in the day and asked for the man recommended by his grandfather. Now he was sitting in a private booth talking to him - a man older than his grandfather even, and a well-known master of his craft. As Carter explained what he needed, the old man nodded with a smile on his face.

"I believe I know just the ring," he said and went to

work showing Carter stones and describing the setting he had in mind.

The next part of his plan, as discussed with Grandpa Will back in the mountains of Peru, was to get Mackenzie up to Freydis for a few days. Carter had to wait another week for the ring to be ready.

Spring had the university bedecked with blossoming cherry trees and flowers. The heavy coats of winter had vanished little by little, and the temperature became bearable outside. He waited until ten in the morning and called Mackenzie in her office.

"You up for a trip this weekend?" He asked.

"Where to?" She asked. "And please don't say Peru. I'm still coming down from that cave. Looks like the government of Peru is working the media big time down there. Everyone wants to see that underground city and the Golden Garden, but they've sealed it off with the army."

"Yeah, so Jacob tells me. I was thinking of a quiet weekend up at Freydis."

"Freydis! That's the best offer I've had in weeks. Exactly what I need after two weeks of sorting through inaccurate data."

"I will have the plane ready by mid-day on Friday. If we leave then, we can be there before sunset."

He checked with the control tower and found out the weather over Canada looked good for the next week. *Excellent*, he thought, *everything is working out perfectly*. He picked up the little box. It was perfect for what he had in mind. With care, he opened it. The box appeared to have been constructed 100 years ago, and it would fool most unskilled observers - such as Mackenzie. Taking his time, he inserted the small envelope on the inside of the lid.

Carter closed the box and put it in a special compartment in his flight bag. He'd already sent an email to his Canadian customs contact about the sensitive little package he would have in his plane this weekend, but decided to call her just to be sure nothing would interfere with his plans. His customs agent seemed impressed when he described the box and the reason for it.

"She'll never know," the woman told Carter. "I saw your email and talked to my supervisors. They told me to physically identify it and see that it matches the receipt you sent us. If all of that checks out, there will be no problem."

Reassured, Carter continued with his plans.

When the plane touched down for the customs check, he told Mackenzie she didn't have to get out, that it was going to be just a few minutes. She was tired and happy to remain on the plane.

"Let's see it," the customs officer said. Carter could swear she was excited. He fished the small box out and showed it to her as she pulled out a jeweler's loupe to examine it.

"It had to have cost you a pretty penny," she murmured. "I'm guessing we're looking at a VVS-1 color F? Seven karats I would say." She referred to the diamond grading system used all over North America and the world.

"You certainly know your rocks," Carter laughed.

"It comes in handy in my line of work," she told him. "You'd be surprised what people try to sneak in across the border without paying duty." She made a few notes on her computer tablet and handed the box back to him. "I'm sure your lady is going to love this ring." She smiled.

The remainder of the trip to the ranch was uneventful. They stayed up late with his grandfather, looking at the latest photographs from the underground city and making plans for the rest of the stay.

The next morning Carter and Mackenzie took off on a hike to spend a few days on the edge of the ranch - his favorite place - where he always went when he wanted to be alone and do some thinking. Now he was going to share it with the love of his life.

It was also the place Ahote had hidden the little box for him. Shortly after arriving at the ranch, Carter had excused himself, borrowed the electric cart, and visited Ahote. He showed Ahote the box and asked him to go out early the next morning and hide it in the specified place. Ahote and Bly were elated when they heard what Carter told them.

"Consider it done," Ahote said.

Carter wanted to arrive at the campsite as the sun was setting. He wanted Mackenzie to see the landscape as he remembered it - with the golden sun setting over the wooded hills. By the time they arrived, the sun was indeed setting, and the land was quiet except for the rustling of animals in the undergrowth and the occasional birdcall heard in the distance.

There was a hidden grove leading to a cave carved out of the hill over the eons by running water. From here, they could see an open valley below, and the river that snaked through it. Mackenzie stood motionless, entranced by the scene as she watched the eagles gliding above. A herd of deer grazed in the distance, the buck watching out for the does with his antlers raised for combat.

"What do you think of this place?" Carter asked as he placed one arm around her. "Do you like it?"

"I am in harmony with the universe," she whispered. "I know it sounds like a cliché, but that's how I feel right now.

I've never felt so much at peace with the world as right now. Do you understand what I mean?"

He smiled "That's why I brought you here. This is my most favorite place on earth; you are the first person whom I've ever shared it with."

"I am privileged." She turned and looked down into the valley. "Are there salmon in the stream down there?"

"You see where it ripples on the rocks? If you're here during the salmon run, you'll see bears fishing for them. It's the most amazing thing in the world to see the bear cubs trying to catch the fish as their mothers toss one to them on the banks."

They went to the cave entrance where he always kept a store of firewood for camping. In minutes, he had a fire going, ringed with rocks to keep the flames under control. Mackenzie hunkered down and warmed her hands over flames. Carter took out a chicken Blythe had packed for them and placed it on a spit over the fire. He turned the chicken slowly to make certain it cooked all the way through while they talked.

Mackenzie looked around. "Another cave? I take it you have dug here before. Any earth-shattering discoveries?"

"I've done some digging," he told her, noting the place where he'd told Ahote to leave the box. What do you say we have a look around together? You never know, I might have missed something."

He stood up from the fire and led Mackenzie a few feet back into the cave and began moving some rocks around on the floor.

"What is it with you and caves?" she laughed while watching him.

"You'd be surprised what you can find in a simple cave," he told her. "The oldest known drawings by humans were found in caves." He turned over a rock and found the hidden box.

"Check this out," he told her sounding very excited. "I think I've found something." He knelt down as if for a closer examination.

She came closer and saw what appeared to be a very old, small box on the floor of the cavern, partially covered by a few limestone rocks. Her scientific curiosity aroused, she leaned down and reached toward it, but paused.

"Is it okay if I pick it up?" she asked.

"Go right ahead. Let's see if there is something inside."

She picked up the box and opened it. Her eyes shone in the dim light of the fire bouncing off the cave walls as she looked at the ring inside. "Wow! Carter! Look at this. There's a ring inside! Can you believe it?"

Carter was still on his knees. "Is there something else inside?"

Slowly she pulled the envelope out and opened it. With care, she pulled the little card out of the envelope. Something was registering in her mind. "This doesn't look very old." She said and started reading the words.

Mackenzie. I love you with all my heart and soul. Will you marry me?
Love, Carter.

Her emerald green eyes grew big and then filled with tears as she nodded her head.

"Is that a yes?" he asked eagerly.

"Yes, yes, yes!" she cried, covering his face with kisses. "Of course, I'll marry you!"

Carter took the ring out of the box and slipped it on the ring finger of her left hand.

"This is so beautiful Carter. I can't believe you've done this." Mackenzie wiped away the tears best as she could.

Carter let out a sigh of relief. He was sure she'd say yes, but there was always the element of uncertainty. After all, she did have red hair.

As they sat down on a blanket, Carter brought out a bottle of wine and two wine glasses from his pack.

They touched their glasses in salute and then sipped slowly on the wine while snuggled up in each other's arms – the happiest people in the world.

"We're spending the night here?" she asked.

"Unless you're afraid of me and want to go home," he laughed.

She threw a playful punch at him and then grabbed him in a hug. "I can't believe how you set this whole thing up. You are a real romantic. I love it."

Mackenzie saw movement outside the cave. "Well, hello there!" she said to the new guests.

On the edge of the clearing were two timber wolves. They stood there watching them, their snouts sniffing the air. *They must have picked up the smell of the chicken.* Carter thought with concern.

He looked at his pack – his pistol was there if necessary, but the animals didn't look aggressive.

Mackenzie looked at the wolves and laughed. "Okay you two, off you go. You can visit us another time. Tonight we would like to have our privacy." She pointed them back to the woods with her outstretched arm and finger.

Carter was surprised Mackenzie was not terrified. He couldn't believe his eyes when the two animals turned around and disappeared into the night as if they understood every word she said.

How is this possible? She grew up in a city. This is probably the first time she's seen wolves in the wild. Yet she has no fear of them. Maybe she really is in harmony with the universe.

He took her face in his hands and kissed her, feeling her respond with an urgency that matched his desire. He brought his hand to her long thick plait of red-gold hair that shone in the firelight. How beautiful it was. Gently and slowly, he unbound it and spread it like a cape around her shoulders.

Chapter Fourteen

DEARLY BELOVED

As Carter and Mackenzie hiked back to the cabin the next day, they became aware of the two wolves following them. Mackenzie saw them first. It was the same pair from the night before, matching pace with them as they continued to the cabin.

When they got close to the homestead, she stopped and turned to the wolves who were still about 50 yards away. She just smiled and pointed them back to the woods without saying a word. The two animals looked at her, turned, and disappeared amongst the trees.

Carter shook his head. Here was a mystery that needed explanation — or maybe not.

Grandfather Will, Ahote, and Blythe were there to greet them. They entered the cabin to find an elaborate lunch set out on the table.

"This is a big surprise!" Carter exclaimed.

"We just wanted to congratulate you," Will said.

"The ring!" Blythe exclaimed as she spied the shiny jewel on Mackenzie's finger. "Let's see it!"

Mackenzie produced her left hand for everyone to inspect. She tried to be as modest as possible, but it was obvious she was thrilled.

Will hugged her and said, "I want you to know, Mackie, I am very proud to have you as my granddaughter. My grandson could not have made a better choice."

Blythe hugged and kissed both of them. Finally, they sat down at the table and enjoyed the feast. Mackenzie knew Freydis was home for her now and a place she would always long for when away.

The first people they intended to see on arrival in Boston were Mackenzie's parents. He told her on the flight back about visiting them first to make sure he had their permission to marry her. As Carter approached the airport in the plane, he finished the story.

"You asked my parents first? You *are* the eternal Gentleman, Carter. I really don't know what to say. But I'm glad you did."

After securing the plane in the hanger, they gathered their luggage and drove to the Andersons' house.

Carter knew her mother would see his car in the driveway before they could get out and wasn't surprised that Mary was waiting on the porch to welcome them.

Mackenzie entered the house with one hand inside the pocket of her jacket. She waited until her parents were in the living room. As they asked her about the trip up north, Carter saw her mother turn and look in his direction.

She knows. Mothers can sense these things.

"So how was the trip?" her father asked. "Did you see any moose up there or make any big discoveries?"

"No moose but I made a major discovery," she smiled from ear to ear. She brought out her hand with the engagement ring on her finger.

Mackenzie's mother cried out for joy and hugged her daughter. Carter shook Steven's hand, then turned and hugged Mary. It was a moment of joy.

"I understand Carter came here first and asked for your permission?" she said.

"That, Mackenzie, is exactly how it's supposed to be done. We didn't say yes on your behalf. We just told him if he wants you, he can have you if you agree!" Steven laughed.

Mackenzie looked at Carter with tenderness in her eyes. "I love you for the way you honored and respected my parents." She threw her arms around his neck and kissed him.

Carter listened to them talking about the wedding arrangements, but there were so many other things on his mind he was not paying attention.

"Where did you find the ring, Carter?" Mary asked. "It's so beautiful!"

He came out of his reverie. "A small shop in the diamond district of Boston my grandfather told me about." He gave her the name of the jewelers.

Carter stood in the church with Jacob by his side as his best man.

It was late August, and the weather had been hot. It was always hot in Boston during the waning days of August as the city approached Labor Day. Vacations were ending, and people would be returning to work. Traffic would soon return to its madness of the school and work year. The end of summer always included more highway accidents and stressed bank employees.

The church they selected was in one of the distant suburbs, as they didn't want to deal with the traffic situation. Their idea was to make the ceremony small and keep it down to as few people as possible. However, one conversation with Mackenzie's mother had torpedoed that possibility. Mackenzie's father had two brothers who were both out of the country. Mary Anderson, on the other hand, came from a family with six siblings. She informed him that all of Mackenzie's aunts and uncles would attend, as Mackenzie was everyone's favorite niece. Carter was glad he didn't have to plan the reception dinner.

Carter glanced over the Anglican Church of St. Ephraim as he walked in with his grandfather. The elder Will Devereux knew the minister of the church and introduced him to Carter. This, at least, made him feel more at ease.

"Remember," his grandfather told him upon his arrival from Freydis earlier in the week, "this is the most important day of your lives. You're not just along for the ride." He turned and looked deep into Carter's eyes, "This is it boy, and you'd better do your very best for her the rest of your life or you will have me to answer to." He reached out and gave Carter a hug. "Love you Grandson." Then turned and took his seat.

He stood nervously waiting, watching the door. Everyone had arrived and taken their places. Will had flown down with Bly and Ahote, who were sitting next to him, quietly waiting and sensing his impatience.

As he glanced around, he saw some of Will's old friends

from Maine, people he'd grown up with, all sitting patiently, waiting to see Will's boy married.

Behind them were a few friends from the university, including Pete O'Connor and his wife.

On the other side, he saw Mary and Ray, who was on special leave for the occasion, along with a few close friends and family he'd been introduced to over the previous weeks.

He turned and smiled at Mackenzie's family. Mary wore an encouraging smile while Ray narrowed his eyes in pretended threat in case Carter took to his heels and ran.

Jacob suddenly jumped and began going through his pockets in a show of jitters.

"What's wrong?"

"I've lost the ring; I can't find it."

Carter was about to put his hands around Jacob's throat when Jacob broke into a grin and pulled it out of his pocket, "Found it."

Ray stifled a laugh as he and Jacob exchanged a grin. "It helps to pass the time Carter. Relax man, she'll be here."

At that moment, the organist started playing the wedding march, and everyone stood. He saw Mackenzie appear in the distant doorway on her father's arm. Slowly, too slowly for Carter, they made their way toward him, giving Carter all the time in the world to take in Mackenzie's beauty.

She wore a dress of pale cream satin brocade, princess line that showed off her slender form. The top was strapless, but the bodice was a beautiful lace with a V-neck and long sleeves, which enhanced and softened the effect around her shoulders and arms.

The skirt she wore was long and moved with a gentle swaying motion as she walked, her glorious hair swept back in a soft chignon and decorated with a cluster of artfully arranged pearls. In her hands, she carried white camellias and pale lemon roses with a small trail of green ivy cascading onto her skirt.

Carter swayed a moment, overcome by the vision of exquisite beauty coming down the aisle. Jacob was alert in case he lost his balance, but he had to admit, this was the most beautiful sight he'd ever seen. Carter was indeed a lucky man.

Eventually, after what seemed an eternity to Carter, she was standing beside him looking up into his face and smiling gently.

"Oh dear God, you are so beautiful," He whispered.

The Minister began, "Dearly beloved …"

They held the reception at a nearby hotel that catered for wedding parties. The large banquet room opened to an expansive garden of trees, their trunks thick with age. The dark green summer foliage cast welcome shade from the heat of the mid-day sun.

Waiters handed out drinks and savory finger foods from silver trays as the guests arrived. The wedding group was kept busy greeting new arrivals for some time.

Mackenzie and Carter made the rounds as the newly married couple, stopping from time to time to chat or to thank someone for their gift.

Finally, they arrived at Will's side of the room where he was holding court with some of his old friends.

Carter introduced the new Mrs. Devereux to them each in turn, and each one gallantly kissed her hand. They complimented her on her beauty and remarked on her bravery, taking on this outlandish young man whose misadventures she must ask them about one day.

Among the group was one James Rhodes, someone not familiar to Carter, and he caught Will's eye with a question.

Will stood and did the introduction, "Carter this is my longtime friend James Rhodes. I know you haven't met him before, but I hope you will forgive me for bringing him along; he expressed a desire to meet my grandson." He turned to James, "And this, my friend, is my grandson Carter."

The men shook hands. Carter expressed his pleasure that James had attended his wedding and moved on to yet another group. Carter would catch up with Will later and ask about the man.

After a delicious buffet lunch, champagne was served, and it was time for the speeches. There was much hilarity as toast followed toast. Of course, Carter stood and thanked them all on behalf of his wife and himself, which brought cheering from everyone and a wolf whistle or two from Ray's corner. Carter elaborated on the beauty of his wife, then moved on to mention the brilliant and scintillating company he found himself in, bringing a laugh from the Anderson family.

At last, Mackenzie drew Carter away, "Come stand with me in the gardens, please. I need a break and a bit of time with you before we make our mad dash to the car."

"You okay?" Carter was a bit concerned.

"I'm fine, really I am. I just need to catch my breath and spend a few minutes alone with you at our wedding reception. She reached up and kissed him. Unknown to either of them, their professional photographer captured the kiss. It was so beautiful it would later be enlarged and framed, always reminding them of a stolen moment on their special day.

As the musicians struck up the gentle tune of a bridal waltz, Carter and Mackenzie returned to the banquet room and stepped onto the dance floor, showing off a skill that few people imagined Carter had. He held Mackenzie close and waltzed her gently around the room allowing her skirts to flare out as they turned. Then Mary and Steven joined in, and soon others followed.

A few minutes later Mackenzie broke from Carter and went over to Will. Taking his hand, she asked him to dance with her. Slowly he moved her around the floor beaming with joy as he held his granddaughter-in-law in his arms.

Chapter Fifteen

I GUESS THAT MAKES ME ADAM

Hours later, Carter flew the plane in a slow pattern over the ranch. He wanted her to see the entire extent of Freydis and the surrounding lands. Deep valleys appeared navy blue in the late afternoon shadows from the setting sun. In the distance, the highest mountain peaks remained capped with snow. Long stretches of grassland spread before them, and clear rivers ran over cliffs, the waterfalls sending sprays up into the sky.

"What do you think of it?" Carter asked her.

"In Xanadu did Kublai Khan a stately pleasure dome decree," Mackenzie quoted from the poem as the plane made another pass.

He landed the twin-engine plane expertly, as usual. This time, his grandfather was not there to greet them, as the older man had elected to stay in the Boston area on some other business – and give the two of them some privacy. He left the electric cart parked in the hangar for them.

Inside the cabin, Mackenzie found the refrigerator fully stocked, firewood stacked in the hearthside rack for use, and wood already laid for a fire in the fireplace. They could easily keep the house warm if need be, should it turn cold at night. It was warm outside now, but this far north the temperature could drop suddenly in the evening.

"Wow," Carter said to her as he opened the liquor cabinet, "you should see what all they've stocked it with. Ouch!"

The "ouch" was from his new bride coming up behind and suddenly grabbing him. It would take some adjustment to get used to living with another person.

"Guess what we're going to do?" she asked.

"You have something in mind?" he said while kissing her.

"Yes," She grinned, "Feeding the chickens. Bly left a note asking me to take care of them until she returns." She laughed, seeing the look of disappointment on her husband's face.

"You've *got* to be kidding!" Carter exclaimed. "On our honeymoon?"

"Come on lover boy, this won't take long," she said taking his hand and pulling him toward the door.

"But…" Carter started to object.

"Oh, it'll be fun. It's just the two of us, and it's a beautiful evening!"

Somewhat reluctantly, Carter followed her out the door, and they left in the cart to feed Bly's chickens.

"Look who's back," she said to Carter as they entered the fenced in coop for the chickens. In the distance, they could see two wolves staring at them with keen interest. She waved at them. "Are you here to celebrate too?" she called to the wolves.

Carter never ceased to be surprised by Mackenzie. It amazed him to see how easily she took to farm life as she went to work feeding the chickens and changing their water just as if she'd done it all her life. She gathered the eggs from the nests and checked their condition before placing them carefully in a basket to take back to the cabin with her.

With the flock fed, they returned home and Mackenzie fixed a light dinner for them.

While she was busy in the kitchen, Carter lit the fire in the fireplace and opened a bottle of wine.

"To us," he said in salute, handing her a glass of wine.

"To us," she replied and sipped the wine, gazing deeply into his eyes.

After dinner, Carter took her by the hand and led her to a seat by the fire.

"Isn't it too warm for the fire?" Mackenzie asked

He smiled mischievously. "No, I don't think so ... I think it will be just about right." He said running his fingers through her beautiful red hair as he kissed her.

She caught his hunger and responded eagerly. Later, the fire's glow warmed their naked bodies as they snuggled before it, resting and peaceful.

"See, I told you it wouldn't be too warm for a fire" he whispered against her head on his shoulder.

She sighed contentedly, drawing gentle circles on his chest with her finger. "Yes, you were right, but the floor is a bit hard. What do you say we move this celebration somewhere a little more comfortable?"

"That sounds like an excellent idea, my love!" Carter helped her from the floor, reached for a bottle of Champagne, and taking her hand, followed her to the bedroom.

The next day they hiked out to their favorite spot, the place where Carter so cleverly proposed and walked along the creek. With summer coming to an end, the water was high on the banks from a recent downpour. He showed her where he used to fish the stream with his grandfather, and where he once met a black bear. "I ran like hell. She had cubs and didn't want me around" he told her.

They set up camp and, later in the evening he started another fire with dry wood from the cave. As they sat around enjoying the cool night air and the warmth of the fire, Mackenzie pointed to the pair of timber wolves who were watching them from a distance.

"Those two again," Carter said. "I wonder why there's just the two of them. Wolves are pack animals and don't travel in pairs unless there is a specific reason."

"Maybe they are planning a pack of their own, or they just like watching us," she snuggled up to her husband under the blanket.

The following morning Carter woke alone. He looked around for his wife and became a little worried. He hoped she hadn't wandered off because it was easy to get lost in these woods if you didn't know your way around. The fire was almost gone, so he added a few dry pieces of wood to it to keep it going.

He was about to call for her when Mackenzie emerged from the tree line with the wolves, one on either side of her. The animals looked at him with their deep gold eyes and stayed close as if to protect her. She was wearing a long white cotton gown from the night before, and her hair flowed down her back. She slowly walked up to him, patted the head of each wolf, and dismissed them both.

"That was...supernatural," he said breathlessly to her. "Just don't tell me you've been out running with them."

"They're my friends," she said as she embraced him.

"You are Freydis incarnate," he whispered as they held each other. He looked into her green eyes and stroked her hair. He stood back and savored this image of her. He wanted to keep this day in his memory forever.

As they hiked back to the cabin later in the day, they watched a herd of deer running in the distance, their white tails bobbing in retreat. It was a perfect day. Foxes scattered along the trail in front of them and an eagle hovered high in the sky. Their footsteps and whispered voices were the only things human heard in nature as they traveled.

Carter took a different route back to the cabin and, saving the best for last, showed her a secluded stream fed by a distant mountain spring. Its flow joined a bigger one further downstream at the bottom of the property.

Stripping down, they both jumped in the stream, frolicking around and splashing up heaps of spray as they fought to pull each other under. For a few minutes, Carter felt like Tarzan with his own Jane. All he needed was Cheetah to come and let him know the drums were pounding in the distance.

"I could live here forever," she said later as they relaxed on the bank. "This place is about as close to the Garden of Eden as you could find."

"Then I will call you Eve, and I guess that makes me Adam."

She laughed as she pushed him away and leaped back into the water.

Part II

Chapter Sixteen

CITY OF LIGHTS

Almost four years after his wedding, Carter's work on analyzing the finds at the lost underground city in Peru continued. Mackenzie still worked on her research in the department of human genetics, and they both tried to avoid the usual university politics and gossip.

Carter didn't care who was up for tenure or which graduate student was sleeping with which teaching assistant. He had his work on the finds in Peru to keep him occupied. Jacob Wilson was still running the university end of the survey and using Resource Alliance Unlimited to bring down people for the dig that passed the strictures placed by the government of Peru and could tolerate the presence of armed soldiers near the site.

The United Nations declared the lost underground city a world heritage site and the Peruvian government was considering sending out a traveling exhibit.

Carter arrived at work this particular morning to find an urgent request to attend a meeting in the Dean's office. *I wonder what this is all about*, he thought as he made his way there as quickly as he could. "Have you had your coffee this morning?" The Dean asked Carter as he sat down. "If not, I suggest you do because you're probably going to need it."

"What happened this time?" Carter asked. In truth, he had skipped his coffee this morning and could use a cup. "Somebody get caught smuggling again? Please tell me it has nothing to do with the site in Cusco because I don't feel up to it."

Before they continued, the Dean asked his secretary to get them each a cup of coffee.

"We've just received another request to do a preliminary survey of a new archeological site, and they specifically asked for you to undertake the survey," the Dean told him.

"Now you have my interest," Carter leaned forward. "Where is this one located?"

"Egypt. You like Egypt?"

"Haven't been there for a while. Please, stop the mystery; I'm intrigued."

"Two days ago," the Dean began, "there was a massive sandstorm in the southwestern part of Egypt. Sand dunes shifted as they always do when a storm of this magnitude strikes. This part of Egypt is pretty remote, and few people live there other than some transitory tribes who follow the caravan route. It's a long way from the Nile or any other river."

"We have no idea how long the dunes have been in that location. The best guess is before the pharaonic times, but they may have been there much longer. With the sand dunes gone, an ancient dry lakebed was uncovered. But, that isn't all. Look at the monitor on the wall."

Carter looked over at the flat screen TV on the wall and watched as the Dean reached over to his desktop computer and pushed a few buttons. The screen saver, which was an emblem of the university, faded and turned into a reconnaissance satellite photograph showing the Egyptian desert. He pushed another button, and the picture zoomed in to show the dry bed of the lake which the moving dunes had uncovered. Another push of the button brought the lakebed even closer, and Carter could see something new on the edge of the dry lake.

A city. There was an abandoned city, which the moving sand had uncovered for the first time in recorded history.

"Who owns the satellite that picked this up?" Carter asked.

"It's a NASA satellite doing some ground work to study weather patterns," the Dean told him. "They informed the Government of Egypt and us first. By noon, every other party with the slightest bit of interest will know. You can't hide something of this magnitude. The story gets even better; they're detecting images of light coming from the city at night."

"Light?" Carter asked. "Any idea what's causing that?"

"We have no clue," the Dean continued, shifting to an image taken at night so Carter could see the cluster of lights around the dry lakebed. "Could be static electricity, could be insects. The only way to know for sure is for someone to go over there and find out."

Carter had the Dean return the satellite images to daytime and enlarge them as best as he could. They could see the remains of dead trees and branches. Everything showed up very clearly, as there was no pollution in the Sahara Desert to impede them. He could see square patterns and shadows of buildings in the daytime sun.

"May I?" Carter asked as he walked over to take the mouse and began to look at the pictures in detail. He stood there enlarging them and moving the perspective around so he could have a better view.

"This is amazing," Carter said as he continued to look at the items he could see on the screen. "Did you say the dunes have been in this location for millennia?"

"Yes," the Dean affirmed. "I've already talked to some people in the geology department. They tell me the dunes in that location don't move very often. But, this sandstorm was huge and lasted the better part of a week. When it was over, the satellites were studying the area and picked up these images."

"Fascinating. When was this discovered?"

"Three days ago. The satellites were in place waiting for the storm to clear before they started their work."

"And the government of Egypt wants us involved?"

"They were the ones who contacted us," the Dean explained. "We're hoping all the recent turmoil is dying down in that part of the world. Can you imagine what it means for their nation to find something like this out in the middle of nowhere? It would be like finding one of the seven cities of Cibola in the middle of the Mohave Desert."

"So when do I get to leave?" Carter asked, trying to hold back his excitement. That 'once in a lifetime' opportunity is what most people in his field prayed for; he was hitting a triple and hadn't even turned 40.

"Get a team together, make sure their passports are in order and they're okay with flying into that part of the world."

"What about taking Jacob Wilson along?" Carter asked. "I know he's still up to his elbows outside Cusco with the underground city, but this is huge. He'll want to be part of the first team doing the initial survey."

"I have no problems with that," the Dean told him. "Find the other people you'll need and get back to me."

Back at his office, Carter had Jacob on the satellite link right away. He was fortunate because it was time for their regular call. Jacob's tired face came up on the screen; nevertheless, he was prepared as usual with a pencil and pad out in front of him.

"Hello, Carter," he said, "I hope your weather is better up there than it is down here. We had some more snow last night."

"Jacob," Carter said, "would you be interested in taking a break from the mountains?"

"This snow is starting to drive me nuts. I would like a change of scenery, yes."

"Do you have someone to cover for you down there?"

"Sure," Jacob responded. "I can always put Andres in charge. He gets along with everyone and knows how to deal with the latest batch of army boys they've dumped on us."

"You up for seeing the Great Pyramid at Giza?"

"Egypt?" "You want me to go to Egypt?"

Carter gave him the information about the city uncovered beneath the sand dunes. He could see the excitement on Jacob's face as he viewed the few select photos Carter had sent him while they were talking. By the time, he was finished, Jacob had written down countless notes on his pad.

"I'll need to get a flight to Cairo. I have a travel agent in town who handles these things for me. The lady will be earning her bonus this month."

"See you there in about five days, Jacob. I have to get the rest of the team together. You take care, and I'll see you soon."

Carter arrived at home after he'd spent the day finding the people he wanted to use. *Why is it always so easy to find your team of highly skilled professionals in the movies?* He should be wearing an expensive suit and arranging this in a luxurious lounge with a fireplace in full view. But, there were no photographs for him to pull out of a pile and select the people he wanted - no prerecorded message to give him his next destination. This was real life and things didn't get resolved in a 60-minute episode, half of which is taken up by commercial breaks.

When he opened the door, the sound of his almost three-year-old son could be heard coming through the house. Liam came running to meet him with a big cry of "Daddy's home!" The little boy rushed to him and let his father lift him from the floor. The kid had two speeds: *Off* and *On*. Right now, *On* was fully engaged.

Carter and Makenzie were elated when they found out that she was pregnant with their first child. Grandfather Will was thrilled when Liam arrived and even more thrilled when he learned his first great-grandson was named after him: William John Devereux. Because it would be too confusing to have two Will Devereux's running around, the family had agreed to call the boy Liam.

"Help!" Carter pretended to yell. "Mackie, where are you? I'm being attacked by a little fox terrier!"

"I'm coming," she yelled back as she came down the hall. She engulfed him in a hug and a kiss. "How was your day?"

"Big," he said putting down his son. "Real big."

"Sounds intriguing."

"It is," he said, "but it's going to take me away from you and Liam for a while."

"Why don't you sit down?" she said. "I'll get us some iced tea and we can talk about it."

When he finished his account of the new opportunity in the Sahara Desert, Mackenzie sat on the edge of the couch enraptured, trying to hear and understand every word he told her. She leaned back and thought for a few minutes.

"At least I can talk to you over a satellite link every day," she said. "It's not like the old days. We can keep in touch, thank goodness."

"Why don't you and Liam go up to Freydis while I'm gone? I know Gramps would love to see the two of you. Ahote and Bly are always asking about the two of you. You can fly up to Quebec City and they can pick you up at the airport."

Mackenzie didn't need any encouragement to spend time at Freydis.

"Are you going to miss me?"

"While I'm at Freydis? Not a bit," she teased, pulling Carter in close to her.

Chapter Seventeen

ARE WE STILL ON EARTH

Five days later, Carter was meeting with his team in the main terminal of Cairo International Airport.

With him were Jacob Wilson, his second in command, Sameha Hannah, a photographer and cartographer from Alexandria International University, and Rafael Gadaway, an electrical engineer also from Alexandria International. His ground radar expert Adam Sinclair, who had done plenty of work with the company they'd used in Peru, and Michael Joseph, a geologist from the same university where Carter taught, also accompanied him.

As the city in the desert had been covered by sand before the beginning of recorded history, they would be the first humans to step inside it in millennia. The purpose of the initial survey was to investigate the site and determine some basic facts before turning the site over to the international community in general and Egypt in particular.

Preliminary research indicated the last time the lake held water was at least 60,000 years ago. If this were correct, it would mean the city uncovered by the storm had

Nothing New Under The Sun

to be the earliest permanent human settlement ever discovered. Even the Çatalhöyük site in Turkey didn't date back further than 10,000 years. The discovery of the 30,000-year-old lost city in Peru had opened up all kinds of interesting lines of examination to archeologists.

The important thing was to begin on the fieldwork and try to figure out what was causing the illumination the satellites picked up from space. Reconnaissance flights by the Egyptian Air Force revealed that the lights were not an optical illusion; they were clearly visible when flying over the city.

A helicopter belonging to the Egyptian Army took them to the site. As in Peru, the government assigned the military to protect the site from anyone looking for buried treasure.

Egypt had a long history of tomb robbing in the Valley of the Kings. The Egyptian government did not intend to allow this site to become a free-for-all to anyone who wanted to ride in and grab something to sell to the collector's market. The team was fortunate to have two Arabic speakers with them to communicate with the troops. While Carter spoke Arabic, it was still best to have a native Arabic speaker talking to the troops.

When the helicopter landed, the team disembarked and stood looking at the city before them. The officer in charge of the protection detail thought of this as an easy assignment and planned to spend the time drinking tea and smoking. He handed Carter a flare gun and told him to fire it into the air if they ran into trouble. They also had radios.

"We think it's full of 'djinn.'" The officer told him. Djinn, according to Muslim demonology, were spirits capable of assuming human or animal form and exercising supernatural influence over people. "But that might have some advantages. I'm told they can grant wishes." The officer said with a grin and a wink. Carter thanked him and began walking, along with his team, across the hot sand toward the city.

Standing before them was the dazzling scene of an intact city in all its glory. It appeared not to have aged in the least - surprising considering no one had the slightest idea how long it had been buried by the sand dunes. Built close to the original shoreline of a lake, they estimated the distance down to the lakebed to be at least 50 feet, perhaps more, as it dropped steeply from the shore.

They spent the first day exploring and photographing the inside of the buildings, which appeared to be made from some kind of brick. Carter couldn't determine the origin of the bricks, but thought they could have been made from fired clay. It would take more work to determine what kind of material was used in their manufacture. He was surprised to note a lack of detrition in the blocks but thought the sand cover might possibly have something to do with their condition.

The floors in the buildings appeared to be made of pale cream marble with fine green veins running through it and were polished to a high sheen. The moving sand left a layer of dirt on the floors both outside and inside the buildings, but it was easy enough to sweep it away. The marble must have been transported here, as they knew of no local source for it.

The most intriguing feature was the enormity of the buildings. The average ceiling height was 18 feet - some were as high as 25 - and rooms measured from 30 to 60 feet across. Amazingly, the colors still held their vibrant appearance. Murals on the walls depicted fish, birds, and animals, which must have been common in the area at the time of their painting. They looked at them and marveled at how well they had lasted through the eons. The team knew experts would debate the meaning of these artistic works for years to come.

To their surprise, the houses were fitted with indoor plumbing - they found evidence of sinks and basins in each of them. Some even had evidence of kitchens with ovens and places to prepare food. By noon, they were exhausted from walking around and absorbing the details.

"So what are we looking at here?" Jacob asked Carter when they sat down for lunch and took out their food.

Carter thought a minute while he munched on a sandwich he'd packed before leaving. "The city we found outside Cusco wasn't too different from the dimensions you would find in our modern homes today. It was built for people of our height and size. They might have been smaller, but advances in nutrition have improved human height over the past 1,000 years."

"But here," he continued, "the buildings were built for people who were a lot taller than us. I've always felt the early humans on this planet were much bigger than we are today, and this city indicates there might be some proof of my theory. I wonder if we're getting smaller over the millennia, although there may be some periods where human height increases and decreases. The Bible talks about giants on the Earth."

"You're trying to tell me this city was built for giants?" Adam inquired with a big frown on his face. All of them were quiet, staring at Carter in an attempt to process what he had just said.

"I can't give you any other explanation," he said.

"I dunno," Michael Joseph the geologist, said. "It all seems so much like Bigfoot, ancient astronauts, and chariots of angels to me. I look for explanations based on natural history."

"We need to open our minds," Carter told them. "Look at this, can you think of any other possible explanation for this city? I doubt it. I am of the opinion it could prove that there were civilizations far older than anything we can imagine. And what's more, these buildings were constructed for people a lot bigger than us."

"I have to agree," Adam added, casting his eyes over the city landscape. "This is far bigger than anything I've ever heard about. It dwarfs what we found in the cave. I've seen some strange things in my time, but this is beyond all of it."

"Well, team," Carter said. "We've got a few more hours of daylight. Let's see what's here."

They followed Carter as he walked down the central walkway between the buildings. The shadows of ancient ancestors loomed long and magnificent over them. Carter and the remainder of the team were constantly taking digital photographs. He had a satellite link on his DLSR camera, which was uploading everything to his secure cloud account. What lay before him was too valuable to leave to chance. He needed to make a precise record of anything and everything they were seeing.

"I don't think this is the main road, Jacob," he said to the other archeologists. "I believe this is some kind of arcade. Look at the width of the fossilized trees and the fountains. Benches to sit on, patterned paving, it would have been beautiful when it was in use."

As they walked, Rafael caught up with Carter. "I'm thinking a lot about the lights," he told him. "I don't see anything electrical at all around here. It's hard to know what I need to find. Those stoves seem to be electrical, they're for sure not wood or gas."

"You see anything that might have carried power to them?" Carter asked. "Any wires, lines, or conduits?"

"Not a thing. I can't see any way power was transmitted around here."

"Hopefully, we'll see something tonight," Carter said. "The satellite picked up something, so I expect we'll see the lights when it gets dark."

They came to the end of the arcade then turned and walked along the streets of the abandoned city until the team reached the outer district. This had to be the equivalent of the suburbs or some housing area away from the major activities of the commerce district. They passed what appeared to be small shops and empty galleries.

"It almost reminds me of Pompeii," Jacob noted. "Thousands of years it lay buried under volcanic ash until it was excavated. When they began digging, they found a preserved city, which had been engulfed by a volcanic eruption."

Sameha wandered over to a counter inside one of the shops and laid her hand on its smooth surface. "Look at this," she said. "I'm five foot six and can barely see over the top of this surface. Just imagine how tall the person who used it must have been."

"I think we've found a hardware store of some kind," a voice called from outside. They went out to join Rafael and Adam, each of them holding a saw and hammer respectively. Each of the tools was far bigger than any they'd ever seen before.

"Check this out," Adam said as he carefully lifted a hammer with his gloved hands. "I would never be able to swing this thing with one hand. I'd call it a sledgehammer, but it's fashioned to be held in one hand. Whoever used it had hands a helluva lot bigger than mine."

Rafael turned the saw over and looked at it. It was huge, almost the size of a lumberjack saw, but it was built with one open handle, which told them the design was for one hand. "I'd like to see the man who handled this."

Inside the workshop were piles of nails and metal tools, which had managed to escape the effects of time. Most of the wood was petrified, but some had disintegrated from the effects of the ages. Piles of sand remained in the corners with more tools sticking out of them.

"I don't think any questions remain about the size of the dwellers of this city," Carter concluded.

Along the lakeside were gardens and courtyards, filled with tall, petrified trees. The effect resembled a garden of stone. Interspaced between the long dead gardens were benches and chairs, also turned to stone over time, where the original inhabitants of the city could recline and enjoy the views.

Scattered amongst gardens and paths stood magnificent statues of metal that had survived the ravages of time. The team walked around them, trying to figure out if the people portrayed in the giant statues were supposed to be life-sized or representative of their status in life.

Next to the dry lakebed, they found a building that appeared to have been used for boat construction and repair. It was long and made of the same hard bricks as found in the rest of the city, and the building was open to where the lake would have been. Inside were the remains of several boats, which were under repair when the city was abandoned. Tools too big for them to handle lined the walls, their function still not apparent to the team as they looked around and took pictures.

As the day turned from afternoon to evening, the group stopped their exploration and sat down in a semi-circle near the dry lake to watch the sun as it traveled down to the horizon. They had enough food and water to last a week, and more could be brought in. In the desert heat, dehydration was a real threat, and everybody constantly sipped from his or her water bottle. The dust coated everything, especially their throats.

Rafael was the first to notice something strange as the sun dipped below the desert landscape, creating long shadows and coloring the buildings in mauve and shades of gold.

"The lights!" he shouted. "Look at them! There are lights everywhere!" He turned to Sameha and exclaimed again in a series of Arabic phrases.

As twilight changed into night, thousands of tiny lights illuminated the arcade and streets. Larger lights shone down from the buildings high above to add their glow.

Inside the shops, more lights came on to show what they no longer had on display. There was no click, no snapping sound of switches activated, nothing mechanical to let them know the lights were coming on. One moment there was darkness, the next, total illumination of the city from thousands upon thousands of tiny lights.

The team sat on the ground, unable to say another word as the abandoned city came to life, the glow of the illumination reaching far into the night sky. Finally, Jacob voiced what was on everyone's mind:

"Are we still on Earth?"

Chapter Eighteen

HAIL UNTO THEE RA IN THY RISING

Ahote was waiting at the terminal of Quebec City's Jean Lesage International Airport when Mackenzie and Liam's plane landed on schedule. He stood at the exit gates waiting for them as they came through, Mackenzie holding Liam's hand very tightly as she navigated through the crowd.

He waited until Mackenzie was just in front of him before he took Liam from her. The boy was excited to see Uncle Ahote after such a long time and Ahote was glad to see him too. Liam reminded him of his own children when they were young - so full of life and energy. He'd never seen such a happy child.

"So good to see the both of you," Ahote said, as he helped Mackenzie and Liam find and claim their bags from the conveyor belt. "Did you have a good flight?"

"About as good as you can have," she told him, holding Liam's hand firmly. "I've become accustomed to Carter's twin engine plane and how it rides. Flying inside a big 737 just put me to sleep. Liam loved the take-off and landing. Kids always love it."

After picking up their luggage, Ahote took them both to the smaller field for light aircraft. It was a little bit different than the big international airport, and Liam's eyes showed how excited he was to see the plane they would use to fly to Freydis. The aircraft had the capacity to hold four passengers, and Liam eagerly allowed Ahote to lift him to the plane's cabin where he quickly climbed into the back seat.

"I get the whole back seat to myself?" he asked his mother.

"Yes, dear," she told him. "Now let's sit quietly because Uncle Ahote is taking us to see Grandfather Will."

Liam was so excited when the small plane lifted off that his mother had to hold him in the seat. He kept up a constant chatter about flying in the air and all that he could see until Ahote landed at Freydis a few hours later. Although firmly buckled into his seat he was still bouncing around when the plane touched down.

As soon as Ahote shut down the engine and opened the door, Liam jumped out and ran into the arms of Grandfather Will, who was just as excited to see his great-grandson and namesake. With a grin, Will lifted Liam into his arms, picked up a suitcase, and with Mackenzie in tow, led them to the electric cart.

Bly was driving the other cart and helped Ahote transfer the luggage and supplies from the plane. She had a chance to chat with Mackenzie while her husband was putting the plane inside the hangar.

"I guess we'll get to see you every time Carter makes another find," Bly laughed while giving Mackenzie a big hug. "So we're good so long as the world doesn't run out of more lost cities."

"Carter is talking about six weeks," Mackenzie told her.

"At least Liam will get to spend some time with his Grandfather Will and you two."

At that very moment, the City of Lights was sparkling with the vast number of small luminaries. Carter's team stood up slowly and began to walk around the vacant buildings and marvel at the sight before them. Had a pyramid risen in the distance they would have shown less surprise.

"I don't know what to make of this," Adam said. "I keep expecting a column of Roman soldiers to march up and inform us we are to be taken to She-Who-Must-Be-Obeyed."

"The officer claimed this place was full of djinn," Rafael recalled. "I'm starting to believe him."

"The city under the mountain was hard enough to describe," Jacob mentioned, "but this is even more fantastic. How can you describe the lights at night and the buildings fit for giants?"

"I understand," Carter agreed. "I just sent Mackenzie an email about this place. She'll have to see it to understand. With the steps and benches, it's difficult to describe." He listened to the sound of the cool evening breeze blowing through the city streets. How long ago had this place been buried by the moving sand?

"It's a painful experience climbing those steps," Jacob pointed out. "They were meant for people a lot bigger than us. I feel like a child trying to go up them."

"What do you make of the murals?" Sameha asked Carter as she adjusted one of her cameras. "Have you ever seen anything like them? I know I haven't."

"I've seen some intricate wall paintings in my time," Carter replied, trying to capture the lights with a camera he carried. "Those tiles are very fine, and I have no clue how they were made. But, some of the work reminds me of cave paintings I've encountered before. Very fine detail - accomplished with skill."

"I still cannot understand how the electrical power is transmitted to these lights," Rafael said, holding a small meter in his hand. It shows a constant flow of electrical current where we're standing, but there are no wires."

Carter took a few steps forward and let his hand travel through a ray of light coming from one of the sources on a nearby building. "We're missing something here," he speculated. "I don't know what it is, but I feel like one of the blind men confronting an elephant. We're allowing ourselves to be blinded by our own preconceived notions. We need to think long and hard about what this city is and who built it."

"I'm sure people are going to be talking about this place for many years to come," Adam gave his opinion. He dropped his camera and looked at the play of light on the tile in front of him. "I wonder if the lights have increased their intensity because we're here. I don't recall them being so bright on the satellite images."

"We'll know when we compare them to the ones it will take this evening," Carter reminded him. "It's too early to know right now."

They made their way back to the helicopter where the Egyptian Army officer was waiting for them. A camp had been set up, tents raised for the group to sleep in, and the Egyptian troops were in a day tent watching a movie. They peered out to see who had arrived, but seeing it was just the scientific team, went back to the movie. "I guess the Djinn have no use for them," Carter heard one of the men comment as he went back inside.

Jacob felt as though he had just fallen asleep when he heard Carter yell, "Time to go," outside his tent the next morning. It was one of the many things you had to be accustomed to while doing fieldwork: you have to make hay while the sun shines. Today's alarm clock was Carter letting everyone know they needed to get out to the site quickly and start surveying.

"Uhhh..." Jacob called out from his tent. "Can't we let the sleeping city of Kitezeh slumber for just a little bit longer?"

"Nope," Carter responded. "We need to get out there as soon as we can."

The team managed to assemble their gear and ate quickly as the hot, red ball in the sky was already starting to bake the dust below their feet.

"Hail unto thee Ra in thy rising," grumbled Adam glancing up at the sun as they headed back to the abandoned city. The Egyptian troops were already up watching them leave. The officer smiled from his chair and told Carter not to forget the flare gun "just in case the djinn become tired of you."

The team noticed the lights had gone out as soon as the sun had risen. It was as if they never existed. With Carter supervising the survey, they decided on a spot near the lake to do some preliminary digging, as it seemed the least intrusive place near the city. In a few hours, they were wearing their sun hats and busy digging the first few pits. They were anxious to see if there was anything of interest below the surface. Adam had his ground penetrating radar set up and started his initial series of readings. If there were any sewer pipes, water ducts, electrical conduits, or the like, the radar would locate them.

It was important to take samples of the soil too so they could take them back for chemical analysis. They documented small portions of the petrified wood as well before packing them for transit. There was plenty to do on the second day and not much time to accomplish it, but this was always the case when a new find was being examined.

By the end of the week, they had identified small rooms and tunnels under the buildings. Some of the rooms contained furniture, which had never been used. The tunnels appeared to be used for accessing the building without disturbing the traffic at street level, much as was done in amusement parks in North America.

"I wonder what brought this city to an end?" questioned Jacob. "No signs of corpses, nothing burned, no loot lying about and no signs of pillage. It's stranger than Angkor Wat."

"I have been thinking about that as well," Carter told him as he screened the remains from the latest hole he'd dug. "It might have something to do with the lake bed drying up - similar to those Olmec ruins in Central America."

"It's hard to tell in these situations," said Mike Joseph, the geologist. Everyone turned to look at him as it was the first time he'd spoken up since arriving, other than a simple yes or no answer. "I've already requested some data on weather patterns going back 50,000 years from the meteorology department at the University. I'll know better when I get them. Of course, it's hard knowing much about anything when you extrapolate back that far."

"Do you think the lake bed dried up before the sand covered it?" Rafael asked. "It would account for the abandonment of the city." He was busy looking at a small artifact he'd located in his latest survey pit.

"Possibly," the geologist responded. "I've already found a strata layer that contains some fossils that are different from the animals and plants that existed here in recent times."

"How and where do you think the dunes came from?" Carter asked him.

This provoked a series of speculations between Carter, Joseph, Jacob, and Rafael, which continued for another hour. In the end, they concluded there wasn't enough data to determine the origin of the dunes, but as there were plenty of dunes all across the desert, it was a moot point. Had there been a climatic change across the planet in the distant past it would account for the dehydration in the landscape, which would have produced plenty of sand.

The days passed without incident. Each evening they would return to the base camp and file reports to Carter, who would put them all together and send them to the University and the Egyptian government. Every evening he would be up late answering a plethora of questions via satellite link from a whole team of other experts: Any clues on the manufacture of the furniture? Did the height of the steps appear to be uniform or were they varied? It would go on until he needed sleep. And in between, he tried to talk to Mackenzie, Liam and Will.

Eventually, Sameha Hanna reported that the photography of all the main buildings in the part of the city they called the arcade was complete. She had made a precise set of structural floor plans and drawings, including the basements. Now she was turning her attention to the murals to ensure they were photographed to completion.

Adam Sinclair was almost finished mapping the underground tunnels, wide hallways and what might have been an underground transportation system. It was only a preliminary survey as he felt the tunnel system extended beyond the boundaries of the uncovered part of the city.

The geologist confirmed the existence of a dry lakebed next to the city, which had contained fresh water. He was able to do this by analyzing the fossils he found and the lack of sea salt on the bottom. He was also convinced that the soil at the time had enough nutrients for growing crops.

Chapter Nineteen

I HAVE A THEORY

Meanwhile, Liam's third birthday was underway. He awoke early in the morning and ran through the cabin. As all young children do when it's their birthday, he was aware of the attention and went into the main room looking for presents. His mother managed to crawl out of bed fast enough to be in pursuit. She had been up most of the night with her husband on Skype while he told her of the wonders of his discovery in the middle of the Sahara Desert.

It was chilly that morning, but Liam was full of energy. Mackenzie couldn't understand where he came by it, but this was her first child, and it took some time getting used to the kind of energy a toddler could generate.

She knew Will had purchased a pony for Liam, and she could just imagine the boy's excitement over the gift. However, Mackenzie didn't want the boy spoiled, and a pony was one quick way to do it. When she expressed her concerns to Will, he had merely laughed.

"Don't worry," he'd told her. "He's a boy, and he'll

remember this gift forever. I chose her carefully from Ned Joy's stables. Nelly's not a skittish youngster. She's well trained to saddle and bridle, and I think she is just right for our lad until he needs something bigger. Then she can retire to live out her days with the horses.

Mackenzie smiled as she watched the joy bloom on Liam's face when his great-grandfather introduced him to Nelly. She wished that some acts of beauty, such as she was seeing at that moment, could last for eternity. She stood watching as Liam danced excitedly around the pony. Nelly was lovely; she was black with a white blaze and came from a very good home.

"You have to greet her calmly Liam, you have to be polite," Ahote said handing him a carrot. "Now put this in your open hand and hold it like this," he said, demonstrating, "and say 'Hello Nelly.'"

"Hello, Nelly." Liam looked deep into her eyes, and she blew a puff of greetings across his dark hair before she accepted the carrot. For Liam, it was instant love.

Mackenzie watched as Ahote led Nelly around the paddock, with Liam sitting tall and straight in the saddle just as Ahote had shown him, and wondered what he would look like when he grew up. He was going to be just like his father; she thought - a true man of letters who had discovered more in one year than most did in their lifetime.

Later that evening, Will Devereux and Mackenzie sat on the veranda of the main house at Freydis watching the sunset. The night was drawing in, and the background sounds matched the nocturnal animals that would emerge when the stars came out. Mackenzie looked up and saw a bat fly across the sky.

"I enjoy my time up here so much," she said to the older

man. "In ways I can't explain, I feel as if I've always lived in this place."

"That first day you got off the plane with Carter," Will said, "I felt you did belong here. I had a vision of the original Freydis when I saw you for the first time. I saw you walking the land a thousand years ago. It was a strange experience."

"I suppose you could say I have always been here. Now I understand why some people believe in reincarnation."

"Could you talk to me a little bit more about your research?" Will asked. His chair was comfortable, but his leg bothered him, so he stretched it out further. "Respirocytes - it's an intriguing concept. I've read a lot on nanotechnology, and your topic fits neatly into it."

"Well, then you would know my research group is trying to build artificial red blood cells. It's the basic definition of a respirocyte. We like to think we could use the technology to enhance the human red blood cells."

"From what I read, these things can hold 236 times more oxygen than natural red blood cells? Is this correct?"

"Exactly. We could use the technology to create artificial blood. Think about it - you could use the artificial blood in place of the real kind. No more concerns about mixing blood types or pathogen contamination. No more blood banks dependent on healthy donors. You could use it in first aid or if a person had just experienced a heart attack. The first aid possibilities alone could revolutionize medical care. We could treat and maybe cure pneumonia, asthma, and anemia, not to mention heart disease."

"Tell me more," Will asked.

"Of course," Mackenzie continued, "a lot of what we're doing is mere speculation. People talk about underwater immersion for up to four hours, runners at full sprint on one breath for thirty minutes, or the elimination of heart disease and diabetes. I'm not ready to go quite that far. It could be decades before this technology is ready for the market. The clinical trials alone would involve years of work."

Will leaned back in his chair again. It was time to open a new line of dialogue. "Have you searched in any ancient texts for evidence this was accomplished in the distant past?"

"People like to think we're the most enlightened group of humans who've ever walked the planet," she laughed. "If I told my colleagues I was looking in ancient texts for signs of nanotechnology, they'd laugh me out of academia. I could kiss any future funding good-bye."

"You might consider all the manuscripts stashed in the alchemical and closed reserve libraries," he told her. "If you search deep enough, you might find what you need. Consider what the Bible had to say about Methuselah and the prophets of the Old Testament. The Bible even talks about giants on the earth. People used to write those stories off as fables. Carter's team just discovered there is some truth to it all."

"In the group I work with, most of the work we do is trying to find a gene for inherited longevity," Mackenzie responded. "However, we haven't made much in the way of progress. I've come around to your and Carter's way of thinking. "

"This is why I suggested a look at ancient manuscripts. There are thousands, if not millions, of them all over the world. I don't mean to push *Morning of the Magicians* on you, but there is data in them no one has ever explored."

"I lack the ability to read most of those ancient languages. What good does it do me to look at them? From what I understand, even if you can read the original language, many of them are written in hidden allegories where you would need a literary background to comprehend what they discuss."

"There are ways, Mackie," he told her. "There are ways to do this. There are also people just waiting to help if you ask. I'm confident if anyone can find mention of respirocytes and nanotechnology in ancient documents; it will be you."

She walked over to Will and gave him a big hug. "I'm so lucky to have you as a grandfather."

She left Will to sit in peace and think about their conversation.

Carter found Rafael staring at the computer monitor, and could see the look of frustration on the electrical engineer's face as he flashed screen after screen with the satellite link they were using. Something wasn't right, and he could feel the man's frustration.

"Is something wrong?" Carter asked. "Do you need help?"

"I have a theory," Rafael started. "However, I don't want you to think I'm going off the deep end."

"Deep end? We've walked through a city thousands of years old, which was built by giants. I don't think you have much to worry about."

"Okay, don't laugh."

"I promise not to laugh."

"Each building," he began, "has a silver disc approximately two inches in diameter set halfway up each exterior wall. I think they're connected with the lights that come on in the evening. Have you ever heard of Wireless Power Transfer?"

"Isn't that how radio and TV's have their signals sent to them?" Carter asked.

"No, this is different. Some people call it resonant inductive transfer. It's a concept that has been under consideration for a long time. Nikola Tesla tried to make it a reality around the turn of the last century with his tower at Colorado Springs, but his investors pulled out. The basic idea is sound: electromagnetic energy can be sent by electrical fields to power motors, speakers and anything that uses it - even lights."

"Assuming your idea is correct, what do you think would be the source of the electromagnetic power?"

"If you consider the Earth as one big magnet," Rafael explained, "which it really is because of the Earth's magnetic field, then you have your source of electromagnetic power. All you would need on the other end would be a receiver, which is what I feel explains the purpose of our silver discs."

"That doesn't sound too deep end to me. I'm sure we can look into the discs as power receivers, which shouldn't be too hard. Do you have any other interesting ideas?"

"The pyramids," Rafael said.

"Go ahead; it sounds like you're on a roll here."

"We know the pyramids were once coated with limestone plates polished smooth. What if the slabs were coated with something else? There are ancient documents that describe the reflection of the pyramids as having sent out rays of light for hundreds of miles. What if the pyramids were originally designed to generate solar power? What if they're part of a vast ancient power grid we don't understand?"

"It does make for some interesting speculation." Carter was deep in thought.

"The problem with this theory is the absence of any solar panels on the pyramids. I don't want to push it too much because of the lack of physical evidence. However, it might turn up some day. This would make the pyramids huge batteries that stored electrical power."

"True. You don't want to discard any idea at this stage; one of them just might be true. If I had listened to reason, we wouldn't know about the underground city in Peru. Just remember, extraordinary claims require extraordinary evidence."

"For instance," Carter continued, "the underground city in Peru. We have all the physical evidence we will ever need to prove it does exist, and yet some of my learned colleagues won't come to visit it because they feel it's another scam like the Tasady tribe in the Philippines - that was proven to be a hoax by a local politician. Now we have photographs, testimony, underground surveys, and hard evidence. The city we've found from the shifting sand dunes is an even better example. How are they going to deny it exists when soon anyone will be able to fly out here and visit it? As far as I'm concerned, we've done due diligence on our job."

"No argument there," Rafael laughed.

"As for the pyramids as a potential source of power, I don't think the idea is too bizarre to investigate.

"Semir Osmanagic has been all but crucified for pointing out that some hills near the town of Visoko in Bosnia are in fact pyramids.

"A team of more than 200 interdisciplinary scientists investigated and found some fascinating things. The largest of the pyramids is about one-third taller than the Great Pyramid of Giza is almost 25,000 years old, and material analysis shows it is constructed from man-made concrete. Now hold your breath for this - there is an electromagnetic energy beam with a radius of about five yards and a frequency of 28 kHz, coming from the top of the pyramid. An ultrasound beam with a radius of 11 yards and frequency of between 28 and 33 kHz has been measured on the top of the pyramid.

"Despite the irrefutable evidence, the man has been called a pseudo-archeologist, a cruel hoaxer, and many other things. Archeologists won't even agree that those hills are pyramids, calling them natural formation flatirons with no signs of human construction.

"It's just like some of my learned colleagues across the world that won't even acknowledge the discovery at Cusco. They won't visit it because they say it doesn't exist."

"Well Carter, it's a relief to know I still have a job, and you're not planning to arrange psychiatric treatment for me!"

Chapter Twenty

INSTRUMENT OF DIVINE JUSTICE

Riyadh, Saudi Arabia

Xavier Algosaibi sat behind his desk and thought about the future. He was a wealthy man. Over the years, he'd learned to be a shrewd businessman, a collector of knowledge, and that knowledge made him a lot of money. He knew how much he was worth at any given time and checked his portfolio at least once a day. Nevertheless, he would gladly spend every bit of his fortune to bring about the one thing he desired in his heart - the total destruction of the House of Saud and the corrupt dynasty within it.

Xavier Algosaibi was one of the ten richest men in Saudi Arabia. Following the teachings of the Wahhabi School of Islamic thought, he performed his five daily prayers in the direction of Mecca, shunned all forms of idolatry, and abstained from alcohol and any pleasures that could distract his thoughts from Allah. He was a devout Muslim and one of the most prominent members of the Wahhabi sect.

The Wahhabi sect, whose members preferred to be called Salafi or Muwahhid, was a religious movement of Sunni Islam. Their ultra conservative and harsh views of Islamic faith helped them attain the dubious honor of having produced infamous extremists such as Osama bin Laden and 15 of the 19 hijackers who killed almost 3,000 American civilians on September 11, 2001. They funded extremist organizations such as the Taliban, Al-Qaeda, ISIS, and many others who could further their beliefs. The Wahhabi believed the Shias were apostates who must all be killed in an act of religious cleansing to establish the only pure form of Islam.

Despite the fact that the followers of Wahhabism in Saudi Arabia constituted only 23 percent of the total population, they wielded the largest political sword. The pact, which their leader made with Muhammad bin Saud more than a century and a half ago, assured the protection and propagation of the Wahhabi movement and its people. This pact guaranteed them power and glory, the rule of land and men, and money from petroleum exports that helped them gain international influence. They were the power base of the House of Saud.

However, the way the House of Saud was squandering the money earned from the national oil treasure was a source of utter annoyance to Xavier Algosaibi. He was raging with hatred and fury while reading a leaked secret report about the fiscal atrocities committed by members of the House of Saud.

Oil was more or less the only source of revenue in Saudi Arabia, and the Saud family used the cover of government ministries to control how that was distributed.

The government dummies made it appear as if oil revenue was an asset of all Saudi citizens and managed for their welfare under the auspices of official government ministries. However, the reality was something entirely different. Many ministries, although fronted by Saudi citizens, were in fact openly, and in some cases from behind the scenes, controlled by an Al Saud.

The King had absolute political power, and he appointed ministers to his cabinet as he pleased - including the Ministers of Defense, Interior, and Foreign Affairs. Additionally, all regional governorships were positions reserved exclusively for members of Al Saud. Commoners fronted all other ministries, but always, without exception, one or more junior Al Saud members acted as deputies.

The 15,000 members of the House of Saud received monthly stipends ranging from $275,000 US for the most prominent members to $800 US for the lowliest members of the family - without having to raise a finger. The finance ministry's Office of Decisions and Rules dutifully processed it all.

The monthly allowances alone took an annual amount of $2 billion out of the $40 billion national budget. Senior princes were enriching themselves out of the money from off-budget programs. A handful of them controlled all revenue coming from one million of the nation's total eight million barrels of daily crude oil production. Al Saud princes, on more than a few occasions, used their power to confiscate land from commoners for a quick sale to the government at enormous profits.

Xavier's face was pale and his hands were trembling as he silently read the conclusion to the report he held in his hands. *"As long as the royal family views Saudi Arabia and its oil wealth as Al Saud Inc., the thousands of princes and princesses will see it as their birthright to receive dividend payments and raid the till."*

He threw the report down on his desk and whispered

through clenched teeth, "You are no better than your godless, infidel allies from America. You are as evil as they are. Your days have grown short; you will be wiped out with them."

There was a time, not too long ago, when he was a prominent man in the *Al Mukhabarat Al A'amah*, also known as the General Intelligence Presidency - an organization similar to the CIA in America. However, in Saudi Arabia, a hereditary King, not an elected president, appoints the director of the GIP. Bloodline – not competency – is the primary criteria, and high-ranking members of the House of Saud needed high-ranking jobs. Therefore, the directorship always went to a member of the Royal Family in the House of Saud.

Algosaibi toiled without much reward or recognition under a director who was qualified only by descent, not proficiency. He spent years working for the man and only grew to hate him.

Eventually, the King had to remove the prince for making one mistake too many. Lives were lost, and the kingdom suffered enormous embarrassment. Everyone on the staff assumed the King would see the logic of appointing an experienced career officer such as Algosaibi, but His Majesty went with another prince as director instead. Thus, yet another prince became deputy director.

Algosaibi was passed over, received a token amount of money, a letter of commendation from the King thanking him for his service and a hint for him to retire. He took His Majesty's advice and handed in his resignation.

"He could, at least, have given me a gold watch," Algosaibi was overheard mumbling the day when he left the office. "They do that in the West."

That day when Algosaibi stepped out the front door, he

became a dangerous enemy to the House of Saud. Algosaibi was a shrewd man. Neither the King nor his new director of Intelligence, nor anyone in the House of Saud for that matter, had any idea about their new enemy. He remained one of their closest friends and confidants.

He had all the insider knowledge and secrets of the government of Saudi Arabia and the Arab world in his head. He had a network of contacts that spanned the globe, and he was a Wahhabi.

He had contacts among the radical Islamic groups, and he was ready to create his own network. Why not? Had he not personally delivered cash to several of the worst terrorists and assassins on the planet to eradicate the kingdom's enemies? Many of those enemies were not even aware that Saudi Arabia was their enemy. He knew things that would destroy the King and his kingdom, and he was going to employ his knowledge to achieve exactly that.

Returning to his business, keeping a low profile and continuing good relationships with the Royal family, he expanded his empire. He knew the King was watching him, but the man had no idea how deep Alogsaibi's network penetrated into his government and outside the borders of the country.

His information officer had gathered a great deal of information about Hassan and his men. It was time to send his emissary to meet and strike a deal with the revered leader of the True Sons of the Prophet, Hassan Al-Suleiman.

Algosaibi felt as if Hassan and his senior officers were old friends. He knew how they were thinking, and he knew Hassan's vision and plans. He even knew the size of the man's shoes and his grades at school. Hassan was not a radical; he was loved and respected by the people in the regions he governed, and he was not on the blacklist of any Intelligence agency. In fact, Algosaibi had it on good authority that the American and British Intelligence agencies were already reaching out to Hassan to form an alliance. It all fit perfectly into Algosaibi's plans.

While the King continued to appoint his family members to important ministry positions, Algosaibi built his own organization. It would bring down the corrupt kingdom and replace it with one pleasing to Allah. He knew the Saudi princes destroyed mountains of revenue each year to support their extravagant lifestyles. He knew the government lied about how the oil income was used and who really benefitted – and it wasn't the Shia heretics or the imported infidel workers who flooded into the country doing the lousy jobs that arrogant members of the aristocracy refused to do. The country would change, and he would be Allah's instrument of divine justice.

Chapter Twenty-One

A FITTING TRIBUTE

Eighteen months after Carter returned from Egypt, very early in the morning, he received a call from Ahote.

"What's wrong?" Carter could tell by the sound of Ahote's voice that something was not right.

"It's your Grandfather Will. He's not well. I think it's his heart."

"What about a doctor?"

"He won't go to the hospital. He refuses to leave the ranch. He saw his doctor a few weeks ago and was warned this could happen."

"Tell him we're on our way," Carter said in a trembling voice.

Mackenzie was awake, dressed quickly and woke four-year-old Liam.

"What's wrong, mommy?" Liam asked with a sleepy voice.

"Grandpa Will is sick. We're flying up to be with him."

Liam's eyes went wide with concern. "Is Grandpa Will going to die?" He started to cry.

"I don't know, my love," Mackenzie said as she dropped to her knees and wrapped her arms around his little body. "We will have to wait and see. Perhaps he will be okay."

The drive out to the private airport was cold. Carter was concerned; he couldn't imagine the world without his grandfather. He knew to expect it someday, but he preferred not to dwell on it. He had watched his grandfather age over the past few years. He'd faced the reality of losing him, but had tried not to think about the day it would come. He was quiet and didn't say much as he helped his wife strap Liam into his seat.

As he started the engine, Mackenzie put her hand on his arm. "I'm here for you," she said. "Don't worry, you won't be alone."

"I know," he leaned over and gave her a kiss, "but right now I feel like that little boy who just learned his family was killed in a crash. My grandfather was all I had in the world. I remember Gramps holding me. I don't know what it's going to be like without him."

"I will show Liam how to do it, so the hugs get passed down," Mackenzie said.

Mackenzie glanced behind and saw that Liam had drawn his blanket around him and was fast asleep. Carter soon had the plane in the air and was on the quickest course he could arrange to Canada.

They landed four hours later and found Ahote on the runway waiting for them. As they approached, he shook his head, and Carter knew he was too late. "I am so sorry Carter."

The big house was warm and smelled of hot-buttered rolls, but the atmosphere was sad. All Carter wanted to do was to sit with his grandfather. Mackenzie sat with them both for a spell but soon left, as she understood Carter's need to be alone with Will.

"Are you alright, Mackie?" Bly asked when she noticed the younger woman sitting alone by the fireplace. "You look drained."

"I feel cold and bleak," Mackenzie told her. "I can't imagine what Carter is going through. It must be beyond understanding for you and Ahote. How are you feeling?"

"The same as you. Ahote is suffering even more; he's going to miss his old friend very badly." She handed Mackenzie a buttered roll and a cup of coffee. When she saw the tears on Mackenzie's face, she sat down and gave her a hug. "We'll survive this. I know we will." Bly poured herself a cup of coffee and joined Mackenzie by the fire.

"He'll be buried here, won't he?" Mackenzie asked her.

A glimmer of a smile lit Bly's face. "Of course. There's not a chance he'd go anywhere else."

Carter sat next to his grandfather's bed and held his hand. "Did you have to be in such a hurry?" he asked; his face ashen and tear ridden. "Couldn't you have waited just a bit longer? Gramps, what am I going to do without you?"

"The Devereux's always survive," he said to his grandfather's lifeless form. Do you remember when my parents, brother, and sister died in that accident, and you picked me up? It's how I feel now, Gramps. I need to be strong, I know, but it's not easy."

Two hours later, he arose from the chair and looked upon the silent face of his grandfather. Carter recited a poem he remembered from his youth:

> *May the road rise to meet you;*
> > *May the wind be always at your back;*
> > *May the sun shine warm upon your face;*

May the rains fall softly upon your fields.
Until we meet again.

He emerged into the kitchen and smelled the familiar scent of cooking bacon. "Trust Bly to cook bacon at a time like this," he said. It was a good strategy; the smell was overpowering and hard to resist.

Liam came over and climbed on his father's lap. Mackenzie came over to them both and wrapped her arms around the two.

"It should be a private funeral, Carter," Ahote recommended. "There's no need for everyone to attend. You can hold a memorial service in Maine."

"It's what he would have wanted," Carter agreed.

The next day, Carter, Ahote, Bly, and Mackenzie carried Will outside, shrouded in a colorful Indian blanket, inside the coffin. Three other people from the town of Saguenay attended. Since the ranch was so remote, a coroner flew in from the nearest town to certify the death. The coffin had been purchased years earlier; Will Devereux was a man who prepared for everything. A local minister performed the graveside service.

It was a cold day, and the wind was blowing the leaves everywhere. Carter looked at the gravesite and noted the foundation for the permanent headstone that he'd poured himself the day before. Both Ahote and he spent the previous day digging the grave. The Canadian government had allowed Will Devereux to be buried on private land because of its remote location.

In the distance, he heard two wolves howl. It was a fitting tribute to a man who had done so much to bring peace and love into the land.

The day after the funeral, Bly suggested they put all of Will's effects into storage right away. No one wanted to endure the pain of sorting through all his papers, books and computer discs that were in the house. Carter was unable to help them pack; his grief overwhelmed him. He spent the day riding the trails on the ranch. Winter was coming, and Freydis was preparing for it.

The trees were a riot of color - Autumn was in full force. The ground was thick with leaves and he heard the sounds of small animals all around him. Only on Freydis could autumn days be so beautiful. Everywhere he felt the presence of his grandfather. The very landscape echoed with his memory. After a few hours of riding, he felt more at ease and knew he could return to the house.

Mackenzie saw him as he walked into the house and Liam raised his arms to his father. He went over and embraced both his wife and son.

A week later when they gathered in Maine, where many of Will's old friends lived, Mackenzie saw the light return to Carter's eyes. His friends from childhood were there as were Ahote and Bly's children. It was the first time she'd seen the look since his grandfather's death.

Bly caught Mackenzie's eye. "It's good to see them together again," she told Mackenzie. "I think he missed being around them."

"Having them here has helped Carter a lot," Mackenzie agreed.

They held the Wake in a large church hall. It

would have been impossible to hold it somewhere smaller, as so many people wanted to celebrate the life of Will Devereux. Bly and Mackenzie decorated the place in bright colors and made sure the serving bowls and plates were made of wood instead of glass or ceramic.

Everyone had stories to share of Will Devereux.

While he sat alone taking a break, Carter watched a man he'd met years earlier walk over to him. He had a difficult time remembering who the man was at first.

"I'm not sure if you remember me, Carter," the man said to him. "Your grandfather introduced us at your wedding. I'm Jim Rhodes." Then Carter remembered.

"Of course! I meant to ask my grandfather about you after he'd introduced us but never got around to it. How is it that you knew him?"

Carter was wondering why Rhodes had an expression of disappointment on his face all of a sudden but didn't bother to ask.

Rhodes continued. "Look, I'll be in Boston in a few weeks. Would you mind if I contacted you at the university? There is quite a bit I need to talk to you about. Perhaps we can do lunch?"

"What's this about?"

"Do you mind if we wait until I can go into further detail? It's about your grandfather and our connection - things you need to know."

"Okay, no problem. Give the archeology department a call when you hit town and ask for me. I'd love to talk to you about him."

When Rhodes walked away, Magi, Ahote's oldest son, came over and sat down next to him.

"You alright?" he said. "A lot has happened. Too bad

your grandfather couldn't be here. He'd love to have heard all the stories people told about him."

"Oh, he's here," Carter responded. "There's no way he would miss out on something like this."

A few days later, his grandfather's lawyer contacted Carter to set up a meeting in his office. Carter dreaded this meeting even though Arthur Winslow was an old friend of his grandfather's. The process of taking care of Will Devereux's estate was painful.

The secretary opened the door and ushered Carter into a luxurious office. An older man in his sixties stood and offered Carter his hand, introducing himself as Grandfather Will's attorney.

"I should have contacted you earlier, Carter," he told him, "but there was so much work to be done with probating your grandfather's estate. At least two countries are involved, but I'm sure you are aware of all the complications."

Carter nodded.

"Carter, you have inherited cash, property, assets, stock, and bonds worth $2.5 billion US. Capital gain taxes and the rest will take a toll, but I feel you will be worth the $1.5 billion figure when it's all said and done. If nothing else, your grandfather knew how to make money grow."

Winslow continued to describe the extent of the fortune, but Carter was speechless. He'd always known his grandfather had done well from selling his interest in the satellite company, but this amount of money staggered the imagination.

"I can't believe all this," Carter said. "How do I handle it all, Mr. Winslow?"

"You can call me Art. Your grandfather did, and now it appears I'm representing you. I suggest we let everything ride for the time being. People will be seeking you out for investments and loans; you don't want to publicize all the funds you control."

"The things I never knew about my grandfather ...," Carter muttered as he shook his head. "I understood he was well-off, but never in my wildest dreams did I think he had this much money."

"As I said," Winslow continued, "he knew how to grow his money from the investments he made. Also, he kept his wealth quiet. Look how far away he lived from everyone else."

"Art, since you're going to manage all this for me, it is of the utmost importance that you keep everything as quiet as you did for my grandfather. As you did for him, I trust you will make sure no one finds out how much money I have."

Winslow smiled. "You can leave that with me, Carter. That's what I do."

Later that evening, after a shot of whiskey and with Liam in bed, Carter told Mackenzie about the meeting with Arthur Winslow.

"He never said a word about his money to you?" she asked while snuggling up to him.

"Not a word. I knew he'd done alright when he sold his interest in the satellite company, but this is hard to fathom."

"He left Freydis to you. That way he'll always be here with us," Mackenzie murmured.

A few days later, Mackenzie called Carter to tell him he needed to see something on TV. He walked into the main room of the house to see a special report on one of the networks. It was a video made with a cheap camera - probably a cell phone. It was a video of the Homs Museum of History in Syria. Why was something like this on television? He understood a few seconds later.

In horror, he watched a group of men clad in black rigging explosives through the museum. It was the Islamic State; it was about to destroy the ancient idolatrous past of Syria to show the world there would be no return. When the men were finished, a masked man praised Allah and pulled a switch.

Before the eyes of millions, the museum vanished; a cloud of rubble was all that remained. Carter could see it was a professional demolition job. Abandoned buildings in the U.S. had less skill displayed in their demolition. However, the fact remained - someone had destroyed Syria's treasures of history.

Carter felt his blood pressure rise. This had happened again, and he wanted to see it stopped. But, what could one man do?

Chapter Twenty-Two

WE CAN'T BE SURE

As promised, James Rhodes made the appointment to meet with Carter a month after Will's wake in Maine. They met in a stylish little coffee shop not far from the University in Boston.

Carter noted that Rhodes sat at a table in the far corner of the room, close to the back door exit. He sat with his back to the wall with a full view of the entry as well as the whole coffee shop. He lifted his finger when he caught Carter's eye as he entered.

Rhodes appeared to be in his mid-fifties, about six foot one, had dark hair just beginning to turn gray at the temples, tan skin, not an ounce of fat on his body and lively dark brown eyes, which constantly and inconspicuously scanned the room.

"I've been looking forward to this meeting for a long time Mr. Rhodes," Carter said as they shook hands.

"Jim will do fine. Most people, including your grandfather, call me by that name."

"Alright, Jim," Carter said as he sat down. "You're the

only one of my grandfather's friends whom I know nothing about."

"Well, I was 20 years younger when I met him." Rhodes smiled. "We became very good friends, and I will miss him very much."

"Yes," Carter responded with sadness detectable in his voice, "it's hard to come to terms with the reality that he's not around anymore."

They spent a few minutes talking about the weather and family. When there was a lull in the conversation, Carter got to the point. "So Jim, tell me all about it. You and my grandfather knew each other for 20 years, and I only hear about it now. I thought I had met all of his friends."

Rhodes's eyes darted around the room again before he turned his attention to Carter. "There is a very good reason for it." His tone dropped to a near whisper. "But I must first have your word that nothing I tell you will ever leave this table."

"So Gramps kept some things from me?" Carter nodded slowly. "Yes, you have my word it stays between us."

"I had hoped Will would have talked to you before he passed," Rhodes began, "When his doctor told him about his condition, I told him he needed to talk to you, but I guess the last heart attack came much quicker than he expected."

Carter looked at him questioningly and wondered. *Talked to me about what?*

"Carter, this may come as a surprise to you. On the other hand, maybe it won't. Your grandfather and I were involved in some very sensitive government work. The two of us worked together on a lot of top secret projects over the past 20 years."

"Top secret," Carter repeated slowly and stared out the

window. It answered many things: the ranch so far from civilization, his grandfather's interest in unexplained phenomena, and long trips to all corners of the globe. Many little bits and pieces he had never questioned suddenly dropped into place. "So my grandfather was an undercover agent?" Carter shook his head slightly. "I never thought of him that way."

"Are you shocked?" Rhodes asked. He sounded a bit alarmed. "Your grandfather was a great man - a true patriot and someone whom I will always admire."

"No not shocked at all, just surprised. So what kind of work did he do? Or is it one of those 'I can tell you but then I'll have to kill you' scenarios?"

"I am more than happy to tell you as much as I can at this stage, but you'll have to endure a little background chatter from me."

Carter nodded. "Yes, I really want to know. In fact, I feel like I almost have the right to know."

"Good," Rhodes started. "As I said, your grandfather began working with me 20 years ago. He did some amazing work for humanity and his country. He had an open mind and was a great asset. At some stage, depending on how far we get, I will be at liberty to give you more specifics about the missions he was involved in."

Carter waved to him to continue.

"As he became older, we started talking with him about retirement and his replacement. I have followed your career since your school days through college right up to this moment. Somewhere along the way, I made up my mind that you should be Will's replacement. After you finished your degree and became a full professor of archeology, I was 100 percent convinced you were the person we needed."

"I will take that as a compliment," Carter smiled. "But to take my grandfather's place in anything is going to be a tall order."

"When you made that remarkable discovery in Peru," Rhodes continued, "I spoke to Will about letting you step up to the plate. At the time, however, he felt we should hold off a little longer. You'd just become engaged, and he felt you needed time to get married and settle down. So, I left it up to him to pick the time and place to tap you on the shoulder.

"When we last talked, he told me he'd received a bleak prognosis from his doctor, and I impressed upon him that it was time to talk to you. He said he would, but, as we now know, he didn't."

Carter shook his head. "No, he definitely did not. It's so unlike him to have left loose ends."

"Yes that's true; he was always a well-ordered and meticulous man." Rhodes nodded. "So Carter, if you haven't guessed by now, part of the purpose of this visit is to see if you are interested in following in Will's footsteps."

Carter was silent for a while. "Please continue," he smiled. "I am still listening."

Rhodes looked Carter directly in the eyes. What he was about to tell him was very sensitive and most important. If it were anyone else, he would've had to go through a long and stringent vetting process first. However, Carter was different; he had been vetted over the past 20 years. Rhodes had no doubt Carter was the man to fill the void left by the legendary Will Devereux.

"What I am going to tell you might help you decide. I wouldn't normally tell anyone what you are about to hear at this stage of the recruitment process, but I have been watching you for 20 years. Your grandfather and I worked together a long time, and it makes the situation different."

Again, he paused for a moment as if to make sure he wanted to proceed. "I work for a top-secret government agency which officially does not exist. I'm not even allowed to give you the name at this stage. It appears on no government documents, and we report directly to the President of the United States. Our funding comes out of the discretionary top-secret black ops budget. If you come to work for us, expect to see a lot of documents with 'eyes only' printed on them and hear the words 'does not officially exist' used on a regular basis."

Carter smiled. He was well aware of the fact that archeologists were used in years past as a cover for covert operations.

"Let me lift part of the veil for you," Rhodes started his explanation. "It might sound crazy at first, but please hear me out. We investigate unexplained archeological phenomena, conspiracy theories, and ooparts. There are so many wild ideas and strange beliefs out there it makes my head swim. I'm talking ancient astronauts, aliens, Star gates, time travel, Atlantis, the lost continent of Mu, or UFOs. You've probably heard about all of them and many more.

"Crazy as some of those ideas might be, for reasons that might become obvious to you momentarily, our government can't afford to ignore any of them. You've unearthed a few history-changing places yourself. You hold very unconventional, and in some circles unpopular, views about human history, just like Will did. But in the end, you were right. Right about the underground city, right about the desert ruins housing giants, and I'm sure you will continue to prove yourself right again in the future.

"This is why the federal government employs us. The

U.S. government can't afford to let some unknown technology, which could be employed for devious purposes, land in the hands of our enemies. No government can afford to do so if they want to survive."

Carter nodded. He understood all of that.

"The problem is," Rhodes continued, "no one wants to be tasked with doing this sort of work. Congress won't have anything to do with it — afraid it would be seen as wasting the budget on crazy conspiracy theories. It could look very bad come election time.

"Be that as it may. We know politics and reality often have very little in common. I don't have to tell you the consequences of what could happen if some ancient technology we don't understand fell into the hands of terrorists. What happens if some lunatic gets hold of a star gate, a death ray weapon, et cetera? Can you imagine what might take place if extremists got their head-chopping hands on the Glocke, that Nazi super weapon? For all we know some kind of rail gun might be hidden under a Mayan ruin. What about some super virus stored in a mound on the tundra? Perhaps the Byzantine's Greek fire was even more deadly than they claimed. The rumors about ancient nuclear explosions abound."

"And these are the sort of things my grandfather was employed to look into?" Carter asked.

Rhodes nodded without replying.

"And I guess you're not telling me more until I sign up?"

"You summed it up," Rhodes confirmed. "Think of it this way, Carter. You unearthed a city under a mountain, which had no reference in written history. You were among the first people, in who knows how many thousands of years, to walk in a city built by giants. Those two discoveries of yours pushed human history back by 50,000 years. The existence of those places was never recorded anywhere, not even in myths and folklore. You know the level of technology both of those civilizations possessed, and we didn't even know it existed. To this day, no one has figured out where the electricity in the City of Lights comes from and how it is conducted. Those giants were using advanced technologies that we can't even begin to explain. To date, no written record left by them has been found. How can we be sure they, or another unknown civilization, didn't create a weapon so powerful it could wipe us all off the face of the earth?"

The implications of what Rhodes was saying hit Carter hard. "No," he whispered, "we can't be sure."

"Well, that's why I'm here today, Carter. We need your help. I'm not sure if you realize it, but you're currently the world's leading expert on lost civilizations."

Carter was a bit startled. He didn't answer immediately; he stared at his empty coffee cup for a while and then looked at Rhodes. "Okay, I have a two-week recess coming up next week. My family and I are flying up to Freydis, and I will think this through. I trust that's okay with you?"

"I understand. We are in a hurry to bring in Will's replacement, but this is not a decision to be made on the spur of the moment. I'll be waiting for your answer when you return."

"You know I'll never be able to hide this from Mackenzie? She didn't fall off a turnip truck."

"I understand that. However, for your family's sake, it should go no further. There are people's lives at stake Carter. There are a lot of power hungry lunatics out there who would go to extreme lengths to get their hands on some of these things if they existed. People could be killed. That's why we work in a world of shadows. If you should decide to come on board with us, we'll need to talk again about what you can and cannot share with her."

"I won't tell her anything for now," Carter said. "I have a lot of thinking and soul-searching to do before I talk to her or make any decision."

"Agreed. It is the best approach for now. But as I have said, you are free to go ahead and tell her what you know now if and when you feel it's necessary."

Rhodes stood and shook Carter's hand, "Would you mind hanging back for a few minutes before you leave?"

"Why ... what ..." Carter stuttered as he looked at him in surprise at the strange request. Then he remembered Rhodes' words. *'We work in a world of shadows.'* This was Covert 101. *That's why he picked this seat, back to the wall so he can see everything, close to the back door for a quick escape, the dark eyes constantly scanning the room. The man is a real spook. Probably packing a gun as well.*

Carter walked around the table and took Rhodes' empty seat; he wanted to observe him as he left. Rhodes went to the counter, paid for the coffee, and walked out without looking back. Carter noticed how he paused for a second before he stepped out. He could see how Rhodes scanned the street to the left and right and across from him in that brief moment before he let his body appear outside. Yet all his movements looked natural. No casual observer would have been able to pick up that transitory moment of observation.

Being aware now of what Rhodes did for a living, Carter paid close attention and was surprised to see how the man moved and conducted himself. He didn't look military. He had a casual style of walking - his head was not pivoting to observe his environment, yet it was certain he knew exactly what was going on around him. Out on the street he could have passed as any middle-aged office worker on his way back to his cubicle after lunch. No one would give him a second look.

Carter smiled. *I'm sure he knows everything about every car and person within 100 yards of his position. He probably registered their faces, clothing, movements, and intentions.*

On the way back to his office, Carter's eye caught another story about the destruction of ancient monuments in the Middle East. It took every bit of self-control for him not to send the newspaper flying into the streets. This time, radical Islamists destroyed an entire ancient temple complex because it violated their sense of historical precedence. Once again, they piled explosives up around it and detonated the entire structure, bringing it down in one hideous explosion.

"They have to be stopped," Carter mumbled as he looked at the paper. *"Something has to be done. This is becoming worse than the destruction of the Library of Alexandria."*

Chapter Twenty-Three

HIS DECISION WAS MADE

The two-week break from school allowed Carter and his family the opportunity to travel to Freydis. It gave him the chance to think about all the things Jim Rhodes told him about his grandfather. Carter made up his mind to talk to Ahote. If anyone of Will's friends knew about the undercover work, it would be Ahote.

The next morning Carter and Ahote rode out on horseback. Carter was hopeful that given their close friendship, Will had confided in Ahote.

About an hour into the trek, Ahote turned to Carter and asked the question on his mind since Carter's arrival. "What's up, Carter? Something is bothering you my friend. I can tell."

"You know me too well," Carter laughed. He turned to watch a vulture soar in the sky, its broad wings riding the up draughts. At that very moment, he envied the carrion bird, as it had none of his responsibilities.

"How many years have I known you, Carter? You are like a brother to me."

"Remember that man, James Rhodes, from our wedding and grandpa's memorial service?"

"Yes, I do." Ahote said. "What about him?"

"I was hoping you would be able to tell me more about him." Carter didn't want to be too direct. "At the memorial service he told me he had been a friend of grandpa for many years. What bugs me is I always thought I knew all of his friends, and now it seems Rhodes was the exception."

Ahote pulled his horse up, turned in his saddle and looked at Carter with a big grin on his face. "Carter, quit beating around the bush. I know you well enough to see that you are fishing for something. Out with it."

"Okay," Carter sighed. Ahote was not going to make it easy for him. "Have you seen James Rhodes on any occasion other than our wedding and the memorial service?"

"No, never. I have been just as perplexed about him as you are. It's obvious the trouble in your mind is somehow connected to this man. Care to talk about it?"

"I'm in a bit of an awkward position at the moment Ahote. I can tell you some of it, but not all. I am sorry my friend; I would like to be able to confide in you, and would do so without hesitation if I had not given my word. Please understand." He almost begged.

"No problem Carter. A man's word is precious. If you have given your word not to divulge certain information, I respect that. Tell me what you feel comfortable sharing, and I will fill in the blanks for myself."

"Thanks for that Ahote. I appreciate that. Grandpa always held you in high regard, and I hold the same view."

Ahote bowed his head in acknowledgement of the compliment and smiled.

Carter told Ahote about the meeting with Rhodes and the fact that Grandpa Will did some sensitive work for the

U.S. government. He skirted around the details of the type of work and ended with the request from Rhodes to take Will's place.

"To take your Grandfather's place? I'm not surprised. It's a great honor, Carter."

"Yes, indeed it is, but I have to think about my family as well. And I don't know to what extent James Rhodes can be trusted."

"I can understand about your family," Ahote said. "As for trusting Rhodes, you have Will's word that he was a friend. I'm sure if Rhodes was not a trustworthy guy, Will would not have invited him to your wedding, and he would have warned you."

"Yes, I guess you're right about that."

"Have you talked with Mackenzie about this?"

"No I haven't, but she will have to know if I decide to proceed with this."

"Why don't we go through Will's papers later and see if there is something we can learn? He might have left something in his desk or books that might tell us what he was doing all those years."

Carter felt it was a good idea, and they rode on in silence. For the time being there was nothing more to say. They continued their ride checking the property for any signs of the wolf pack, which had grown over the years. As the day drew to a close, they finished it by inspecting and cleaning around Will's grave before returning to the house.

Later that evening Carter told Mackenzie about his meeting with Rhodes. She listened quietly to everything. When he was done, she said, "I have faith in your decisions, Carter. I know you'll do the right thing for both Liam and me. If you feel this is the right path to take, go ahead – you have my support."

"Thank you, Mackie. I love you. No man could ever hope to have a better wife than I have."

"Carter Devereux, secret agent," she laughed. "As far as I am concerned, if that is what Will was involved in, then whatever they want you to do is all right with me. I never knew him to do anything that wasn't honest and good for everyone. We can check through your grandfather's papers in the morning. For now, why don't we turn in early?" She said leading him down the hall to their bedroom.

Carter and Mackenzie walked into the storage room the next morning and looked at all the boxes stacked on skids to keep them off the floor and dry. They were organized by the date compiled and stacked in the best order possible at the time they moved them.

"It's strange seeing a man's life packed away in such a fashion," Carter said. "Where do we begin? I can't even think where to start?"

"At the beginning," Mackenzie laughed. "We just start with the first one we can reach and go through them one by one."

"Hmm... forever logical! That's my Mackie." He gave her a hug.

They spent the morning going through all the boxes. They would open one, check through it, and place it to one side if it contained nothing of interest. Most of them were full of old bill receipts, which his grandfather was meticulous about keeping, in the days before digital storage.

After lunch, Bly and Ahote joined them and helped go through even more boxes. By early evening Carter despaired, he would never find anything in them that might help him make his decision. It was obvious Will Devereux kept nothing at Freydis relating to his government work.

Just as they were about to stop for the day, Mackenzie

opened a small box containing the contents of the bedside table in Will's bedroom. She found his personal Bible on top of the items and held it up.

"How lovely; this was given to your grandfather by his mother when he went off to college. It's a leather bound red-letter edition - an original King James Version. What an incredibly wonderful gift." She read the inscription on the inside cover aloud. *"To my dear son William, may you find wisdom and comfort in this book all the days of your life. Let this be the lamp unto your feet. Your loving Mother. 18 July 1950."*

They both had tears in their eyes as Mackenzie flipped through the Bible. Suddenly, her fingers found a single sheet of folded paper inside the pages. She took it out, noticing the name "Carter" handwritten on it and handed it to Carter.

Carter took the paper, unfolded it, and with shaking hands read:

To my dear Carter

In Psalm 103:15 the psalmist says, "The life of mortals is like grass, they flourish like a flower of the field; the wind blows over it and it is gone, and its place remembers it no more."

The sand in my hourglass is at its end. I look back at my life and, with the wisdom of hindsight, there are things that I would have done differently. If I got a second chance, there is also much I would not want to change.

God blessed me beyond description when He gave you to me as my grandson and my friend for 38 years. God's blessing went far beyond my wildest dreams when He also granted my desire to meet my wonderful daughter-in-law and my great-grandson. I am at peace when I leave this place to meet my Maker.

Nothing gives me more joy than the knowledge that you, Mackenzie, and Liam are happy and that you love and respect each other.

There remains but one matter that I never spoke to you about. That is about the work I did with my friend James Rhodes. You will never know how desperately and for how long I have wanted to share it with you.

I took pride in the work I did with him. I have no regrets. I don't have to go into the details here; James will no doubt contact you at some stage after I'm gone and will tell you all about it. You can trust and believe him.

For some time now, James has wanted you to step into my place, and as far as I'm concerned, there's no one better or more capable of doing so than you. Still, every time I saw you and your family, I wanted time to stretch further, to hold you all close, and so I have delayed the moment. Alas, I have held on for too long.

James was a true friend and I can assure you he will be for you. It doesn't matter what your decision is – he will remain a loyal and trustworthy friend just like Ahote, Bly and my other friends you have met.

Nonetheless, as James will tell you, it is dangerous work - sometimes more so than you can imagine. There is your young and growing family to consider. Therefore, I ask you to think carefully before taking my place.

You have always made me so proud. You, Mackie, and Liam have filled my life with joy – you made it a life worth living.

It's time to say goodbye my son. Never forget I will always be somewhere nearby.

Your loving grandfather.
William Devereux

Carter's eyes filled with tears and his hands shook when he gave the letter to Mackenzie to read. When she finished reading it, she passed it on to Ahote and Bly.

Mackenzie hugged her husband and cried for a long time. Later, Carter walked outside and listened to the sound of the wind in the trees. In the distance, he could see Mackenzie's wolf friends watching him.

His decision was made.

Chapter Twenty-Four

THEY HAD A LOT TO DISCUSS

South Eastern Syria, close to the Iraqi border

Hassan Al-Suleiman stood and looked around the room that was now his office, admiring its size and symmetry. The tiled floor and high arched windows pleased him. He'd decided to move into the building a year ago, as he believed it was time to improve his public image.

He spent most of the morning listening to various complaints from his commanders in the field about what the official Syrian government was attempting to do now. Hassan did not give a flea-bitten donkey for the official government or the clan who ran it. They did not fit into his plans – he would deal with them in due time.

He was about to meet with a delegation from Saudi Arabia. Not knowing much about them, or whom they represented, he was prepared to listen to them. He had reached the stage in his plans where he could use the financial backing of someone who shared his vision. Many delegations had visited him in the past, but he had yet to find one that held his views on the future of Islam. All of them were only interested in one goal – to wipe out the Jews and turn the entire world into one big Sunni Islamic state.

He was in no hurry to form alliances he might regret later. He would wait for the right one to show up. He understood the wisdom of 'making haste slowly' – a philosophy that had served him well in the past and would continue to serve him well in the future.

"You may send in the delegation," he told his aide.

Hassan shut down his computer and pulled out a pad of paper. He took his automatic pistol from its holster and put it in the drawer. It was a gift from an American CIA representative, who had visited the week before.

Khalid Abdul Bashir and another man, who was introduced as Saad Abdullah, entered his office. He offered them tea, coffee, and food, and then showed them to their seats.

Abdul Bashir was the spokesperson. Contrary to Arab custom of making a lot of small talk before getting to the real purpose of a meeting, Khalid asked Hassan if he would be okay to get right to the point.

This pleased Hassan, as spending hours chitchatting was not his way of getting things done.

Abdul Bashir smiled when he saw Hassan's positive reaction to his suggestion and thought, *our agents did a good job when they built Hassan's profile.*

He proceeded to explain that they represented a very influential man in Saudi, who was not part of the royal family, and wanted to remain anonymous for now. He gave Hassan a glowing reference about the man and assured him that he was probably the most trustworthy person anyone could ever hope to deal with. The truth was that Khalid Abdul Bashir didn't know who sent him. He believed he was on a top-secret mission for Youssef Bin-Bandar, the third highest member of the General Intelligence Presidency.

Hassan was a good listener. Although he felt some apprehension dealing with intermediaries for a phantom, he kept his facial expression and his body language neutral. He nodded, "I understand. No problem with that. If we were to reach a mutually beneficial agreement, there would be enough time to become acquainted with him." Hassan smiled.

Abdul Bashir nodded while thinking, *that's not going to happen, but you will find that out later. Now is not the time for you to know that.* He continued to convey his congratulations and admiration for the achievements of Hassan and his True Sons of the Prophet. Admittedly, they had been studying various groups and warlords all over the Muslim world, in search of someone wise and truthful and who had the guiding hand of Allah. He was pleased to tell Hassan that their information about him and his successes were what brought them to his doorstep.

Hassan was quite surprised to hear how much they knew about him and his group. His esteem for them kept growing as they heaped the praises on him.

Abdul Bashir was a skilled negotiator, interrogator, and judge of people's behavior. He had a doctorate in clinical psychology and worked as an agent for *Al Mukhabarat Al A'amah*, the Saudi General Intelligence Presidency. He had been studying Hassan for months and knew exactly which emotional buttons to press, and which ones to avoid.

"We are impressed with the happiness, stability, and prosperity you have brought to the people you govern." He laughed. "I have to admit; many didn't think you would last a year when you took control of your first valley. However, you have survived and continued to expand. We have been following your progress for some time. We would like to invest in you - help you thrive and flourish and bring your vision to reality." An hour later Hassan was eating out of his hand.

Hassan leaned forward, "You know what my vision is?" he smiled because he thought he was about to hear the first lie out of Abdul Bashir's mouth.

"Oh yes, we do. It's the same as ours – one big consolidated Muslim Empire. Stop fighting the entire world. Stop trying to control the world. Consolidate the people of Islam and bring peace and prosperity to them."

Hassan almost went slack-jawed. *This was the hand of Allah. This is what he had been waiting for.* "And you share and support that vision?" He queried making sure he sounded a bit skeptical.

"Yes, 100 percent without any reservation whatsoever."

Hassan got up and started pacing around the office. Everyone was quiet when Hassan's back was turned, Abdul Bashir slowly moved his finger to his lips to show his companion, Saad Abdullah, to remain absolutely silent. Abdul Bashir knew this was an important moment. Hassan had to feel in charge. No one would say a word until he had a chance to organize his thoughts and speak aloud.

He was of two minds. On the one hand, he was shocked about the profound knowledge these men had about him. *Where and how did they get it? Did someone in his inner circle talk too much? For how long had they been watching him? What else did they know about him? He didn't even know who sent them. Could he trust them? On the other hand, he had been waiting for this opportunity.*

A few minutes later Hassan stopped pacing and stood behind his chair, looked at them and said, "I am impressed by your preparation for this meeting; you have honored me by your visit. Nevertheless, I have a few questions, and I trust you will answer me honestly as you have been doing up till now."

Abdul Bashir nodded, "Of course we will answer your questions honestly, and I would have been very disappointed and doubted our decision if you didn't have any questions." He smiled.

Hassan sat down. "It is obvious to me that the man or organization you represent has money and influence. Why did you choose me, a humble servant of Allah? Why do you need me if you can set up and control your own group and land? If it is indeed true that we have the same vision, then we will meet again in the future, and we will join forces. Won't we?"

"Yes, that's true. We had that choice, and I guess the option is still there. But, why would we want to ignore what you have achieved. You have the expertise. The people you govern love and respect you. They support and trust you. Their lives have been changed – for the better. They have a better quality of life than anyone else in the rest of Syria does. They are happy and gratified."

Hassan smiled, and Abdul Bashir knew they were almost there. He continued. "Do you know by what name you are known by your people and the many others that are eagerly waiting for you to arrive and set them free from the chains of poverty and strife?"

Hassan shook his head. He had no idea he had another title or name. His men called him prince and he was not aware of any other title.

Abdul Bashir smiled. He knew he had Hassan in his hand. "You are known as the Sultan of Syria. The people are honoring you."

Upon hearing those words, all of Hassan's doubts disappeared, and he relaxed. Abdul Bashir saw it.

"What exactly is it that you have to offer my people and me, and what part do you play in fulfilling our shared vision?"

Abdul Bashir took some documents out of his briefcase.

Hassan called his aide, told him to cancel all his meetings for the rest of the day and night, and ordered him to get the women to prepare a feast for their guests. They had a lot to discuss.

Three days later Xavier Algosaibi was studying the detailed report and listening to the recording of the meeting with Hassan Al-Suleiman.

Xavier was a happy man. He had taken the first real steps toward the destruction of the House of Saud and the establishment of world domination by the Wahhabi Muslims.

In one day with a well-planned and orchestrated meeting, he had acquired, land, people, and an army. There was still a lot to do, but with the guidance and help of Allah, things were going to fall into place.

Chapter Twenty-Five

THE ANNIVERSARY

It was their sixth wedding anniversary, and Carter made a dinner date with Mackenzie. He found a babysitter and let Mackenzie know by way of a bouquet of flowers delivered to her office.

As the Maître d seated them, Mackenzie looked around the restaurant and turned to her husband. "You know I am still thinking about the first time we went out to coffee," she had a puzzled look on her face. "I still haven't figured out how you managed to pull that one off."

"I can't tell you all my secrets," he laughed.

The wine steward came with their order and filled the glasses as Carter handed Mackenzie a small box wrapped in red tissue paper and tied with a white ribbon. She picked it up and smiled at him.

"Why Professor Devereux," she exclaimed, "whatever could this be?"

"Something to show how much you mean to me."

"Can I open it now?

"You most certainly can."

Mackenzie looked at the box with glee and slowly removed the wrapping, being careful not to damage it in any way. Inside the gift box was a small jewelry case. She opened it to find a silver key ring with what looked like a small flash drive attached. Turning the flash drive over, she saw it contained a digital display screen.

"This is beautiful, Carter," she said as she looked at it. "I love the design on the key chain. What's this small thing attached to it?"

"It's a miniature camera and digital display," he explained to her. You can take pictures with it and use it to look at them. You can even upload hundreds of photos on it and look at them whenever you want."

"Where on earth did you find it?"

"I had it made for you at the little shop over in Washington - the same place that did such an outstanding job on the engagement and wedding rings."

"Thank you... I love it," Mackenzie said as she looked into his eyes. "Over the past six years, you've made me the happiest woman in the world!"

Dinner passed pleasurably as they finished their appetizers and waited for the main course. The food was excellent; Carter had chosen the little French restaurant based on recommendations from his colleagues at the University. While they ate their food, he asked about her research into ancient medicine.

"I'm so glad Grandpa Will steered me in this direction. In the beginning, I was skeptical, but boy have I been pleasantly surprised. Just this morning I found some information that shows how the Incas used obsidian knife blades for surgery. They're sharper and less dangerous to living cells than the platinum scalpels used today."

"Has anyone tried using obsidian surgical tools in modern times?"

"Yes, in fact, a doctor in Idaho used an obsidian blade to remove a tumor from a patient's lung. He had to make a huge incision, but the cut was so precise it healed up with barely any scarring."

Carter was smiling as he could see the look of excitement on her beautiful face.

"There are schools of medical thought dating back thousands of years that worked to treat diseases we can't cure today. I know of several people who are in the process of translating the ancient texts from India in hopes of finding new information."

Carter listened to Mackenzie, asking occasional questions, as she filled him in on all she had discovered. He found what she had to say endlessly fascinating and wanted to hear more.

She played with the key chain as they talked - the tiny camera captivated her. He could tell by the way her green eyes sparkled when she looked at it. Later he'd show her how it worked and within a day or two, she would have all the pictures of Liam she could find on it.

Carter checked his watch and regretfully told her they needed to get home because the babysitter could only stay until midnight.

They left the restaurant and strolled along the street, admiring the displays in shop windows as they made their way to their car. Across the street, students were heading to late-night parties and bars.

"Do you remember being so young?" Mackenzie said as they watched the undergraduates walk past. They were a mixed lot, dressed in all manners.

"No, I don't recall ever being *so* young," Carter grinned.

"At their age, I was busy working on my degree and spent all my time with my nose in the books."

Chapter Twenty-Six

A PACK OF INFORMATION

Hassan had another request for hire from a nearby ISIS chapter for his demolition crews to destroy some pagan ruins in an area under their control, which Hassan accepted. It did not matter all that much to him. If the Daesh wanted the ruins destroyed, let them use their own explosives and pay for the work. He planned to incorporate this area into his own sphere of control but was not yet ready to make his move. This job would diminish their arsenal of explosives, weakening their defenses when he attacked, and add some funds to his bank account.

He was well aware of the Westerners' concern for the old broken stones and ancient idols. Hassan understood they would use it against him if he were connected to the destruction of these old pillars. Therefore, he instructed his men to make sure they were not photographed in their uniforms. They were to wear ISIS uniforms and make it clear to everyone this was an ISIS action.

With the financial backing and the blessings of the Saudi's, he started preparations for the next expansion. He consolidated what had been conquered before, and the people in the areas under his control were happy and safe. It was time to increase the influence of The True Sons of the Prophet again. There were still vast areas about him under the control of fanatics and incompetents - ripe for the picking.

Upon proclaiming a new and independent territory, his first act was to create the resemblance of a state. He understood man's need to belong to a large tribe - one that was on a winning streak. His march across the hills and valleys did not go unopposed, but he triumphed everywhere his troops went, receiving a hero's welcome in each new territory conquered. The people were eager to greet the arrival of the Sultan of Syria.

He took a second wife, one of the beautiful daughters of a tribal leader, and cemented his link to the powerful families in the land. His second son was born, and within the same week, Adeela gave him a beautiful dark-eyed daughter.

His troops trained regularly, maintaining their reputation as the best and most disciplined in the region. They knew he would tolerate nothing less.

The Saudi partnership was working very well. Very soon, he would welcome five new instructors who were ex-special forces. They would launch the Special Forces division of the armies of the True Sons of the Prophet. The services of these highly trained men, who had served in the much-feared Russian Spetsnaz, were easily bought at the right price.

In a secret lab in the lower part of Mecca in the district of Misfalah, Saudi Arabia, very close to Jabal Thawr, also known as Mount Bull, three scientists were working on a project. One was Chinese, one Pakistani, and one Bulgarian.

The lab was close to the famous cave, Ghar al-Thawr, Cave of the Bull, in which Muhammad and his companion, Abu Bakr, hid from their persecutors, the Quraish, during their migration to Medina.

It is said that with the help of Abu Bakr's family and slave, Muhammad and Abu Bakr took refuge in this cave. When the Quraish came seeking them, Abu Bakr was worried and told Muhammad, but Muhammad assured him that Allah was in the cave with them. When the Quraish reached the cave, it was clear to them no one was in the cave because there was a spider web spread across the mouth and birds nesting nearby.

The Pakistani medical doctor, a professor in human respiratory sciences and the Bulgarian, a professor in medical nanotechnology, entered the lab and watched the mice running on treadmills.

"Look at that!" The Chinese microbiologist shouted. "Mickey and Mini have been running full out for one hour already, and they are still going at the same pace! Tom and Jerry here didn't even last five minutes."

The others checked the stopwatches on the cages and nodded. "Looks like we got it right this time." The Pakistani said.

The Chinese nodded. "Yes, the information we got out of the American labs was excellent."

"Almost time to start human trials, what do you think? That would be the next logical step wouldn't it?" The Bulgarian questioned.

The Chinese and Pakistani nodded in agreement.

"I know you have done some calculations. What performance can we expect from a human?" The Bulgarian was looking at the Pakistani.

"Well, let's consider a real life situation. The current world record for 100 meters is 9.58 seconds, and the same man holds the 200-meter record at 19.19 seconds. So, as you can see, his endurance starts to fail over that distance. Instead of double the 100-meter time of 19.16 seconds, it took him an additional 0.03 seconds, the difference is minuscule over such a short distance, but it's there.

"However, let's look at the longer distances. The 400-meter world record is 43.18 seconds, so the pace is close to 11 seconds per 100 meters. The 1500-meter world record is 3 minutes 26 seconds – a pace of about 13.5 seconds per 100 meters. Over the half marathon of 21 kilometers, that speed drops to about 16 seconds per 100 meters, and over the full marathon, 42 kilometers, it drops to 18 seconds per 100 meters.

"If we take a very mediocre athlete that would normally run 100 meters at 11 seconds and inject him with this stuff, he will not win any 100 or 200-meter races, but he will come in third in the 400-meter race. In the 1500-meter, he would break the current world record by 41 seconds with a time of 2 minutes 45 seconds. In the 21-kilometer, the half marathon, he would smash the world record of 58 minutes 23 seconds by more than 20 minutes. Over the 42 kilometers of the full marathon, his time would be 1 hour 17 minutes, 45 minutes quicker than the current world record of 2 hours and 2 minutes."

"Of course, that's the theory. We will have to show that it will actually work like that in humans," the Bulgarian responded.

"There's only one way to find out I guess." The Pakistani smiled.

The telephone started ringing, and the Chinese answered. A voice spoke on the other end saying, "I am sending you a pack of information which might be of great help in your research. It will be delivered by hand tomorrow. I want you and your colleagues to study it and let me know if it is useful. It's the latest information from the American labs."

"Yes, sir I will do that. Thank you."

Chapter Twenty-Seven

THEY SHOOK HANDS

A week after his sixth wedding anniversary, Carter met with Jim Rhodes again and told him about the letter he'd found in Will's Bible.

"I'm glad you found it. I have this feeling you might have turned me down if you hadn't found that letter."

"It did sway my decision." Carter smiled

"So I take it, it's in order to say welcome aboard?"

Carter nodded. "Do you want me to sign my name in blood?"

"Nothing so formal," Rhodes laughed. "We'll look each other in the eyes and shake hands on it. I will let my people know, and that is all we need to do. Twenty years ago, it was good enough for your grandfather and me. Today it will be good enough for his grandson and me."

They shook hands.

Over lunch, Rhodes told Carter about some of the work his grandfather had done. Carter listened intently and connected the stories with some of his grandfather's long absences over the years. It explained why he would vanish for months at a time, then return carrying a chair from Afghanistan or a woodcarving from Borneo. Rhodes talked about his grandfather's sense of humor and duty.

"He never let a job remain unfinished and managed to see humor in every situation. He was deadly serious about everything he did," Rhodes explained. "At the same time, he could come out of left field and hit us with a quirk that would make us explode in laughter. I remember the director of the CIA glowering at him for 30 seconds after one very tense meeting when your grandfather had fun at the director's expense, and the man failed to see the humor."

"I'm glad to know I wasn't his only victim," Carter grinned.

Over lunch, a partnership was born between the two men.

"There are countless things we can't afford to ignore," Rhodes said and repeated some of their previous conversation. "Through history, governments and kings have tried to get their hands on holy relics and artifacts which were supposed to bring them power. Most were mere symbols, but even a symbol has a power all of its own.

"Before the Second World War, the SS sent an entire detachment to study in Tibet, assured they were tracing the origins of the lost Aryan race. It didn't stop there. We know the Nazi scientists of the Third Reich were developing a machine called 'Die Glocke.' Apparently, it was a device made out of a hard, heavy metal about 9 feet wide and 12 - 15 feet high, and shaped like a bell - hence the name Glocke.

"It is thought to have been operated with a metallic liquid substance, code-named Xerum 525. When this machine was in operation it would crystalize animal tissue, turn blood into a gel-like substance and plants into a greaselike substance in an area up to 200 yards around it. A reported eyewitness said that five of the seven original scientists working on the project died in the course of the tests.

"We still don't know its purpose or even if it really did exist. Some say it was some kind of time-travel machine, that it showed images of the past. Others say it was a death-ray weapon, and some people think it was an effort to build a star gate. Most scholars assume it was a ruse to deceive the Office of Strategic Services, the predecessor of the CIA. We may never know, but the fact is there is some truth in the whole story. The Nazi's were working on Die Glocke, and no one knows what happened to it – where it ended up. For all we know, it could be sitting in a cave or an underground chamber somewhere."

"One would hope the good guys would get it before the bad guys." Carter murmured.

"That's our work Carter; we can't sit back and hope that it turns out okay. We have to be proactive. These are the types of things we have to pursue. We have to get them in our hands before anyone else does. As I mentioned the last time we met, we are up against some deadly people, and it is not preordained that good will win over evil. In this shadow world, you can trust very few people."

"I get the picture," Carter commented.

"Let's talk about your training," Rhodes continued. "You'll start with a one-month orientation course. Afterward, we'll call you for two weeks or more of specialist training as opportunity permits. Do you have some free time coming up in your university schedule?"

"I can arrange for it and let you know."

The conversation continued for a while longer, and then Rhodes left.

Carter watched him out the window as he crossed the

street to his car and wondered about the opportunities and challenges this new chapter in his life was going to bring.

The next day he spoke to the Dean of the faculty and arranged for a one-year sabbatical from the university. His official reason was to pursue independent research and spend more time with his family.

Chapter Twenty-Eight

GIVE THIS TO THE SULTAN

Hassan sat in his office reading one of the many foreign news feeds about the continuing conflict in Syria and Iraq. Hassan had matured over the years. His beard now had white streaks in it, but he had not lost his strength or vigor for his cause.

He bookmarked a few stories to read later and paid close attention to what his rivals on either side of him were planning. He trusted the Allawi in Damascus only a little less than the people who ran the Islamic State. Either one would kill him the first time they felt it expedient to do so.

Leaning back in his chair, he recalled the destruction when the Islamic State took control of the ancient city of Palmyra. It was horrible what they did to anyone against them, and the ruins of a beautiful city showed the kind of barbarity they were prepared to unleash on the world should they ever have the opportunity. They dynamited and tore down Roman and ancient temples that were the pride of Syria. In their savagery, the Islamic State used the ancient amphitheater for public beheadings of their enemies

It was abhorrent what they did to the elderly government archeologist who tried to stop them. Dr. Khaled Assad was butchered for the crimes of 'overseeing idols' and 'attending infidel conferences' as the official representative of Syria. The man was in his 80's, and they decapitated him in a public square. They hung his body from a Roman column he'd spent his life trying to preserve.

Hassan thought about the gruesome death as he looked at another email from a representative of the Islamic State to his south. They had some ancient sandstone tombs in the way of an anti-aircraft battery. They claimed it was necessary to remove the tombs to provide their weapons with an unobstructed view to keep out the Russian bombers. Hassan was puzzled as to why the Russians had not carpet-bombed their holdout by now.

Hassan dispatched a team of men to take out the towers with the standard instructions for payment. They were to receive half of the money before, and the other half after the job was completed. His team was also to bring back any artifacts they could safely transport, and that might be of interest to him.

A week later, his demolition crew carried out their assigned task, wiring the charges in the old towers, while representatives of the Islamic State looked on. One of the towers, built to hold the ancient remains of the town's once great families, stood four stories in height. It exploded in one flashing ball of white fire while the spectators roared and chanted in approval. Hassan's men, dressed in the black robes of the Islamic State, waited until the dust settled and walked up to the rubble to inspect it. They didn't think it would take long, and then they could go home.

The rubble, however, revealed something unexpected as they approached the site of destruction. Their commander ordered the men to halt, and he went forward alone to examine a large hole in the ground where the building previously stood. The hole was much bigger than he expected. With his rifle slung over his back, the commander, a man named Moussa from Homs crawled around the rubble and leaned over to look into the hole. He was worried the explosion had opened up a cavity beneath the former building, which might create a sinkhole in the middle of the town. It wasn't his concern, but he didn't need Hassan giving him the order to return and clean up the mess he'd created. There was something down there, but with all the dust in the air, he couldn't tell what. He motioned for the rest of his men to approach. The other members of his demolition squad came closer and took position behind their commander.

It was a hot day, as most are in the Syrian lowlands, and the dust had coated everything when the charges destroyed the buildings. They moved carefully behind him as he began to navigate his way down the rubble that partially filled the opening at the bottom of the crater caused by the explosion.

After a half hour of removing and clambering over the debris, they reached the bottom and looked around. It was cold and clammy below the surface, and the men with Moussa were nervous.

He produced a flashlight and examined their surroundings. They appeared to be in a chamber 15 x 24 feet and approximately 30 feet below the surface. Moussa left one member of his team alone at the entrance to the hole with a machine gun and told him not to hesitate to use it should someone try to follow them down.

They found no inscriptions on the walls and were about to return to the surface when Moussa felt a rumbling beneath his feet. One of the stone slabs on which they stood broke loose and tilted downward, dropping him and his squad onto a subbasement floor. They praised Allah for surviving the fall and shone their lights around as they regained their footing. The slab remained in place behind them, which meant they, at least, had a way to get back up.

Their lights illuminated a scene the likes of which they could not describe. Directly in front of Moussa and his squad was a table with a group of shapes sitting around it. He walked closer to it and blinked his eyes a few times. The figures appeared to be human skeletons but were made of crystal. The flashlight sent rays dancing off the crystal shapes and sparkled across the room.

"Beard of The Prophet!" one man exclaimed behind Moussa. "What kind of hell have we found?"

Moussa walked closer to the table to inspect the crystal statues. He pulled his cellphone out and started taking photos. A few minutes later, he told his men, "We're going back up, but we're not leaving this area unattended. I need to let the Sultan know what we've found."

When they emerged from the hole in the ground, Moussa went up to the nearest ISIS representative and told him they'd found a staggering amount of unexploded bombs underground in a chamber no one knew existed. He would send the youngest member of his squad back to the Sultan and ask for guidance. They would need men to help disarm them. In the meanwhile, they would guard the entrance from anyone who wanted to look, since one wrong move might detonate the bombs and destroy the entire town.

The ISIS soldier saw the wisdom in what Moussa

wanted to do and ordered the crowd back to the edge of the city.

When they were told about the unexploded bombs, the people quickly lost their curiosity and vanished.

"Give this to the Sultan," Moussa instructed the young man he was sending back to Hassan as he handed him an SD card that contained the pictures he had taken with his cell phone. "Tell him what you have seen, but tell no one else."

Moussa made camp that night with his squad. He looked up at the stars and waited for Hassan to arrive with his troops.

Chapter Twenty-Nine

A-ECHELON

On the first day Carter reported for the orientation course, he learned the name of the organization he would work for in the future - A-Echelon. The A was for Archeology. Their covert workspace and offices were hidden in some of the secret underground facilities below the Smithsonian Institution Building known as The Castle. The Institution hosted a number of different research centers, as it was involved in a wide range of top-secret initiatives and programs across the globe.

A-Echelon's location was specifically chosen to be out of the public eye, close to the Smithsonian Institution's secret vaults, libraries, and research facilities, and in close proximity to DARPA's headquarters as well as Capitol Hill. The organization had no official existence. It did not have an official address where its offices were located, and only a select few people knew it even existed.

The director, Hunter Patrick, did not appear on the list of federal employees. None of his employees, research associates or field operatives could talk about their work, past or present. Their families only knew it was connected to the Smithsonian. Each employee of the institute was sworn to secrecy under an obscure act of Congress, which allowed the executive branch of the government one agency for which it would never be held accountable. The people involved in the institute, all of them, liked their jobs and knew that keeping them was contingent upon not discussing them. The institute employed two people for internal affairs, and it was their duty to run background checks on any potential candidate for employment.

The first four weeks after Carter's arrival, he was put through a demanding crash course in basic spycraft. He quickly confirmed his suspicions that James Rhodes was an ex-CIA spy instructor and field agent.

Although Carter was not entirely unsuspecting of what his training would entail, he was surprised at the level of physical and mental intensity required of him.

His days would start at 7:00 am with a one-hour self-defense session conducted by Rhodes, followed by one hour on the shooting range with various types of handguns.

The first morning's sparring session with Rhodes reminded Carter of the second day he attended Master Hong's Center of Harmonious Gratitude where he endured the humiliation of 30 minutes of beating by the other students. Despite Carter's years of tai chi training and managing to beat Rhodes in the end, after 20 minutes on the mat sparring with the older man, he could see why Rhodes was in such good physical shape at his age. He moved around and fought with the skill and ability of a man half his age.

A-Echelon had a close working relationship with the CIA and DARPA, as they would, from time to time, request skilled resources to assist with their covert operations. The

Directors of the CIA, DARPA, and their agents, who had worked with A-Echelon before, were counted among the few people who knew of the institute's existence and the nature of its work. For Carter's orientation, a few CIA instructors joined the training team.

In addition to the hand-to-hand combat and weapons training, he was also tutored in secured electronic communications techniques, encryption of messages, covert surveillance and counter surveillance techniques, and a lot of human behavior related psychology.

Rhodes and the CIA instructors were hard taskmasters. Carter received no TLC from any of them. They pushed him to the limits on all fronts and didn't allow him much sleep either. But Carter persevered. He absorbed everything they threw at him and thrived. He never second-guessed his decision to take up his grandfather's place.

At the end of the second week, Jim attended an assessment meeting with Director Hunter Patrick. "Jim, how is young Devereux holding up?" Hunter inquired.

"Hunter, we've got a winner here." Rhodes smiled. "The guy is an enigma; he's like the Rock of Gibraltar. He has had no military training and spent most of his life behind a desk or in a classroom full of starry-eyed students, but I have yet to hear one single complaint out of his mouth. Whatever we throw at him he takes on with a smile on his face. I think he's actually enjoying all of this.

"He has a photographic memory. I've never seen anything like this. No wonder he can speak seven languages, and God knows, understand and read how many more. The instructors feel like morons most of the time. There's nothing wrong with his attitude either. He is a very humble man with the best attitude I've ever encountered. His questions reveal deep insight; his observation skills are unparalleled. To see the ease with which he assimilates new information and how he masters skills in one session, which would take others weeks and months is just mindboggling."

Hunter smiled. "That sounds like Will Devereux's boy. I'm really glad to hear that."

The fifth and final week was set aside for briefings and mission preparations with Director Hunter Patrick and James Rhodes, who would be Carter's handler and partner for the future.

Patrick was a stocky man, in his mid to late sixties, who radiated self-confidence. This was the first time Carter had met him. He reminded Carter of a career government man, such as Allan Foster Dulles, who ran the foreign office after World War 2.

"I'm impressed with your results, Carter," Patrick beamed. "I don't think we have ever seen anyone who did as well. I believe you out-scored your grandfather. He did great work for us, and I expect you'll do the same."

"My grandfather will be a hard act to follow, Sir," Carter told Patrick. "In my eyes, there have been few men of his caliber in history."

"You may call me Hunter." He smiled. "At least you have your grandfather's example to follow. Not too many men have such an exemplary role model."

"Thank you, I appreciate it."

"Time to get down to business," Patrick said as he brought up a file on the large screen on his office wall. "Here are the essentials of the mission - Jim can fill you in on the finer details later."

Carter and Rhodes nodded.

"You may have heard rumors about evidence of nuclear weapons used in prehistoric times," Patrick said. "Do you have any opinion about it?"

"I've heard about it and done a bit of reading on the subject, but I haven't seen much physical evidence in support of it," Carter responded. "Have you found something worth investigating?"

"Rumors and second-hand information are widespread. As Jim has already told you, we can't ignore it -- that's our job. We have to investigate. You know even Robert Oppenheimer, the Professor of Physics, known as the Father of the Atomic Bomb, must have had some notion of an ancient nuclear blast if you read between the lines."

Carter must have had a frown on his face when Patrick said that, because he continued.

"Yes, that's right. Dr. J. Robert Oppenheimer quoted from the Bhagavad Gita, a Sanskrit text dating from 300 – 400 BC when he spoke those famous words, *'Now I am become Death, the destroyer of worlds.'*

"Seven years after the first nuclear bomb exploded in New Mexico, Dr. Oppenheimer gave a lecture at Rochester University and got the following question: *'Was the bomb exploded at Alamogordo during the Manhattan Project the first one to be detonated?'* Dr. Oppenheimer's peculiar answer was, *'Well…yes. In modern times, of course.'*"

"That's intriguing; I have never heard that," Carter frowned.

Patrick continued. "I don't have to tell you the implications if a terrorist organization found such a weapon or a description of how to build one. I'm certain they wouldn't hesitate to deploy it."

"Yes, I agree with you on that point. There are a lot of irrational people out there."

"Lunatics, Carter -- real, dangerous, radical, lunatics who would not hesitate to blow us all to kingdom come at the first opportunity. We need to know if someone in ancient times had a nuclear weapon. We need to know if one or more of these weapons survived into modern times. And let me be honest with you, I will definitely be very happy and sleep a lot better if you could debunk it all as a myth."

Hunter concluded his briefing by handing Carter a flash drive with all the documents and texts collected from all over the world. Some of the texts were in private collections and would not be easy to obtain. All of the information on the flash drive attracted the interest of the Institute due to apparent references to nuclear weapons.

The scope of Mackenzie's medical research had been rapidly expanding since she started digging into ancient medical practices. She read everything she could lay her hands on during her spare time. She devoted her free lab moments to testing some of the new theories and ideas she learned from her reading. She kept her private research away from her University research work. To suggest the investigation of ancient medical texts as a way to solve some of their current problems would have caused too much of a stir. She wanted to learn a lot more before she would be ready to take a stance.

Carter had introduced her to Liu Cheun, a woman of Chinese descent who was a professor of ancient languages at the University. She had done a lot of translation work for Will and Carter in the past and turned out to be very helpful to Mackenzie as well.

Over lunch, one afternoon while Carter was away, Liu asked Mackenzie how she was progressing with her research. "I know I'm not the only one doing your translation work," Liu said while their food was placed in front of them. "I'm sure you've found some surprises along the way." She smiled as she tucked into her lunch.

"Quite a few," Mackenzie replied. "I'm astounded almost every day as I discover what medical knowledge existed in times past. We never thought to look at some of these ancient texts, let alone believe them, and yet the solutions to so many problems are staring us right in the face."

"I think more people are waking up. After your husband's discoveries of those two lost cities, there is just no way anyone can deny the existence and value of past knowledge anymore."

"Well, he has certainly turned the applecart over." Mackenzie chuckled.

"I have the feeling you're on the verge of something big yourself?"

"It's too early to say, Liu." Mackenzie laughed. "I still have a long way to go."

"Care to talk about what you've learned so far?"

"Sure. I've found some new things, and by 'new things' I mean things that *I* didn't know about, and have been organizing them into five categories: internal procedures, instruments, diagnostics, surgery, and dentistry."

"So you are telling me you've made discoveries in each of these areas?"

"I wouldn't call it discoveries per se." Mackenzie took a sip of her tea and caught her breath. "For me, at the moment, it's new information. It's my personal journey of discovery more than anything else. However, I'm already convinced, even with the little bit of study I've done so far, that some ancient civilizations possessed much more medical knowledge than we thought."

"Examples?" Liu asked.

"The Ancient Indians and Egyptians from BC times already understood the relationship between the nervous system and how limbs function. There's a whole school of medical thought going back to prehistoric times in India called Ayurveda, which deals with the balance between the mind, body, and spirit. They understood how the heart and the circulatory system worked; yet in our time, we didn't figure out any of this until the first part of the 17th century. Our knowledge comes from Europe and William Harvey, who described completely, and in detail, systemic circulation and properties of the blood.

"I've also found some Chinese texts from 500 BC, which appear to describe the function of an X-ray machine. They were using a mirror to push light into the body from an element described as a 'gem'. It might have been a source of radiation. I can't figure out what they would have used as a photographic plate, but we only started on this particular text last week, and it might refer to something else; I'm not sure at this stage. If it's true though, it's amazing because X-rays were unknown to us until the end of the 19th century.

"The details and accuracy of some of the ancient diagnostic manuals are astounding. I cannot believe how many diseases they list and all the categories for them. I'm in the process of talking with more people who are experts in the history of medicine."

Liu was leaning forward, elbows on the table, absorbing Mackenzie's words enthusiastically. "Are you planning to publish some of your findings at some stage?"

"Yes, that's the plan, but it's not going to be very soon. I still have a lot more work to do before I will put my name on a publication that has the potential to cause a lot of controversy."

Liu pushed her plate to one side and picked up her bag.

"Mackenzie, thank you for the lunch. It was exciting to hear about your progress. Let me know if there is anything else I can do to help; I have plenty of grad students who need to be put to work."

Mackenzie thanked her for the offer and assured her she would definitely take her up on it.

After the meeting with Hunter Patrick, Rhodes and Carter spent time in some of the secret underground vaults below the Smithsonian collecting every bit of information they could get.

"Any ideas how you would like to approach this Carter?" Rhodes asked when they settled back in his office.

"Well, we have to do our research first. I suggest we do a quick review of all the material we have collected so far, look for references to other material and then decide how we would like to proceed from there."

Rhodes nodded. "You're the research buff. I'll do what you tell me."

"That's a welcome change in attitude after trying to kill me the last four weeks!" Carter quipped.

Rhodes laughed. "I can just hope there are no grudges left my friend."

"Nah, I actually enjoyed most of it. I learned a lot of new things."

"You did great my friend; Hunter wasn't just blowing sunshine up your ass when he complimented you this morning. He was serious - you did exceptionally well the past four weeks."

"Thanks for that Jim." Carter was a bit self-conscious. "Okay, let's get down to business."

Rhodes nodded for him to continue.

"I'm assuming, for now, that the site of an alleged explosion won't necessarily be the location where the alleged weapon would have been manufactured."

"That sounds like a reasonable assumption for now," James replied. "At least, until we can find evidence to show they have somehow managed to destroy themselves either deliberately or by accident."

"Yes, there is always a chance of that, but highly unlikely it could have happened at all of the sites. Nevertheless, before we go much further, I think we have to get verification that those sites are indeed radioactive. If that is so, then we will have to find out what caused the radioactivity.

"You know the discovery of a prehistoric nuclear chain reaction in that uranium mine in Gabon, West Africa caused a lot of speculation among scientists. Some swear it can be explained as a natural phenomenon. Others swear it's impossible; it can't be natural. They have the luxury to speculate, but we have the job to find the truth.

"We will also have to talk to someone who has a better understanding of nuclear science than the two of us. Do you happen to know someone?"

James grinned. "No problem, those are a dime a dozen around here in D.C. Anything else you can think of?"

"Other than a Starbucks coffee," Carter laughed, "nothing else I can think of for now."

"Okay let me go and take care of both of those right now."

A while later, Rhodes walked back into the office with two Starbucks coffees and announced he'd booked a meeting with Dr. Mark Adalbert of CENPA, the Center for Experimental Nuclear Physics and Astrophysics at the University of Washington, for 9:00 am the next morning.

"He consults for the CIA from time to time, so he has the necessary security clearances."

The next morning at nine, James introduced Carter to Dr. Mark Adalbert and explained the purpose of the meeting. They quickly brushed aside the formalities and called each other by first names.

"Mark, I have a few questions for you and hope, in the future, I might be able to knock on your door again if I need more information?" Carter started the conversation.

"No problem, anytime, just let me know what I can do to help. I'm also available on secure video conference if necessary."

"Thanks, it's good to know I will have your knowledge readily available. My first question is this. What type of instruments would one require to be able to measure one-hundred-millionth of a second?"

"The Japanese developed a high-speed camera, the HPV-1, with which they can take photos at a rate of one million frames per second. The atomic clock can measure up to one billionth of a second."

"For how long have we been able to make those sorts of measurements?"

"I will have to go back in history if you don't mind."

Carter nodded.

"The Persian scholar al-Biruni first used the term 'second' in the year 1,000 CE. He defined it as 1/86,400, which he got from multiplying the 24 hours of a day by 60 minutes and then again by 60 for the number of seconds in each minute. That definition remained unchanged until 1960 when it was redefined based on the period of the Earth's orbit around the sun in the year 1900.

"In 1967, however, the International Committee for Weights and Measures changed the definition. Since then it is based on the number of periods - about nine billion - of the frequency of radiation from the cesium atom in the so-called atomic clock. Since then we have been able to measure subdivisions of the second, such as a millisecond, a microsecond, and a nanosecond which is one billionth of a second."

"Why do you think someone would want to measure time in a specific range from three one-hundred-millionths of a second to 4.32 billion years?" asked Carter.

"That's a very wide range, Carter." Mark laughed.

Carter smiled as well and continued to explain. "We found an ancient Hindu book called, the Bihath Sathaka in which reference has been made to those time frames. The 'kashta', which is three one-hundred-millionths of a second and the 'kalpa', a period of 4.32 billion years. Sanskrit scholars have no idea why such a small fraction of a second was required in ancient times. All they know is that it was used in the past, and they feel obliged to carry on tradition."

"Well, if they used time divisions, it implies that the duration of something has been measured. How they did it at that minuscule level without today's precision instruments beats me. But I can tell you the only phenomena in nature that I am aware of that is measured in billions of years and in millionths of a second is the disintegration rates of radioisotopes of elements like uranium 238 with a half-life of 4.51 billion years to subatomic particles with mean half-lives of millionths of seconds."

"I was afraid that's what you were going to say." Rhodes had a frown on his face. "You see we are looking into the possibility that some of the speculations about ancient nuclear weapons could be true. If so, we will have to make sure none of the crazies get their hands on it."

Dr. Mark Adalbert looked troubled when he shifted in his chair and said, "That would be a catastrophe."

"Are you familiar with the Oklo phenomenon, the ancient nuclear plant in Gabon, West Africa?" Carter asked.

"Yes, I am. In fact, I did a study of it a few years ago."

"What were your conclusions?"

"I am of the opinion it is a natural phenomenon. I know the chances of a nuclear reaction happening without human intervention, sort of 'by accident,' is extremely small, but the evidence and reasoning that I studied led me to that conclusion. I have seen nothing from the people on the opposing side that even tries to give a logical explanation. They only hammer on the idea that coincidences such as that don't happen in nature. Their biggest problem is that no evidence of human activity has ever been found there."

"Are you aware of any other places on the planet where natural nuclear reactions are taking place or have taken place in the past?" Carter asked.

"None that I know of, but I can tell you in the 1950s, Dr. Paul Kuroda from the University of Arkansas described the probability of naturally occurring nuclear reactors lurking in the crust of the Earth. That was more than 20 years before the Oklo discovery.

"He theorized that if enough of an isotope of Uranium called U-235, which occurs naturally, collected under particular circumstances, a natural reactor could activate and perpetual fission would occur. He did, however, point out that such a reactor could not exist today since too much of the Earth's natural U-235 has decayed over billions of years.

However, a billion or so years ago, there was enough of it to make it happen, which is of course exactly what I think happened at Oklo."

A smile broke across Rhodes's face. "I am feeling a lot better already Mark."

"We're not out of the woods yet, Jim." Carter responded. "We only have good reason to believe the Oklo phenomenon is not going to cause us sleepless nights. The other sites across the world, even some here in America, are still waiting for us."

James nodded. "Mark thank you for your time. I'm sure once we get under way with our research we will be back with a lot more questions."

"It is my pleasure. As I have said before, you are welcome anytime. I will be more than happy to help."

Carter left Washington early the next morning.

Chapter Thirty

I HAVE NO DOUBT

Khaled, a good 40 feet underground, looked at the scene inside the chamber before him where, until ten days ago, a sandstone tower rested for the past 2,000 years. He made notes on a plain paper pad with an ordinary pen as he looked around the room. Strapped to his belt was a portable Geiger counter, and the device was sending him all kinds of bad signals.

Fear started to settle in his stomach as he realized the background radiation in this chamber was powerful enough to kill him if he stayed more than an hour.

Every member of the first team that entered the chamber exhibited all the signs of radiation poisoning just two days after they'd found it. The team made several trips down to the bottom of the shaft to take photographs and they'd worn no protective clothing at the time. Three of them had already died, and four more were on the verge of death. It was not a pretty sight to see how their bodies were wasting away. It started with nausea and vomiting, diarrhea, headache, fever, dizziness and disorientation. Within a few days, the victims were showing weakness, fatigue, hair loss, bloody vomit and stools. In the final stages, their skin started to peel off, infections broke out all over their bodies, and death had come as a relief.

When Khaled determined the life-threatening levels of radiation, he decided that from now on, no one would be allowed into this area without protective equipment. They needed to seal the hole at the top just to be on the safe side.

Khaled had a degree in engineering from Purdue University in the United States, which was why the Sultan had wanted him to go down and look at the chamber. He wanted Khaled's opinion on what caused the formation of the crystal skeletons. Sultan Hassan Al-Suleiman would take no chances when it came to the safety of his men.

He climbed out of the cavity and made his way to the surface where the battalion of the Sultan's men waited for him. Five days ago, Hassan's troops had taken the ancient city without firing a shot. Before the sun rose, they swarmed over the small contingent of Islamic State militia and took their guns away. The locals were relieved to see the orderly transfer of power. They knew Hassan ruled in peace over his lands, and no one disappeared in the middle of the night at the whim of some local commander.

"Don't come near me!" Khaled screamed at the Sultan's men who approached him. "I'm contaminated! I need soap, water, and an isolated tent. When I'm clean, my clothes will need to be buried at a remote site."

When the troops brought him what he needed, Khaled took out his cell phone and transmitted a message to the Sultan. He told Hassan that Allah had smiled on them this day. Down inside the shaft was a level of radiation too high for a natural cause. Someone had worked with nuclear materials in the ancient past, and if they did that, they probably had the technology to create a nuclear weapon. If the ancients had built nuclear weapons, so could the Sultan.

Twenty-four hours later, Hassan was in his office with his advisors. His council consisted of the four men he trusted most. These men had been with him a long time and owed their rise to power to him alone. Still, he didn't fully trust anyone and ensured all four were under constant surveillance. After his experience with the traitor Ali, Hassan was careful to make certain none of his inner circle felt so confident they could make deals without his approval. He didn't care what they thought about him as a man, so long as they gave him good advice and followed his orders.

"Is he serious?" Haji, a small man from Damascus asked. "Does Khaled expect us to believe he's found a nuclear blast underground?" Haji was a former doctor and ran Hassan's medical corps.

"Why don't you go see for yourself?" stated Bakr, who'd been with Hassan since leaving Mosul. "I trust Khaled's opinion on what he found down there. As you are a medical man, I understand your shock about the dead men of the first team who went down there."

"I would like to point out that our brother Khaled is not a nuclear expert," Haji returned. "The last time I checked he was a chemical engineer who managed an oil refinery."

"Agreed," Bakr responded, "but we would be stupid if we didn't go and investigate it thoroughly. The radiation level was confirmed by the Geiger counter; I would like to point out."

"Who do we know with a background in nuclear physics who could investigate this site?" asked Youssef, another member of the inner circle from Mosul and a former Iraqi army colonel.

"I will be in contact with our friends among the Saudi's," Hassan interjected into the discussion from behind his desk. "This will be of great interest to them. I suspect we have an area of mutual interest. Perhaps they would have someone to send to the site."

He adjourned the meeting and went over to the nearest barricaded window to stare at the wind sweeping up dust into the air. *Nuclear weapon capability? Right under my feet?* He smirked. *What would the members of the nuclear club think if they discovered they no longer had a monopoly?*

Two days later in Riyadh, the capital of the Kingdom of Saudi Arabia, Xavier Algosaibi read a decoded message and almost dropped the paper on which it was written. With shaking hands, he took the paper to an ashtray in his office and burned it.

"Allahu Akbar," he whispered while flushing the ashes down the drain, "If this is true, we have earned favor with Allah."

Four days later, a three-man team of experts, including one Dr. Ishrat Sadiq, arrived at Hassan's compound and asked for permission to see the Sultan. He met with them in private and then wrote a letter that guaranteed them safe passage to the site of the radioactivity. Each man had expertise in the nuclear program of Pakistan, and each was contracted by an anonymous company in Riyadh to perform the survey.

At the site, Khaled, who was now also suffering the

effects of exposure to radiation, told them what he found when he went down into the chamber. Only one man remained alive from the original team who had discovered it, and the doctors didn't expect him to live much longer.

The hole now had a concrete cover over it and was accessible only through a manhole installed at the time it was poured. The experts from Pakistan suited up in radiation suits and air masks before the portal was opened. Using a ladder installed by Hassan's men, they ventured into the lower reaches of the chamber while monitoring the background radiation. As they reached the table and crystal figures, one of them checked the Geiger counter and found the radioactivity level lethal after prolonged exposure. Then they began the time-consuming work of documenting everything they found.

Three weeks later, Dr. Ishrat Sadiq of Islamabad, Pakistan, booked into Dubai's Grand Hotel for a vacation with his family. The same evening, he had a secret meeting at another hotel with Dr. Abu Al-Assad of Riyadh, Saudi Arabia, who was also on vacation with his family.

They had the hotel room where the meeting was taking place swept for any listening devices, and when assured that the room was 'clean', they entered and started their discussion.

The two men, who had never met before, shook hands, exchanged a traditional greeting in Arabic and sat down. Both were scientists. Sadiq taught nuclear physics at a university in Pakistan, and Al-Assad was a teacher of chemical engineering at a university in Saudi Arabia. They were aware of each other's work and agreed to use first names during the meeting.

"Ishrat, as you know I represent someone else," the Saudi scientist said. "I am not allowed to give you his name. I bring you his greetings and blessings. He is very pleased with the work you have done for him at the site."

"Thank you," the scientist from Pakistan responded. "Let him know I was honored to be contracted to do the work he needed. Please send him my blessings too."

Sadiq handed Al-Assad a flash drive and told him it contained everything he would need. The small piece of plastic and circuitry held the results of lab tests, field surveys, photographs, and many other supplementary items. All of it would prove to be useful.

"Please forgive me for all the questions I must ask," Al-Assad explained. "These are questions I have been instructed to ask and to report back the answers."

"I would be very surprised if you had no questions," Sadiq laughed. "I am happy to answer them all."

"Tell me in detail what your team discovered at the site. I want to know the conclusions you reached."

"Let me begin with my suppositions. First, the background radiation is abnormally high inside the chamber. Second, it is the product of a nuclear explosion. Third, the nuclear explosion occurred a long time ago. Without any scientific dating, it's difficult to say, but I would guess more than 10,000 years ago."

"You are sure of this?"

"I have no doubt in my mind about the cause of the explosion, but I can't commit about the time when it occurred."

"Do you have any thoughts on what might have caused the nuclear blast?"

"Initially, I believed it might be from a natural reaction, such as the Oklo site in West Africa. However, the background radiation is far lower at Oklo, about half of what you would receive from a chest X-Ray. Furthermore, the Oklo reaction did not result in an explosion, just a sustained nuclear reaction, and it took place almost two billion years ago."

"Are you telling me this nuclear blast was the product of a human action?"

"I can't say for certain. With the passage of time, you can't tell much. But off the record, I would bet money this was the result of a battlefield nuke."

"Are there any other instances in recorded history of sites where nuclear blasts have taken place in prehistoric times?"

"There are several where a nuclear blast may have taken place. Right now, it's a matter of speculation because the physical evidence is so slim. We have found several in the Gobi Desert, and at least one in India. There are others in America, Africa, and South America, but no one that I know of has done any serious scientific investigation. For every argument supporting the supposition that a nuclear blast took place in ancient times, you will have more that push for a different interpretation. Most scientists don't feel enough evidence exists in favor of them. I have included everything on the flash drive."

"Can you tell me more about these other places?"

"Years ago," Sadiq continued, "I visited Mohenjo-Daro and Harappa in India. We know little about either city or the civilization that built them. We know the destruction of each happened overnight, and their surviving populations abandoned them.

"And there is a new site inside Kashmir which has yet to

be explored in depth," Sadiq confided as he leaned closer to the scientist from Saudi Arabia. "We have found a significant level of background radiation and a blast zone with a 150-foot radius. Everything inside it was crystallized, fused, or melted. Several hundred human skeletons with burn marks are there, suggesting a massive heat flash, such as you might see from a nuclear blast. No one has found anything to account for the background radiation or the effects of a large firestorm. Based on the best evidence, I concluded it was from a nuclear explosion."

"How extensive is the underground chamber? Was the blast limited to what your team found or did it cause more destruction?"

"Actually, we found an entire city buried beneath the surface - at least the remains of one. From what we can tell, a thermonuclear weapon leveled it. It could have held 10,000 people at one time, perhaps more. We didn't have a geologist or archeologist on the team, unfortunately. We think the city was buried by several later generations each erecting new structures over the top of the original structures, even with the residual radiation. It is smaller than the site I examined in India. I'm certain a nuclear blast destroyed this ancient city though. There is no doubt in my mind about it. All the photos we took and maps we made are on the flash drive."

"Given the ancients found a way to build a nuclear bomb, we have to wonder how they did it. Do you think it would be possible to reverse engineer their methods and find out how it was done?"

"We would need more time. I understand the original team down there found some codices, but they gave them to the Sultan, who controls the region. I also know he annexed the town a few days after his men found the entrance to the site.

"If we want to find out how the bomb was built, we need more information. I think those papyrus texts might have the information. Why else would they have been left in front of the crystal skeletons?"

Al-Asaad was quiet for a moment, "Yes, and who put them there and when is a good question." He paused again, "Are those codices where you would start looking to find out how the ancient nuclear weapons were constructed?"

"Yes. I would also look in the ancient Babylonian and Sanskrit texts. If you start with the texts we do have; you might find the clues where to look for the others. There are many thousands of pages we need to read."

"Ishrat," the Saudi scientist said. "Thank you for your efforts and devotion to the work. I know the money we promised you has cleared your bank account. I will give this flash drive to our benefactor and tell him of everything we discussed. We will be in touch should your services be required again." The two men bid each other a pleasant evening and left the room.

Dr. Sadiq, who already had the money spent in his mind, died instantly ten minutes later. Witnesses told the local police about a speeding car which turned a corner and struck him as he was crossing the street. He was dead on arrival at the hospital, and the police were never able to identify the car. His widow found the money in the bank account but never knew where it came from.

The same night in Islamabad, the two men working with Dr. Sadiq vanished into the night and fog. Men who claimed to belong to the Pakistan Intelligence Bureau arrived at their homes and arrested them. No one heard of them again, and the Bureau vehemently denied any involvement.

Two days after the meeting between Al-Assad and Sadiq, Carter arrived home from his visit to A-Echelon headquarters. As he held little Liam in his arms, 6,300 miles away, in Riyadh, Xavier Algosaibi pushed a flash drive into his laptop computer and began to review the information about the ancient nuclear blast site.

Chapter Thirty-One

A TIME BOMB WAS ALREADY TICKING

Carter dove into the material he and Rhodes had collected while at A-Echelon. He had three objectives. First, establish if there had been an ancient civilization with enough technological knowledge to create a nuclear weapon. Second, find out which sites had evidence of a nuclear blast. Third, make an in-depth study of ancient texts that might contain information about nuclear technology.

He already knew that references to the 'infinitely small,' in ancient Indian texts, could possibly be referring to an understanding of atomic theory. The small timeframes mentioned in the text corresponded closely with the disintegration rates of the radioisotopes of uranium used in nuclear weapons, or as fuel in a nuclear reactor.

He discovered that many writers from ancient times indicated an understanding of atomic theory, even if metaphorically. From Ancient Greek writers to the Buddhist Sutras, there were references to the knowledge of atomic structures.

The planetary model of the atom, Carter thought to himself, *is quite recent. Although it was now supplemented by newer concepts, for 100 years this was the one everyone used. It's taught in schools at the introductory level. Could it be this was a rediscovery of something known much earlier?*

Roundabout 460 B.C., The Greek philosopher Democritus said, *'In reality there is nothing but atoms and space.'*

The Roman poet Lucretius, who lived between 99 and 55 B.C.E, wrote extensively about the theories of the atomic structure of matter. *'Atoms rushing everlastingly through all space undergo myriad changes under the disturbing impact of collisions. It is impossible to see the atoms because they are too small.'* Lucretius' ideas would in due course create the foundation for the development of western science.

The writer of one of the Buddhist Pali sutras knew something about the molecular composition of matter, *'There are vast worlds within the hollows of each atom, multifarious as the specks in a sunbeam.'*

It was apparent that the authors of those documents, at least, had an understanding of the science of the atomic and molecular structure of matter. Somebody told them about it; there was no doubt. Someone in ancient times recognized and understood it. And, there was a good chance that this knowledge had been handed down from a time before them, a time of which very little knowledge exists today, a time, according to modern scientists, when man would not yet have invented the wheel. In fact, a time when man would just about have learned how to walk upright.

Carter was talking to himself. "It is only in recent times we understood that each atom is like a mini solar system, consisting of a core with electrons moving around it in set patterns as the planets move around the sun. I have to wonder how much of what we claim to discover for the first time has actually been rediscoveries. I think Solomon was right when he said, *there is nothing new under the sun."*

On July 16, 1945, the first nuclear bomb, in modern times according to Dr. Oppenheimer, exploded at the Trinity Site in New Mexico. The explosion, equivalent to 18,000 tons of TNT, created a crater 800 yards in diameter. The heat melted the desert sand, and when it solidified, a light olive green, glass-like substance remained. This substance was named Trinitite. Chemical analysis found that it consisted mostly of pure melted silica with traces of Olivine, Feldspar, and other minerals found in the desert sand.

Time Magazine, September 17, 1945, reported: *Seen from the air, the crater itself seems a lake of green Jade shaped like a splashy star, and set in a disc of burnt vegetation half a mile wide. From close up the lake is a glistening encrustation of blue-green glass 2,400 feet in diameter, formed when the molten soil solidified in air.*

Carter wanted to know if there were other places on earth where Trinitite had been found. He was not taken by surprise when he discovered many references to a green glass-like substance found in a number of places across the globe.

In 1947, in modern day Iraq, archeologists digging at a site uncovered evidence of four civilizations layered on top of each other. The final layer consisted of fused green glass.

Some scientist immediately pointed out it could have been caused by lightning, but they failed to explain that although lightning can fuse sand, it does so in a characteristic, root-like pattern and that only a nuclear explosion would have rendered an entire stratum of fused green glass.

Glassy sand, present for thousands of years, was found in the Gobi Desert in Mongolia. In Israel, archeologists dug up a layer of fused green glass measuring several hundreds of square feet, a quarter of an inch thick, and 16 feet below the surface.

It surprised Carter to learn that even in the United States, ruins existed in southern California, Colorado, Arizona, and Nevada, where at some stage in the distant past there would have been an event, which caused heat so intense it liquefied the rock surface. In the Mohave Desert, several circular patches of fused glass were discovered.

While Carter progressed on his work, Mackenzie did the same on hers. It was clear to Carter that Mackenzie enjoyed everything she did, and it made him happy to see her doing research with so much excitement. He wondered if he could add to her research in some way that would extend her work.

After Liam was in bed, they had time to spend together. Over a glass of wine, they talked about the work they were doing at the university. Mackenzie shared her discoveries with Carter, which he found absorbing and sometimes even running a close parallel to his own work, although he was unable to share this with her.

"Carter, it's been a profound experience to delve into ancient medical mysteries," she said. "If only I had more spare time to spend on the subject. I can't read enough about it."

"I'm glad to know Gramps was able to push you in a new direction with those suggestions he made," Carter sipped on his wine. Then he had a thought. "Have you ever considered resigning your position at the university and pursuing this full time? It's not as if we can't afford it. You could hire a team of linguists and researchers to help you out."

"I don't know," Mackenzie said thoughtfully. "I've spent so much time in academia I can't imagine life on the other side of the wall. However, I do have to admit I'm getting less and less satisfaction out of my university research project since delving into this ancient medicine stuff."

"You should do what you enjoy. As I just said, we don't have to worry about money. It's about doing what gives you the most satisfaction. We are fortunate to be in a position where both of us can do what we feel passionate about."

"I suppose I could - I'd not thought of that," Mackenzie agreed with him. "I have an office at home, and anyone I hire to work for me could do it remotely. We can see each other more, and I can be home with Liam all the time."

"We just have to keep the distractions at a minimum," Carter joked.

She knew what he was trying to say. "Well, I guess we will just have to learn how to control our hormones during work hours then!" She had a mischievous little smile playing on her face.

"It also means we can go up to Freydis any time we want," Carter pointed out.

"I'll talk to the Dean tomorrow," Mackenzie responded. "Liu was interested in having her students work for me. I think this would be the best way for them to gain experience. I still don't know what to do, but I'm sure by tomorrow I'll have a grasp on it. I'll talk to Liu and see what she thinks."

"Let me know. If you decide to do it, we'll take a trip to the ranch and get you set-up there. You'll have all the space and resources you need at Freydis."

Mackenzie walked around the campus of the University

the next day, during her lunch break. *How many times have I walked the pathways and toured the parks that dotted the university? It seemed a magical place when I arrived years ago. Now I only see the bitter infighting between departments and the continual suck-up to whatever department head is on the rise.*

She knew some graduate students who were so deep in debt from student loans they would never climb out. She was a mere assistant professor who did research for someone who would take all the credit. If she was excellent at politicking and published the right amount of papers, she might find a position at a peripheral college somewhere in the Midwest. The big chairs went to famous people who knew how to be 'noticed' by the people with influence and money. She was never one to be competitive and claw her way to the top. *Had I not bumped into Carter that day, I would still be just another academic researcher pursuing one more obscure set of data.*

Carter was offering her a chance to leave this shark pool and build her own pond. She would miss the camaraderie and friendships at the university. Her parents wouldn't see their grandchild as often. However, Carter promised to help her get a pilot's license so she could fly down south and visit her family whenever she wanted. She would have an office and a real Institute with funds in Canada where she could pursue the kind of work her heart desired.

Mackenzie sat down on one of the benches and watched a couple of undergraduates toss peanuts to a squirrel. They were so tame down here - not at all like the ones at Freydis. Perhaps they were soft after all the years of living on a guaranteed allotment of peanuts.

She made up her mind sitting on the bench, listening to the students talk about the classes. They sounded just like her not too long ago - full of hope and desire to make a name in the world of higher learning. Most of them would learn the hard way and fall by the wayside. A few, like her, would continue to push, wanting to be the esteemed scholar at the front of a lecture hall everyone looked up to in awe. However, the chances of achieving a tenured position were slim. Why not start from the beginning and do it her way?

She returned to her office and looked up the procedure to start a private research corporation in both the United States and Canada. If it was a non-profit, the paperwork and legalities made the creation of it almost impossible.

Mackenzie decided to make her institute a profitable venture, even if she never expected to see a dime out of it. She created a special file for her soon to be institute on her tablet and put everything she could find into it.

By the end of the week, she had a business plan and a lawyer to help her get the venture started. Carter looked over her plans and was pleased that they were so robust. He helped her work out a budget for the first year and set up the necessary financing. She had everything ready to launch by the end of the month. After meeting with the head of her department to discuss her plans, she gave him her resignation. He accepted it, although not without protest, and promised to give her a glowing reference should she ever need one.

Carter arrived at the conclusion that ancient civilizations had an understanding of atomic theory and energy. Everywhere he searched, he found evidence of ancient writers who were firsthand witnesses to the effects of nuclear weapons.

When he read the work of Professor Frederick Soddy, a nuclear scientist, Nobel Prize winner, and discoverer of isotopes, it became apparent that they held similar views about advanced past civilizations. The difference was that Soddy already had those views in the early 1900's.

He couldn't stop a sneaking sense of unease when he read what Professor Soddy said in 1909, 36 years before the 'first' atomic bomb was detonated, about a past civilization that had mastered atomic energy. *Can we not read into them (the prehistoric traditions) some justification for the belief that some former forgotten race of men attained not only to the knowledge we have so recently won but also to the power that is not yet ours?*

It was a nerve chilling experience when he studied the ancient Sanskrit text of the Mahabharata. It was as if the cold terror of the survivors lived in the pages of that compilation of 200 verses, referring to events that had taken place thousands of years ago.

In 1884, the chief translator of the Mahabharata noted that much in the text would seem ridiculous to the reader, and back then it would have been true because it was decades before the first aircraft took to the skies, and long before rockets and nuclear bombs. In 1884, no one would have been able to describe radiation sickness, simply because such a disease did not exist at the time.

The similarities between a description given in the Mahabharata and the description of a nuclear explosion by a modern day observer were terrifying. The modern day observer described the brilliance of the explosion, a mushroom cloud of rising smoke and fire, forceful shockwaves and heatwaves, the appearance of the victims and effects of radiation poisoning.

The ancient observer writing in the Mahabharata

described it as '*An iron thunderbolt contained the power of the universe. An incandescent column of smoke and flame, as bright as ten thousand suns, rose in all its splendor. Clouds roared upward. Blood-colored clouds swept down onto the earth. Fierce winds began to blow. Elephants, miles away, were knocked off their feet. The earth shook, scorched by the terrible violent heat of this weapon. Corpses were so burnt that they were no longer recognizable. Hair and nails fell out. Pottery broke without cause. Birds were turned white. After a few hours, all foodstuffs were infected. Thousands of war vehicles fell down on all sides, thousands of corpses burnt to ashes. Never before have we seen such an awful weapon, and never before, have we heard of such a weapon.*'

Carter comprehended that those verses were not ridiculous; they were reality, a deadly reality for the author from the distant past, giving an eyewitness account of the horrors of a nuclear explosion.

In the ancient Babylonian text of the Gilgamish Epic, he found another account of such a terrible day when "*the heavens cried out, the earth bellowed an answer, lightning flashed forth, fire flamed upwards, it rained down death. The brightness vanished; the fire was extinguished. Everyone who was struck by the lightning was turned to ashes.*"

At Çatalhöyük, South-Central Turkey, archeologists reported about thick layers of burned brick - blocks fused together by heat so extreme it penetrated more than three feet below floor level, where it carbonized the soil.

In images of woodcarvings from Easter Island, he found the unambiguous dreadful symptoms of humans exposed to nuclear radiation. The carvings depicting shrunken bodies with swollen goiters, clenched mouths, sunken cheeks, swollen groins, popped eyes, and swollen stomachs—all in incredible detail.

He was wondering if those pictures related to the blazing destruction discovered on the island by archeologists.

The royal buildings at Alalakh, North Syria, showed melted and crystallized wall plaster - even basalt wall slabs had melted.

The Popul Vuh, the sacred book of the Mayas, according to ethnologists the oldest surviving document in human history, described a fire from the sky that burned out eyes and consumed flesh and entrails.

Carter spent a lot of time wondering if the knowledge of atomic power, so recently gained, existed in prehistoric times and was lost. Could it have been similar to the knowledge lost on how the pyramids were constructed? Examples existed in Egypt of pyramids used as test runs for the ones that came later. The collapsed pyramid at Dashur, built after the Great Pyramid, proved to be a failure when the angle used was too great to support the weight of the construction.

Perhaps, he wondered, the Great Pyramid came about at the beginning of the pyramid construction, not toward the end as was assumed. If this was the case, the lesser pyramids came later because the knowledge represented in the Great Pyramid was lost to history. If this was the case, the Egyptologists had everything backward.

Slowly, Carter put together a theory of declination of knowledge. It proposed a way to account for the loss of scientific, medical, and engineering knowledge.

The more research he did, the more Carter worried about ancient nuclear warfare as a reality and not some daft ancient astronaut concept. The language in ancient texts describing the destruction of whole civilizations would have been recognizable to anyone who studied the blasts at Hiroshima and Nagasaki.

If such devices existed in the past, they might still be around. All it would take would be one person finding one and activating it. He needed physical evidence. As far as he was concerned, a time bomb was already ticking.

Chapter Thirty-Two

MORE THAN ANYONE WOULD CARE TO ADMIT

Shortly after Mackenzie submitted her resignation to her department head, the Dean of the faculty called her into his office. He told Mackenzie she was an exceptional researcher and instructor, and he didn't want to lose her. He asked if there was anything he could do to make her reconsider. When she indicated that she was not going to reconsider, he offered her a research fellowship that would still give her a connection to the university. She thanked him for the generous offer and told him she had to think about it.

She did offer to share a paper she was preparing, in her spare time, with the university. The Dean assured her she still had access to the university facilities whenever she needed them. This would allow her to use the library system and consult with her former department whenever she needed their help. They would assist and help her with the publication of her work. It was a good arrangement and Mackenzie was pleased with the plan.

She agreed to stay on until the end of the semester. This

would avoid any disruption with her research and instruction.

Mackenzie devoted her free time to organizing her new venture. In due time, she hired staff to assist her with translations and other research. Liu and Carter helped her find the people she needed.

Mackenzie thought long and hard on what to call her new organization. It had to reflect her purpose and the people who made it happen. After an afternoon of deep thought, the name hit her. She would call it The Will Devereux Medical Archaeology Foundation.

When Carter arrived home later that day, Mackenzie greeted him with excitement, told him of the name, and asked for his opinion.

"I think it's a great name, Mackie! I really like it. You should contact our lawyer to help you set it up. I think it should be done as a subchapter S corporation."

"I know your grandfather would approve." Her face went sad for a short while, "I miss him so much Carter. I can't imagine what it must be like for you to be without him."

Carter said nothing but nodded. He was still struggling to get used to the idea that Gramps was not there anymore. Many times, he'd pulled out his cell phone ready to call his grandfather and ask for an opinion about something, only to remember before touching the number pad, Will Devereux was no longer with them. The passing of the old man had left an emptiness inside him he strove to fill with his work and family.

Mackenzie phoned Bly and Ahote to let them know they would be flying up to see them soon. They were excited and told them everything would be ready for their arrival. Liam was excited too and couldn't wait to see Nelly, his pony, again. He was worried she had forgotten all about him.

By the time Mackenzie was ready to leave the university, they had accumulated a large amount of material for her to review.

While he awaited the test data from several possible ancient nuclear explosion sites, Carter offered to help Mackenzie with her work. He became her research assistant and did what he could to help her index the information the university sent to her. He also helped to collect new sources of information she might need in the future.

"So how do you plan on paying me?" Carter asked her one evening. He had a large stack of folders in his hands.

"The usual way," Mackenzie told him as she winked and pinched him in the side while passing close by him, a smile playing on her beautiful face.

Mackenzie's last day at the university arrived, and the three of them were excited about spending the next few months up north at Freydis. They had to explain to Liam, ever excited, why he still had to wait two more days to see his pony.

Two days later, Bly and Ahote waited for them on the familiar landing strip as the plane landed and taxied down to a full stop. The doors opened, Carter jumped out, and then went over to the passenger side to help Mackenzie and Liam. Ahote and Bly were driving the electric cart with a trailer hitched to the back for the luggage.

Knowing how excited Liam was to see his pony, Ahote had Nelly saddled and ready at the edge of the runway. Thrilled to see him, Ahote helped Liam on the back of the pony and walked him around. Bly and Mackenzie stood and watched while Carter used the time to put the plane inside the hangar.

Carter soon joined them and noted how much bigger Liam was on the pony compared to their last visit. His legs were dangling down the side.

"He's going to need a real horse soon," Carter noted.

"He'll be a tall man," Mackenzie proclaimed proudly. "Just like his father."

Over the next few days, they settled down to a routine. Mackenzie would do her daily video conferences with the staff she'd hired. Carter situated himself in his grandfather's old library, which he kept intact as if the old man would step into the room at any moment.

Liam was in heaven. He was the only child around the adults and had plenty of attention. He spent his days with Bly and Ahote, and learned the basics of horsemanship from Ahote. In the late afternoon, his parents would drag him away from Bly and Ahote, but only after he'd fed Bly's chickens and made sure they were safe for the night. They also encouraged him to help in the garden as it gave Liam a sense of responsibility.

Ahote taught Liam about the plants and animals in the forest, showed him how to fish and gather wood, and told him many stories about the forest. Ahote even did an overnight camping trip with Liam in a cave. The little boy was so excited he couldn't stop talking about it to his mom and dad when he returned.

It brought joy to Mackenzie's heart to see her son attaching himself to the older couple. They could never take the place of his great-grandfather, but she enjoyed watching the close relationship they were building emerge. It also made her very happy to see Liam's growing love for nature and the ranch.

A daily routine developed at Freydis. They made time for work and play, filling their days with research and long trips horseback riding on the property. They went fishing or just enjoyed long walks. Freydis was huge and it was easy to find some new place or animal. They visited Bly and Ahote, and sometimes flew out of town to replenish their supplies.

Carter still did not tell Mackenzie the specifics about his research. She understood his secrecy, knowing it was a reflection of his concern for her and Liam's safety.

He had Mark Adalbert's offer of assistance, but felt he should learn as much as he could on his own. He needed to prove his theory about ancient civilizations having technology superior to ours. He needed to open his mind to possibilities other than the ones currently accepted by modern science.

He spent most of his time reading about the advances in nuclear and nanotechnology, believing that the ancients had a better concept of both fields than anyone suspected. He had the evidence from the city found in the Sahara Desert and some of the research on what they found in the underground city in Peru. There was more out there for discovery, more than anyone would care to admit.

Chapter Thirty-Three

THEY TRUSTED NO ONE

Many revolts had failed in the Saudi Kingdom. The attempt at seizing the Great Mosque in Mecca, put down in a few days, was the result of bringing in foreign mercenaries to do the job. French troops did the hard fighting after taking a temporary conversion to Islam. Algosaibi remembered that day and the humiliation he endured while watching phony Muslims do the task his warrior ancestors would have done with glee. How ashamed they must be in heaven to know their own descendants were incapable of battle!

It would soon change.

The King and his spies didn't know about the ancient nuclear weapons, but Algosaibi did, and he would find them, even if it took him to his last breath. He booted his computer to look at the document provided by the late Dr. Sadiq again.

His computer was a special one, made to his specifications by a group of technicians in Sweden. It was not cheap, but it was impervious to all hacking methods. A specially trained technician performed a daily check to ensure that his computer would never be compromised. He almost never connected it to the Internet, although it did have the ability to find designated places on the Dark Web if needed, but any data fed into it passed through anti-intrusion software. This was the same software used by the most sophisticated intelligence organizations on the planet. The wrong thumbprint or an attempt at entering the wrong password more than three times would erase all the information on the device and trigger a power spike that would turn the sophisticated machine into a heap of slag.

Algosaibi was proud of this investment and entrusted his best-kept secrets to it.

He had Dr. Sadiq's report on the screen in front of him. He'd been studying this report repeatedly for weeks. The evidence gained from the buried city site in Syria pointed to a nuclear blast thousands of years in the past. The late scientist was of the opinion there were other bombs, similar to the one detonated thousands of years ago, just waiting for discovery.

All Algosaibi had to do was find them - or the plans to build them.

Youssef Bin-Bandar was an important member of the Saudi establishment. He was the third highest member of the General Intelligence Presidency, directly beneath the director and deputy director. He sat across from Xavier Algosaibi at the restaurant in Riyadh. Over the past 35 years, the two men had formed a close friendship, and they shared an absolute hatred of the Saud royal family. They were united in their desire to bring down the House of Saud and unify the world under a new Islamic caliphate.

"I have a lot of new information for you," Algosaibi told his friend Bin-Bandar as they sipped their coffee.

"Let's hear it," Bin-Bandar said after he had scanned the rest of the restaurant for anyone who sat too close.

Algosaibi told him of the report pertaining to the new site under the control of the Sultan of Syria. He told him of the underground city destroyed by a nuclear blast thousands of years ago. Most importantly, he let his friend know that he had unambiguous physical proof that nuclear weapons were used in the location.

"Allah showed us the way," Bin-Bandar commented as he smiled. "You have my full support. Just tell me what I can do to help."

"You have connections with the American intelligence community," Algosaibi said. "Can you find out if anyone over there is working on something similar? I doubt we are the only ones trying to find an ancient nuclear weapon. We must know who else seeks them and discover who they are. They might lead us to the weapons."

"I think it would be a good idea to have our own people on the ground near this site," Bin-Bandar said. "We could find some scientists to place at the site. I don't trust that Sultan one bit. He's using us for his own purposes. Why let him control everything at the site?"

"I've thought along those lines myself, but right now, the Sultan is a good ally, and we need to keep it that way. We risk losing everything by upsetting him. In addition, if we move our own technical people into the region we are taking the risk of too many people knowing about the ancient nuclear weapons. The fewer the people who know about it, the better."

"That's a wise decision, my friend. I agree; we must handle this one with care and assiduousness. If there is an ancient nuclear device somewhere, I want to be the one who finds it."

When they finished their coffee, they left with the traditional promise to meet up again when the time was favorable. Each man took a different exit and doubled back to make sure no one was following. Although they were on familiar territory, they trusted no one.

Meanwhile at Freydis, Carter was looking at the vast amount of material Mackenzie had accumulated about ancient medical practices.

"So are you still working with the respirocytes?" Carter asked her one afternoon as he watched Mackenzie examine an obsidian surgical tool from the Inca period. She looked up at him and put it back in the box gently.

"Yes I am," she replied. "It was one of the terms of my fellowship with the department. I have to review all the work they're doing in Boston. I may not be in the lab every day, but they send me regular reports about their progress."

"Let me know if there are any other ways I can help you," he smiled. "Your husband is a professor of archeology, after all. You can tap me for anything you need."

"I know," she winked. "You are my pillar of strength."

Carter walked over and hugged her.

"I'm looking at the latest reports coming from Peru. The inhabitants had a clinic down there where they performed all kinds of surgeries." Mackenzie pointed to images on the laptop screen. "They still haven't located a manual or anything textual, but there's always hope. Jacob and his team sent me some digital pictures of a wall diagram which is pretty astounding." She spun the screen around so he could see it.

"Impressive," Carter said while looking at it. "They had the major organs mapped out."

"I understand why you want to share all this with the world. Science does not advance in a sealed container." He shuffled through some of her papers and looked at photographs she found in his grandfather's library.

"Don't you find it a little strange?" She asked. "You are working for this covert government agency and are a university professor at the same time? What happened to the free flow and exchange of ideas?"

"There's a long tradition of academics who worked for their country in secret. Some information just cannot be allowed to become public knowledge."

"As long as you feel it's for the best, but I worry about you at times. All these secret meetings where you fly off and can't talk about what you're doing. I worry about you not coming back."

"At this stage there's nothing to worry about," he assured her.

He picked up another one of her papers and looked at it. This one had to do with nanotechnology and scanning electron microscopes - information useful in the design work for respirocytes.

Chapter Thirty-Four

WE NEED MORE INFORMATION

In Washington, D.C., Patrick and Rhodes met with Carter at the A-Echelon offices. It was a cold day; Carter had flown in the night before from Freydis and stayed overnight at a hotel.

Now he sat in front of the director with Rhodes seated to his right. "So what do you have for us?" Patrick asked.

"This," Carter said as he handed the director a flash drive. "All my research, findings, and conclusions are on there."

The director took the drive, placed it in front of him on his desk, and went quiet for a minute while his mind drifted. *Ten years ago, Carter would have given me a laser disc, before that it would have been a floppy disc. Does anyone still use paper these days? Maybe I am getting too old for this job.* During his annual physical, his doctor told him it was time for him to think about retirement. The 40-plus years in the high-stress world of covert operations had taken its toll. He was overweight, had high cholesterol, high blood pressure, and arrhythmia - irregular or abnormal heart rhythm. He was a walking heart attack waiting to take place.

He cleared his throat, "Thanks for that Carter, I'll read all the details as soon as we are done with the meeting. Perhaps you can tell me what have you surmised?"

"My inference is that we have prima facie evidence of the use of nuclear weapons in the distant past," Carter stated.

Hunter sat forward - Carter had his attention.

"I'm basing my findings on physical evidence taken from the sites under investigation. I used my study of ancient texts to identify the sites and Jim dispatched people to do the actual surveys on location. The reports that came back from the field technicians show they measured significant levels of background radiation. The specifics are in the report, including data charts, photographs, geological analysis, results from Geiger counters and more."

Hunter looked worried. "I have to meet with the President later so I suggest you don't leave town right away - I might need you."

"No worries. I hadn't planned to leave immediately. Just let me know when you need me."

"Hunter, if you have a few more minutes?" Rhodes asked. "I would like Carter to give you the particulars of a discussion he and I had this morning over breakfast."

Hunter nodded and looked at Carter with interest.

Carter leaned forward. "I am probably preaching to the choir, but I think it's worthwhile saying. If nuclear weapons were used in ancient times, they could still be out there. We need to locate them before someone else does. Even if they don't succeed in deploying them, the residual radiation from a leak could be horrendous. I'll let you imagine what would happen if the plutonium core of such a device is opened."

Hunter shook his head, "I don't need any convincing. We have a serious situation on our hands. I have some ideas but would like to hear what you think."

"We have data from places all over the world, but it's inconclusive as to which ones actually had nuclear explosions. Once we know which sites in fact witnessed the use of nuclear weapons, we can try to determine what they have in common. I suspect there was an ancient civilization that learned how to use atomic power and deployed it as a weapon."

Patrick stared at Carter, slowly nodding his head in agreement. "This idea of an advanced civilization is mind-altering, yet no one can doubt it anymore. You have proved it twice already." He turned and looked at Rhodes. "You have any ideas, Jim?"

"I think we need to start putting tabs on everyone we can," Rhodes responded, "conspiracy nuts, nuclear physicists, archeologists, anthropologists, people who read ancient languages." He paused for a moment and before anyone could reply, he continued with his list, "nuclear engineers, rocket scientists, and science fiction writers. Did I leave anyone out?"

"Psychics and fortune tellers?" Carter deadpanned.

"Yes include them. At least we will be able to gaze into a crystal ball and see in advance how this all turns out." Hunter laughed.

"Alright," the Director of A-Echelon concluded, as Carter and James stood to leave. "I will study the report and prepare for the meeting with the president and whomever he wants to bring along tomorrow. You two don't go far. Stay close; I might just have a need to see one or both of you on short notice."

"Yes boss," the two smiling men replied and left the

office.

The following afternoon, Hunter Patrick had his meeting with the President of the United States. He was surprised when he walked into the Oval Office and realized that in addition to the President, the Vice President, two members of the National Security Council, and the Secretary of Defense were present as well. The President didn't feel the matter yet warranted the attention of any other members of the National Security Council.

So much for keeping A-Echelon's work under wraps, Patrick thought.

With 15 minutes to make his presentation and another 15 to answer questions, he started by going over the field evidence and showing them how it correlated with modern day atomic blast sites. Next, he presented a summary of the data regarding the radiation levels found at some of the sites they were investigating.

Taking note of the attendees' body language, Patrick quickly perceived that the President appeared to be the most interested of the five. The Secretary of Defense seemed curious, but Patrick could tell his mind was somewhere else. The Vice President appeared bored by the whole affair - almost to the point of rudeness. The rest of the audience barely had lukewarm interest and, he felt, were having a hard time suppressing their yawns. It was just as Patrick feared; if it depended on anyone but the President, he would see his budget blue-penciled.

When he completed his presentation the President stood up, his hands in his pockets, pacing back and forth while everyone watched him and waited for him to talk. He was shaking his head slightly. "So Hunter, you are telling me that sometime in the distant past, nuclear weapons were used on our planet?"

"We have strong evidence of that, yes, Mr. President," Patrick replied. "Although it might sound outlandish, I would like to remind everyone of the discoveries that Professor Devereux made in Peru and Egypt not too long ago. There is, as far as I am concerned," Patrick was looking at the Vice President while he talked, "at least face value evidence to prove the existence of such an advanced lost civilization."

"Sounds like *Chariots of the Gods* stuff to me," the Vice President snorted. "If someone used a nuke before, why don't we know about it already? Or are you saying you are the first one to think about this?"

"No sir, I am not saying we are the first to think of it, which is precisely the reason why I am here today. There could be many reasons why no one has discovered this before Mr. Vice President." Patrick remained calm and collected despite the Veep's incredulous and silly little smile. "Most of the sites are not visible anymore. They have been covered by millennia of movements in the earth's crust, the explosions themselves, earthquakes, tremors, meteorite strikes and even sand. Those are all reasonable explanations as we have seen in the cases of the lost city in the mountains of Peru and the City of Lights in Egypt."

Patrick saw his reply stirred up a bit of interest amongst the others, except of course for the Vice President.

"Yeah, yeah I've read some of Devereux's publications. So what? Archeologists have miscalculated the age of human civilization by a few years. That doesn't prove there was an ancient civilization that built and detonated a nuclear bomb."

Patrick opened his mouth to say, *have you been listening to a word I've said? Did you not hear when I told you we already found the sites?* But, he had been in Washington long enough and understood the political grandstanding game. Instead, he said, "Mr. Vice President, with all due respect, 50 millennia can hardly be called a few years. Before Professor Devereux's discoveries, every school and university taught students that our civilization was no more than 12,000 years old. His discoveries, however, forced a few updates to the history curriculum. I brought this matter to the attention of the President and all of you because I am just a little bit worried that human history could very well be due for a few more, and may I add, potentially explosive timeline revisions."

Patrick observed what he perceived to be a little smile playing on the President's face. It was no secret, at least not to high-ranking government officials in DC, that the President did not get along very well with his Vice President. The President hadn't wanted him on the ticket in the first place, but he had to accept the man's nomination to win California and thus the presidency. The man was exceedingly well off with a huge amount of influence. In fact, he was by far the richest politician in Washington. The family wealth was unbelievable, with wide-ranging business interests including pharmaceutical, medical, and real estate.

The President was in his second term and had no further political dreams. He just wanted to serve the American people as best he could for the remainder of his term and leave behind a lasting legacy. The Veep, on the other hand, had higher ambitions. He was already in the image building stage of his campaign to run for the highest office, and nothing else mattered to him.

It looked as if the Vice President had his mind set on

getting the last word in the argument with Patrick. However, the President would not have any more of it.

"Hunter, what would be a worst case scenario here?"

"Mr. President, if someone built a nuclear device in the past, there could still be some of those devices waiting to be found, and there might even be blueprints somewhere." Patrick felt he didn't need to explain the implications of that scenario. After all, these were supposed to be intelligent people.

The president looked at him, nodding his understanding. "Well Hunter, you haven't let me down yet. You've helped to prevent some nasty things happening in the past." He looked around the table. "I think this is important. It can't be swept under the rug."

He looked back at Patrick and continued, "We need more information and I will ensure that you get the full cooperation of the FBI, CIA, and NSA."

The President lifted his eyebrows questioningly while he looked at each of the men in the room in turn and got agreement from them all including the Vice President's half-hearted nod.

He got up and shook Patrick's hand. "Thank you for your time Hunter. Keep me posted, and if you need anything just let me know."

Chapter Thirty-Five

A FUN EVENT

Riyadh, Capital of Saudi Arabia

It was the annual Riyadh Road Runner Marathon, a big fun event, not an official sports event. Thousands of people were lining the sidewalks along the route to encourage and cheer on their friends and relatives among the more than 8,000 participants.

Twenty minutes into the race, a lean man in a white vest, black shorts, and the number 7012 stuck on his back was leading the field. He had just crossed the ten-kilometer mark, eight minutes ahead of his closest rival.

The sports commentators were perplexed. Their lists, mapping the numbers to names, indicated the man's name, but no one had ever heard of him. He'd never won any marathon – no history about him – just his name, Bashir Mohammed.

"It's impossible," one of the sports commentators told his audience. "I have never seen or heard of anything like this. He has been running at the same pace for the last ten minutes - two minutes per kilometer. He cannot maintain that pace for the entire marathon. No human can."

Bashir's eyes were fixed on the road in front of him about 20 paces ahead. He didn't notice the buildings or the people; he didn't hear the spectator's cheering; his mind was blocked out.

In a TV vehicle leading the race, three men - one Chinese, one Pakistani, and one Bulgarian - watched the athlete on their screens, now almost four kilometers ahead of the world class Kenyan and Ethiopian runners.

Micro monitors strapped to his chest recorded every step, every heartbeat, and every breath. His heart rate, oxygen levels, blood pressure and other bodily functions transferred wirelessly in real time and displayed on an array of monitors in front of the three men in the TV van.

An hour before the race started Bashir received a transfusion of artificial red blood cells which were now pumping through his entire body, feeding his muscles and brain with rich oxygen.

"Tell me more about these chemicals you are going to inject into me tomorrow," Bashir asked the three men the night before. "What effect will they have on me? "

"Nothing to worry about Bashir," the Pakistani medical scientist told him while the other two scientists present nodded their agreement. "It will make a hero out of you tomorrow. No side effects at all. This is going to change your life."

"You are going to be endowed with super human capabilities, the first super soldier of the army of The True Sons of the Prophet," the Bulgarian medical nanotechnology scientist told him.

"I can't wait for the race to start," Bashir could barely hide his excitement. Hassan Al-Suleiman, the Sultan of

Syria, assigned this special mission to him and he was not going to disappoint his Sultan.

Bashir had just passed the halfway mark, leaving another 21 kilometers to go. He crossed the halfway point in exactly 42 minutes; the second man would only reach that point in 63 minutes - 21 minutes behind Bashir.

The sports commentators were dumbfounded. They sensed that something was going on. No human being could do this. No one in history had even come close to this pace over that distance. In Saudi Arabia, journalists and commentators knew how to choose their words very carefully, and they kept on singing the praises of Bashir Mohammed and his wonderful performance. When they looked at each other, however, they were shaking their heads and whispering behind their hands that something very strange was playing out right in front of their eyes.

The Pakistani doctor sitting close to the screen blinked his eyes. He was sure he saw Bashir cough. Checking the monitors, he noted that the runner's heart rate was slightly up from a few seconds ago, but the oxygen levels remained constant. *Must be my imagination.*

Not a minute later, they all observed Bashir coughing twice in short succession. They looked at each other. "How much more time before the effects of the injection wear off?" The Pakistani asked the Bulgarian.

"He should last another hour at least. He should be able to finish with ease."

About three kilometers from the finish line, the TV cameras flicked back to the rest of the athletes. They looked tortured, the pain and anguish clearly visible on their faces and bodies. Many were bent over, sweat streaming from their faces and bodies, their muscles cramping. The cameras flipped back to the leading runner, only two kilometers from the finish line, on his way to smashing the world marathon record by 40 minutes.

Bashir's world record would never be recognized. It was a fun event, and there were no Olympic officials to record and verify his time.

As the scientists watched, Bashir crossed the 41-kilometer mark, coughing again. The monitors showed an increased heart rate, rapidly dropping oxygen levels, and he was sweating more than at any other time during the race. It looked as if his skin has turned pale.

As the finish line came into view, Bashir closed his eyes. *Not far to go. The Sultan will be very happy. I am going to be a hero when I get back.*

He coughed again and wiped his mouth with the back of his right hand. When he took his hand away, he noticed the streaks of bright red blood. *What the hell? Where is that coming from?*

He dashed across the finish line and raised his arms in victory. The crowds were screaming their excitement. Bashir felt dizzy; his ears were ringing, and the people and buildings started to spin. He started coughing again, and everything went dark around him. He didn't see or feel it, but one of the TV cameras and a few hundred spectators caught a glimpse of the blood streaming from his mouth.

"Well, now we know it works!" The Bulgarian shouted excitedly as he opened the back door of the van and scrambled out with his two colleagues to collect Bashir from the ground and carry him to the van, away from the prying eyes.

TV crews, journalists, and spectators descended on the van – all of them screaming and shouting questions and comments. What is going on? Who is this man? Where did he train? What is wrong with him? Why is he bleeding?

As the van doors closed, the Chinese man put the van into gear and drove out of the crowd. The tinted windows helped to protect them from curious stares. They were not allowed to answer any questions. They had to get Bashir out of there, to a private and secure location quickly. They had many tests to run on him, and he didn't look all too well.

As they left, someone from the crowd yelled, "You have drugged that man! There is no way any man can run like that without drugs!"

"How do you feel?" the Pakistani asked when Bashir moaned and started opening his eyes.

Bashir coughed again, and more blood spat out of his mouth. He held his stomach. "Incredible race ... never got tired, ran flat-out the whole time ..." he stuttered as he whispered into the Pakistani's ear.

All of a sudden, Bashir's body went into a spasm. He pulled his knees up and started vomiting.

"The side effect is kicking in fully now," the Bulgarian commented.

Bashir struggled to raise his upper body from the floor and fought to speak. "You said ... no side effects!" His face was contorted and ashen, his eyes were rolling, and he was struggling to breathe.

The Pakistani tried to display a sympathetic look. "Sorry Bashir, something went wrong. It was not supposed to happen. The pressure within the capillaries in your lungs has increased, and they are bursting open."

"You bastards! You knew! You ..." he fell back to the floor, gave one more cough and stopped breathing. He was dead.

The Pakistani smiled. "The trial was a success, although it's a pity the patient died."

"What a glorious death for a brave warrior!" The Bulgarian chuckled to the amusement of his two colleagues.

Three days after the race. Washington D.C., USA.

An important looking man in a charcoal business suit lifted his glass filled with very expensive whiskey. "God underestimated man. There are no limits to man's capacity. Within the next two years, we will prove that."

His two guests raised their glasses. "Hear, hear!" they replied enthusiastically and drank a toast to their host's words.

"We will have to keep on monitoring those researchers out there and pass on all the information we can get to our guys over in Saudi." The man in the suit said.

They all raised their glasses in acknowledgment and toasted again.

Chapter Thirty-Six

LITTLE MYTHICAL GOLDEN BIRDS

Earlier in the evening, Carter went to the cellar and got a bottle of Napa Valley, Cardinale 2006 Cabernet Sauvignon, which he opened and left to breathe. He and Mackenzie curled up in each other's arms on the sofa in front of the fireplace, Liam fast asleep after the day's outdoor activities.

Mackenzie held out her glass for a refill. "I've finally caught up with the information the team translated for me before we arrived. Every day I've been finding new things in those translations. It's been very exciting. I just can't believe that all this information is available, but so few want to read it."

"Story of my life Mackie, I have always said it's all out there waiting to be uncovered. We just have to go out, lift the veil and see it. But as you know, it's hard to change your mind, and it's very hard to admit that you've been wrong."

"Yeah, that's so true. I have firsthand experience."

Carter smiled. "Well, maybe in your case it was a bit different. Will and I didn't give you much of a chance did we?"

"Yes, there is that of course, but it still took an effort to admit I'd been barking up the wrong tree. Can I show you what I have discovered, or unveiled as you said, so far?"

"Oh yes," he smiled. "I was going to ask had you not offered to do so."

Carter relished the way Mackenzie's eyes lit up as she pulled her laptop closer and opened it.

"I've organized the information into a few main categories. You see here: medical care and programs, dentistry, surgical instruments and surgery. Under each of them, I've stored the related information I got from the team."

"I'm eager to see what you have there."

"Okay. Let's start with medical care and programs."

Carter took a sip of his wine, picked up the laptop, and started reading. "The Chinese in 300 B.C. already had government medical aid. Doctors received their compensation from the government and medical aid was free to all?"

Mackenzie nodded.

"Well, I suggest you send that to Congress and tell them to get their act together. What they have been struggling to do for decades can't be that difficult, considering it was done more than 2,500 years ago already."

"Good idea. They might just learn something in the process." She laughed.

Carter kept on reading about Chinese pharmacologists, specialist doctors, and veterinarians dating back to hundreds of years B.C.

Excavations at the Great Pyramid in Egypt showed workers received excellent medical care. There was a man who lived for 14 years after a leg amputation; another survived brain surgery. Skeletons found onsite showed broken arms bound with wooden splints. The Egyptians had contraceptive jelly and urine pregnancy tests and could determine the gender of an unborn child. In Alexandria, they had a college of medicine to train surgeons and GP's.

In India 4,000 years ago, they had immunization and inoculation programs. Two thousand years ago, they had a pharmaceutical encyclopedia listing over 500 herbal drugs and drug prescriptions with instructions, such as *take before going to bed*, or *take twice a day*.

"So they didn't have the 'take two and call me in the morning' prescription back then?" He quipped.

"No." She laughed. "Well, not as far as I can find."

Carter shook his head. "I think its gross negligence to be as deliberately ill-informed and self-centered as our medical scientists are. I am getting the impression they don't want to hear about these things."

"Carter, what you have seen so far is minor. Wait 'til you read the rest of what I've found, especially in the surgery folder. And as you know, I've just begun to scratch the surface."

Carter opened the dentistry folder and read about discoveries of a type of cement filling in tooth cavities found in Egypt. In other parts of the world, discoveries were made of crowns and cement fillings in cavities that were still holding after 1,500 years - even gold inlays, caps, and artificial teeth.

"Those are all techniques and procedures which we claim to have *discovered* quite recently," she remarked. "If you ask me, I would say we *re*discovered them."

"It is indeed as Solomon said in Ecclesiastes," Carter contemplated as he quoted. "'*That which has been is what will be. That which is done is what will be done, and there is nothing new under the sun*'."

"I have to agree with Solomon, especially if one looks at

all this medical stuff and what you have unearthed in Cusco and Egypt already."

"Okay let me see what else you have here," and he turned his attention to reading about surgical instruments found by archeologists.

He started reading aloud. "'*Obsidian instruments, a thousand times sharper than modern day platinum surgical blades - so sharp they do not bruise the cells.*' I wonder if Obsidian instruments could transform surgery, especially today's cosmetic and plastic surgery. What do you think?"

"Definitely, but as you know, to persuade physicians to start using them will be another battle."

Carter continued reading about discoveries at Pompeii, Italy, where they found adhesives, tourniquets, forceps, gauze, absorbent cotton bandages, plaster of Paris, and a whole raft of surgical instruments made as well as anything used today. Even surgical screws as delicate and capable as anything we have now.

He was shaking his head in amazement when he read about the discovery of more than 100 different surgical instruments in India, dating back to 500 B.C. that included curved needles for sutures.

In Egypt, they found instruments equaling those of modern times such as forceps, scalpels, and clamps. Discoveries in other countries around the world brought evidence of artificial nourishment by tubes and life-support systems.

He shook his head. "Mackie, this is mind-blowing stuff you have here."

"Well, I have you and Will to thank for all the pleasure I am getting out of this research. It's still early days, but it appears to me that ancient medical practice was much, much more than herbs and witchdoctors. I get the impression that advanced medical science existed worldwide at some stage in the distant past, and we are only now relearning it, and I can't help but add, the hard way."

"Yes, that's surely the case. We will probably never know it all, but we can be pretty confident about the wealth of medical knowledge and skill that existed before us. This information sketches an entirely different picture of the practice of medicine millennia ago than what we have always been led to believe."

"Wouldn't it be great to find a site somewhere that will reveal all this information in detail?"

"Yes, like the medical version of Cusco or the City of Lights. However, I can't help but think what an uphill battle is awaiting the one who will try and convince the FDA that some ancient medicine could actually be beneficial for us today."

"I guess we will have to cross that bridge when we come to it. But it's definitely not going to be easy."

Carter refilled their glasses, sat down, pulled Mackenzie closer to him, and started reading the next folder.

His eyes almost immediately caught an article published in the National Enquirer on September 10, 1972. William Dick and Henry Gris wrote about a delicate head surgery performed 3,500 years ago, at Ishtikunny, near Lake Sevan in Armenia.

Professor Adronik Jgaharian, anthropologist and director of operative surgery at the Erivan Medical Institute in Soviet Armenia, performed the examination and reported his findings in the article.

Apparently, surgeons removed bone splinters from a woman's brain after a blow to the head that punctured her skull and fractured the inner layers of the cranial bone.

They did it by cutting a larger hole around the puncture, removed the splinters penetrating the brain and she lived for another 15 to 18 years.

"How challenging would surgery like that be for us today?" he asked.

"I emailed the article to the Dean with that same question. He was stunned to learn about this and commented that even by modern standards, the operation would be considered extremely challenging."

"Ishtikunny, Lake Sevan in Armenia?" Carter mumbled. "That's a place we will have to visit for a look-see. What do you think?"

"Life with you is never going to be boring Carter Devereux. Of course we will have to go!"

"Just let me know when we have to start packing. I've never been there; I like to see new places, especially new old ones."

"Okay. What you've read so far is background information. The stuff that has me really excited is in the surgical folders."

"Do you think you are getting closer to finding something about respirocytes?"

"I haven't found anything explicitly describing it yet, but considering ancient Egyptians had a plasma generator, and some civilizations were doing blood transfusions, I'm sure I'm heading in the right direction."

She flipped to the next document and pointed to it.

"In Peru, a carving was found that shows pregnant women donating blood to organ transplant recipients. It had me wondering if there could possibly be a yet undiscovered substance, such as a hormone, produced by pregnant women, which could prevent the body's immune system rejection response."

"That's a fascinating thought."

"You will see there is evidence of open-heart surgery about 1700 years ago. There were lung, kidney, and liver operations - even organ transplants. In Peru and China 400 B.C., it looks like they had the ability to perform heart transplants."

"What! A heart transplant?"

"Yes, there are images showing how a heart was taken out of the patient and a new heart implanted while tubes were feeding him with infusions."

"If I'm not mistaken the first heart transplant ..." Carter hesitated for a moment, "in our time, was performed in South Africa in the late sixties."

"Let me see." Mackenzie took the laptop and found the file. "Yes, it was December 3, 1967, by Professor Christiaan Barnard, performed at the Groote Schuur Hospital in Cape Town, South Africa. The patient's name was Louis Washkansky – he lived for 18 days after the operation."

"And let me guess, at the time it was heralded as the biggest medical achievement in human history?"

"Verbatim, from one of the articles here." She laughed. "Listen to this. In Peru, the discovery of stone carvings from the pre-Inca era, led Dr. E. Stanton Moxey, Fellow of the American College of Surgeons, to believe that open-heart surgery was a known procedure to the medical community of that civilization. Here's what he said, *'In the photographs of stone carvings depicting heart surgery, the detail is clear, the seven blood vessels coming from the heart are faithfully copied. The whole thing looks like a cardiac operation, and the surgeons seem to be using techniques that fit with our modern knowledge'*".

"Nonetheless, the world's scientists of today are flattering themselves with the idea that never before has there been such a smart lot of masterminds. To me, it sounds more like pride capped with ignorance," Carter said, shaking his head.

"The thing that excites me the most about all these bits and pieces of information from old documents, clay tablets, and pictures on cave walls from across the world, is the feeling that there are many more sources somewhere, waiting to be discovered. It's as if the authors of those bits and pieces were intentionally leaving clues and pointers to a time before their own, a time when much more knowledge existed."

"That's the essence of archeology Mackie. You sometimes have to run after the sniff of an old oil rag - bits and pieces left for us by our ancestors long ago.

"Many great discoveries have been made from what was once believed to be myths. Just think about the myth of the lost golden gardens. Jacob found that little golden bird and it led us to Cusco and the mythical golden gardens.

"Troy was always believed to be a mythical place, a flight of fantasy of the Greek writer, Homer. Nevertheless, a German businessman, Heinrich Schliemann didn't want to believe it was a myth and hunted down every clue he could find. His reward was the discovery of the city of Troy in northwest Turkey in 1869. Today it's on UNESCO's listing of World Heritage Sites."

"Well, to use your analogy, I think I am holding quite a few little mythical golden birds in my hand at the moment," she smiled.

"Definitely, you have more leads to follow than many archeologists who made great discoveries ever had."

"You know I have been wondering lately. Those inscriptions and carvings on cave walls all over the world – were they left there as messages? Or are they advertisements of their achievements?" Mackenzie asked.

"That, my dear Mackie, is a refreshing thought. I will have to think about it, but my initial response would be, they are messages for us to dig deeper."

Chapter Thirty-Seven

THIS NAGGING FEELING

Just as dawn broke through the darkness, on the lawn in front of the cabin back at Freydis, Carter's graceful movements flowed freely as he practiced Tai Chi. He held the sword in the way he'd been taught. Looking at the tiger, he could see it hovering in the background before him, looking for that opening. Carter snapped up the sword, and the tiger held back when it saw the blade. The tiger was careful this time.

The ritual came to an abrupt end when his cell phone rang with a sound indicating the call was coming in on the secure line. Very few people had access to that line; it had to be important.

"Good morning, Carter." It was James Rhodes. "How are you doing there in the backwoods?"

"I'm in God's own country, Jim," Carter laughed. "You should see this place. The sun is breaking through the trees, and everything is glowing. The birds are singing, and the air is fresh! This, my friend, is what I call paradise."

"Your grandfather loved the place. I've never been there, but the pictures he showed me were beautiful."

"That chasm in your life can be rectified easily if you would come up for a visit. Say the word and I'll pick you up in Quebec City. We have plenty of room for you to stay and a horse to ride."

"You know, I was actually calling to arrange for you to come down to D.C., but your offer is very tempting..." He went quiet for a few moments. "I guess whether we meet here or there won't make a difference, and that way I get a chance to see the place you Devereuxs have been yapping about so much."

"Done deal, your life will never be the same after this!" Carter laughed. "Just let me know when to pick you up at the airport. Oh, and don't forget to bring your hiking boots, you're going to need them."

At noon the next day, Carter greeted Rhodes as he came out of the terminal at Jean Lesage International Airport. Shortly after, they were in the air, soaring over the Canadian countryside. James' mouth was agape as he took in the spectacular beauty of the scenery below them.

Over the sound of the plane's engines and the distraction of the beauty below, Rhodes filled Carter in on the latest test data collected by the survey teams out in the field. Fifteen sites were being examined as possible locations for the nuclear explosions in ancient times. Nine sites had been ruled out after thorough testing and analyses. Five locations had all the telltale signs of a nuclear explosion: inordinate amounts of Trinitite, soil and rock fused into a glass-like substance, indications of a blast radiating from an epicenter, and abnormally high levels of radiation.

The sixth location revealed extensive damage from a

heat blast, similar to what would be expected with a nuclear explosion, but had low levels of radiation and startlingly high volumes of Helium-3. This site had the scientists scratching their heads.

"Low levels of radiation and high levels of Helium-3?" Carter looked at Rhodes. "That's noteworthy. Do they have any suppositions about it?"

"Well, as I've said, the first five sites can be explained, but that last one is flummoxing their brains. I brought all the test results and reports along for us to study."

When they landed, Mackenzie was waiting for them. James got out of the plane and looked around him. The air was fresh. It smelled of life and vigor. He took one deep breath of the fresh mountain air and said, "Now I know what you meant yesterday when you said this is God's own country. This is unequivocally awe-inspiringly beautiful. No wonder Will and you have been tied to this place."

"Not just the two of us my friend, Mackie thinks she has lived here in a previous life! And Liam – I don't know how we are ever going to get him back to the city with us when the time comes."

Mackenzie came up, hugged and kissed Carter and pecked James on the cheek, welcoming him to Freydis. While Carter put the plane in the hangar, Mackenzie helped Rhodes load his luggage into the electric cart.

"I was just telling Carter how beautiful this place is."

"It's the most beautiful place on Earth," she said. "I don't know how we're ever going to be able to go back to Boston." Carter got into the back seat while Mackenzie drove them to the cabin.

"Carter I have something fascinating to show you both later tonight. I made an intriguing discovery today."

"Carter told me about your research on the way here. I

am fascinated and very keen to hear more about it." Rhodes replied.

Later that night, after a dinner of fresh salmon caught by Ahote and Liam earlier in the day, and fresh homegrown organic vegetables, they settled down in front of the fireplace. That's when Carter reminded Mackenzie about the surprise she promised them earlier.

While Carter opened a bottle of vintage port and prepared a platter of cheeses, dried fruits, and walnuts, Mackenzie showed James the research she had been working on and had already shared with Carter a few days earlier.

"So where are you heading with this research Mackenzie?" James asked.

"At the university I have been working on an absorbing project about the improvement of the function of human red blood cells." She stopped and got a devious little smile on her face. "And it was all going fine until someone body-slammed me outside a building on the campus." She was looking at Carter.

"Accidents happen, my dear," Carter grinned. "As I accidently took you to coffee a few days later."

"I still haven't figured out how you pulled that one off."

Carter laughed. "Jim wait, let me just set the record straight. The accident was real, not arranged. The most fortunate accident of my life, but I have to admit the first coffee date was a brilliant scheme."

"Aha, there it is! You have admitted it, scoundrel. So it was a scheme and all these years I have been worried I was losing my mind!" Mackenzie looked at Rhodes. "And you employ criminals like this?"

James put his hands over his ears and laughed. "I'm not listening. I like both of you very much, so please don't ask me to choose who I believe."

Carter handed them each a glass of port and placed the platter on the table in front of them.

When the laughter subsided, Rhodes looked at Mackenzie to continue. "Okay, so despite the endless distractions caused by Carter's incessant nagging to marry him, I managed to carry on with my work and started looking at respirocytes."

Carter was just shaking his head at Mackenzie's witticisms.

"Respiro what? Just don't ask me to pronounce that word three times in a row quickly."

"Respirocytes. An artificial red blood cell. Right now, it's still a theoretical concept. It's a nano-synthetic red blood cell, which can outperform the natural human red blood cell. It may well be up to 200 times more efficient than the natural cell and can supplement, or entirely replace, the function of the body's normal respiratory system."

"Amazing! So is that where you are heading with your current research?"

"Yes, my primary objective is to find something in ancient history that could perhaps help us build such a respirocyte generator."

Mackenzie went on to talk about her work. She told him how the respirocyte could be of great benefit to humanity by way of disease eradication. She also talked about where the idea had originated.

"I can see how significant that would be. I'm intrigued. So what's next?"

Nothing New Under The Sun

"Mackie," Carter said, "Why don't you tell him what you've found from the survey work that's been done in the underground city in Peru?"

"A while back," she began, "I found a paper on blood transfusions from younger mice to older ones. The older mice had increased vitality, and now some researchers are talking about trying it on humans. The technique has been around since the 19th century. Parabiosis, they call it."

She explained that the effects lasted only for a limited time, but were still regarded as a significant discovery by the project team, which was at the stage of getting ready to start trials on humans to see if they could bring relief to the elderly with diseases such as Alzheimer's and Parkinson's.

"Our team down in Peru," Mackenzie continued, "sent me a picture of a wall mosaic showing a pregnant woman donating blood. It's obvious what is happening, and I've never seen anything like this before. Whoever lived in the city knew about this method to restore vitality to aged cells. Don't you find this fascinating?"

"It does seem like more than a coincidence to me," Rhodes agreed. "Don't the aboriginal people in Australia practice blood transfusions with a hollow reed? I can recall reading about that somewhere and always wondered."

"They do. I've seen Chinese medical texts dating back to 2,650 B.C in which the doctors described the function of the heart and exactly how it pumped blood through the arteries and the human arterial circulatory system."

"It falls in line with a theory I'm developing," Carter explained. "I have a strong sense an advanced civilization may have existed thousands of years before recorded time. What if some of the things we've been uncovering are part of that lost civilization?"

"Lately, there's certainly a lot of evidence coming to

light that supports that hypothesis of yours," Rhodes agreed." I'm getting the feeling that in one way or another, these people were heir to ancient knowledge."

"I was interested in Mackie's research on the respirocytes as a way to account for evidence of gigantism in prehistoric humans," Carter said as he took a sip of wine. "The Earth might have had a higher oxygen concentration in previous ages. We know the atmosphere has changed drastically over the millennia."

"Carter and I had that conversation a long time ago, come to think of it. It was during that first bogus coffee date!" Mackenzie laughed and pointed a finger at him. "He told me then how he learned about respirocytes when he was looking into the reason for gigantism amongst humans in the past."

"And what did you find?" Rhodes asked.

"When I remembered about the conversation, I started wondering if higher levels of oxygen did indeed exist in the atmosphere back then. And I found quite a few scientific studies, showing that sometime in the distant past, the world had about 30% oxygen in its atmosphere compared to only 20% that we have today."

Rhodes was deep in thought as he looked at Mackenzie, waiting for her to continue.

"There is plenty of evidence from the City of Lights in the Sahara Desert to back it up," Mackenzie pointed out. "Everything I've read and seen shows a city built for people who were much taller than we are. Even air analyzed from bubbles inside amber drops shows a higher concentration of oxygen in the atmosphere. Humans are limited by how tall we grow because of our skeletal structure, but high levels of oxygen in the atmosphere could provide a feasible explanation for gigantism. Just look at the dinosaurs and how big they were. Granted, they were probably a lot slower than elephants because of the time it takes for neurons to fire, but we haven't seen creatures of such size for millions of years."

Carter and Rhodes stared at her. It was obvious she had a lot more to reveal.

"Based on what has been discovered at the City of Lights, I set out to find more supporting data about giant humans, animals, and plants. I was not disappointed. There are masses of evidence from all over the world. Houses and graves, fossil footprints, bones, artifacts, the Bible - all these tell the same story about the existence of Titanic humans, incredible lifespans, superiority, and nobility. But, sadly it seems we, their descendants, have all but forgotten them."

She pulled her laptop closer and searched for a file. "Dr. Carl Baugh, of Glen Rose Texas, constructed a large high-pressure oxygen chamber, also known as a hyperbaric biosphere. His purpose was to recreate the conditions of our original world.

Here's what he says: *'We've been doing extensive research into the ancient atmosphere, the one that produced the fossil record. Our research indicates that essentially everything was larger in the past. For instance, the club mosses, which today reach sixteen to eighteen inches, often approach two hundred feet in the fossil record. The great dinosaurs, with their relatively small lung capacity, reached tremendous stature. Seismosaurus could reach his head almost seventy feet in the air. Something has to explain this anomaly in terms of today's atmosphere.*

In today's atmosphere, we have fourteen point seven pounds atmospheric pressure per inch at sea level. But to oxygenate the deep cell tissue of these great dinosaurs, we need much greater atmospheric pressure. Research has shown that when you approach two times today's atmospheric pressure, the entire blood plasma is saturated with oxygen.

Our research indicates there was about 27 pounds per square inch of atmospheric pressure in the past. That would beautifully solve a problem even paleontologists admit exists.

In addition, the oxygen supply in the fossil record has been found to be 30 percent oxygen compared to 20 percent today. Ancient air bubbles trapped in amber have been analyzed and revealed this heavier concentration of oxygen. If we had those conditions today, we could run two hundred miles without fatigue.'"

Carter started laughing. "Mackie, now you will have to admit how valuable that first coffee date turned out to be!"

"Yeah, but only if you will admit that you were a tricky rascal in setting it up!"

Carter held his hands up in surrender. "I admit I am guilty as charged."

Rhodes just shook his head at their little quips with each other. "Mackenzie, I'll see what help I can get you with your work. This research of yours is of great consequence. You need access to all the resources we have and everything we can get for you. I have a higher level of clearance than most people because of my position in the federal hierarchy, and there are people I know who can help you in big ways."

"That will be magnificent! Thank you very much."

"It will require special clearance for you, but I don't think it will be a problem once I tell Hunter about your research."

"And I have to ask you," Rhodes said while nibbling on a bit of cheese, "what are you doing to protect this research of yours?"

"Protect?" she asked. "Protect it from what? I'm not trying to patent anything. This information should be freely shared with all scientists."

"I am not so sure about that. In fact, I'm definitely not at all sure."

"Why is that?" Mackenzie frowned at him.

"Do you realize what the implications of your respirocyte research could be?"

"I'd like to think it would improve our quality of life and cure a lot of hematological diseases."

"Yes, I agree it would indeed. Nevertheless, this technology could also have all kinds of negative uses. Suppose someone decides to build an army of super-soldiers with it. Think of what terrorists could do with men who could run for ten miles on a single breath or stay underwater for hours at a time with no scuba gear. And then we haven't even considered greed – money. Can you imagine to what lengths big pharmaceutical companies will go to get an exclusive hold on this technology?"

Mackenzie and Carter went quiet when the reality of what Rhodes was saying dawned on them.

"He's got a point there, Mackie," Carter responded. "The implications of this technology go further than human health. Remember, the same fire that heats a home can also burn it down."

Mackenzie stared into the fireplace. She was troubled - she had enjoyed her research so much and had only noble intentions, but what Rhodes was saying was true. She never gave it a moment's thought that anyone could possibly have malicious intentions. "So how do I begin to protect it?"

"I'd backup everything on a dedicated server that is never connected to the Internet," Rhodes said. "At least, make sure you have copies of it all. Make hard copies of the most important data. If you have a set of notebooks, make sure each of them is signed and dated. You can't be too safe these days. There is an old motto in the archeological world, which I am sure Carter will confirm. Good archeologists keep their work secret until they have confirmation."

"Okay, point well made. I can set up a system to secure my work and make sure it's safe."

Carter nodded in agreement.

The next morning Rhodes sat on the deck outside and watched Carter show Liam the complicated moves of Tai Chi. Carter had promised to take the boy with him to his class next time they were in Boston and introduce him to his master. It was good to see Liam so close to his father. The boy was at the stage in his life where his dad was his superhero. *Carter is the best role model any boy could have;* Rhodes thought to himself.

After breakfast, Carter and Rhodes strolled to a ledge where they could look out over a large part of the ranch. It was a beautiful lookout point where Carter liked to go when he needed time to think in private.

Rhodes briefed him on the meeting Hunter Patrick had with the President, Vice President and the others. "Hunter said the Veep acted like a jackass. He told me the man thought A-Echelon consists of a bunch of Don Quixote's. However, on the positive side, the President took him seriously and promised him the full cooperation of the other national security agencies. He is adamant that he wants to have more information about this."

"I can understand when the few people who know about us here at A-Echelon sometimes think we are in the crazy business Jim. It's because the blind are leading the blind. We, especially you and I, on the other hand, don't have that luxury; we can't afford to make assumptions."

"Exactly," Rhodes nodded. "Okay, let's take another

look at our discussion of yesterday. Have you got any initial thoughts?"

"Well, since I last saw you I've been studying as much as possible about the latest nuclear and nanotechnology developments. The sites showing high levels of radiation have been explained – I think. However, the site that doesn't, still begs for an explanation, and I have been wondering if a hydrogen fusion bomb could be a possibility."

"You mean like a hydrogen bomb?"

"No, I'm thinking of something different. You see, with a hydrogen or H-bomb, also known as a thermonuclear bomb, they still use a primary nuclear explosion to compress and fuse hydrogen. The first explosion is an atomic explosion that creates the secondary explosion, which is a nuclear fusion reaction. The result of that is an enormous increase in explosive power compared to a single-stage atomic fission bomb."

"Okay, so far I'm still with you."

"What I'm proposing is fusion technology, the very same way the sun works. In a nuclear reaction, the splitting of an atom causes a chain reaction, which generates the massive energy. In the sun, the reverse process takes place. In other words, the nuclei of hydrogen atoms are fused, and in the process, an enormous amount of energy is released. The sun is one big ball of hydrogen plasma in which fusion reactions take place at a rate of about 700 million tons per second. This reaction releases heat energy so intense we can feel it 93 million miles away.

"The idea of fusion power has been around in theory ever since the first atomic bombs were exploded, but no one has found a sound way to start a self-sustaining fusion reaction for more than a few microseconds."

"So do I understand correctly that you believe they may have been able to build a fusion bomb?"

"Yes, I think we have to, at least, consider it. Even though modern day scientists have not mastered the technique yet, we can't summarily discard the idea. A pure fusion weapon does not need a fission explosive to ignite the fusion. They might have found an easy way to do it. And keep in mind that because such a weapon wouldn't require any fissile material it would be very easy to build in secret, far easier than conventional nuclear weapons."

Rhodes looked at Carter, concern showing on his face. "The process of preparing high-quality fissile material to build a nuclear bomb or reactor requires an enormous investment and infrastructure. That is why it has always been relatively easy to detect the facilities and to block the sale and transfer of the equipment. When you build a pure fusion weapon, it can be much easier to hide your activities."

"How much more or less energy would a fusion bomb release compared to that of an atomic bomb?"

"My understanding is that the fusion reaction would produce hundreds of times more energy than an atomic fission reaction."

"So, the explosive power of a hydrogen fusion bomb would be... what? How much trouble are we talking about?"

"Let me put it this way. A one-kiloton atomic bomb, like we used at the end of World War II, has the explosive power of 1,000 tons of TNT. It takes 1,000 kilotons to make one megaton."

"Ok, I'm still with you," Rhodes nodded.

"The atomic bomb we dropped on Hiroshima in 1945 was a 15-kiloton bomb - the equivalent of 15,000 tons of TNT.

"In 1952, we successfully test detonated the first hydrogen bomb, code-named Ivy Mike, on an atoll in the Pacific Ocean. Its explosive power was 10.4 megatons, equivalent to 10.4 *million* tons of TNT. A pure fusion bomb would have a far greater lethal area per unit of explosive than a large fission bomb. For example, it is estimated that a pure fusion bomb, with the same TNT equivalency of the Hiroshima bomb, would have a lethal radius hundreds of times larger than the Hiroshima bomb."

"Oh my God!" Rhodes stared at Carter in shock. "I honestly hope you are wrong."

"I hope so too, but I have this nagging feeling I am not."

Chapter Thirty-Eight

VISIT THOSE SITES

Carter and Rhodes returned to the cabin and settled in Will's study where they busied themselves with the review of all the reports. Carter, staring out the window deep in thought, startled Rhodes when he suddenly exclaimed, "Space archeology! Of course."

Rhodes looked up, staring at Carter in surprise. "We haven't been in the sun that long, have we, my friend? Please tell me you are not thinking of ET or The Final Frontier."

"No, I haven't gone that far around the bend yet," Carter laughed. "I'm talking about satellite reconnaissance photography and mapping - the way we found the City of Lights in the desert. Over the past 20 years as satellite mapping has established itself, and people use it to look for lost civilizations. Lately, that type of research has turned up thousands of new archeological sites we didn't even know existed. Sarah Parcak is a leading expert in space archeology, and she has already discovered some amazing stuff."

"Oh ok, now I know what you are talking about." James

sat back, visibly relaxing. "Man, you had me worried there for a minute."

"These days, desktop archeologists, as they are also called, are finding thousands of sites never seen before using Google Earth." Carter elaborated. "I remember reading about a Ph.D. student at one of the Australian universities uncovering hundreds of previously unknown sites in Afghanistan that way."

"Well, that is certainly worth looking into. With the president's promise of cooperation from all the security agencies, we will probably have access to the most comprehensive satellite images on the planet."

Carter walked to the window and watched a herd of deer wander across the yard in front of the house. There were less of them since the wolves returned. Wolves were the best way ever found to keep a deer population under control.

"Another thing we still haven't figured out is how they powered the City of Lights," Carter commented. "We think we know how they conducted power; those silver discs on the buildings seem the best candidates for power transmission. I think they found a way to tap into the magnetosphere, the interface of the Earth's magnetic field with the solar wind from the sun."

"How does that tie in with our research?"

"I'm not sure there is any connection; perhaps Mark Adalbert could shed more light on it for us. Do you think he will agree to a video conference?"

"Only one way to find out," Rhodes replied. "I'll give him a call."

An hour later, thanks to having good relations with a satellite internet provider, they were sitting in front of a screen talking to Dr. Adalbert. .

Carter began by thanking him for looking over the reports he'd sent him. Adalbert told him it wasn't any bother; he'd found his research fascinating. He agreed with Carter's supposition; there was enough evidence to show that nuclear power had been used before recorded time. It was the type of information every scientist lived to discover.

"It's the sixth site in the report which has me perplexed," Adalbert said. "We have the typical Trinitite residues, the spread of the blast from an epicenter, but no significant levels of radiation. It could have been a thermonuclear explosion, but even then I would expect the radiation levels to be much higher."

Rhodes cleared his throat. "Mark, Carter has a theory which I think you might want to hear."

Mark listened intently while Carter described his fusion weapon theory.

"My understanding is that in order to create a hydrogen fusion reaction, the hydrogen isotopes tritium and deuterium are required. I also understand that those isotopes are not hard to come by. I'm aware that current scientists have never been able to create a nuclear fusion reaction long enough for it to sustain itself. My question is, hypothetically speaking, if it was possible to build a fusion bomb, do you think that could explain the evidence of the release of extreme heat energy at those sites?" Carter asked.

"Absolutely, no doubt about it. During a fusion reaction, hundreds of times more energy is released than in an atomic fission reaction."

Rhodes sighed and shook his head. "I was hoping Carter was wrong about this. So now that we know it is a possibility do you have any ideas how they could have done it?"

Adalbert took a deep breath. "Keep in mind that what I am about to say is all theory and speculation."

Both Carter and Rhodes nodded for him to continue.

"To get a fusion reaction, deuterium and tritium isotopes have to be heated to more than 200 million degrees Fahrenheit, which requires enormous amounts of energy, as you can imagine. Our scientists are doing that with electromagnets. At those temperatures, gas turns into a liquid, that we call plasma.

"The primary benefits of fusion reactors would be no carbon emissions, energy efficiency, and short-lived radioactivity.

"The scientists estimate that two and a half pounds of fusion fuel will produce the same amount of energy as 25 million pounds of fossil fuel.

"As for radioactivity, it won't last for more than 100 years."

Carter nodded. "So going back to my hypothesis, a hydrogen fusion reaction can explain why the radioactivity levels are so low at that site?"

"Yes indeed, it could explain the anomaly. My question is how would they have produced the enormous heat required to create fusion? For that answer, I guess we'll have to think outside the box."

"Way out of the box, I would say. How about laser? Could that create enough heat for fusion?"

"Yes, a laser could definitely turn gas into plasma. In fact, it has been demonstrated, but it lasted only for a split second. You will need a laser beam generator that can produce continuous petawatt beams – 1,000 trillion watts and more.

"The Japanese recently built a generator that produced 2,000 trillion watts, and the beam lasted for one trillionth of a second. The generator is as big as a basketball field, and the electrical power required to generate that beam was almost unfathomable."

"So in theory again, it is possible, but with our current level of scientific understanding we would not know how?" Carter asked.

"Yes, that's correct. The problem is that our ideas and visions are limited to what we understand today. Anything outside of that becomes science fiction. Many scientists wouldn't pay a moment's notice to the notion that what they are trying to achieve today might have been accomplished thousands of years ago," Mark chuckled.

"Well, with the potential danger this poses to our entire civilization, we don't have the luxury of thinking like that," Rhodes commented.

"Remember, in defense of some of my colleagues," Adalbert continued, "the era in human history we are looking at here was, according to most scientists, when our ancestors had just moved out of caves and had not yet invented the wheel."

Carter smiled. "The reality is we have to consider the possibility that those cave dwellers might very well have been using more of their brain capacity than we do. They could have been technologically advanced to levels we can't even begin to conceive."

Mark laughed. "I agree. Nonetheless, that thought won't go down well with many of them, I can assure you."

"I can tell you all about that." Carter smiled. "One more crazy idea; how about electricity? Would that produce enough heat for fusion? If, for instance, they were able to tap into the unlimited power available in the magnetosphere."

"Again, yes indeed, it's possible with enough electricity,

but we don't have a power plant on the planet today that could generate enough electricity to drive a continuous fusion reaction. Not even lightning could do it - even if you could harness the power from thousands of lightning strikes. The only source of electricity, which could produce enough to generate the required levels of heat, would be the earth's magnetosphere as you have mentioned. And again we know it's there but have not figured out how to tap into it yet."

"Isn't that the idea Tesla played around with?" Rhodes asked.

"Yes, that's Nicola Tesla's brainchild. We know there is an unlimited supply of electricity running at millions of amperes in the magnetosphere. But as I've said, we haven't yet discovered how to get to it."

"I guess there is not much point in deliberating things such as zero-point energy and dark matter then?" Carter smiled.

Mark nodded. "Yep, we are only beginning to understand what those things mean. To be honest, scientists are sometimes still arguing about their existence. Therefore, although nothing can be ruled out, I am afraid there are very few, if any, who will be able to come up with even a theory of how they could be used as a weapon. You would probably get better ideas by watching sci-fi movies or read books about them than talking to scientists."

James sat back. "So it boils down to five sites with a definite 'yes' as having been destroyed by a nuclear explosion. The last one, the sixth site, is a definite 'maybe it was obliterated by a fusion weapon of some sort, but we have no clue how it was done'."

"Yes, that sums it up fairly accurately I would say." Mark smiled, but then got a serious look on his face. "However, I have to leave you with one very disturbing piece of information, and that is the fact that an uncontrolled fusion reaction has the potential to turn this planet of ours into the second sun of our solar system."

"Oh my God!" Rhodes shook his head. "The news can't get any worse."

Carter and Rhodes thanked Mark for his help and ended the videoconference. Carter got up and poured them both a coffee. "I doubt we can find more than what our field teams have discovered so far. Nevertheless, I think it is important that we visit those sites. You never know what a fresh pair of eyes and a different viewpoint might uncover."

"Agreed. Let's finish our meeting with Hunter next week and then start making arrangements."

Rhodes checked his email and got a message from Hunter Patrick. "We have a meeting in Washington with Hunter Monday afternoon. He has to brief the President again on Wednesday. I guess you would rather videoconference in on the meeting?"

"No, I have actually been planning to go down to D.C. in the next two weeks. I want to spend some time down in the archives to see if I can dig up more information. Now is as good a time as any to make the trip."

"Excellent. I'll let Hunter know you'll be there."

"So that leaves you with a few more days to enjoy Freydis before we head down to the concrete backwoods."

Rhodes laughed. "Yes, I guess you can call it that after you have experienced this place."

Chapter Thirty-Nine

NEEDLE IN A HAYSTACK

Shortly after 11:00 am Monday, Director Patrick listened carefully as Rhodes summarized his discussions with Carter at Freydis. Hunter questioned them in detail about the hydrogen fusion theory and probabilities. Carter relayed the conversation with Mark including the conclusions they had reached. A hydrogen fusion reaction would explain what they had found at the one site, but modern science had no idea how it could have been created.

The Director stood behind his chair in silence, looking at the two of them and glancing at the painting on the wall behind them. When Rhodes finished, he sighed. "Listening to you two, I get the nauseating feeling this problem is not going to land in the crazy basket. Fusion and nuclear weapons sitting somewhere in a cave or at the bottom of the ocean," he said. "This job is beginning to resemble a doomsday movie."

"There's no director to yell 'cut!'" Rhodes pointed out with gallows humor.

"I wish there was, it would make my life a hell of a lot

easier. At least, I would have the chance to edit out everything I don't like. Now I have to tell the President we think there are not only ancient nuclear bombs but also fusion weapons, and the latter could turn the whole damn planet into a burning ball of fire."

"Unfortunately, that seems to be the case," Carter replied. "Our challenge now is to find them with the help of a scientific community who still regards it as science fiction."

"So this is not like looking for the proverbial needle in a haystack, it's more like searching through a haystack to find the brightest straw. What's the next step?" Hunter inquired from Rhodes.

"Carter and I are going to visit a few of the other agencies to see if we can get access to concise satellite maps which we would like to study in the hope of figuring out where to start our search for an answer."

"Desktop archeology," Hunter responded. "That would be an interesting and significant starting point. You can get a much better idea of what's down here with satellite probes from up there than you can from down here." Hunter smiled.

Rhodes continued. "Carter also thinks it's a good idea to visit the sites in person, so I will make the necessary arrangements over the next few days."

"Sounds good to me," Hunter concluded the discussion and sat back. "So Jim, tell me what was it like out there in the boondocks the last few days?"

"Hunter let me tell you, that's what I thought about the place until I saw it. For me, it was heaven. I can't recall when I've had such a nice break and seen such beauty. It's spectacular, and to top it all off, Carter and Mackenzie were the best hosts one can hope for - gave me five-star treatment all the way."

Patrick laughed. "Yeah I know, I have been out in those areas once before, and it's spectacular as you said."

Rhodes looked at Carter and then at Hunter. "If you have a bit of time, this might be as good a time as any to tell you about Mackenzie's research project."

"You caught me at a good time. My next meeting isn't until late afternoon. Let me order us something to drink and you can tell me. I'm sure if her project has interested you so much; then I must hear about it." Hunter called his secretary to place their coffee order.

After an hour of listening and questioning, Hunter took his glasses off, folded them into a triangle, and placed them squarely in front of him on the desk. He looked at Carter and said. "Do you and your wife have any idea what a shit storm this work of hers can stir up?"

Carter was slightly surprised by his tone. He hadn't known Patrick long enough to be familiar with his body language and mannerisms, but he was sure the man was deadly serious.

"This is the second time in a week I've heard that question." Carter glanced at Rhodes. "Do you two know something you are not telling me?"

Rhodes had his hands up shaking his head. "There's no conspiracy here Carter. The answer is plain and simple; Hunter came to the same conclusion I did when I heard what Mackenzie is working on."

"So I take it you have asked them the same question?" Hunter asked while looking at Rhodes, who was nodding.

"Well, Carter if your wife happens to make any discoveries of the magnitude of yours, she is going to stir up a hornet's nest.

The stuff she is working on is part of what we at A-Echelon must know about. Breakthrough discoveries in that field can hold not only enormous benefits but also terrible perils for our country and the world. Her work must be safeguarded, and the release of information managed and controlled properly. We don't want to see that stuff in the hands of our adversaries."

Carter was a patient man, but Patrick's choice of words was beginning to test his endurance. He leaned forward, closer to Hunter's face and said in measured terms, "I sincerely hope that was not a threat to take it away from her Hunter."

"Oh my God no! Sorry Carter that was not my intention." When Carter saw the genuineness of the apology on Patrick's face, he relaxed and immediately regretted his reaction. "I was just trying to convey my perception of the gravity of what your wife is dealing with. Please accept my apologies. I am very interested in this, and I would like to offer her any resources we have to help further her research."

"My apologies, I overreacted." Carter smiled. Patrick waved his hand, dismissing the issue.

"No problem. Let's get back to it then." Patrick continued. "I was going to ask if you think she would consider working for us. That will give her access to resources and material she would never have otherwise." He chuckled, "just think about it, you two could be A-Echelon's Mr. and Mrs. North."

Carter was quiet for a few moments, and then a smile broke across his face when he replied, "you or Jim will have to talk to her about that. When Jim gave you his account of his visit to Freydis, he left out a tiny but vital bit of information. Mackenzie has naturally red hair. I would not dare make a decision on her behalf!"

"Well, she was very kind to me all the time I was there," Rhodes laughed. "I'll take the risk and talk to her."

"I think it will be best if we both sit down with her," Patrick suggested. "There will be a lot to discuss and agree upon, and of course, security clearances and background checks to follow."

Carter didn't listen anymore; his mind was racing with thoughts. Although he hadn't yet experienced any danger, he knew it was never far off, and he wasn't sure how he felt about Mackenzie stepping into this cloak and dagger space as well. Additionally, there was Liam to think of. However, it was as he told them; he would not make her decisions. He would back her, whatever she decided, and they would agree, as they always did, on how to handle things from there.

"I have my weekly meeting with the Director of the CIA tomorrow morning. I'll discuss both topics with him and see what he thinks," Hunter said as he concluded their discussions.

Carter and Rhodes spent the next day examining the maps given to them by the NSA. The plan was to visit a site in North India, close to the Pakistan border, first. Many charred ruins, appearing as huge masses fused together, had been found at this location. Some reports gave descriptions of glazed walls and surfaces of stone furniture vitrified by incredible heat.

Next, they would visit the Saad Plateau in Egypt where a geologist discovered big sheets of solid yellow-green glass in 1932. At the time of the discovery, he had no idea about the origins. It was only many years later, while visiting the

Alamogordo's White Sands missile range, when he saw the chunks of glass left there by the nuclear tests, that he realized they were identical to what he observed on the Saad Plateau.

Geologists concluded that the heat, which produced the glass in the African desert, must have been 10,000 times more powerful than the heat caused by the first nuclear explosion in New Mexico.

The third location was the City of Lights, where they would spend a week.

The fourth location to be visited was the 8,000-year-old Çatalhöyük in South Central Turkey, one of the earliest civilizations recognized by conformist archeologists. There were reports about signs of heat so extreme it had penetrated over three feet below ground level, fusing brick blocks together and carbonizing the soil.

Wednesday morning while Carter was in the Smithsonian's vaults, he got a call from Rhodes. "Carter I hope you brought a suit with you."

"Yes I have. What's the occasion?"

"The President wants to see you."

"What? You must be joking. Why would he want to see me? I didn't even vote for him." Carter laughed, still thinking Rhodes was fooling around.

"Carter, I'm not joking. Hunter's meeting with the President has been moved to Friday and we have to attend."

"Why does he want to meet with us?"

"Well as you know, Hunter had his weekly meeting with the CIA boss yesterday and told him about the nuke project and also about Mackenzie's work. When he heard what Hunter had to say, he apparently became very excited, especially about those respiro thingamajigs." Carter smiled at Rhodes who still couldn't get the pronunciation right. "The

CIA Director went straight to the President and told him about it, and now the big boss and his sidekick want to talk to you."

"Sidekick?"

"Vice President," Rhodes chuckled.

"I told you before I can't make decisions on Mackenzie's behalf. I will, however, support her, whatever she decides."

"Carter, at this stage, the President, and the Veep are very interested in both her work and yours. They are not going to ask you to decide for her. As far as we are concerned, this is a secret meeting and not to be discussed with Mackenzie yet – unless, of course, it's decided to approach her to join A-Echelon in the same capacity as you did, and she agrees."

"I thought the Veep was of the opinion we belong in the looney bin. What got him so excited all of a sudden?"

"I don't know, but we will find out on Friday when we meet with them."

Carter, still a bit flabbergasted, started to mumble. "I'll be damned ... meeting with the President and Vice President of the United States, and the Director of the CIA. That's enough to get anyone on the most wanted list!"

"I warned you when you joined – you are moving into a weird world," Rhodes laughed.

"Is there anything I need to prepare for this meeting?"

"I guess they may ask you about your discoveries in Cusco and Egypt, and maybe your radical ideas about human history!" Rhodes laughed. "But you can be 100 percent sure they will want to hear about the ancient nukes and Mackenzie's research."

"So who else is going to be at this meeting?"

"The President, the Veep, and the Director of the CIA. It's supposed to be informal and unofficial. My guess is that they don't want it leaked to the press that he's meeting with a couple of guys who believe in ancient nukes built by a race of giants."

Carter, still shaking his head, remembered to call Mackenzie and tell her about the change of plans. However, he did not tell her the reason.

Chapter Forty

MR. PRESIDENT

Friday afternoon, three black SUV's with dark-tinted windows, to hide the identity of the occupants from anyone on the outside, arrived to take them to the White House. The Secret Service agents escorting them were quiet and no-nonsense. It was their job to take the bullet for the President should the need ever arise, and they knew it. The Service had experienced some bad publicity in recent times as to their effectiveness, and they were in no mood to let anyone think they treated their duty lightly. Carter could see in their demeanor that these agents were efficient and every bit as professional as he always believed they were.

Nearly half an hour later, the gate to the White House grounds opened, the SUV's rolled into the perimeter, and made their way into the underground parking lot. Once inside the security zone of the White House, they became the responsibility of the Secret Service.

An aide to the president met them inside and escorted them to the Oval Office. She was a rather nice looking young woman, athletic in appearance, with the build of a gymnast. Carter noted the enhanced security features everywhere - security cameras, Secret Service men standing around with earpieces. No one was taking any chances. It was rumored a nuclear blast-proof bunker was beneath them. *This has to be the most secure place on the planet,* Carter thought.

"I must apologize," the aide said to them. "The president is on the phone and will be slightly delayed."

Carter wondered if the call she referred to had something to do with the news that broke earlier - a Chinese warship that drifted into US territorial waters.

She seated them in ornate chairs in a waiting area outside the President's office and asked if they needed anything. When they declined, she took a seat close to the door and waited.

Carter glanced around the room and wondered how many important people in history had sat in this very place. His skin tingled at the thought. He'd heard about the White House all his life, but never thought he'd find himself inside it. Here he was, Carter Devereux, waiting to meet with the President of the United States. *Grandpa Will, wherever you are, I hope you're seeing this!*

He glanced over to one of the chairs across from him and noticed an Air Force officer holding a plain leather briefcase. For a second, Carter thought this man was also going to attend the meeting, but then he realized the man carried the 'football.' 'Football' was the code name for the briefcase containing the nuclear attack instructions and missile launch codes. It contained everything the president needed to authorize an immediate response. The officer carrying the briefcase had to be within voice-calling distance of the President at all times. It was a grim reminder of the nuclear Damoclean sword that still dangled over the world despite the end of the cold war.

Close to half an hour later, the door to the Oval office opened. The aide stepped in and motioned for the three of them to follow her.

Behind the desk sat the most powerful man on earth. He wasn't impressive to look upon, but the desk and office, which Carter had seen on TV and the Internet as long as he could remember, lent him an awe-inspiring aura of authority and dignity. Next to the President sat the Director of the CIA and the Vice President. Large windows allowed the fading sunlight to stream inside. The Oval Office was definitely an imposing place.

The President stood to welcome them and, coming around from behind his desk; he pointed to where everyone should sit. Carter's group took one couch, the President and his men the other. Looking around, Carter noted the aide had left the room.

"Sorry to keep you waiting, gentlemen," the President said. "Can I ask Nakesha to get you something to drink?" They all declined politely.

"Professor Devereux, may I call you Carter?" the President asked.

"You may Mr. President."

"Hunter, I see you've brought your brain trust," the President said as he turned to the Director of A-Echelon and smiled. "If you don't mind, I would like to get right down to business."

Everyone agreed, and he continued. "So what progress has been made since our last meeting? So far the press hasn't found out about it, and I hope it stays that way."

Director Patrick gave a quick but effective summary,

telling how they planned to use satellite imagery to locate the most probable nuclear explosion sites. Then he mentioned the possibility of a fusion weapon and the supporting evidence. He also explained the significant difference in destructive power of a fusion weapon compared to a nuclear weapon and ended by saying, "This means, we might have a much bigger problem than we initially thought. The fact is we are looking at potential annihilation of all life on the planet."

"Well, that just added a ray of sunshine to my day," the President said with a wry smile. "And I don't have any illusions that given half a chance, some of those fanatics in the Middle East will not hesitate one second to set off an explosion that will send them all to their version of paradise and us infidels to hell."

The President was up, hands in his pockets, pacing behind his desk - a sign for everyone to be quiet and allow him time to think and speak first.

"If what you are saying is correct – if there is scientific confirmation that five of those 15 sites were targets of ancient nuclear explosions, then it is fairly obvious, at least it is to me, that we are due for another about-face regarding human history. In which case, we will undoubtedly quickly come to terms with the reality that our ancestors were probably not swinging around in trees, eating bananas and insects." The President was not talking to anyone in particular. "Damn. If only they would have left a bit more information, it would have made life a lot easier for us." He stopped and looked at Carter. "I'm told that you hold an alternative theory about human origins. Would you care to tell us a bit more?"

"Mr. President I would not call it a theory just yet, at least not the academic definition of a theory. I still need a lot more information before I can call it that. However, I am leaning toward the idea of the existence of an antediluvian civilization, far more advanced than ours."

"On what basis? What real and concrete evidence do you have?"

"The discovery of the site at Cusco down in Peru has pushed human history back by almost 30,000 years. The discovery of the site of the City of Lights in Egypt has pushed it back by at least another 20,000 years. So, instead of the generally acceptable 12,000 years of human history, we are now looking at 50,000 years.

"Archeologists are frequently uncovering artifacts that do not seem to belong where they are found. For instance, micro gold spirals found in Russia, 20,000 years old, which appear to be human made with technology that we can't explain. Also, human and dinosaur footprints have been found in the same strata. Human tracks next to and inside those of dinosaurs, and even dinosaur footprints on top of human footprints."

The President nodded. It was obvious the information captivated him.

"Sir, I am told you have been informed about my wife's research?" The President nodded. "Well, after our discovery of the City of Lights, she has undertaken a limited study to see if she can find supporting evidence of gigantism in other sources. She has found a great deal of data from all over the world: dwellings, graves, fossil footprints, bones, artifacts, the Bible, and they all point to the existence of gigantic humans, incredible lifespans, intellectual superiority, and nobility in a time for which we have no recorded information."

"That's another thing we have to discuss – your wife's research - but let's finish this nasty nuke thing first. What do you propose we do about finding these nuclear weapons should they be out there?"

Carter went over their plans to use satellite imagery to locate more sites from orbit with the help of the NSA and any other government agency they could bring to their assistance. He also explained their plans to visit some of the sites in person.

"In your opinion, how imminent is the threat?" the Director of the CIA asked.

"Sir, I apologize in advance if my answer sounds dubious. As far as we have assessed to date, there is no concrete evidence of someone out there actively looking for those weapons. However, while it may not be considered 'common knowledge,' there are many people out there who do speculate about the destruction caused by ancient atomic explosions. The Internet has a plethora of sites on the topic, and even though no one seems to be seriously researching it, I believe it's sensible to assume that someone is indeed looking for an atomic device or its plans."

"Yes, you're right. It is sensible to go with the belief someone else will be interested."

"I'll make sure you have all the clearance and help you need," said the President. "One of my secretaries will draft a letter to the directors of the CIA and FBI, so you have their cooperation as well."

"Which sites are you planning to visit?" the President wanted to know.

Carter gave him the names.

"Çatalhöyük? In Turkey?" The Vice President asked. "What could you possibly expect to find there?"

Well, at least he's paying more attention this time. Patrick thought to himself. *I wonder if someone hit him on the nose with a folded newspaper and scolded him after our last meeting.* He had to suppress the grin he felt at the thought. *I sure would have liked to see that!*

"Mr. Vice President, Çatalhöyük is just beginning to give up its secrets and in doing so is mystifying archeologists and scientists alike. Not only did they find evidence of an atomic explosion there, but we also learned about the mind-boggling technological achievements of its inhabitants thousands of years ago."

"Such as?"

"Slag. Slag is the stony waste matter that is separated from metals during the smelting or refining process. This suggests that copper was being extracted from its ore. To do this requires extreme temperatures in excess of 3,330 degrees Fahrenheit. However, according to current belief, 8,000 years ago, the current estimated age of the city, man had only just about discovered fire – not how to build furnaces. The question then becomes, when and where did they learn to extract and smelt metals in 6400 BC?" Carter paused.

"Don't stop now! Please continue; this is fascinating," the Director prompted.

"Discoveries have shown that they could polish a mirror of obsidian, which is hard volcanic glass, without scratching it." Carter's enthusiasm was now showing. "They drilled minuscule holes through stone beads, including obsidian, that are so small even a hair-thin, modern, steel needle can't penetrate them."

"It will be interesting to read your report when you get back," the Director responded.

The Vice President moved to the next item on the agenda. "Carter, would you mind telling us about your wife's research? We are all very interested to hear more about it."

Carter had thoughts similar to those of Hunter a few moments ago. *At least we have his attention this time. Someone must have thumped him behind the ears hard enough to make his feet sting!*

Carter gave them an overview of Mackenzie's research and her goals and then went into a bit more detail about the respirocytes and what progress she had made on that front.

"She has a foundation devoted to the study of ancient medical practices?" the President asked when Carter ended his narrative.

"Yes, Mr. President. She dedicated it to my late grandfather - The Will Devereux Medical Archeology Foundation."

The three Leaders continued asking questions about Mackenzie's research and foundation for another 15 minutes. James, Hunter, and Carter were pleased that they showed a lot of interest in her work.

Finally, the Vice President asked, "Is there any possibility you could convince her to come work for A-Echelon?"

Carter smiled. "Mr. Vice President, as I have told Hunter and Jim, my wife has red hair, and I know better than to make decisions on her behalf."

Everyone exploded into laughter, and the Vice President remarked, "Yes, I understand those red heads can be quite fiery sometimes! Okay, so that we don't get you into trouble with her, how do you suggest we go about recruiting her then?"

"Mr. Vice President, with your permission I will pave the way for Hunter and Jim to talk to her, but I have to state that I will not try to persuade her. This is her research and expertise, and she will make her own decision. I will support her decision, of course, whatever she decides. That's all I can promise."

"That's good enough for me," the Vice President said. He looked at Hunter and Rhodes. "You two just let me know if you need my powers of persuasion. We can always invite her to dinner at the White House if it helps." He laughed.

The President nodded.

The Vice President wanted the last word. "We," he pointed, including the President and the Director of the CIA, "discussed her work yesterday and believe it is crucial that we help her achieve her goals and protect the information from landing in the hands of our enemies."

Carter nodded. It was obvious there was a very definite 'squeeze' going on to get Mackenzie involved.

Mackenzie was waiting for him in the electric cart when he landed at Freydis. He taxied the plane down the runway and into the hangar, contacted the tower at the Canadian airport to let them know he was safely on the ground and gave them his coordinates.

Joining her beside the cart, he took Mackenzie in his arms, gave her a long and lingering kiss and told her how much he had missed her. Then he looked around, "no Liam?"

"He's out fishing with Ahote," Mackenzie said as they got into the cart. "They will be back later."

Carter breathed deeply of the fresh air. "I have always loved it here, and the more often I'm gone, the more I appreciate it when I get back." He started the cart, "especially with you and Liam here waiting for me," he said with a smile as he drove toward the cabin."

While Mackenzie got the espresso machine going, she asked, "So what kept you away from me for another day? Or are you not allowed to say?"

"I am allowed to say, but you won't believe me." Carter smiled.

"I've known you long enough to be sure it could not have been trivial, so out with it."

"It was a meeting with the President of the United States, the Vice President, and the Director of the CIA."

Mackenzie stopped in her tracks and looked at him with distrust. "Carter Devereux, you'll sleep with Bly's chickens tonight if you don't tell me the truth right now!"

"Mackie, I'm not joking. It's true!" He laughed. "I told you; you wouldn't believe me!"

"At the White House? ... That big white building there in Washington D.C? ... The one where the President of the United States lives and works? ..." She looked at him, still very doubtful.

"Yep, that's the one! The White House," he confirmed. "That big white building there in Washington D.C."

"Am I really to believe you? Why did they want to meet with you? You didn't even vote for them."

"I don't think they cared about my vote. They wanted to know about the project I am working on, the one I can't tell you about. But I got the impression the meeting had an additional purpose."

"And you can't tell me about that either?"

"Oh, I can tell you about that," he said with a devilish grin, "but I won't until I have a nice coffee in my hand."

She handed him his coffee and said, "I am listening. Just remember Bly's chicken coop is still available as your bedroom tonight."

"You certainly know how to put pressure on a fella," he laughed.

She just grinned; her curiosity had the upper hand.

"I will give you all the minor details later because I

know you will want to hear them as well. For now, I suspect the part you would be most interested in is that they asked me about your research and were wondering if you would be interested in working for them. It's the same organization I work for."

"Work for them? ... me ... how did they come to know about my research?"

"Easy, it was a chain reaction. Jim told his Director, who was instantly intrigued. He then told the Director of the CIA and got him very excited. The CIA Director, in turn, told the President and Vice President. Needless to say, they also got enthusiastic and wanted to hear more about it immediately."

"So what exactly did you tell them?"

"You mean apart from you being the most beautiful and clever woman on earth?" He teased.

"You like to live dangerously don't you?" she grinned.

"Okay, okay." He held his hands up in defense. "I told them everything about your research, what you have achieved so far and what your primary goals are - as close to verbatim as I could to what you gave Jim and me the other night."

"And how did you answer them when they wanted to know if I will work for them?"

"Well, I told them you're a redhead and that I was in no way going to risk my life to tangle with you on this. I told them they could take the risk; I am not prepared to." He smothered a laugh and tried to keep his face straight, but it didn't work.

"You said what?" She shoved him, and he fell off the couch onto the floor laughing. She jumped on top of him and thumped him again. He thought he heard her murmur something about Bly's chicken coop.

"Ow! That hurt."

There was silence for a moment. Another moment passed and for a little while, they were quiet. Carter reached up and undid her hair, letting it flow around her shoulders, watching it glint in the afternoon sunlight seeping in through the window. "My wild Freyda, my beautiful woman, I have missed you so much," he murmured.

She leaned over and kissed him slowly, deeply, passionately, her hair creating a curtain, cutting out the rest of the world and their thoughts, as they came together. Time ceased to exist for them.

Sometime later, they regained the couch, and he spoke. "Mackie, you know you don't have to say yes, it could turn out to be dangerous. Don't forget the warning Jim gave you.

"You wouldn't work for the President personally, but the organization does report directly to him. We'd have to move down south again. Of course as Liam's starting school soon, that will be necessary anyway. The good news is, you would be near your parents, and I know they want to see Liam more."

"I'd have to share my research with these spooks, wouldn't I?"

"Watch it, your husband is a spook."

She stared out the window, "Did you really mean what you said when you told me you will back whatever decision I make?"

"Yes, and I told them so as well. You will have my support whatever you decide to do."

"And based on that, I now have a job offer from this organization?"

Carter nodded. "They would want to review everything - national security interest and all that. However, you would have access to all kinds of classified data few people are allowed to see. I can't promise you'll find the answers to all your questions, but you will definitely be in a position to get a lot closer."

She went quiet for a while. "This requires some serious thought. We need to consider the ramifications to Liam and our life here."

She got up and walked out onto the porch where she stood deep in thought for some time. Carter knew better than to interrupt her. If nothing else in his six years of marriage, he understood her need to have some time alone to think things through. She stood on the porch hugging the rail while Carter watched her. He had a vision of the earliest Freydis in full battle armor on the deck of a Viking long ship. He could feel the sea breeze, smell the salt, and hear the sound of waves crashing against the hull.

About an hour later, she came back into the house and went up to Carter. "We still have the house near Boston. We'll use it as our primary residence and Liam can start school in the fall. If that works for you, I'm in."

"You have my full support," he said taking her in his arms and holding her close to him.

"Does this 'organization' I'm going to be working for ... we work for, have a name, or is it too secret for that?"

Carter laughed. "It's called 'A-Echelon'."

"What a strange name."

"Mmmm" Carter murmured as he kissed her brow. "You will learn more about it in the orientation and training classes you will attend."

As he expected, once Mackenzie got over the surprise, she peppered him with questions - about the meeting, everything leading up to it, and afterward. Carter had to give her everything in minute detail from the moment he received the invitation: what he was wearing, what the room looked like, what they talked about, and what sort of people are the President, Vice President and the Director of the CIA. She didn't allow Carter to miss one bit of detail.

Once Mackenzie was satisfied that Carter had given her a complete brain dump, they talked about their plans for the immediate future. Returning home to Boston was sensible because Liam was about to start school, and being close to her parents when Carter was away would be an added bonus.

To say that Liam was not pleased with the idea of leaving Freydis was an understatement. Once he heard about it, he came up with many excuses to stay with Ahote and Bly. The only way they could console him was by promising him they would come back as often as they could, and that he could video conference with Bly and Ahote anytime he wanted, so he could see Nelly and hear about the wolves, the deer, and Bly's chickens. He brightened up when they also told him he'd be able to see Grandpa Steven and Grandma Mary anytime he wanted to, when they moved back south.

Chapter Forty-One

NOT NEGOTIABLE

A week later, the Devereux family arrived back at their home in Boston. "Looks like the maintenance company has done a good job of keeping the place in good condition," Mackenzie noted after she did her inspection. She took her shoes off and sat down on the leather couch as Carter brought in their luggage.

During the flight from Freydis, she'd pummeled Carter with questions about the Institute and how it functioned. He told her all he could, but many times had to let her know there were some things he was not allowed to discuss. Besides, he was clueless on many aspects of the Institute. He had no idea how many field agents worked for them or the number of staff and contractors.

Carter had passed Mackenzie's willingness to work for A-Echelon on to Hunter and James but, at the same time, also told them that before she would agree to come onboard, they would have to negotiate the terms and conditions with her.

As the first step in the recruitment process, three days after their arrival in Boston, Hunter Patrick and James Rhodes met with Mackenzie at a local Boston restaurant. Although Carter was invited, he did not join them. Mackenzie was more than capable of handling it on her own.

Mackenzie looked at Patrick and tried to sum him up. He was probably in his late 60's, overweight, balding, and wearing wire rim glasses. Not the sort of person you'd look at twice while walking down the street. However, Mackenzie soon concluded that the gentle exterior concealed a sharp and clever mind.

Once they were seated and had placed their orders, Hunter got right to the point. "So, Dr. Devereux, can you tell me more about your work?"

"You can call me Mackenzie. I trust it's okay if I call you Hunter?"

"Of course, Mackenzie," he continued. "People have called me much worse." They all laughed.

"I'm spending the bulk of my time on the respirocyte technology which Carter told you about," Mackenzie answered. "It has the greatest potential to change the world for the better. As you may have noted in my papers, creating a more efficient red blood cell using nanotechnology would advance the human race and cure many diseases."

"So how does that tie in with your archeological work on ancient medical practices?"

"The idea of expanding my research into ancient texts actually came from Will Devereux, Carter's grandfather, whom I believe you knew. With Carter's, and other's discoveries of lost civilizations and artifacts, it makes sense to explore the possibility that this technology could have existed in ancient times, especially if you are prepared to admit they could have been much more advanced than we are. It wouldn't surprise me if they already had this technology. That's why I'm 'digging' around in the past."

The restaurant was quiet, but Mackenzie noticed they were right next to a water fountain. The sound of the water annoyed her for a while until she realized that Hunter probably placed them there for a specific reason. The noise created by the water fountain created a blanket of white noise, making it impossible for anyone to eavesdrop on the conversation even with a parabolic microphone.

Patrick nodded his understanding.

"So, why don't you tell me a little bit about what it is you do, and how you see my role in your organization?" Mackenzie asked.

Patrick explained A-Echelon's mission - to investigate ancient history and identify potential benefits and threats originating from discoveries. He went on to explain to Mackenzie how he saw her work tying in neatly with A-Echelon's own efforts and objectives.

"Your work has a lot of potential benefits, but in the wrong hands, it could easily become a major headache."

"I have recently become aware of the perils," she said while looking at Rhodes. "Since Jim and Carter made me aware, I have become more conscious of the potential negatives." She was shaking her head, "I just can't believe there are people who would want to take something as useful as this and use it for evil purposes."

"Mackenzie, don't doubt that for a moment. There are people who, for their own purposes, would go to extremes to get their hands on this information, and, as you said, use it to strengthen their own powers."

She nodded her agreement.

"I'm glad we're in agreement about that aspect. So I have to ask you then," Patrick continued, "what would it take to have you come on board?"

"There are a few things we will have to agree on before I will get on board. First and foremost, I need to understand how it will affect my family, especially my time with our son Liam. Second, we have to reach an agreement under which I would be able to preserve my independence while working for the Institute."

"Good," Patrick nodded. "Please go ahead and give us your terms."

Mackenzie placed her coffee cup down. "I suggest that I telecommute from Boston and only go down to D.C. for meetings and research as required."

"No problem with that," Patrick agreed.

"I keep the Will Devereux Medical Archaeology Foundation going, which means I will be continuing my research on ancient medicine, and the only part of my research that will come under the auspices of A-Echelon will be the respirocytes." She paused and looked at them. "And that is not negotiable."

Patrick and Rhodes both had to suppress a smile when they heard her choice of words and saw the determination on her face. Carter was right about the fiery temperament going with the red hair.

"Agreed," Patrick said, "but I would like to add one condition, and that is you will tell us about any discoveries you make outside of the A-Echelon project."

As he saw her body language stiffen and she started to object, he quickly raised his hand in a stopping gesture and continued. "The reason being, we would like to assess the implications and offer you the necessary protection and support if required."

Mackenzie paused and then relaxed. "Okay, no problem. I can see the logic of that, as long as you won't try and direct my research or claim it as your own."

"Don't worry, it won't happen. Our interest is purely about national security."

"Next, I want full access to the Smithsonian archives and any other information you might have for both the respirocyte project and my foundation research."

"No worries," Patrick smiled. "I have been ordered by the President and Vice President to arrange that access for you as soon as your security clearance comes through."

"Finally, I will need Liu Chuen's help for translation, which means you will have to get security clearance for her as well."

Rhodes grinned. "It seems we are a few steps ahead of you Mackenzie. You might not believe it, but the truth is Liu has been working for us for a few years already!"

Mackenzie shook her head in disbelief and then remembered, "Of course Grandpa Will! He is the one who introduced me to her."

Patrick and Rhodes laughed while they nodded.

"Okay, so those are the main points I had to clear with you. Now it's your turn." She smiled.

Hunter looked at Rhodes raising his eyebrows, "Other than wanting to know when you can start, I have nothing. What about you Jim?"

"No, nothing else from me," Rhodes responded. "As soon as we have completed your security checks, we will have to get you to D.C. for a month of orientation, just like Carter did."

"So does that mean we have reached an agreement?" Mackenzie asked.

"Yep, that's all there is to it." Rhodes nodded and extended his hand.

"Welcome aboard Dr. Devereux!" Hunter said, also shaking her hand.

Mackenzie smiled brightly, "Thank you!"

Chapter Forty-Two

YOU'VE NEVER BEEN TO JERUSALEM

Hunter Patrick found it difficult working out the weekly budget for his institute since officially it didn't exist. In the past, secret agencies didn't have such problems. They were handed a lump sum of money, and in return, gave the patron the information they needed or results they wanted. The money vanished into a black hole and, if the results and information were good, the spy agency would get more funds the next time. In such a manner, secret intelligence gathering agencies found their budgets and the employee roster expanded quickly. If, however, the information and results were bad, they found themselves curtailed, and a new agency would come into being. In such a fashion, the OSS had given way to the CIA when the cowboy phase and prep school atmosphere of the Second World War replaced the need to become professional.

The institute found itself in the peculiar situation where its activities more often than not, produced nothing of value. Its adversaries on Capitol Hill, who did know it existed, compared A-Echelon to the boy who went around snapping his fingers every day until someone asked him why he did it. He told them it kept the monsters away. When informed there were no monsters, he offered this as proof that his method worked.

A-Echelon existed because, when the institute did produce something of value, it was revolutionary. A budget crisis in Congress a few years ago didn't happen because of a vast influx of cash into the federal budget from unknown sources. At the time, government critics accused the Federal Reserve of playing with the gold supply in Fort Knox to manipulate the budget, but what they didn't know was that A-Echelon had discovered a massive amount of gold bullion stashed in the Southwest. The horde was unknown for centuries until an A-Echelon researcher found the location by examining a map in Catalan from some conquistador centuries ago.

Another text, translated 20 years ago, gave the institute credence when they found an anti-radar coating for aircraft. An Italian alchemist working on an ointment to give its user invisibility found something extraordinary. He managed to write down the formula in his notebook in a secret code no one had ever cracked until a genius mathematician, working for A-Echelon, found the key. Legend had it that the alchemist vanished into history and, some said, with the contents of a duke's treasure room. The notebook, seized when the duke's troops raided the alchemist's lab, ended up in the ducal library, but the duke's daughter vanished with the alchemist. The author of the notebook found out there were things more useful than the discovery of turning base matter into gold.

Rhodes told Mackenzie these stories as he took her on a tour of the A-Echelon offices, housed inside the Smithsonian in Washington, D.C.

He took her through a back door, badly in need of a coat of paint. Once past the musty museum, Mackenzie found herself in a carpeted hallway that led to a suite of offices. People roamed past her with bound copies of books and ancient artifacts held carefully in hands wearing cotton gloves.

This royal tour of the facilities, led by Rhodes, was the first step in her month-long orientation course. Her orientation course was structured very different from Carters. Although it included some self-defense and weapons training, her course was designed for someone who would be working as an A-Echelon researcher with very little requirement to go out in the field, like Carter would have to do.

At the end of the course, she and her handler, Irene O'Connell, met with Director Patrick, the same as Carter had to do at the completion of his orientation course.

Patrick had Mackenzie's results in front of him and looked at her where she sat opposite him, with Irene on her left. He smiled broadly. "I thought Carter was the brightest candidate we have ever seen in this place, but I think he has some serious competition now. You did very well Mackenzie. I'm impressed."

"Thank you, Hunter. I enjoyed it very much." She smiled.

For the next hour, the three of them discussed the logistics and administration of her project. After reaching an agreement, the meeting adjourned and Mackenzie picked up some documents from Irene before making her way to the airport to fly back to Boston.

"So how long have you worked for the Institute?" Mackenzie asked Liu when they had lunch together the following week. "I requested they hire you on as a translator and was informed you've been one of them for a long time."

"About seven years," she laughed. "Will got me in."

"I was surprised when I heard about your involvement but also very happy," Mackenzie said.

"So was I when they told me you were coming onboard," Liu told her. "You'll have access to libraries the Vatican doesn't even know about. The Institute has a listing of every single obscure book in the country and all the private collections that interest them. I don't think even I have any idea what information they have available at their fingertips. Come to think of it, I don't think there is one single person in A-Echelon that knows."

"It sounds like we are going to have a lot of fun with all these new resources becoming available."

"Oh, I can assure you of that. You will lay eyes on information that will go beyond your wildest dreams. Some of it might be scary, I warn you, but for most of the time, you are going to have a ball."

Mackenzie's parents were excited and very helpful when they heard the family would be returning to Boston. Her mother was elated when Mackenzie asked her to help take care of Liam for those times when she had to be in Washington. Liam was their first and only grandchild, and they wouldn't pass up any opportunity to see and spoil him.

After returning to Boston, Carter, Mackenzie, and Liam took frequent walks in one of the parks near their home.

Liam enjoyed running around and playing with his newfound love, a three-month-old puppy named Jeha, a Cavoodle - a cross between a King Charles Cavalier Spaniel and a miniature Poodle. The two of them were inseparable. Jeha even slept with him on his bed at night. She was a birthday present from his grandparents soon after they returned from Freydis. Of course, Steven and Mary checked with Carter and Mackenzie first to be sure that they would be okay with having a dog in the house.

"So what plans do you have for the upcoming months?" Mackenzie asked Carter.

Now that she was also part of A-Echelon, it was possible for them to exchange information on their work.

"I've got a lot of traveling coming up soon," he exhaled. "And I'm not looking forward to being away from you and Liam, but there are just so many places where those nukes could be. Working on the assumption that we are not the only ones looking for them, we, unfortunately, don't have time on our side."

Carter didn't tell her he was worried about the contents of a CIA report shown to him by Rhodes. A ground penetrating radar satellite image picked up abnormal radiation from a location inside Syria. The CIA was being their usual tight-mouthed selves about the specifics – telling Rhodes that they would investigate further and keep him in the loop. They had been sitting on the information for weeks already.

Carter didn't hold out much hope for a quick answer from them. The importance of information sharing between security agencies was still being paid lip service only. Despite foreign and local terrorism threats, every one of them still protected their own little information empires as if their personal lives depended on it rather than all the lives of the very people they were supposed to be protecting. With the civil war raging in Syria, there was nothing that A-Echelon could do but wait. They also hoped the CIA understood the importance of the matter, and would give it the proper priority.

"I take it that whenever the need arises for me to travel incognito, abroad or domestic, A-Echelon will take care of the necessary ID documents?"

"You really are into this 'cloak and dagger' stuff aren't you!" Carter laughed.

Mackenzie gave him a playful kick on his butt.

"Don't worry, they will get you whatever documentation you need," he told her. "We work closely with selected people at the CIA at times, and they can create some bizarre, but possible scenarios to get you where you need to be. Remember, these are the guys who created a fake film studio just to rescue some embassy employees during the Iranian Hostage Crisis in 1979."

"So if I need to be a member of the National Archives ..."

"They'll find a way to make you all the credentials you need. One word and you'll be anyone you need to become. I haven't needed their I.D. cover services yet, but I'm sure they could turn you into a Carmelite nun if you needed to become one."

"Somehow this doesn't make me feel a whole lot better, but whatever it takes to get the job done I guess."

"You've never been to Jerusalem. Would you like to see it?" Carter asked.

"I would definitely love to see it."

"I'm thinking about meeting up with you and Liam there at the end of this big survey tour. I thought maybe we could spend a few days in Jerusalem and then take a nice one-month Mediterranean cruise before we come back."

"Oh yes, that would be nice! But isn't Jerusalem a risky place to visit?"

"It's been quiet the past year. I'm not too worried about it. Things do flare up from time to time, but you shouldn't let that keep you from seeing what most people believe to be one of the most historically significant places on Earth."

"That's going to be a very pleasant holiday." She winked at him with a 'you-just-wait-and-see' smile on her beautiful face.

Chapter Forty-Three

WHERE WOULD IT ALL END?

It was almost midday in northern India when the passenger jet touched down. Chandigarh International Airport in Punjab was very busy, and Carter and Rhodes watched fighter jets lift off on training exercises on the adjacent runway as their plane taxied up to the airport terminal. The airport handled many commercial flights, although it was also part of an Indian Air Force base. The military in India had no issues with the civilian sector using their runways. However, judging by the number of uniformed personnel around the terminal, there could be no doubt as to who ran the show at the airport.

Two porters offered their services as Carter and Rhodes left the terminal after clearing customs, but Rhodes already had a flight and transportation lined up with the Indian Air Force. He'd arranged it through the Indian embassy in Washington.

A secret GPR – ground penetrating radar – satellite controlled by the CIA produced some very intriguing anomalies at a location in Northern India. It was of interest to

Carter for many reasons. Most important was that the GPR data, rendered as 3-D images by special geological survey software, showed multiple layers of structures more than 50 feet below the surface. From what they could figure out from the pictures, there were, at least, two layers, and possibly a third. The only way to get better information was to visit the site and undertake some ground based GPR surveys. It was of some concern that the site was in very close proximity to an unstable border with Pakistan.

On closer scrutiny of the images, maps, and other information, Carter and Rhodes learned that an archeological dig under the direction of Professor Chandra Pillay, an archeologist lecturing at Guru Jambheshwar University, was already established.

Carter found pictures of some of the artifacts that Professor Pillay had put online and saw that some of them were modeled out of Trinitite. The satellite radar images also showed that Pillay's crew was just scratching the surface. There were structures more than 50 feet below the levels where Pillay's crew was digging, and he was, no doubt, unaware of what was going on deeper down.

Carter contacted Professor Pillay and told him about the interesting anomalies he found on the radar images and asked for permission to visit the site, and to be able to explore and map it out in detail.

Pillay was delighted to oblige, especially after he heard about the financial contribution he would get for his research project if he were willing to let Carter and an associate spend some time on his dig. Of course, Carter and his associate could work on their own as long as they would share their findings with him when they were done.

Carter and James hadn't been waiting more than a few minutes when a military vehicle from the nearby base pulled up in front of them. A uniformed orderly stepped out and held the door open for them, informing them that their flight would be leaving in the next 30 minutes. They placed their luggage in the trunk; then they were quickly taken to the military section of the airport.

A Chetak helicopter was waiting on the tarmac outside a large hangar. It was an older model, one of the many aging helicopters in the Indian Air Force fleet. Carter and Rhodes weren't overly worried. Although it was not exactly a Black Hawk or Apache, the Chetaks still had a very good reputation as a reliable mode of air transport.

"I take it you are Professors Blackmore and Hayden?" the Indian pilot asked in perfect but accented English.

Both men had to suppress a smile - Carter, because of his name change to Blackmore, and Rhodes for acquiring a professorship. They pulled out their passports and showed them to the man who nodded and handed them back.

"I'm Captain Singh. I'll fly you to the archeological site near the border. Your equipment arrived yesterday and is in a crate behind your seats. I hope you're used to the heat, professors, it is very dry and very hot where you are going."

They both nodded as Rhodes commented, "So I've heard. Can't say I'm looking forward to that part of our excursion."

They strapped themselves in for the flight. The officer told them over their headphones about the uneasy peace, which existed between Pakistan and India. Both countries, and what would become Bangladesh, were formed out of the dissolution of the British Empire in the 1940's. At that time, Hindus set up their state in India and Muslims established themselves in Pakistan. Bangladesh was originally part of Pakistan but went its own way in 1971 after a bloody war that pulled India into the conflict. The main reason for the ongoing animosity between the two countries was Pakistan's claim to the province of Kashmir, which India controlled.

Carter and Rhodes looked out the windows at the desolate land below, hot and dry, peppered with many small rivers and farms. Carter could not help but compare what he saw below with the natural beauty of Freydis – there was no comparison. Now and then, they would spot a packed train making its way across the land.

Rhodes took his headphones off and motioned to Carter to do the same. He leaned over and, relying on the noise of the engine and the fact that the pilot had his earphones on, murmured, "I saw at the terminal we've already picked up a tail."

Carter looked at him in surprise. "Really. So soon?"

"Yep, saw two guys taking photos of us on their cellphones."

"Should we be worried?" Carter asked.

Rhodes shook his head. "No, I don't think so. I think the photographers were just confirming and reporting our arrival. We're going to a very remote and strictly controlled area, so I think we'll be okay while we're there - unless they start shooting at each other across the border. However, we can never be too careful. Let's keep our eyes and ears open when we get to the other side."

Carter nodded. He had received a bit of surveillance and counter-surveillance training during his orientation month at A-Echelon, but it was nothing compared to the skills of an experienced ex-CIA field operative such as Rhodes. He would have to stay close to Rhodes and get his mind into paranoid mode very quickly. It wouldn't hurt to be vigilant.

The helicopter soared over fields of mustard and wheat,

and a few hours later, they watched the ground rise up at them as the helicopter began its descent. It was with relief they felt the bump when the chopper made contact with Mother Earth.

"Be quick!" the pilot yelled from the front of the chopper. "They don't get too many helicopter landings around here, and I don't want them to rush in." He was pointing at the crowd of children and adults a few hundred yards away.

While the blades kept spinning, Rhodes and Carter grabbed their luggage and the crate of equipment and jumped out. It would only take one of the people in the crowd to decide to try to get a ride in the chopper and a wholescale charge on the helicopter would follow.

Luckily, two of the archeological students were waiting for them and quickly helped them take their equipment and luggage over to a nearby Land Rover.

Rhodes gave the pilot a thumbs-up and his lips formed the words 'thank you very much.' The pilot returned the thumbs-up. Seconds later the helicopter rose into the sky and headed out. The crowd cheered and waved as it soared up and away.

Carter looked around. In these hills, time moved at a different pace than in the city. People planned and lived their lives in accordance with the harvest seasons and how many children they planned to have. They were extremely poor. It was a hard way to live, which is why the best and brightest traveled to the cities for work and never came back. It had been this way in India for more than two centuries, and modern transportation only accelerated the depopulation of the rural areas.

The ancient settlement had been uncovered a few years ago, and Professor Pillay and 12 students were in the process of mapping it out and excavating certain areas.

Carter watched them at work for a moment and then left the Land Rover. He looked up to see a man he recognized walking toward them slowly.

Professor Pillay wore light cotton clothes, a pair of leather gloves, a cap on his head, and sunglasses to cut back on the glare to his eyes.

"Professor Blackmore!" he called out. "Welcome to India and to my site."

"Good afternoon, and thanks for having us. Please call me John."

"Good, John. Please call me Chandra."

"I take it this is your associate, Professor Hayden, who you told me about?"

Rhodes had to suppress a smile for a second time. He had used many different aliases and titles on his travels over the years, but 'professor' had never been one of them. He did his best to portray an academic as he imagined one would look and act.

They shook hands, and the three of them walked to the tents where they would be staying for the next two weeks. Pillay made sure it was as comfortable as he could afford, scraping together sleeping cots and furniture out of the meager furnishing available.

It was almost dark, so he suggested they unpack their stuff, take a shower and then join him in the mess tent for a few beers and dinner. They would start their work the following morning.

During happy hour, dinner, and for the duration of their stay, Carter and Rhodes made sure that they never let Professor Pillay know the real purpose of their visit. They showed a lot of interest in his work and flooded him with many questions and praises, which kept him talking for most of the time they were together. Professor Pillay enjoyed their company, although he still felt he had to do a sales pitch to secure more funding for his project.

"How was the city discovered?" Carter asked Chandra and took a sip of his beer.

"A local farmer found it," Professor Pillay explained. "His plow hit something as he was plowing a new furrow in the wheat field. It was a clay jar with bronze artifacts in it. He took it to the local government office, believing he might be able to sell it, or, at least, claim a reward.

I came out here two years ago and did the initial work. From what I found, I was able to convince the government to buy the land from the farmer, who is now living comfortably with his extended family near Mumbai."

By sunrise the next morning, the three of them were out on the dig where Pillay gave them a tour with running commentary.

The university paid a few of the local farmers to help with the excavations, but the students with their notebooks and trowels carried out the bulk of it. Carter bent down and looked at the mud bricks beneath the dry earth they were removing.

The complex uncovered by the students was impressive. They could walk between buildings lost millennia ago and get an idea of the grandeur of the place as it once was. Chandra showed them some of the artifacts and more buildings. Carter and Rhodes carefully studied the Trinitite artifacts and questioned Pillay about the places where they were found.

"I'm sure this is not as impressive as the city in the desert you visited," Pillay said. "Still, there is much to be learned here. This may be the oldest permanent human settlement we've ever found in India."

"Every site has its own magic and character," Carter

replied as he looked over the ruins. "Archeological sites are like women. Every one of them possesses some form of beauty and intrigue, and it's unfair to compare them."

They all exploded in laughter. "I will remember that one!" Pillay said.

As they crossed the field to a new and recently opened location, Rhodes noted two men about 150 yards away, aiming cameras at them. He touched Carter's arm and whispered, "three o'clock, two men with cameras."

Carter didn't look immediately. He took a few more paces, stopped and turned around slowly as if he was taking in the surrounding landscape. He saw the two men and memorized their features and clothes as best he could from that distance.

They wore simple clothes and carried rakes. They looked like farmers, obviously of lower caste. The cameras were totally out of sync with their general appearance. *A real oopart* Carter thought. He found it strange that the two men didn't try to hide the fact they were photographing them. Either they were simply stupid, or they were sending them a message – *take note, you are being watched.* Either way, there was no doubt someone was interested in their visit to the site, and most likely, their activities. Carter's mind filled with many questions: who, why, how? But he could not discuss it with Rhodes, as Pillay was close by.

It was midday when Pillay finally completed the tour and stopped talking. For now, he had nothing more he wanted to show, or tell, them. He asked if it was okay for him to leave them on their own so that he could get back to his work and his crew. They assured him they would be fine, and he let them know they were welcome to wander around and investigate anything they wanted.

While Carter and Rhodes appreciated the information

from the tour, they felt it had gone on for far too long and were glad to have time on their own. It was a relief to be free from the constant stream of information flowing from their host. Finally, they were able to discuss the more important aspects of their visit to the site.

They walked over to a quiet spot and sat down on one of the ancient stone walls. Carter first wanted to talk about their uninvited camera crew first.

"Don't worry about them. They were just there to let us know they were watching us. Maybe to scare us, I would guess," Rhodes explained.

"Okay, I'll accept your advice, but on whose orders are they watching us? Who the hell knew we were coming here? According to my calculations, there is only a handful that knew about our trip."

"Hold your horses; don't let your imagination run away with you," Rhodes smiled. "There is a good chance those guys are working for artifact collectors. They could very well be just the 'unofficial guards' tasked to make sure their boss stays in the know regarding anyone coming and going at this site."

"I have to confess, since yesterday I've become a bit paranoid. Professor Hayden, this whole thing of traveling with fake ID's and being photographed every time I show my face outside has me a little nervous."

"Yeah, I can understand that, it's your first time. But, if there were more ominous forces at work, I would have expected those guys with the cameras to at least try to hide their activities from us. Nonetheless, it's a good idea never to take anything at face value. It's always wise to be a little paranoid and a little nervous when you're in the field."

"What about those two back at the airport yesterday?"

"Military. The short hair and disciplined demeanor gave

them away. Remember it's a military base, and they want to know who is coming and going."

"I would have thought they would be a bit more inconspicuous about that, such as using hidden surveillance cameras."

"Make no mistake, there were surveillance cameras as well, but having a few guys out there for everyone to see sends a message – *you are being watched ... don't try anything stupid.*"

Carter nodded. "Good point. Let's go back to that new trench Chandra showed us this morning. I saw a few things there I'd like to have a closer look at." They stood and walked over to the trench.

Carter took out the maps and satellite radar images to pinpoint the areas of interest on the ground. After they located them and marked the borders with flags, they took their Geiger counters and checked the area for any sign of radiation. When they were sure there was no radiation hazard, they assembled a small one-man-operated, but very sophisticated, GPR system with which they could scan and map the area up to 100 feet below the surface.

The GPR device produced much better images than the satellite GPR did, but it was slow and painstaking work. The data had to be transferred from the little GPR to a computer, and then converted and rendered as 3-D images. They had to scan the area layer by layer a few feet at a time. Every few hours they stopped and transferred the data to the laptop. The laptop could do some of the data conversions and give them some information, but it was not powerful enough to give them the high-quality 3-D images they wanted.

Rhodes uploaded the day's data every night via the secure satellite link to the A-Echelon offices where specialists, using powerful equipment and state of the art software, rendered the data as high-resolution 3-D images and sent it back to them. His daily data uploads were also accompanied by an encrypted progress and status report to Hunter Patrick.

As the first week came to an end, Carter and Rhodes were able to see that there were clearly three different layers of ruins on top of each other. "This is something that has happened all over the world in the past," Carter explained. "Cities were destroyed and abandoned, and hundreds of years later, people returned to build on top of the ruins of the previous city. I have seen a few places with three layers of cities constructed on top of each other over thousands of years."

"So I guess the million-dollar question is, how old are each of these cities below our feet?" Rhodes asked.

"Chandra told me the part he has been working on has been estimated to be between 8,000 and 10,000 years," Carter replied. "What lies below this layer and how old it could be is anybody's guess at this stage. One thing is for sure, the next two layers will be even older, but we will have to dig down to find out how much older."

"That's going to present us with a few hairy scenarios," Rhodes said under his breath.

Carter frowned. "What are you thinking?"

"If we were to start digging here, we need manpower and equipment. The moment we bring those in from outside, we will have to protect the site to make sure no one else gets near it. We can't use the locals, as we already know they are probably all on the payroll of the illicit artifact merchants. We can't ask the Indian military for help as we are two miles from the Pakistani border, and if a lot of soldiers turn up here all of a sudden, we might start a nasty incident with some gun-toting, trigger-happy idiots running around. They have hated each other so much and for so long it wouldn't take much for them to start pushing buttons which would launch a few nuclear missiles. If your theories about the past are correct, that's exactly what people in these parts of the world have been doing in their past for many thousands of years. We want to make sure we don't repeat the mistakes of the past."

"Mhh, we have a bit of a dilemma. I guess eventually we'll have to kick this up the chain to the President," Carter responded. "He can negotiate with the leaders of Pakistan and India on our behalf."

Rhodes agreed. "Let's continue our survey work from above the ground, dig no holes, make sure we get every bit of data we need, and then move on to Egypt and Turkey. When we have all our data, we can go back and discuss our options with Hunter and, if necessary, the President."

"Okay, I'm in agreement." Carter shook his head. "To tell you the truth I am itching to start digging a few deep trenches right now. But," he hesitated for a few moments, "I guess not if it is going to start a nuclear war."

"Yeah, I have been trying to avoid those my whole life," Rhodes deadpanned. "The next two weeks we will have to come up with a plan of what we are going to share with Chandra before we leave. I'm sure we won't be able to show him everything. On the other hand, we will have to give him some information to keep his loyalty."

Carter nodded.

He spoke to Mackenzie and Liam on Skype every night, but as agreed, they kept the conversations to the personal and family level, and any details about their research work were kept off the agenda.

One morning, two days before they were scheduled to

leave, Carter was up early, studying the 3-D images that came in overnight. "Jimmy boy wake up!" he shouted to his tent mate. "Get your carcass over here. You gotta to see this."

Rhodes was sitting up trying to rub the sleep out of his eyes. "What the hell — it's five o'clock man. Go back to bed. It's in the middle of the night."

"Get your lazy butt over here and have a look at this." Carter insisted.

"Ah, shit; okay then," he growled. "But my eyes won't see and my brain won't fire on all cylinders until I get coffee into my body."

"I will make you coffee, but when I get back here you better be seated in this chair right here," Carter pointed to the seat next to his in front of the laptop on the table. "Be warned, I'm bringing a glass of cold water with me."

Carter returned with two mugs of coffee and found Rhodes sitting in the chair as ordered. However, it looked as if he was sleeping again — his head was nodding. Carter kicked the leg of the chair. "Wake up Professor Hayden! Thy humble servant has brought thee coffee."

Rhodes almost fell off the chair. "Devereux, this better be good. There are very few things in life that I rank higher than my uninterrupted sleep."

"Look at these dark parts here on this image," Carter pointed to the area of interest. "Keep that in your mind, and now look at these images." Carter slowly flipped through four more images for Rhodes to study.

"Same area but much more detail and much clearer than the first one," he mumbled. "Am I looking at a flight of stairs going down below from the third layer, or do I need more coffee?"

Carter started laughing, "Coffee definitely kick-starts

your brain. Yes, that's exactly what that is - stairs going down. We will have to go back to those coordinates and set the GPR to its maximum to see how far down they go. The top end of the stairs is 50 feet below ground. The GPR can do another 50 feet. Depending on how compact the soil below is, we might get lucky and see another 20 or so feet deeper."

"Well, I would certainly like to know what is at the bottom of those stairs."

"So would I," Carter concurred. "We could be looking at yet another city, in other words, a fourth layer." He opened a few of the topographical maps and stared at them. "We will have to get a geological survey done. I suspect this area has seen a few big land shifts over the ages, which could be what has covered the cities in the layers we have detected."

"So other than trying to get down as deep as we can below ground with the equipment we have, there is not much more we can do?" Rhodes inquired.

"Yes, and then we will have to come back or send a team with better equipment to get to the bottom of it," Carter replied. "I suggest we talk to Chandra and tell him we found more layers and that we would like to bring in better equipment and maybe more people."

"You think he will agree to that?" Rhodes asked, lifting his eyebrows.

"I am sure he will agree if we tell him about the three layers we already discovered," Carter replied with a devious smile. "And when he hears about the additional funding you will give him, he will definitely be amicable."

"We are going to give him more money? When did ..." Rhodes looked up in surprise and saw the smile on Carter's face. "I guess you're right. It might be a small price to pay."

That night during their usual happy hour and dinner, Carter and Rhodes informed Pillay about the discovery of the second and third layers. They had decided not to say a word about the stairs and the potential fourth layer. Pillay was ecstatic, and when Rhodes offered more funding, he immediately agreed to their proposals.

"You've done a great job here Chandra, especially when taking into account the limited funding and resources available. Hopefully, things will now gain more momentum when you get the additional funding," Carter told him the next day as they waited for the helicopter to arrive. "I don't think anyone could have done better."

"Thank you, John," Chandra told him. "I know it's not impressive to look at right now, but we feel it will be a major site in a few years. We just need to put the time into documenting the work we've done."

And pray another border war doesn't erupt, Carter thought. Conflict had done more to destroy archeological sites than anything else in history had. During a war, no one cared about the ancient significance of anything. If it stood in the way of reaching the target, it was destroyed. For the Taliban and ISIS, the chosen target was based on religious reasons.

As they left the dig site, Carter looked across the border and saw the Pakistan military conducting training exercises. Would this part of the world always be under a perpetual threat of nuclear annihilation? Where would it all end?

Chapter Forty-Four

BOOKS OF THE ELDERS OF MEDICINE

Mackenzie stopped to look at the impressive castle-like building in front of her on Constitution Avenue. It was her first day of a planned three-day trip to do some research. She, Carter and Liam had a long Skype session the night before - the day after he and Rhodes arrived at the dig in Northern India. This morning, Liam and Jeha, the Cavoodle, had gone to stay with her parents for the few days while she would be in Washington. She was happy, her family was all safe and sound, and she looked forward to entering the secret underground vaults of the Smithsonian in front of her for the first time. Not many people knew about the vaults, and even less ever got the opportunity to set foot inside them.

There was only one way to get to the A-Echelon offices. You had to pass through the museum to the secure door in the rear, and then use a special swipe card to enter through the door. On the other side, there was a small reception area and a guard who would only allow people he knew past his checkpoint, swipe card or not. It was the first time he'd met Mackenzie, so she had to tell him that she worked with Irene O'Connell, who he phoned to come and fetch her in the waiting room.

Irene turned up shortly after, and the guard showed Mackenzie to the scanning area, which everyone at the institute called 'The Airlock.' She had to step into the vestibule and place her briefcase on a conveyor belt, similar to the ones used by airport security. It traveled through a sequence of scanning devices that made sure nothing harmful or unauthorized entered or left the institute. Finally, she had to step through a body scanner.

It only took a few minutes, and she understood the need for all the security. The institute housed plenty of valuable manuscripts, which were irreplaceable. Furthermore, many things in the institute vault should never see the light of day.

Irene stood on the other side of the Airlock waiting for her.

"Welcome to the cave, Mackenzie." She smiled as she handed Mackenzie a badge she had to wear at all times while inside the A-Echelon area. The badge activated as she pinned it on her blouse. It tracked her every movement until she left the premises and handed the badge back to security.

Mackenzie liked Irene. She was always nice and kind to her and very helpful. She was a slender woman in her mid-forties, married with two children, and had shoulder-length auburn hair she always kept in a ponytail. She had a Ph.D. in Human Biology and was an employee of DARPA on special assignment with A-Echelon to assist Mackenzie with the respirocyte research.

Mackenzie suspected Irene had worked for one of the government security agencies in the past - CIA or FBI.

She'd never ask, though. Irene would tell her if she needed to know.

Irene smiled. "It's exciting to finally have you here and, hopefully, raring to go with this project."

"Thanks for the welcome Irene, and yes, I doubt you can even begin to imagine how excited I am."

"That's good to hear. Okay, how about we grab something to drink in the kitchen and then go to my office. I've lined up a meeting with some very clever people whom I think will be of great help to us."

With their hot drinks in hand, they walked to Irene's office where she told Mackenzie about the two DARPA medical nanotech scientists they would be meeting with at ten.

Mackenzie frowned. *DARPA? That means the military is thinking respirocytes could play a role in warfare.* This research of hers had certainly stirred up interest in strange and unexpected places.

Irene laughed when she saw the worried look on Mackenzie's face after she ended her narrative of the two scientists' background. "Don't worry Mackenzie, when I told them about you, they already knew all about your work at the university and are thrilled for the chance to meet with you. You know a lot more about the subject than they do."

At ten, the four of them gathered in a secured meeting room, safe from any eavesdropping.

Irene introduced the DARPA scientists, Dr. Cate Nelson, and Dr. Scott Watson, and once seated, they agreed to do away with formalities and call each other by their first names.

The first 40 minutes or so of the meeting consisted of exchanging information about their various work projects. Cate explained that DARPA didn't have an active respirocyte program but that they were eagerly following the research of universities and pharmaceutical companies on that front.

Mackenzie had to ask, "I take it your interest is because you have some military use for the technology?"

"Indeed," Cate replied. "On the battlefield, if wounded soldiers could be treated with this, it would save many lives and prevent many injuries from becoming crippling afterward."

"In other words," Mackenzie smiled, "you are not thinking of constructing cyborgs?"

"That's still a bit too sci-fi for us," Scott laughed. "Our interest is purely medical applications at this stage. I can't say that someone won't try to build a super soldier in the future, but for now, we won't waste time and money on it."

The highly scientific but interesting discussion continued for another two hours. Afterward, the DARPA delegates left promising to give Mackenzie any help she might need, and Irene's promise to share Mackenzie's research with them.

Irene and Mackenzie went back to her office and finalized the schedule. Liu, having been notified of Mackenzie's visit, was already on site, and Irene called her to join them. The three of them made their way down to the vaults where they would be spending most of their time over the next few days.

The room custodian, Mike, looked at their cards when they entered, punched their numbers into his computer to make sure they had the necessary clearance and waved them inside. This vault, one of many, was a special room with controlled temperature and humidity to preserve the delicate contents.

Mike pulled out a pair of cotton gloves from the box on his desk and put them on. He walked through a shadowy room filled with shelves of books and vanished, returning shortly with the documents they requested. As he left to locate another book, Mackenzie noticed the holstered gun on his left side.

The books in this room were not allowed to be removed. She glanced at the titles in the cart next to Mike's station. Most of them were quartos, printed documents folded over and left unbound in a file. Not one of them was in English, at least, no English writing she recognized. They all had tags sticking out of them that indicated where they were supposed to go. Mackenzie noticed the tags were of different colors, which had something to do with their nature. One of them had a red tag, meaning the book was restricted to only those with special permission to see it. She wondered what it contained.

"Here's the book you asked for, Doc," he said. Mackenzie immediately noticed the red tag. He handed her a pair of cotton gloves and waited while she put them on before he would let her touch it.

Once Mackenzie and Liu were settled and happily reading, knowing they had all the help they needed, Irene returned to her office.

Mackenzie and Liu both brought laptops and were busy collecting references, paraphrasing texts, and taking snapshots of pages, which they stored on their laptops for reading and translation. They also kept Mike busy, asking him to do searches to find the referenced material.

By five o'clock, their table was swamped with documents and books. "Organized chaos," Mike observed when he turned up with the latest folio they'd requested.

"Will it be okay with you if we leave everything here, as it is, for the night?" Mackenzie asked, waving her hand over the documents. "We will be back early in the morning to continue and don't want you to have to run around retrieving all of this again."

"Yeah, no problem," Mike shrugged.

Over the next two days, they collected enough information to keep Mackenzie and Liu busy for at least two weeks. Mackenzie stopped by Irene's office late in the afternoon on the third day to give her an update before she returned to Boston.

"Found anything of value down there in the vaults?" Irene asked.

"Oh yes," Mackenzie replied with the excitement clearly noticeable in her voice. "I've gathered enough information to keep me busy for at least the next two weeks. I'm overwhelmed by the sheer volume of information down there."

"Yes, it's tantalizing, isn't it?"

"That's for sure. I wish I could transfer this place to Freydis and sit there for the rest of my life reading everything."

"You won't get through all of it in one lifetime, Mackenzie," Irene laughed.

"I came across two references today about documents kept at the Mesrop Mashtots Institute of Ancient Manuscripts in Armenia, which might be of interest. Do you know someone who might have connections with them? Maybe we can ask them to send us copies of the documents?"

"Armenia you say," Irene paused. "Yerevan ..."

"What was that?" Mackenzie asked, not quite hearing what Irene murmured after her question.

"Yerevan, the capital of Armenia. I can't think of anyone right now but leave it with me; I will find out and let you know."

"I have a vague idea of where Armenia is," Mackenzie

smiled "but that's the extent of my knowledge about the country."

"It's a small country of about three million people, democratic, Christian, and has been around since 2,400 B.C.," Irene rambled off the basic facts. "It's a beautiful place."

"You've been there?" Mackenzie was surprised. "Business or pleasure?"

Irene got a solemn expression on her face. "Business."

Mackenzie wanted to ask more but got the distinct impression Irene was probably not going to be very forthcoming. It just confirmed her suspicions that Irene had worked for the CIA or one of the other secret organizations in the past, or might even still be working for one or more of them.

After they had scheduled their conference call times for the next few weeks, they said their goodbyes and Mackenzie caught a flight back to Boston.

Carter had arranged for them both to be issued secure satellite phones so they could communicate with each other, and with people at A-Echelon. They also both used the secured links to upload their research work through the impenetrable firewall at A-Echelon and onto their servers. None of their laptops carrying their research was ever connected to the internet.

Mackenzie and Carter had a long Skype session that night after she returned home from D.C. Of course, Liam and Jeha joined the first part of the conversation, with Liam insisting that Carter also talk to Jeha because he was sure the little mutt was missing Carter just as much as he did.

Mackenzie told him she had finished most of their travel arrangements for the trip they planned to take when they met in Israel in about five weeks' time. "A Mediterranean boat cruise of discovery just for us." She sounded excited, "Going to all the new places we always wanted to see and taking our time to do it."

"I can't wait for it to start," Carter laughed.

The next day Mackenzie started working through the data she and Liu had collected. Late that afternoon she received a call from Irene letting her know she had made contact with the Mesrop Mashtots Institute of Ancient Manuscripts in Armenia, and that they were happy to help in any way they could. However, she needed to understand that some of the documents could not leave the Institute due to their fragile condition and, in some cases, the documents also required special authorization from certain government agencies.

"Thank you for your help, Irene. I will work on getting you a list of these documents first. I might need to go back to D.C. to finalize that part of the research next week."

"No problem. Just let me know when you want to come in and I'll make the necessary arrangements."

Mackenzie went back to her work and within a few days, had more references to texts held at the Mesrop Mashtots Institute of Ancient Manuscripts. These she added to her list for Irene. The enticing part was that she found various documents written by different authors and at different times referring to the ancient Armenian manuscripts. Unfortunately, she ran into some problems when the translation of some of the texts proved to be beyond Liu's capabilities.

Mackenzie called Irene to arrange for another visit to the vaults and to find out if A-Echelon had access to any ancient language specialists. Irene told her not worry about that; she had a person with the right security clearances who would help. "I sometimes get the impression Harry Auden can speak all languages ever known to man," she chuckled. "I will make sure he is available to help you."

After two days back in Mike's vault, five levels below ground, with the help of Harry Auden, a linguist specializing in ancient languages, Mackenzie made the first significant breakthrough.

Harry was a short, thin, man with silver hair in his mid-sixties. He wore gold-framed glasses, and those in A-Echelon who knew him referred to him as a genius.

"Harry, I think I've found something important here." She had memorized the keywords in this ancient script so she could quickly scan a document and find the words she was looking for. The Latin text in the document in front of her had quite a few of those keywords. "I'll take a picture of the pages and would appreciate it if you could translate it for me."

She handed the camera to him after she took the photos and Harry got busy while she continued searching.

About an hour later, Mackenzie heard strange noises coming from Harry's side of the table. "Mhh ... I see ... aha ... got it, is that what you mean, mhh, okay."

Mackenzie stared at him waiting for him to say something, but she soon realized he was not aware of her staring. To her, it looked as if Harry was in a trance. Then she remembered Irene telling her that Harry had a habit of talking to himself while he was translating and that he should not be disturbed when he does this. Those sounds and mumblings were usually a good sign.

A few more rumblings and mumblings came from Harry, and then he went quiet and started typing.

Mackenzie had to use all her willpower to remain in her seat and not jump up to go over to see what he was typing.

Another tense hour went by with Mackenzie trying to concentrate on reading more but unable to do so in anticipation of Harry's translation. Finally, he rolled over next to her in his office chair and placed his laptop on the table so that she could read the screen.

"That's the first rough translation, but it should give you a good enough idea of what the author tried to say."

Mackenzie started reading, and her heart began to race.

I have learned about a medical procedure used by an ancient people, long before our time, during with which they cured patients who had difficulty with breathing. I have learned that when a patient's breathing becomes difficult, originating from lung dysfunction, airway obstruction, or injury, the problem can be solved by infusing oxygen into the bloodstream. They say that the procedure will prevent heart failure and brain damage.

I undertook a study of this method of treatment to learn how they did it and found some books about it. These books describe how molecules/particles/atoms are surrounded with oxygen before being injected into the patient to supply critical oxygen to the body. I have not been able to find out precisely how it is done.

Due to my illness, I cannot continue, nor do I have enough time to complete, my work on this very important matter. I can only hope that someone will continue and complete the work I started.

The books/library of the Elders of Medicine contains all the specific information on how to perform this procedure and how to make the oxygen molecules/particles/atoms.

Mackenzie did not even read any further. She swung her chair around, barely able to keep herself from leaping from it and dancing with joy, "Mike, can you please call Irene and see if she can come down here right away?" Then she swung back to Harry, grabbed his head, and planted a kiss on his mouth. "You ...are ... a ... genius! You've done it! We've found it!"

Harry was stunned and blushed deeply. It was not everyday that a woman as beautiful as Mackenzie laid a kiss on him. He could feel his heartbeat speed up and his blood pressure increase. He was fumbling around with his hands, not sure what to say or do, so he just sat there displaying a befuddled grin.

Mackenzie's head was still spinning with elation when she said, "The Books of the Elders of Medicine? Wait a minute, I have seen that name a few times lately. Let me get it." She pulled her laptop closer and opened the document where she was storing all the references. "There, I've got it. Three references."

"You have other documents referring to The Books of the Elders of Medicine?" Harry asked still a bit overwhelmed by that kiss. "Does it still exist? Do we, by chance, have it here in the vaults?"

Mackenzie shook her head. "It exists, but it's in the possession of the Mesrop Mashtots Institute of Ancient Manuscripts in Armenia."

"Shit! ... sorry about that," Harry apologized. "Do you think they will allow us to see it?"

"That's for ..." At that moment, Irene walked in, "her to find out," Mackenzie said pointing at Irene.

Irene immediately felt their excitement. "Okay, tell me about it."

Mackenzie didn't say a word. She pulled a chair up for Irene and turned Harry's laptop to face her, pointing to the screen with a shaking hand.

When Irene finished reading, she looked up at Harry

and Mackenzie. "Let me guess. These Books of the Elders of Medicine are in the Mesrop Mashtots Institute of Ancient Manuscripts in Armenia?"

Mackenzie nodded, "Yep."

"Excellent work you two. I will get onto it right away."

Five days later, Mackenzie and Harry were on their way to Yerevan, Armenia. The Institute had confirmed The Books of the Elders of Medicine were in their possession; however, they were so fragile they could not be moved or copied, and that access to them would require permission from the Armenian Minister of Health.

Mackenzie was still wondering how Irene managed to pull it all off in five days. She must have called in the help of quite a few high-ranking officials and politicians in D.C., possibly even the President or Vice President. Nevertheless, they got the necessary permission from the Armenian Minister of Health, and the USA embassy staff was waiting for them in Yerevan.

Mackenzie arranged with Hunter to include a message for Carter in the daily encrypted communications between him and Rhodes. Carter replied that he was very happy and excited for her and hoped she would make a big breakthrough during her trip.

They still communicated via Skype every night, and although it was extremely difficult not to talk about the Armenian trip and Carter's work, they stuck to the agreed security protocol and kept the conversations on the family and personal level.

Armenia was a small and beautiful country, just the way

Irene described it, landlocked, south of Georgia, next to Turkey and tantalizingly close to Mount Ararat.

Mackenzie and Harry stood and looked at the imposing building hosting the Mesrop Mashtots Institute of Ancient Manuscripts. Inside this building, she hoped she would find the elusive bit of knowledge that would open up the world of respirocytes and finally make them available to the world.

Chapter Forty-Five

HE KNEW THEY EXISTED

Cairo, Egypt

Carter and Rhodes landed in Cairo. They were going to spend one day in the capital of Egypt and then two days on the Saad Plateau inspecting the area where a geologist discovered big sheets of solid yellow-green glass in 1932. After that, they would visit the City of Lights for four days. Although no one had found any evidence of a nuclear explosion in that area, Carter felt it could hold the answers to many of their questions.

The final leg of their tour would take them to the ancient town of Çatalhöyük – until recently regarded as the oldest human settlement. Carter's discovery of the buildings under the mountain near Cusco in Peru and the City of Lights in Egypt moved human history back by almost 50,000 years.

In Cairo, Carter's credentials opened many doors, including access to Zahi Hawass, the long-reigning former Egyptian archeologist and Director of Antiquities. Although

Hawass was no longer Director, he still had much influence and access to various parts of the museum. It was for this reason Carter wanted to meet with him.

Hawass was a loud and dynamic man. His grip on Egyptian antiquities was powerful, his knowledge and understanding beyond any others in his field. From Carter's point of view, the museum lost a notable and powerful Director when he was ousted.

Because Carter was well known amongst archeologists in Egypt, he didn't use an alias while they were there, but Rhodes remained a professor of archeology. "So Carter," Hawass challenged him after they shook hands, "What is it you wish to see and ask me about?" It was clear Hawass was used to leading, ruling and having the last word.

Carter looked at Hawass for a moment, summing him up, before he said, "What I wish to see is the pectoral found in 1998 in Tutankhamen's tomb. I believe the scarab is carved from Libyan Desert Glass, and I wish to have a close look at it."

Hawass stared at him, grinned, took his hat off, dusted it on his trouser leg and replaced it. "Maybe we find a quiet place for coffee and talk, eh?"

"That sounds like a good idea."

Later Carter held the pectoral in his hand and looked carefully at the scarab made of Libyan Desert Glass. The carving was perfect in every way. The light that glowed from the glass gave it a mysterious shine. "How old do you reckon this is?"

"Hard to date it, except to say it was found in Tutankhamun's tomb and, therefore, is considered to have been made by craftsmen from that era. However, now that we know the scarab is Libyan Desert glass, it's possible it was carved many years before. It has been said to be older than Egyptian history." Hawass shrugged expressively "We can only guess."

Carter nodded and handed it back.

Saad Plateau, Libya

The next day Carter and Rhodes flew from Cairo to Tripoli in Libya. From there they chartered a flight to the Saad Plateau where they were finally able to walk across the ground and feel the crunching slivers of glass under their boots.

In 1932, geologist Patrick Clayton discovered pieces of incredibly clear, yellow-green glass among the black charred rocks of the desert floor while walking through the area. He was mystified by it but it wasn't until many years later, while visiting Alamogordo's White Sands missile range, that he saw the chunks of similar glass left by nuclear tests and realized what he'd found on the Saad Plateau was the same.

It was an eerie experience walking across the glass and wondering about it. Alone in the vast expanse of the desert with the plane some distance behind the hills, Carter experienced a sense of the enormity of the event that created this haunting wasteland.

The sound of the glass crackling as they wandered around was eerie. Wherever he looked, Carter could see pieces of the stuff that were big enough to trip over. When he picked up a sample and held it to the sun, it gave off a translucent sheen and was so pure he could see tiny bubbles of air within.

They collected a few more samples and found a nice comfortable outcrop of rock where they sat down to look around and talk.

"What happened here?" Rhodes inquired. "Did mankind have some hand in this?"

Carter was quiet for a while. *Was this before or after the City of Lights? Obviously, it hadn't affected the city. Maybe it's too far away? Were there no other explosions? Why here? Was it a test site?* Carter had read all the available information on the glass. There were anomalies here that drew him towards considering a nuclear explosion.

"I'm not sure Jim. Everyone is still guessing," he explained. "At first, some people thought the glass dated back 19 million years, but if that is the case, then it could not have originated in the Sahara because the sand of the desert is no more than one million years old."

Rhodes looked around, "Could it have been caused by a meteor impact?"

"I think we can rule that out," Carter said. "The glass is a form of tektite which would indicate it was not formed by a meteorite strike. Compare this area with the meteor impact site that created the Kebira Crater in Egypt's Western desert millions of years ago. That impact created the biggest crater on the planet, larger than the Meteor Crater in Arizona. Here there is no crater - no impact center. Everything is flat for many miles around us."

Time passed as they sat taking in the silent emptiness. Once there'd been a sea here, with marine life, where people lived, fished, and swam near the shores. They knew this by the cave paintings found nearby and the geology of the area that spoke of the sea waves carving their way into the cliff faces. Once there had been life in abundance here, now there was only desert, and the ever-present sand dunes to be seen across the land.

The next day as they left, Rhodes looked down from the window of the plane and turned to Carter. "It's a relief to be leaving this place. I have no doubt it is thousands of years old, but it gives me the creeps."

City of Lights, Egypt

On their arrival at the City of Lights, they found the expedition leader was none other than Daan Hannah, a professor at Alexandria International University and father of Sameha Hannah. She had been the cartographer and photographer who was part of Carter's team when they did the first site survey on behalf of the Egyptian government.

Daan was pleased to see Carter. He owed him a lot of gratitude for selecting his daughter for that first expedition. The work she did under Carter on that trip assured her a permanent position on the current team. Daan spared nothing in his display of hospitality. He did everything in his power to ensure Carter and Professor Hayden were treated like royalty at all times. Rhodes commented after a while, "The only things missing are the red carpet and the harem of belly dancers!"

Carter chuckled; however, he was disappointed with the progress made since the initial survey. It was obvious the project was underfunded, poorly equipped, and understaffed, with only about 20 people on the team. The area was under the protection of the Egyptian military, which was patrolling the perimeters, which were set at about a mile around the area.

Daan showed them the GPR maps and shared every bit of information he had collected. Unfortunately, it was not much more than Carter already knew. "The problem is," he explained, "our GPR equipment is old and unreliable. We can't see more than a few feet below the surface, and we don't have enough people. If we could just get more funding, we could learn so much from this place."

Carter felt sorry for him and quietly resolved to have a word with Rhodes to see if some strings could be pulled to get proper funding and impetus going. He agreed with Daan – there was a lot to be gained from this site. It was depressing to see the lack of interest in a discovery as significant as this.

After their orientation, Daan gave Carter the 'freedom of the city' allowing him to take Professor Hayden on a full tour through the entire area and beyond if he so wished. He told them they were welcome to use their own equipment and do as much surveying as they wished – of course, with the proviso they had to share it with him before they left.

Rhodes was dumbfounded as he walked through the ancient city. If he had any remaining doubts about Carter's notions of the existence of antediluvian advanced lost civilizations and giants, it disappeared within the first hour of the tour. He didn't need any more convincing; he was sure Carter was right.

However, as illuminating as that realization was, it immediately moved the entire ancient nuclear threat to center stage in his mind. With the realization that the people who once occupied this city were probably one of Carter's advanced lost civilizations, Rhodes recognized that they probably had the proficiency to build nuclear weapons, which increased the possibility that those weapons or their blueprints were just waiting to be discovered by someone. It was a thought that made Rhodes shudder.

After their four-hour tour, they sat down in one of the tents and started to study the information provided by Daan.

There was still no acceptable answer for the power

source of the city's electricity. Speculation was rife among those who examined the silver disks, although they agreed the disks acted as receivers. They also agreed that electricity was transferred wirelessly from the disks to the lights and other electrical appliances, but the technology and the source of the power to the disks still begged for a plausible explanation.

It was astonishing to them that many scientists still didn't want to hear anything about the City of Lights. The lightbulb had been 'invented' by Edison in 1880, and that was as far back as they would allow their minds to go. To those people, the City of Lights was a myth - dating it back 50,000 years was a bedtime story to be told to small children, not well-educated scientists.

Carter and Rhodes, however, kept open minds to all arguments and concluded the most likely answer for the source of the electricity remained the magnetosphere. Tesla proved the existence of this unlimited source of free electricity in the atmosphere around the earth, even demonstrated how it could be tapped. They couldn't help but wonder if it was also the source of energy used by the ancients to set off a fusion bomb.

Another quiet observation they made was the total absence of written information anywhere in the city. There were no inscriptions on the walls, no clay tablets, no papyrus, copper, or golden scrolls. There were no written records whatsoever. There was no doubt that the inhabitants were technologically and socially advanced, and it was highly unlikely they'd never had a written language - so where were the records of themselves they'd left behind?

When they were alone, Carter mentioned this to Rhodes. "Jim, do you also find it strange that these giants didn't leave us a library? In fact, they didn't leave us one single word."

"Yeah, the thought crossed my mind. It is just as mystifying as the question about what happened to them. Where did they go? No graves, not one single body, not even one human bone thus far." He shook his head. "Do you have any theories how that could be?"

"I think the simple answer is that it hasn't been discovered yet," Carter reflected. "It must be here. It's either deeper down below the surface where they can't see, or further away from where they are digging at the moment. I just can't accept that a society as sophisticated as this never recorded anything and that no one who lived here ever died."

"You might be right about that," Rhodes mused, and then all of a sudden broke out in laughter. Carter looked at him in surprise with raised eyebrows. "What do you reckon the chances are that they had computers and were storing information like we do these days – on disks and drives?"

Carter stopped and looked at Rhodes and then, he started laughing too. "If I were on the record, I'd say it's time for us to get out of the sun, Jim, you have been out here for too long. As I am off the record, I'd say yes, of course, that's entirely possible. These people had electricity and electrical appliances. Why not computers?"

Rhodes smiled, "you see, I do have the occasional moment of brilliance."

"Yeah, I know - as long as we keep the emphasis on the word 'occasional'," Carter said grinning. "You know what would be nice?" Rhodes was shaking his head no. "To pick a team of open-minded expert scientists, come back here with enough funding and the best possible equipment, and find that damn library... because intuition is telling me that this place is hiding some earthshaking information. Who knows, the answer to our nuclear predicament might even be waiting for us here."

Rhodes was of the same mind. "Well, what I can do is get a message through to Hunter asking him to support the idea and get the ball rolling. I have one condition, though."

"And that is?"

"I want to be part of that team of yours."

"No problem. You get approval and funding, and you're on board." Carter started smiling, "we always need someone to cook for us when we are out in the field!"

Rhodes just shook his head in amusement, quietly laughing to himself. Carter was quite a partner.

On the morning of the second day, while Carter and Rhodes finished their first cup of coffee of the morning with the maps of the site spread out on the table in front of them, Mackenzie and Harry walked through the entrance of the Mesrop Mashtots Institute of Ancient Manuscripts in Yerevan, Armenia. They were accompanied by a member of the USA embassy staff who would introduce them to the Director of the Institute, vouch for their credentials, and then left them in her care for the duration of their research.

Carter studied the layout of the city on the maps provided by Daan. He was trying to get an idea of how much had been uncovered and how much could still be hidden under the sand - and maybe even below the structures currently visible. It was clear that far less than 50 percent of the city had been uncovered so far. He and Rhodes planned to use their GPR equipment to scan for more structures that had yet to be uncovered, as well as any signs of hidden chambers, tunnels, and cavities below the structures already uncovered.

Riyadh Saudi Arabia

Xavier Algosaibi was in his office with his purpose-built laptop open, studying the reports from Youssef Bin-Bandar, one of his very few confidants and the number three man in the General Intelligence Presidency of Saudi Arabia. He was very satisfied with the progress of the foundation's plans on all fronts.

He had taken painstaking care to set up the foundation. It took him a few years to select and approach the right people to join him. He had them checked and rechecked, and there was nothing about them he didn't know. Only when he was absolutely sure they could be trusted did he approach them, and never directly at first. He always used an intermediary to plant the seeds and pave the way.

The result was that the foundation consisted of five members. Algosaibi was the leader, and the remaining four members were all wealthy and influential. The foundation had access to the revenue from a quarter of a million barrels of oil per day.

The foundation was set up like a well-planned and organized terrorist organization. It was nearly impossible to infiltrate as it operated in isolated independent cells and the only person who knew how far and wide the foundation reached was Algosaibi. The five board members knew each other but went to great lengths to ensure they were never seen together in public. Their meeting times and places changed every week and were held during and after daily prayers in various secret underground facilities at mosques and other secure venues throughout the city.

Two of the board members were also members of the Royal Family of the House of Saud. One of them was a flamboyant international businessman with his fingers in many pies all over the world. The most lucrative of his business ventures was from a drug trade joint venture with a corrupt general of the Cuban Air Force. Algosaibi hated this drug business as it was strictly forbidden by the Koran. However, he could not turn away the millions of dollars streaming into the coffers of the foundation every week. He honestly believed Allah would understand, that sometimes the end justified the means, and would not hold it against him when his own day of judgment arrived.

Algosaibi smiled broadly when he read Khalid Abdul Bashir's report. The partnership with Hassan Al-Suleiman and his TSP - True Sons of the Prophet - in Syria had been a brilliant move. Hassan had liberated more areas since the formation of the partnership, and with the financial backing of the foundation, the TSP's sphere of influence was gaining momentum. Hassan and his TSP were welcomed like real heroes wherever they set foot. The people saw them as liberators and bearers of good fortune.

The areas under the control of the TSP saw economic growth, peace, and stability. New schools were opened, new clinics and hospitals provided medical care, and local councils were established which provided potable water, electricity, and sanitation. Farmers got financial assistance to help them get their farms back into full production, which helped the region become self-sufficient in food. The first University of the TSP was about to open. Madrassas, teaching Wahhabism were established all over the province.

Algosaibi was particularly pleased when he read the section on the growth of the military arm of the TSP. The money and arms provided by Algosaibi's foundation had turned the TSP's military arm into a highly efficient and disciplined fighting force. The Special Forces division now numbered close to 100 soldiers trained by some of the world's best Special Forces instructors. The TSP elite force now had experts with skills in reconnaissance, surveillance, counter-surveillance, hostage and prisoner extractions, abductions, assassinations, and snipers. To top off the capabilities of the special forces, Algosaibi now had a list of 20 martyrs, ready and even eager to sacrifice their lives in exchange for the once in a lifetime opportunity to go straight to paradise upon death.

The next report was not as encouraging as that of the TSP. Nevertheless, it was still early days for the secret underground lab below a mosque close to Jabal Thawr. More money, resources and equipment would have to be invested in this operation before it would produce results. Algosaibi was a patient man; he was in it for the long haul. This lab was another venture he was very proud of, and sometime in the not too distant future, he expected this operation to pay off big time.

He formed this joint venture with two American businessmen. As always, he remained in the shadows and did his negotiations through a trusted intermediary, so the Americans didn't know he was behind it. Through their network of industrial spies, they had placed tabs on all respirocyte research conducted in the USA and other countries. They knew the names, addresses, and personal details of each and every respirocyte researcher, and had unfettered access to all their research.

Every bit of information was passed on, eventually landing in Algosaibi's hands. With all this information available, the scientists at the lab in Jabal Thawr were way ahead of everyone else. They had been conducting human trials for almost six months while no one else in the world was even close to running human trials. The results were mixed. Initially, it was a disaster - subjects died almost instantaneously after receiving the respirocyte infusions. However, over the past few months, they were able to keep the subjects alive for much longer. One of them recently unofficially broke the World Marathon record but, unfortunately, died half an hour later. Lately, they had made more progress. They were now able to keep subjects alive for up to twenty-four hours. It was slow work, but it was steady, and it was in the right direction.

The project that had Algosaibi most excited was the search for the ancient nuclear weapons. The discovery of the underground site by Hassan's men had triggered this new project. The onsite investigation by the late Dr. Ishrat Sadiq from Pakistan and the deaths of some of Hassan's men caused by radiation had been unfortunate. However, the discovery of a metal box with the papyrus book containing a full description of the horrific events on the day of the explosion, many thousands of years ago, all provided proof beyond a shadow of a doubt that thousands of years ago nuclear weapons were used to wage war.

Algosaibi again turned to his American joint venture partners, of course as always, through his trusted intermediary, and struck another mutually beneficial deal. Again the Americans would use their extraordinary resources and extensive networks to find out if anyone was already investigating this matter and collect information about their activities and progress.

It was not entirely surprising to Algosaibi when he got the message that a very small top-secret government organization in America had a team of experts working on the ancient nuke problem. He smiled when he looked at the information in front of him. Professor Carter Devereux and James Rhodes were the investigators. He already had a copy of every report the two men had produced - even the

PowerPoint presentations made for the President of the United States. They knew as much as he did. In fact, they actually knew a bit less than he did, because they were still speculating about the existence of the nukes, whereas he *knew* they existed.

Algosaibi couldn't help but laugh when he thought about the number of American scientists that he had working for him indirectly, without them having the slightest idea they were doing so.

Chapter Forty-Six

WHAT INFORMATION DO YOU HAVE?

Yerevan, Armenia

Mackenzie and Harry found the Director of the Mesrop Mashtots Institute of Ancient Manuscripts to be a very friendly and helpful person. Once the embassy official introduced them and verified their credentials, she went out of her way to assist them. She assigned an assistant to help them find what they were looking for and assured them she would be on hand if there were anything else they might need.

The assistant, Meryl, took them down to the climate-controlled room, located the first of the Elders of Medicine books, and placed it on the table in front of them. She then took a seat at the one of the desks a few yards away from Mackenzie and Harry and unpacked her laptop to continue with her work while she remained close to them to assist them with what they needed.

Mackenzie couldn't help but notice the strange looking miniature dish-like apparatus clipped to the top of Meryl's laptop screen. She'd never seen such a tiny antenna and had to ask Meryl about it. Meryl explained, in broken English, that it was the antenna for her wireless modem so that she could have access to the Institute's network as well as the Internet. In truth, it was a directional parabolic microphone designed to collect and focus sound waves onto a receiver. Her command of English was not adequate to explain that the real purpose of the device was to make sure every word Mackenzie and Harry uttered to each other would be recorded on her laptop. She also didn't divulge the fact that she was going to receive a princely sum for the recordings, and that was on top of an all-expenses paid four-week holiday in the South of France for herself and her boyfriend.

The Books of the Elders of Medicine were fascinating, and before long, both Mackenzie and Harry were so absorbed they ceased to be aware of what was going on around them. They frequently experienced slack-jawed moments as they read the documents. Mackenzie was making notes as fast as she could and only wished she was allowed to make copies or take photos of the pages, but that was strictly forbidden by the Director. They could read and make notes, but no copies of any nature were allowed. There was a lot of information related to her non-respirocyte research, and she jotted down the page numbers and made short notes. She was going to get back to those pages when she had collected all the respirocyte information.

As expected, the Books of the Elders contained more detailed information about the blood oxygen treatment alluded to by the Latin author who had led them to the Institute.

Hours went by as she and Harry discussed and questioned the information. They were profoundly involved with the subject as they considered ways and means for the information to be used for the future.

They learned that oxygen-filled microparticles covered with a layer of fatty molecules, each molecule encapsulating a tiny pocket of oxygen, were injected in a liquid solution into the patient. The text described how the infusion of these microparticles into patients with low blood oxygen levels restored the blood oxygen to near-normal levels within seconds. The author of the article quoted another text in which an observer described the effects of the treatment. After the injection, *he saw blue blood, a sign of low oxygen, turn red, almost instantaneously - reversing brain damage, restoring respiratory functions and damage to the heart.*

Despite the thrilling discoveries in the Books of the Elders during the first two days, they reached what they initially thought was the end of the road. On the morning of the third day, when Meryl placed the final volume of the books on the table, they discovered there was no more information related to their search to be found within them.

Although they had progressed in their knowledge, there were still many unanswered questions. The most important was, *how were the oxygen-filled microparticles created?*

The information in the Books of the Elders of Medicine was based on inherited knowledge passed on from another civilization long before the time of the Elders. Possibly the author was not able to take his information further. Maybe the knowledge had been lost in some cataclysm.

Mackenzie and Harry looked at each other when they got to the last page in the last of the books. The question was on both their faces, "Where to from here?"

Mackenzie looked over the stack of documents and books littering their workspace. "We need another reference. We have to find the original source - the one the

Elders used. Or, do you think it's possible the knowledge was passed on through the generations verbally?" She shook her head and answered herself, "No, I don't think so. It would be too easily misinterpreted."

Harry was quiet for a while, looking around the secured room and the shelves of books. He shook his head, "Neither do I. There was too much detail in those sections of the Books of the Elders. It must have come from a written account somewhere. Something as technical as that would never have survived thousands of years of oral transmission, as you said."

"Let's go back and study each section in detail," Mackenzie suggested. "We could easily have missed the reference to the earlier sources."

For the next few hours, that's exactly what they did, and their effort paid off when they found three references to the same source. It was a big relief. They had not reached the end of the road, as they previously believed. They just hoped and prayed that the Institute had the document to which the Elders referred.

Harry had been staring at the strange letters on the page for a long time. Mackenzie had no idea what they were. They could have been Arabic, Chinese or anything in between. Harry started mumbling incomprehensible words and Mackenzie held off – she knew not to interrupt him. After a while, he wrote down the word, '*sirralnnudam.*' He looked up and said, "That word is related to Arabic. It's made up of three different words which might be related to modern-day Arabic 'Sirr' which could be linked to the Arabic word 'alssrr' which means secret, 'allnnu' which could be related to the Arabic word 'alnnusi' which means script or text, and 'dam' which likely is the Arabic word 'alddam' which means blood. I would guess a sensible

English translation would be something like 'the secret book of blood' or 'the book of the secret of blood' maybe."

They had forgotten Meryl's presence by now and spoke freely; they had no reason to distrust the friendly young woman.

Mackenzie shook her head in wonder. She could speak English and French and still remembered how hard it was to learn another language. Listening to Harry switching between ten different languages over the past few days, as if most of them were his mother tongue, was an extraordinary experience.

They called Meryl over, showed her the reference and asked if she could try to find it on the computer index system. It took the young assistant a few minutes to trace it, but then she smiled. Yes, they had it, but it was flagged and required special permission to access. They thanked her and went to see the Director.

The Director wasn't too fussed about all these protocols and authorizations. She was more concerned about keeping the high profile researchers from America happy rather than enforcing government red tape. She gave them the approval to access the document and told Meryl to take them to the room where the book was located. It was in a different area from the one they were working in before.

Once they returned to their main working area with the newly retrieved document, Meryl settled down with her laptop and continued with her work.

Mackenzie was given pause when she read a passage in the English document accompanying the Sirralnnudam. The paper was a history of the origin of the Sirralnnudam text: where it was found, who found it and how. It also explained how it came into the possession of the Institute and its estimated age. The part that gave her reason to pause and increased her heart rate was that the document was found in Çatalhöyük about 50 years ago. She was deeply in love with a man who would be visiting Çatalhöyük in the next four to five days and was wondering what the chances were of surprising Carter on his arrival there. She missed her man so much; she was giving the idea some serious thought.

However, Harry snapped her out her reverie. "Mackenzie" he laughed, "I think you will find what we are looking for *inside* the book rather than in the English document you have been staring at for the past five minutes." That got her back to reality.

She only had to see the first page to know that she would rather be staring at the English document; she was looking at those strange letters again. She pushed the book to Harry and said in a mock-serious tone, "Harry how is your gobbledygook? I haven't had much practice lately."

Harry looked at the first page for a minute and said, "If only it were gobbledygook," he chuckled, "I would be able to read it, but this is going to take a long time. I can only make out every tenth word. It's a language I haven't seen before. It's vaguely related to Arabic, but the emphasis is on 'vaguely.' I'm sure it can be read, but I will need help and time."

"How much time and help?"

Harry shrugged his shoulders, "I have no idea. Give me an hour to page through and see how much I can understand."

Makenzie nodded and sat back – her brain was working overtime. They were not allowed to copy the book - it was in a very fragile state; they were not allowed to take it out of the room, and they couldn't rewrite it. Yet it was potentially holding the key to a secret that could change the world of medicine.

She watched Harry as he slowly paged through the book, his lips moving, his head shaking every now and then, and lots of strange noises coming from his side of the desk. Frequently he stopped and wrote something on the pad next to him.

A plan was slowly taking shape in her head. She was not going to rush into it, and she was definitely not going to drag Harry into it. She needed time to think it through very carefully. She got up to stretch her legs and walked around the room while she waited for Harry to finish.

As she walked, she appeared to be looking at all the documents behind the glass on the shelves. She took great care to inspect every wall and every corner of the room for security cameras. Stopping under the two overhead air vents, she checked them as well while pretending to stretch her back. It was surprising to find there were no security cameras she could see. Either the cameras were undetectable, or they were obviously not as security conscious at this Institute as the people responsible for the contents of the vaults at A-Echelon.

About an hour later, Harry looked at her and said. "Okay here are a few of the main keywords which I picked up and might interest you - molecules, atoms, blood, blood cells, oxygen, generator, diamonds, carbon ..."

"Thanks, Harry," Mackenzie interrupted, "I get the gist of it. All the right keywords are there. That's good news. We just have to work out a plan to produce a reliable translation. How much time do you think you will need?"

"My guess is, if I can get three of our linguistic experts to help me, we could achieve it in two to three weeks. That's a rough estimate. It could be a bit quicker as we learn the meaning of the words. Once we get going, things will speed up. There are also some diagrams and sketches in the book. Perhaps we can reproduce them on paper for a start."

"Okay. We have two more days left. I don't think we will be able to get approval to stay much longer, nor could we get everything organized in the next two days to get linguists over from the States. I suggest you take up the embassy's offer of a guided tour of the city tomorrow while I come back here to gather information for my non-respirocyte research."

Harry nodded, "Okay that sounds good to me. I would certainly be interested in looking around the city, compliments of Uncle Sam."

"Alright, I suggest we call it a day."

They packed their laptops and left for their hotel. There were a few shops close to the hotel, and Mackenzie wanted to do a bit of shopping before she went back home.

That night when Mackenzie and Carter had their regular Skype session, he could immediately see she was excited about something. He made a few passing comments about her jubilant mood, and she showed him a double thumbs up without saying anything. He knew then that she was onto something significant. Later during the conversation, Mackenzie's parents, Liam and, of course, Jeha joined them from Boston in one big cyberspace family gathering.

City of Lights, Egypt

The next morning, Rhodes showed Carter an encrypted message that arrived during the night. It was from Hunter informing them that A-Echelon got a positive response to the request for additional funding and resources for Professor Chandra Pillay's expedition in North India. The details would be finalized when Carter and Rhodes returned to the USA, but they were welcome to share the good news with Professor Pillay in the meantime.

After breakfast, Carter and Rhodes unpacked their mobile GPR and other equipment and started a meticulous underground survey of an area on the western side of the city that Carter had marked out the day before.

With the experience of being followed and photographed during their trip in India still fresh in their minds, they continually checked the people around the site, including the military contingent, who were showing the same kind of interest in their activities.

"Jim I haven't noticed any photographers since our arrival," Carter noted. "Have you seen any?"

"No, I haven't, but that doesn't mean there's no one out there watching us," Rhodes replied. "I'd feel more comfortable if I had. The problem is not the ones who show themselves; it's the ones who don't that are the worry."

The two of them would have been far more concerned if they had known there were, at least, two people in Daan's team watching their every move. They would have been severely shocked if they knew that some of those dish-shaped antennas in the site's military base and on some of their vehicles were powerful directional parabolic microphones, which had been recording their conversations since the moment they set foot at the dig.

Soon after they started scanning, the little screen on the GPR alerted them to the fact that there were structures below the surface, the top of which was no more than four feet away. The images displayed on the small screen of the GPR were not clear enough to enable them to make out what they were. They transferred the data to the laptop, converted them and got a better idea. There was definitely a massive structure, and it went down as deep as the GPR was capable of detecting. That afternoon they uploaded the day's data to the A-Echelon servers with enthusiastic anticipation of what the 3-D images would reveal.

Yerevan, Armenia

Mackenzie was back at the Institute shortly after breakfast and arranged with the Director for Meryl to set her up in one of the rooms for the day.

She started by asking Meryl to bring her the collection of the Books of the Elders of Medicine and the Sirralnnudam, and then took a seat at the table that allowed her to have a good view of Meryl. Pulling the reading light closer to the books, she made sure the pages of the book in front of her – the Sirralnnudam – received the best possible illumination from the light. She stacked the other books in heaps around her so that it would be impossible for Meryl to see what exactly she was doing.

All the while, there was a painful moral battle raging in her mind. On the one hand, she heard one voice accusing her – *'This is wrong, it's plagiarism; you're abusing the trust and hospitality of these people. You are not allowed to do this.'* The other voice was saying, *'You have no choice, you must do it, humanity needs it, get it done and get out of here.'* Yet another voice kept questioning - *'What if someone else gets their hands on this book? What if this place burns down? Remember the loss humanity suffered when the Library of Alexandria was set on fire? What if someone steals this book? What if they won't give you access to it again?'*

Mackenzie didn't know what to do. She was torn between what was right and what was wrong. In the daylight and with the books open in front of her, she had second thoughts. Doubts began to sneak in; maybe this wasn't such a good idea anymore. What if there were security cameras that she hadn't detected? What would be the consequences if they discovered what she was doing? Her actions could reflect disastrously on the USA. The relations between Armenia and America could quickly escalate into a serious political issue.

Yet something persuaded her in the end to go ahead and do it. Something that she couldn't explain motivated her to continue.

When she saw Meryl get bored and plug her earphones into her mobile phone while she was reading, probably a fiction book, she started paging through the Sirralnnudam very slowly pretending she was comparing pages from there with pages in the Books of the Elders – stopping every now and then to make notes on her laptop. Every time she turned a page in the Sirralnnudam, her hand would hover over the page long enough to take a photo with the miniature camera Carter gave her for their sixth wedding anniversary.

It took her the best part of five hours of careful inconspicuous maneuvering to photograph the entire Sirralnnudam. It was easily the most uncomfortable, nerve-wracking five hours in her life. The constant indictments by her subconscious mind made the whole experience ten times worse than just the fear of being caught.

At four o'clock, a very relieved Dr. Mackenzie Devereux walked through the front door of the Mesrop Mashtots Institute of Ancient Manuscripts after she had thanked Meryl and the Director for their help. She promised that she would return, in all likelihood, within the next few months with a team of linguists to help her translate the Sirralnnudam and a few other documents. Once the translations were complete, of course, she would happily share them with the Institute.

When she got outside, she looked up and saw there was a big thunderstorm brewing. She shuddered at the portent and hastened to wave down a taxi to take her back to her hotel before the downpour started.

The mini camera was safely stashed away in her handbag. There was no need to tell Harry or Irene about it; she wanted to talk to Carter first. Of course, Carter was going to be furious, yet she felt she had created a backup plan. There was no logic, no moral justification, yet it seemed wrong to delete the data from the mini camera just yet. If Carter told her to do it, she would, but until then it was staying exactly where it was. Should Irene and A-Echelon get the funding to send Harry with a team of linguists back to translate the book, she would also delete it - but not until those arrangements were certain.

Mackenzie would have been shocked, or even possibly relieved, with what she did that day had she known what happened just minutes after she left the building.

Shortly after five, with the rain bucketing down, Meryl ran from the entrance of the Institute, rushing to get through the deluge to the car waiting for her on a nearby side road.

There was a small bundle wrapped up in a scarf under her right arm; her handbag was in her right hand and her laptop bag in her left hand. About two yards from the car her foot slipped and she fell. Her arms instinctively reached out to prevent her face from hitting the concrete of the sidewalk. She managed to hold onto her handbag and the laptop, but the bundle under her arm slipped out and landed in the gutter right behind the car. Instantly, the raging gush of water caught up the bundle and rushed into a nearby storm water drain.

She watched in despair as the book, free of the scarf, disappeared out of sight as it was pulled down into the sewers far below and out of reach.

With the book gone, there would be no money and no all-expenses-paid holiday in the South of France.

The car door on the passenger side opened, a man got out, ripped the laptop bag from her hand, got back into the car, and drove off. Tears were streaming down her face as she stood up and watched the red taillights speeding away from her. She was soaking wet and suddenly very cold.

City of Lights, Egypt

That night during their Skype session, Carter noticed that Mackenzie was not as cheery as the night before, and it frustrated him that he couldn't ask her outright what was wrong. He kept throwing hints at her during the conversation, but she either didn't get it or didn't want to discuss it. Carter decided it couldn't be too serious, because if it were, she would have at least shown him a thumbs down. It was probably just her missing Liam and him. They would be in each other arms in two weeks' time. When he reminded her of that, he got the magic smile out of her he longed to see.

The next morning Carter was up early and very surprised when he saw Rhodes was awake as well. They both scrambled for the laptop to start it and download the images. They were not disappointed. There was a strange looking walkway of sorts, about 20 feet wide, spiraling down more than 100 feet, which was as deep as their GPR could detect. It could have been going down even further than that.

For the next hour, they studied the images and speculated. How far down did it actually go? Was it leading to chambers down there? What was the real purpose of this walkway?

Carter suggested it was time to bring Daan in and show him what they'd discovered. Daan was elated when he saw the images, "Carter, what are we looking at here?"

"Well Daan, there is one easy way to find out. Let's get your team to remove the topsoil, and then we'll drill a hole through the wall and send one of our robots in."

"You can do that?" Daan asked with eagerness.

"Yep, if you can get a team of diggers over there, Professor Hayden and I will bring all our equipment over, and we can do it."

Daan didn't bother to discuss it any further. Without a word, he spun around and, at a near run, started calling members of his team to him.

The underground structure was covered in sand, which made it easy for Daan's team members to dig down and expose the entrance to the walkway. Two hours later, they all looked at the enormous granite door in front of them. It was more than 15 feet high.

The first thing they noted was the engravings. They looked like pictures, but Carter soon pointed out they were not pictures, but words - the first written words found in the City of Lights. The problem was, none of them could figure out what they said. None of them had ever seen any language even remotely related to the words they were looking at now.

After studying the GPR images closely, they located a place on the door where they could safely drill while causing the least amount of damage. It was a shame to deface the door at all, but sometimes a small amount of scarring is necessary for the greater good – like surgery in the medical profession. They were archeological surgeons and, like their medical counterparts, they were careful, conservative, and precise. It took them another two hours of hard labor to drill a hole through the door and insert the little remote controlled robot. Their sudden burst of activity at the dig raised the interest of the commander of the base, which rapidly brought him and three of his men in a military vehicle to the spot. Daan met with them and explained about the discovery. The commander was keen to stay and see what was going on. He walked back to the vehicle, equipped with a dish as well as a 20-foot whip antenna, and spoke on the radio.

Carter, who was fluent in Arabic, followed the conversation as the commander relayed the details of the discovery to his second in command back at the base.

There was absolute silence when Carter activated the robot and steered it through the hole in the granite door. He enabled the onboard light and video camera, and a few seconds later they got the first glimpse of what lay beyond. Now, after more than 50,000 years, human eyes saw once again what was on the other side of that door. Everyone, except maybe the commander and his soldiers, appreciated what a momentous event this was. The Commander was more interested in the report he'd be sending back to his superiors.

As the robot slowly made its way along the walkway, following the instructions given Carter via the remote control panel, stopping and turning, moving the spotlight to various areas of interest, they all looked on in awe.

After half an hour, everybody had formed their own opinion about what they were seeing, but no one wanted to voice it first. The only voices were eager requests, *"Wait, hold it there ... can you turn the light and camera to the right? Sorry, can you back up a few inches? Wait, I thought I saw something ... can you stop there? Don't leave yet, let me have a closer look."*

Carter already knew what it was. Rhodes tapped him on the shoulder and raised his eyebrows as if to say, *what are we looking at?*

It wasn't often that Carter was moved by something that brought him close to tears. This, however, was one of those moments. He knew he was looking at something way beyond anything he could ever begin to imagine in his wildest dreams of archeological finds.

Once past the magnificent entrance, the robot slowly descended, exposing the paved walkway spiraling down deep into the earth. High stone walls faced in white marble rose above them before being blocked by something. On each side of the ramp, deep holes appeared, taller than they were wide and completely smooth on the inside. They were all uniform in height and depth - almost like huge manufactured vertical storage tanks. As the passageway sloped down, more and more of the mysterious cavities were exposed.

Carter knew he was looking at the catacombs of the distant past, the tombs of the people who had lived here long ago and walked the roads of this ancient, magnificent city. For the first time in his career, his head was spinning as he realized the enormity of the discovery.

He whispered to Rhodes, "We've found them, the inhabitants of the City of Lights. Can you imagine that?"

"You're for real?"

He nodded. "Watch," he turned the robot so its light shone directly into one of the cavities. Inside, although hard to discern, the visual showed what appeared to be a figure. It was clearly mummified. What were once robes still draped the body. What was hard to accept was the size of the person. Even without proper clear light, and even as the light from the little robot reached its limits, it was beyond doubt they were looking at giants. People, Carter quietly estimated, to have been between 12 and 14 feet tall

Rhodes' breath was rapid as he stared at the screen, "This is incredible. Carter, are you sure?"

He nodded, then stood, and said to everyone, "Okay, I'm sorry folks, but I'm going to retrieve the robot now. We can't go any further until we have the proper personnel. That means anthropologists, biologists and every other sort of 'gist' you can think of, out here with their equipment so a professional research project can be launched."

As they walked back to their tents, Rhodes spoke to Carter. "My friend you are a remarkable scientist. You've been here for two days and discovered more in that time than Daan and his team could do in years."

Carter was a person who disliked the limelight. "To be fair Jim, if Daan had been given more staff and the proper equipment, he could have done it." He was uncomfortable with Rhodes' praise.

Carter changed the subject. "Jim there are a few things we need to do. You have to let Hunter know about this and get the videos across to him. Then we need to ask him again to get approval for more funding and resources for this site. This is not just a matter of 'want,' it's much more serious than that. Should this discovery be leaked out before we are ready, it could lead to all sorts of mischief. The site must be secured quickly."

Rhodes nodded his agreement.

"My next suggestion is that we change our travel plans. I believe we should postpone the trip to Çatalhöyük to another time, stay here and start looking for that library. I can feel that library is somewhere near, and the answers to those damn nukes are somewhere inside it."

"Well, I have all the reason to trust your gut instincts. I'll get right on it with Hunter."

Later that night the Commander collected all the recordings and pictures of the past 24 hours and sent it off to his superior in Cairo, just as he had been doing for so many months.

Riyadh, Saudi Arabia

Xavier Algosaibi saw the call coming through on his mobile phone; it was Youssef Bin-Bandar, calling him on an open, unsecured phone. Youssef had recently been promoted to one of the deputy director positions in the Saudi secret service, the General Intelligence Presidency. He should know, better than anyone, not to use a mobile phone - unless it was a matter of extreme urgency.

"Xavier, how are you, my friend?" Youssef kept his voice calm and neutral.

"I am good Youssef, and I would be pleased to hear that you and your family are also well."

"Yes, indeed my friend everyone is doing just fine."

"To what do I owe the honor of this call from you my friend?" Xavier wanted to get to the reason for the call as quickly as possible.

Youssef laughed. "I am flattered by your kind words Xavier. It's nothing urgent." It was their code for *it's critical*. "It's just a social call to make sure my old friend is still in good health and enjoying the grace of Allah." The code for *something urgent has come up.* "We haven't seen each other for such a long time I thought it was time to fix that problem." The code for *we have to meet as quickly as possible.* "My wife and

I would be honored if you and your wife would join us for dinner at six tonight at my house."

Xavier looked at his watch it was four o'clock. *This must be really urgent.* Usually, they would plan their meetings a few days in advance.

"Of course Youssef, it will be a great pleasure and honor for us to be in the company of the Deputy Director of the General Intelligence Presidency."

Youssef Bin-Bandar's residence was a fortress, protected by guards, state of the art electronic security systems, invisible infrared trip wires, motion sensors, and reinforced bulletproof walls, doors, and windows. The entire house was scanned once a day for listening devices, and the windows were fitted with high-tech electromagnetic and vibration devices that would foil any attempt to eavesdrop on conversations by using directional parabolic microphones. Xavier and Youssef were both comfortable that their conversation would never reach the ears of anyone other than themselves.

"Xavier, there is some good news and some bad news. We will have to act immediately," Youssef started once they were both seated in the secure room two levels below the ground floor of Youssef's house.

Xavier nodded and smiled, "That much I gathered from our conversation earlier. Tell me about it."

"Three hours ago I got a report through our network coming from our American partners about both of our joint ventures. I'll start with the details of the nuclear business first?" Lifting his eyebrows questioningly.

Algosaibi nodded for him to continue.

"As you know, Professor Carter Devereux and James Rhodes, who are both working for that secret organization A-Echelon, went on a global research trip to find more information about ancient nuclear weapons." Youssef looked at Xavier waiting for his acknowledgment and then continued.

"The first site they visited was in North India close to the Pakistan border. This site also has all the signs of an ancient nuclear explosion." Youssef turned the screen of his laptop to Algosaibi so that he could see the pictures.

"Did they find anything there?"

"Yes, they did. Here are the 3-D images and the report they compiled for their Director, Hunter Patrick. See here," Youssef pointed to a photograph on the screen, "it's a flight of stairs going down deep below the current excavations. The current expedition leader, Chandra Pillay doesn't know what they found. It looks like this site consists of four layers of civilizations, one on top of the other, stretching back for many thousands of years. The Americans have approved additional funding for the dig and are planning to send a team of experts out there soon."

Algosaibi smiled. He was happy to hear all this. "It will be very interesting to know what they find at the bottom of those stairs."

Youssef smiled. "We will keep a close watch. I'm just as curious as you are to know what is down there." He continued, "Next they went to the Saad Plateau in Libya and spent a day there. There is nothing in their report to get excited about. We already know there must have been a massive nuclear explosion in that area a very long time ago.

"From the Saad Plateau, they went to the City of Lights in Egypt. Again, I have all the reports, 3-D images, and recordings of their conversations. Although the site is still largely unexplored, and to date no evidence of a nuclear explosion has been found there, Professor Devereux seems to be convinced that the answer to the ancient nuclear explosions lies within this City of Lights."

"So he believes the Giants knew about these nuclear weapons or were the ones who built them?" Algosaibi sat forward in his chair. "Does he have any proof yet?"

"There is nothing in the reports or the transcripts of their conversations to indicate that they have concrete evidence to support that theory. The transcripts show that Devereux is going on a hunch."

"Not a very scientific approach." Algosaibi commented, sounding a bit disappointed.

"Well, I agree it's not very scientific, but don't write him off yet. The man is a legend in archeological circles and beyond. He has made a few major discoveries based almost solely on hunches. I got the impression that his latest discovery at the City of Lights came from such a hunch."

"And what was that?"

Youssef gave Algosaibi a detailed account of the catacombs discovered by Carter two days before. He showed him the videos, reports, and transcripts of the conversations between Carter and Rhodes.

"I guess you are right about this man's hunches. We should keep a close watch on him." Algosaibi started laughing, "I have a hunch he might lead us to the nuclear weapons."

"Would you like me to tell you now about the respirocyte venture?" Youssef inquired.

"Yes, I am eager to hear about that. I take it this is where I will hear the bad news now?"

Youssef shifted with a bit of unease. He would not hide anything from his friend, but it would have been much easier if what he was about to tell him was all good news.

"As you know, this Professor Devereux's wife, Dr.

Mackenzie Devereux, is now also working for A-Echelon. Her task is to conduct research into ancient medicine to find out if respirocytes were known to the ancients."

"I was aware that she had become an employee of A-Echelon and was doing research on ancient medicine, but not that she had been looking at respirocytes. I'm struggling to tell my brain that it's not too farfetched."

"True, it's hard to believe, but if the ancients did build nuclear weapons, it's possible they could have built respirocyte generators as well. These days I am not prepared to believe that anything can be too farfetched."

Youssef continued giving Algosaibi a detailed report of the work that Mackenzie had been doing and her discoveries. He included all the details of Mackenzie's discovery of the Books of the Elders of Medicine that led her to the Sirralnnudam texts. He showed him all the reports Mackenzie had sent back to Irene and the transcripts of the conversations between her and Harry, recorded by Meryl.

The excitement was clearly visible on Algosaibi's face when Youssef paused. "Youssef, please tell me you have that book, the Sirralnnudam."

Youssef couldn't meet Xavier's eyes. He stared out in front of him. "I am sorry to say, my friend, but that's the bad news. We had a woman on the inside that did excellent work. She followed Dr. Devereux and recorded all her conversations with the linguist helping her. After the doctor left the last day of her visit, she stole the Sirralnnudam and got it out of the building. However, there was a severe thunderstorm with pouring rain. As she was running to the car, she slipped and fell, and lost her grip on the book. It was washed away into the storm water system of Yerevan." Youssef sighed when he completed the narrative.

Algosaibi had his hands in a steeple over his mouth

while he considered what Youssef just told him. A few minutes of uneasy silence followed, and then he asked, "Do you think there is a chance that this woman, Dr. Devereux, has made a copy of the Sirralnnudam?"

Youssef shook his head. "No, I don't think so. In the transcripts, you will see that she and her linguist have agreed that they would have to go back to the Institute in Yerevan with a team of translators to help them translate the text."

Algosaibi was quiet for a few moments. "And that was the only copy of that text in the world?"

Youssef nodded slowly. "I am afraid it's now lost to us and the world."

Algosaibi formed his hands in a steeple over his mouth again and stared at the floor for a few minutes again. "What information do you have about Professor Devereux and his wife? Do you know where they live, their movements and habits?"

Chapter Forty-Seven

THE SIRRALNNUDAM

Much to Daan Hannah's delight, Carter and Rhodes had changed their travel plans to remain onsite at the City of Lights for an additional two weeks to continue the GPR surveys. Their research had indicated there were a vast number of underground structures waiting to be explored.

Daan's eyes filled with tears when Carter told him they were in the process of requesting additional funding and resources for the excavation of the city. He didn't mind that the acquisition of funding from America would mean the entire operation might be managed by Americans eventually. He was just happy that the site would get the attention it deserved, although he did request that he and his daughter be allowed to continue as part of the team.

On her return to Boston, Mackenzie wrote a detailed report about her trip to Armenia that she would submit to Irene in person. They had arranged to meet at A-Echelon a couple of days later.

They met at the exit to the Airlock after Mackenzie cleared the usual security check and Irene handed her the security card, which authorized her to move around the A-Echelon offices.

After they'd prepared their drinks in the kitchen, they went to one of the secured meeting rooms where Mackenzie provided a detailed account of her research at the Mesrop Mashtots Institute of Ancient Manuscripts. She didn't mention that she'd copied the Sirralnnudam.

"So let's see if I understand the significance of what you've unveiled," Irene said when Mackenzie finished her report. "The Books of the Elders of Medicine contained the first major breakthrough in the sense that it confirmed the existence of, what we today call, respirocytes in antiquity?"

"Yes indeed," Mackenzie smiled. "I think that was a substantial leap forward. Up to now, we were just poking around in the dark trying to find out if prehistoric practitioners of medicine knew of the concept. Now we have confirmation that is indeed the case. They did."

"Do you think the information you have at hand could already be useful to researchers in this field?"

Mackenzie had been thinking about it since she first laid eyes on the translation of those passages by Harry. "I have been giving that idea much thought over the past week or so. Yes, I think what we have can be useful. But there ..."

Irene held her hand up. "Apologies for interrupting. If you don't mind, I would like to get Hunter and the DARPA people in here so we can discuss this in one meeting. That way you won't have to repeat the whole thing three times over." She looked at Mackenzie for approval.

"No problem at all."

Irene used the phone in the meeting room to call Director Patrick and Drs. Cate Nelson and Scott Watson.

They were all available and joined Irene and Mackenzie in the meeting room shortly afterward.

Irene gave them a brief overview of Mackenzie's trip and then handed off to Mackenzie for the detailed narrative.

Mackenzie started off by describing the discovery of the Latin text they'd found in the A-Echelon vaults and how that led them to the Books of the Elders of Medicine in Armenia, which then referred them to the incomprehensible Sirralnnudam text.

A short discussion followed ending with Hunter promising to secure funding for a team of linguists to visit Armenia and begin translating the Sirralnnudam text as soon as possible. They agreed it would be necessary for Mackenzie to accompany the team; therefore, it would have to wait until she returned from her holiday.

"Okay, Mackenzie, this is very exciting," Cate Nelson said as she leaned forward. "Would you mind sharing with us all the technical information you have gathered so far?"

Mackenzie looked at Patrick and Irene, who nodded for her to continue. "It was fascinating reading finding out how they did it. They used oxygen-filled microparticles covered with a layer of fatty molecules as the transport medium. Each molecule encapsulated a tiny pocket of oxygen. The microparticles were injected into patients in a liquid solution."

Cate and Scott each started shaking their heads. "What?" Mackenzie asked a bit worried. "Have I said something wrong?"

"No, no, sorry. It's just such a huge mind shift," Cate laughed. "Here we live in the 21st century, believing we are the most advanced, scientifically knowledgeable human beings ever to walk the planet. I suspect we are in for a rather large serving of humble pie."

Mackenzie nodded with a smile. "I know the feeling. One day when we have a bit of time, I'll tell you all about my metamorphosis."

"Have you found anything that explains the benefits they derived from this treatment and exactly how they did it?" Scott wanted to know.

"The answer to your first question is yes, the second no." Mackenzie continued. "The text we found described how the treatment restored the blood oxygen to near-normal levels within seconds." Mackenzie looked at the notes on her laptop. "Here is a translated quote from one of the authors ... *'I saw blue blood, a sign of low oxygen, turn red, almost instantaneously - reversing brain damage, restoring respiratory functions and damage to the heart.'*"

Mackenzie's audience was agog. "So that means," Hunter started with a soft voice which grew louder as he kept on expressing his thought, "you have found confirmation about the use of respirocytes by the ancients!"

Mackenzie looked at Irene, who came to the same conclusion earlier in the morning. Mackenzie smiled, "Yes that's correct. It's amazing isn't it?"

Hunter laughed, "Mackenzie that is the biggest understatement I've ever heard. It's not only amazing, it's earth-shaking!"

A few moments of quiet descended upon the group as they digested the information. "Mackenzie," Scott broke the silence, "you'd been doing a lot of research on this topic before you started digging into history. So I guess you have a good handle on the approaches current researchers use? Is there anyone that you know of that has ever looked at the approach you have just described to us?"

"I don't know of anyone doing this," Mackenzie replied. "All of the research projects that I have been privy to are trying to build an artificial red blood cell. They are attempting to follow Robert Freitas's ideas as described in his 1998 paper titled, *A Mechanical Artificial Red Blood Cell: Exploratory Design in Medical Nanotechnology*. They're all using artificial materials to create a generator to produce these respirocytes to replace human red blood cells and hopefully, do a better job than our natural red blood cells do."

"That means we have to find out how they built those ancient respirocytes. I just hope we'll get the answers in that strange book you mentioned," Hunter commented.

"The Sirralnnudam," Mackenzie noted. "Yes, I'm keen to see what we can learn from it. It's difficult to predict what we'll find. It certainly contains the right keywords as far as Harry could understand. If it doesn't have all the details we are looking for, we might, at least, find references to more documents."

"So in summary then," Hunter started to wrap up the meeting, "we have enough information to encourage us to continue our research, and we have information which could be useful to modern day researchers. But, it might be wiser to see what we get out of the translation of the Sirraln-what's-a-name text first."

Mackenzie and Irene nodded their agreement.

"Thank you for the update, Irene, and Mackenzie. Excellent work. I will give the President a report early next week," Hunter said as he stood to leave.

The rest of them continued for another half hour, to discuss more of the technical details. By midday, Mackenzie wrapped up her meeting and was on her way home. She was looking forward to a six-week Mediterranean holiday and luxury cruise with Carter and Liam.

Back in Boston, Mackenzie made sure she had all her research backed up and safely stored, including a copy of everything on the miniature camera, which contained the copy of the Sirralnnudam. Sooner or later, Carter would have to know about her illegal activities in Armenia, and broaching the subject with him would be difficult. Other than the miniature camera, which she'd take with her, everything else, including her laptop and tablet, would be securely locked up in the vault.

For the next six weeks, it was going to be family time. If it happened that she and Carter did discuss her work, she could plug the miniature camera into his laptop.

She and Liam started packing. Mackenzie did a last minute check to make sure all their travel documents were in order and double-checked with the travel agent to make sure all the booking arrangements and itinerary were still as agreed.

She had a hard time explaining to Liam that it would be impossible to take Jeha with them on the trip, but that his grandparents would take loving care of her while he was away, the same way Ahote was taking care of Nelly while he was away from Freydis.

Riyadh, Saudi Arabia

Xavier Algosaibi smiled when he got the coded message from Youssef Bin-Bandar to meet about an urgent matter in two hours' time at one of their secured meeting venues. He had been waiting for this message for the past two days and was getting a bit impatient.

"Xavier my friend," Bin-Bandar smiled as the meeting began, "We have everything we need to give the go-ahead for the operation." Bin-Bandar was keen to try to please his friend after the messy end to the operation in Armenia when they lost the Sirralnnudam.

"What do you have?" Xavier asked with raised eyebrows.

"I have here two reports that might be of great interest to you. The first one is a copy of a report by Dr. Mackenzie Devereux, which Hunter Patrick, the Director of A-Echelon, handed to the President earlier in the week. It contains all the details of her research."

"Have they made a copy of the Sirralnnudam text?" Algosaibi leaned forward eagerly in the hope Youssef would give him some good news.

"Unfortunately not," Youssef replied in a somber voice. "From what I gather, they are still unaware that the text has been lost. They are planning to send a team to Armenia to do the translation."

Algosaibi nodded the disappointment clearly visible on his face. "This report contains information we don't already know?"

"Very much so, my friend," Youssef replied, the excitement returning to his tone. "This Dr. Devereux has solved a big part of the puzzle for us. She discovered how the ancients used respirocytes. I have to admit she didn't get all the information, but she found enough for our scientists to work with."

"That's very encouraging Youssef. It's not the Grand Prize, but I guess without the Sirralnnudam this is the only prize we can hope for."

Youssef smiled. He was starting to feel a lot better now.

"What's in the second report?" Algosaibi inquired.

"Not as exciting as the first report, but still very important, I dare to say," Youssef answered. "It's the complete report created and submitted to A-Echelon by Professor

Carter Devereux. It contains all the details about his exploration of the sites in North India and the City of Lights in Egypt. He hasn't found any nuclear devices yet, but he clearly stated in his report that he has absolutely no doubts about their existence. He also reiterated the importance of the two sites in the search for those nukes."

"Good. I'm very pleased with our achievements." Algosaibi stated. "Can you give me the assurance that you have everything ready to launch our planned operation?"

"Yes, hand on my heart," Youssef said and put his hand on his chest. "Everything has been planned in minute detail. Now I only wait for you to say the word, and the operation will kick into action."

Algosaibi had his hands in a steeple under his chin, his elbows resting on the armrest of the chair, staring at the table as though considering the next move in a complex strategy game. After a few minutes, he looked up at Youssef and said, "Let's do it. Allahu Akbar." With that, he took the last sip of his coffee, stood, shook Youssef's hand, and left.

Chapter Forty-Eight

THE TRIANGLE

Tel Aviv, Israel

Carter was waiting for Mackenzie and Liam at Ben Gurion International Airport, Southeast of Tel Aviv when their El Al flight from Boston landed shortly after midday. He had been there for a few hours already since he had to see Rhodes off to Washington D.C. earlier.

It was a non-stop 11-hour flight, and Carter made sure that the two of them were booked in first class so they would be comfortable enough to enjoy the trip and get some sleep. They would only have two days in Jerusalem, and had a lot to see in those two days before they embarked on the cruise ship.

Carter spotted Mackenzie and Liam before they saw him. Carter was amazed at how it never ceased to set his heart racing to see Mackenzie after any period of absence. Despite the long flight, casual loose fitting clothes, and minimal makeup, she remained a vision of natural beauty and elegance that melted his heart. Mackenzie caught

Carter's eye, then bent down and pointed Liam towards him while she followed with the baggage trolley.

Liam raced through the crowd, sidestepping people like a major league quarterback, straight into his dad's waiting arms. Mackenzie, arriving shortly after, threw her arms around his neck and kissed him. "I missed you so much," she whispered in his ear.

"I missed you too, Mackie. I can't believe you're finally here. We're going to have a great time."

Security was tight at the airport. Liam stared openly at all the heavily armed soldiers and security personnel. He didn't seem to be frightened by their presence - just interested. A few of the soldiers made his day when noticing his curiosity, they smiled and waved at him.

From the airport to their hotel in Jerusalem was about 30 miles, and Carter had a taxi waiting for them outside. On the way, the driver gave them a running commentary about the sites they were passing in accented, but excellent English. Liam had his face next to the window staring at all the people in their strange looking garb with headdresses, and leading animals. He swung around to stare out the window when he saw a few men riding camels.

The terrain reminded Mackenzie of Arizona. There was not a lot of rain in this part of the world, and she smiled when she recalled that one of the former Prime Ministers of Israel, Golda Meir, once joked about Moses wandering all those years in the wilderness to find the one place in the Middle East that didn't have oil.

Jerusalem, Israel

Carter loved Jerusalem and always looked forward to

visiting it. He was sure his family would soon embrace his sentiments as well.

Their hotel was not too far from the Downtown Triangle, a dense concentration of shops and entertainment venues. As in every part of the isolated nation, security was tight. Each hotel had three men in uniform at the entrance and four more outside doing perimeter checks. It was obvious that the Israelis took the safety of their people very serious.

They had a two-bedroom suite on the tenth floor with a lovely view over parts of the city. The quickest way to get their body clocks in sync with the new time zone, they decided, would be to stay awake until nightfall. Both Liam and Mackenzie had been able to get some sleep during their flight and were too excited to go to bed now in any event. They unpacked some of their things, making sure they locked up all their valuables, including Carter's laptops and tablet, as well as Mackenzie's miniature camera, in the safe inside the room. They all took quick showers and then went down to the hotel restaurant for a snack and something refreshing to drink.

The hotel room furnished its own coffee maker, but Carter appreciated the stronger grades of coffee of the Middle East, especially the coffee prepared by the corner vendors who made fresh cups over a fire.

They sat down in the restaurant on the ground floor of the hotel and placed their orders. Carter sat back, "So tell me about all your travels and exploits since we last saw each other. From our Skype sessions I got the impression you've been having a ball the last six weeks."

Mackenzie mustered one of her mind-numbing smiles, "Okay let me give you the summary version now and the details later."

Carter nodded, and Mackenzie gave him a brief version of the discovery of the Latin text in the A-Echelon vaults, which led them to Armenia and the Books of the Elders of Medicine. She then elaborated on what they found in those books."

Carter was ecstatic when she explained that she had found confirmation of the use of respirocytes in prehistoric times. "Mackie you are a genius! That was a brilliant piece of research!"

Mackenzie laughed. "Coming from you Professor, that is a big compliment. I'm going to put that on my resume! I can just see the smile on Grandpa Will's face."

"Well in the Books of the Elders we found various references to another text, called the Sirralnnudam ..."

Carter held his hand up, "Sirralnnudam ... mhh ... that's an ancient version of Arabic, mhh, *the scroll of secrets of blood*." he murmured.

Mackenzie looked at him, utterly flabbergasted. "You took less than thirty seconds to translate that word which took Harry almost an hour! How did you do that?"

Carter shrugged his shoulders and smiled, embarrassment showing on his face.

"We should have flown you over to Armenia the moment we got that book. Harry is a brilliant linguist and I am told he can speak ten languages fluently, and read a dozen more, but the language of the Sirralnnudam he could not." She seriously considered telling him the whole story but then decided it could wait -she had it on the flash drive of the miniature camera. There would be enough time for him to look at it later. "So when we got stuck at that point, we went back home and reported to Irene and Hunter. They immediately agreed that we should return to Armenia with a team of linguists to translate the document. Hunter even got the go ahead from the President."

"Sounds like you will have your work cut out for you when we return after this cruise." Carter took her hand and pulled her up. "Okay, let's try and put that away for now and go out to see a bit of Jerusalem before it gets dark. There is a nice little street café, not too far from here, where I would like to take you and Liam for dinner later. They serve the best kubba I have ever tasted, and that is only the appetizer, their food is exquisite."

"Kubba? Never heard of it."

"It's a dish brought to Israel by Iraqi Jews. They make it with rice, onions, and finely ground meat - beef, lamb or chicken - with the most delicious and tasty spices you can imagine."

"That doesn't sound too outlandish to me. I'm game for it. If you like it, then I'm sure I will like it too."

They kept Liam between them while they made their way towards the hustle and bustle of tourist attractions in the Downtown Triangle.

The Downtown Triangle, also known as 'The Triangle,' was the central commercial and entertainment district in Jerusalem. It was Jerusalem's most famous district and covered an area of more than 300,000 square feet. An open-air pedestrian mall, it contained many outdoor cafes, souvenir shops, and the Zion Square.

Carter would not have brought his family to The Triangle 15 years ago due to the terror groups who delighted in bombing the area. Since 1948, bombs in this area had killed and maimed hundreds of innocent people. However, since the last attack occurred in 2001, and the Israeli government's increased security measures in the area, it was now believed to be one of the safest places in Jerusalem to visit.

The three of them walked, looked, and shopped for almost three hours around the mall in the Triangle, gathering a bag full of trinkets before Mackenzie and Liam announced, almost as if they had rehearsed it, that they were hungry.

"Good timing," Carter laughed. "There's the café where I wanted to take you." He pointed to a little street restaurant less than 50 yards away on a corner across the road.

The owner was a short, stocky and jovial man. He welcomed them with a big smile. Speaking to them in perfect English, he inquired where they came from and what brought them to Israel. He seated them at a table outside, right next to the sidewalk, as they requested. He took their drinks order and handed them the menu.

While Carter and Liam settled into their seats, Mackenzie entered the restaurant to use the bathroom. Liam was like a bottle of champagne, bubbling with energy and questions. "Dad, look at that. What is that? Why do the men wear dresses? Why aren't there any camels here? When can I see a camel again?" Carter smiled, enjoying the enthusiasm of his son. He just couldn't keep up with the answers for the flood of questions streaming out of the youngster's mouth. He was still busy answering one question when the next one was already out.

When Mackenzie returned from the bathroom, they looked at the menu and placed their orders. All of them would have Kubba for an appetizer, and then share a platter with a variety of dishes to give them a taste of almost all the main dishes served.

Now it was Carter's turn to use the bathroom while Mackenzie had to front Liam's next barrage of questions.

Shortly after Carter disappeared to the men's room situated at the back of the building, Mackenzie and Liam heard screaming and shouting coming from across the street. Liam immediately jumped onto his chair to get a better view. Mackenzie rose to stand next to him, her arm around him, protecting him from accidently being bumped off the chair if someone passed by too closely. A crowd quickly gathered on the other side of the street. It looked like people were fighting.

Armed soldiers and police were rushing to the scene from all directions and started breaking up the crowd. As the crowd made way for the police, Mackenzie could see two men throwing punches at each other; she didn't notice the van racing towards them on the street behind her...

United Airlines flight 6 hours out of Tel Aviv

James Rhodes tried to stretch his long legs to ease the discomfort of being cramped for so long in the airline seat. His thoughts briefly turned to his friend Carter and his family, well into the first day of their six-week holiday, as he flipped through the channels on the small TV screen in front of him.

Carter had accompanied him to the airport to see him off and to wait for the arrival of his family on a flight from Boston, which was scheduled to land within an hour after James' departure.

He found the CNN channel just as a red, flashing, breaking news banner flashed on the screen ...

Northeast Canada

Ahote turned over in the dark and lay on his back. *What was it? Something's seriously wrong; I can feel it, but what?* He shifted uneasily in the dark. Moments later he heard wolves howling, was that what woke him?

Bly touched his shoulder. "Those are Mackie's wolves."

He turned to face her, "How can you tell they're Mackie's wolves?"

"Their howl is different from the others."

The wolves' howls came closer, and Bly got up to look out the window. Ahote joined her.

"This is odd, they don't come around while Mackie and Carter are away, yet here they are, actually in the compound near the barn staring up at the house."

Bly stood watching them. "They howl to get Mackie's attention; they're looking for her." Then she whispered, "They know something we don't, and have come to tell us something is wrong."

Ahote sighed, "Oh hell Bly I hope you're wrong. If they are looking for her, then something bad has happened."

The moonlight reflecting off the glistening snow illuminated the two wolves. Ahote and Bly felt shivers tingle their spine as Keeva and Loki, so named by Mackenzie, continued their eerie, mournful howl …

Next in the Carter Devereux Mystery Thriller Series

vinci-books.com/freydis

Uncover the traitor. Stop the evil. Save the world.

Carter Devereux and his team of Special Forces operatives must race against time to uncover a traitor, rescue captives, and thwart an unspeakable evil from altering the course of history. As they navigate a treacherous landscape of international conspiracies and hidden agendas, Devereux confronts challenges that test the limits of his resolve.

Turn the page for a free preview…

The Wolves Of Freydis: Prologue

Ahote turned over in the dark and lay on his back. He considered turning the bedside light on but didn't want to disturb Bly.

Something had woken him, but he couldn't identify what. He frowned. For some reason, he felt uneasy. Bly stirred beside him, "Ahote? You okay?"

"I suppose so."

She leaned up on her elbow, "That's a strange answer."

"Hmm..."

He got out of bed and restlessly went over to the double glazed window to look out over the snow-covered landscape. High above, the full moon caused the trees to cast their shadows towards the house.

He put his head against the cold glass and rested there a moment as Bly got out of bed "Well dear, whatever it is, you will need a nice warm drink to get you back to sleep." She pulled on her slippers that matched her floor-length pink flannel nightgown and wandered off into the open plan living quarters looking like a waif in the light cast by the glowing embers of the fire.

A moment later the light in the kitchen came on, and he could hear her fixing a saucepan of hot milk for them both.

What was it? Something's wrong; I can feel it; but what? He shifted uneasily in the dark.

Moments later, he heard wolves howling; was that it? Is that what woke him? No, he was used to the wolves howling, he'd know something was wrong if they didn't howl.

He gave up and wandered into the kitchen. "The wolves are giving voice tonight, must be the full moon."

"Maybe it's them who woke you."

"No. Well, they might have, but they aren't what's giving me this presentiment of something being seriously wrong."

The wolves' howls came closer, and Bly went to open the upper half of a Dutch door and peer outside. "Now, that's odd. Those are Mackie's wolves."

"How do you know? We don't usually see them while Mackie and Carter are away. In fact, come to think of it, they haven't been here for a couple of months."

"Well, we're seeing them now. They are actually in the compound near the barn, staring up at the house. They've never done that before. Come and see."

He got up and moved to her side. "Are you sure they're Mackie's wolves?"

"Oh yes. I'd know their howl anywhere; it's different from the others. They howl to get Mackie's attention. I'll bet if you check around Carter's house and buildings in the morning, you'll find their footprints. They're looking for her."

Ahote sighed, "Oh hell Bly I hope you're wrong. If they are looking for her, then something bad has happened."

The next morning, they took off on the snow sled and covered the mile to the Devereux homestead in a short time. There they dismounted and walked around the buildings.

Sure enough, there were wolf prints in the snow up to the main house door and the windows. There were even signs the wolves had stood on hind legs to look inside.

"This just isn't normal wolf behavior, Bly." Ahote was disturbed.

"No, but these are not ordinary wolves Pet. They know and love Mackie, and they know something we don't."

"How on earth can they do that?"

"Perhaps the same way you woke up last night feeling something was wrong." Bly shrugged, "There's no way they'd come into close contact with the buildings here or at home if there were nothing wrong. We wouldn't normally see them until Mackie returned; you know that."

When they arrived back at their house, the wolves were waiting for them.

Bly told Ahote to wait for her and started to walk towards them. "Don't do that Bly; they may not be all that friendly while Mackie's away."

She turned back, "Don't worry, we've been introduced. I know their names." She smiled mysteriously at him.

She drew closer, "Keeva, Loki, come." She beckoned with her hand, and they moved closer. They stared into her deep brown eyes with their equally dark gold ones. She put out a hand and placed it on Loki's head. "You're looking for Mackie, eh? Something's wrong, isn't it? Keeva moved in and welcomed Bly's touch with a soft whine as if both of them were feeling lost and needed some reassurance.

Bly smiled to herself. Ever since the Wolves met Mackie,

and indeed even before that, they'd been around. They never caused any trouble but if Carter took a horse out for the day or chose to camp out for a while, they would go with him. When Mackie arrived, they seemed drawn to her, and she to them. She had never been afraid of them, and they came in close to walk side by side with her.

Bly spent a few minutes just patting them and crooning a little Indian song, the sort she used to sing to her babies before they grew up.

Eventually, they moved away and quietly vanished into the trees.

She returned to the back porch and accepted a cup of hot coffee from Ahote, then settled down next to him on a bench, hunching deep into her all weather poncho.

"Will you tell me their names?"

Bly smiled, "Of course. The female is Keeva, which means beautiful and gentle, and the male is Loki, which means Wolf Spirit."

Ahote nodded and asked. "So, do you think they will come back?"

"No, they don't need to. They've done their bit; told us something is wrong. Now we have to worry about it." She sipped her coffee.

Ahote was silent for a moment. "You're right though aren't you? Their instinct for things goes far beyond what we can see, hear, and touch. Animals have instincts – no, they have knowledge about this world we live in – knowledge that we just don't understand, although it's not as though people haven't tried."

Bly nodded, "Yes they have, but people want it all to be so cut and dried and it isn't. Look at you; you feel something's wrong, you can't explain it but you know it's real.

They do too, they may even know what it is, but could never tell us how they know."

"Like the elephants in Indonesia that knew about the Tsunami days before it hit and moved up into the mountains for safety."

"Or birds that vanish before an earthquake."

They fell silent again then Ahote added "Like dog owners who claim that their pets know when they are due to come home even if they change their routine and arrived at different times. Still, without fail, the dogs go and wait for them at a door or window ten to twenty minutes before they come home just as always."

Bly giggled, "Do you remember that little dog we had when the children were small – the one who always knew when a visitor was due even though we weren't expecting one?"

Ahote laughed, "She was always right. So we just accept that Loki and Keeva know. No scientist on earth can explain how, all we can be sure of is there's a link – an invisible cord – between them and the family. So something is wrong, and they came to tell us. Now that we know, they trust us to sort it out. Is that how it goes?"

Bly nodded "I'm afraid so. We are now sure something is wrong, and the wolves expect us to fix it. It would help to know what it was."

A phone call to the Andersons went unanswered so there was nothing more they could do.

It was two days later, when James Rhodes called, that their presentiments became real.

The Wolves Of Freydis: Chapter One

United Airlines flight 7 hours out of Tel Aviv, 5 hours after the bomb explosion in Jerusalem's Downtown Triangle

James Rhodes tried to stretch his long legs to ease the discomfort of being cramped for so long in the airline seat. His thoughts briefly turned to his friend Carter and his family, well into the first day of their six-week holiday, as he flipped through the channels on the small TV screen in front of him.

Carter had accompanied him to the airport to see him off and to wait for the arrival of his family on a flight from Boston, which was scheduled to land within an hour after James' departure.

He found the CNN channel just as a red, flashing, breaking news banner flashed on the screen …

Bomb explosion in Jerusalem. 15 killed, 35 injured.

News about bombs killing and maiming people in the

Middle East, especially countries such as Iraq, Afghanistan, and Syria, was an almost daily event. However, bomb blasts in Israel were not such a regular occurrence, even more so in Jerusalem. But that was not what set the alarm bells off in James' brain. Those stomach-churning sounds in his brain were triggered by the thought of his friends, Carter and Mackenzie Devereux with their six-year-old son Liam, who were on holiday in Jerusalem.

Oh God, please don't let them be part of this, was his first thought as he grabbed the earphones out of the seat pocket, plugged them in and started pushing buttons to find the one that controlled the volume.

He'd set out from Tel Aviv's Ben Gurion International airport seven hours earlier. He and Carter had just finished a research expedition to India and Egypt, and he was on his way back home. Carter and his family were getting a six-week holiday under way, starting with two days in Jerusalem and the rest of the time on a luxury Mediterranean Cruise ship. Carter had accompanied him to the airport to see him off and to wait for the arrival of his family on a flight from Boston, which was scheduled to land shortly after James' departure.

Finally, he found the right button and raised the volume to hear the news. As the facts were announced, a nauseating foreboding started to wash over him. The bomb explosion happened about five hours after he departed from Tel Aviv. It happened in the Downtown Triangle of Jerusalem – that was very close to the hotel where he and Carter stayed for the last two days before he left. The two of them had visited the Triangle the night before, and Carter told him that he was planning to take his family there on the first night after their arrival.

The Triangle is a big place; he kept telling himself. *Maybe they weren't even in the Triangle when the bomb exploded.*

The fact that thus far four American citizens were amongst the dead and injured did not help to alleviate his disquiet. Neither did the notice that the final death and injury toll was still unknown but would undoubtedly increase over the next 24 hours, as rescue teams sifted through the rubble to locate additional victims. No names or details would be released until next-of-kin were notified.

James spent the remaining hours of the flight looking out the window, torn between hope and fear for his friend and his family. After hours that seemed like an eternity, the plane finally landed at Dulles International in Washington, DC. As it touched down, he had his cell phone ready in his hand, waiting for the announcement, which would allow passengers to switch on their mobile devices. The announcement came as soon as the plane started taxiing to the main building. He could not switch his phone on quick enough to suit him.

The moment the phone connected to the cellphone network a series of loud beeps sounded, there were two messages – a voice mail notification and a text message. He read the text message first. It was from Hunter Patrick, the Director of A-Echelon, where he worked: *Contact me the moment you land. It's critical.* He pushed the speed dial button to retrieve his voicemail messages. It was Hunter Patrick's voice – *"Jim, I know you will still be en route when I leave this message, but I just want to make sure that you contact me the moment you get my messages."*

Grab your copy…
vinci-books.com/freydis

About the Author

JC Ryan is a bestselling author renowned for his intricate espionage, archaeological thrillers, and conspiracy mysteries. With over 30 acclaimed novels, including the popular Rex Dalton K9 Thrillers, Rossler Foundation Mysteries, and Carter Devereux Mystery Thrillers, Ryan has captivated readers around the globe.

Drawing from his diverse professional background—as a military officer, lawyer, and IT manager—Ryan creates compelling narratives that skillfully blend historical accuracy with thrilling adventure. He is celebrated as a master storyteller, known for crafting riveting plots, meticulous historical details, and engaging, multidimensional characters. Ryan's meticulous research lends authenticity and depth to each story, immersing readers in richly constructed worlds filled with intrigue, suspense, and adventure.

Fans of David Baldacci, Lee Child's Jack Reacher, Tom Clancy's Jack Ryan, Nelson DeMille's John Corey, Vince Flynn's Mitch Rapp, Mark Greaney's Gray Man, Gregg Hurwitz's Orphan X, Robert Ludlum's Jason Bourne, Daniel Silva's Gabriel Allon, Brad Taylor's Pike Logan, Brad Thor's Scot Harvath, James Rollins' Sigma Force, Steve Berry's Cotton Malone, and Dan Brown's Robert Langdon will find JC Ryan's novels equally compelling and unforgettable.

When not writing, Ryan enjoys spending time with his college sweetheart, whom he married in 1978. They are proud parents of two daughters, have two sons-in-law, and are grandparents to two grandchildren.